THE PROMISE OF TOMORROW

ANNEMARIE BREAR

ALSO BY THE AUTHOR

Historical

Kitty McKenzie

Kitty McKenzie's Land

Southern Sons

To Gain What's Lost

Isabelle's Choice

Nicola's Virtue

Aurora's Pride

Grace's Courage

Eden's Conflict

Catrina's Return

Where Rainbow's End

Broken Hero

The Promise of Tomorrow

The Slum Angel

Beneath a Stormy Sky

Marsh Saga Series

Millie

Christmas at the Chateau

Prue

Cece

Contemporary

Long Distance Love

Hooked on You

Where Dragonflies Hover (Dual Timeline)

Short Stories

A New Dawn

Art of Desire

What He Taught Her

THE PROMISE OF TOMORROW

AnneMarie Brear

PROLOGUE

Warwickshire
May 1912

*V*ernon McBride was a happy man. As he sauntered along the sharply trimmed gravel path meandering through the bountiful garden beds and lush green lawns, he chuckled at nothing, bowing and tipping his hat to anyone who passed. The smell of spring and early summer flowers that he couldn't name filled the air. Contentment and pride straightened his spine, squared his shoulders and brought a smug smile to his face.

'Will you stop grinning, McBride? You look like a circus performer strutting about like that.' Neil Featherstone, his friend, mocked him as they walked along the path, the women in front.

McBride's smile widened. Nothing and no one would ruin this day. 'It is my birthday, my good fellow, allow me the pleasure of it.'

Oh, yes, life was good, brilliant even, and the reason for this vast improvement to his world was the arrival of Charlotte Brookes, and her sister Hannah, distant cousins who, after losing their last closest relative, was now under his care. Years ago, their father, Jeremy, for reasons no one will ever know, selected Vernon as guardian to his two daughters in the unlikely event of the girls being left without family. No one expected that to happen, of course. The girls grew up being loved by not only their parents, but their grandparents as well. When Jeremy died five years ago, and his strange request was read out in the will, no one, especially not the girls' mother, Imogen, expected anything to come of it, for Imogen and her parents were in good health. Yet, within four years of Jeremy's death they too were gone, and Charlotte and her younger sister Hannah were alone.

Featherstone shortened his stride, allowing Mrs McBride and the Misses Brookes to walk further ahead so he couldn't be heard. 'Your birthday is the only reason? It's not that you're now in care of heiresses? Or is it that you sampled the fleshy delights at Madame Carling's establishment last night?'

McBride flashed a look ahead at his wife, and content that Featherstone hadn't been heard, let out a breath. 'I haven't frequented Madame Carling's for some days. I've been too busy.'

'Yes, counting the young ladies' money, no doubt.' Feather-stone, a reedy framed man with feline eyes gave him a knowing wink. 'Lucky swine.'

'Come now, Neil, don't let envy get in the way of our friend-ship.' Slapping him on the shoulder, McBride strode on.

'Oh, I won't, especially if you send some of it my way. I tell you that Chigwell land holding will make an excellent develop-ment. The plans—'

'Yes, yes, don't keep harping on about it. It's my birthday, the sun is shining, and we have Charlotte to look at as we dine later. I don't wish to talk business today.' Seeing Featherstone's fallen expression, McBride sighed. 'We'll discuss it tomorrow, I promise, but today we enjoy ourselves. You know, Featherstone, you should find yourself a wife.'

'Someone like Charlotte perhaps?'

'No!' he yelled, causing those people closest to stare and his wife to stop and turn to frown at him. He lowered his voice. 'Charlotte isn't for the taking.'

'I didn't mean it, of course, McBride. You know me, always one for a jest.' Featherstone had the good sense to make it a joke.

McBride smiled and waved his wife and the girls on. 'Well, don't jest where she is concerned. Charlotte is mine.'

'Yes, you're her guardian, I know, but she'll marry one day and then—'

'Oh yes, she'll marry all right. She'll marry me!'

Featherstone jerked to a stop and stared at him as though he'd sprouted horns out of the top of his head. 'You? But you're already married.'

He leaned in close to Featherstone. 'A minor detail, friend, a minor detail.'

'I'm all for going after what you want, McBride, but to rid yourself of a wife?'

'You don't understand. I married Deirdre for her father's money, as he had promised me I would get it if I took Deirdre off his hands, and of course I expected a son to carry on my line. Well, I ended up not receiving a penny and she's barren. I've had to get where I am today by years of wheeling and dealing until I can't think straight. Nothing has been given to me. I've earned everything I have, but I want more. Now it's time to try again and Charlotte is my ticket to a life I should have had when Deidre's father passed. I'm due, wouldn't you think?'

Featherstone glanced at Deidre's straight, narrow back and grimaced. 'I suppose you could be right, McBride.'

McBride chuckled, knowing exactly what was on his partner's

mind. Deirdre was a sour apple and sharp-tongued. She rarely smiled and never paid a compliment to anyone. She saw fault in everything, and he couldn't remember the last time she looked at him in kindness. His gaze drifted to beautiful graceful Charlotte and his chest swelled at her innocence, her air of fragile sophistication, and the creaminess of her skin. Oh yes, she was perfect and she *would* be his wife. And the money she'd inherit at twenty-one would be his also. He just had to start putting his plans into action.

Straightening his shoulders, he quickened his pace. 'Now, I want you to take my wife's arm and young Hannah's and go buy them a toffee apple each from the stall at the end of the park. I need to talk to Charlotte.'

Featherstone sighed and hesitated. 'Be careful. She's young, what is she seventeen? But from what I've seen, not stupid.'

'Charlotte is eighteen in October.'

'And her inheritance. What does she know about that?'

'Very little. Her family solicitor is an old man and he has dealt with me and my solicitor only. We kept Charlotte out of any discussions and since she was busy grieving, it was easy for me to persuade her to let me handle everything. She believes she will come into a small amount of money when she's twenty-one. I've deliberately allowed her to presume the inheritance is several pieces of jewellery and a few hundred pounds. Nothing for her to worry about.'

Featherstone brushed the tip of his shoe over the gravel path. 'Very clever. She is totally dependent on you until she's of age.'

'Yes. I know what I'm doing. She's looking for security after the trying times she's had and her sister is of the upmost importance to her. She will do anything for Hannah.' He rubbed his hands together and smiled. Yes, her devotion to her sister will be of tremendous help in obtaining his goals.

'Including marrying you once Deirdre has gone? That alone is going to take time. How will you do it?'

'Never you mind about that.' He stared coldly at his wife and knew just how much money it would take for her to be erased from his life. Charlotte, on the other hand, would need careful handling and time. He just had to be patient, cautious and at his most charming. Smiling again, he quickened his step. He could be all three.

CHAPTER 1

September 1913
Yorkshire

Charlotte stopped walking along the York Road and stared through the sleeting rain at the signpost. She looked down the lane running to the left. 'Belthorpe is one and a half miles from here. Shall we go there and find a bed for the night before it gets dark?'

Her sister, Hannah, kept her head bent slightly, having worked out a way to keep the rain from dripping off her sodden hat and running down the back of her neck under her collar. 'I don't care. I'm so wet and cold. I just want to stop walking. My feet hurt.'

'Your feet always hurt.' Charlotte gripped the portmanteau more firmly and shivered as rain hit her face, momentarily blinding her. 'Come on. We'll see if we can stay somewhere, even if it is just a farmer's barn.'

'I'm hungry.'

'You're always hungry too.' She'd forgotten what it was like to have a full stomach herself, but complaining about it didn't make it any better. Her stomach contracted with the familiar ache of hunger.

Trudging along the rutted dirt road, bordered by thick hedges and wide fields, Charlotte ignored Hannah's grumbles. She couldn't make it stop raining and Hannah's whining gnawed on her last reserves of patience. 'Stop complaining, Hannah! I'm doing my best.'

Falling into a sullen silence, they walked on. After a year living on the road they were now used to the country. The smells and noises were known to them, they didn't jump every time a cow bellowed, or a stoat ran out from under a hedge. Despite the disadvantage of being out in all weathers, and the uncertainty of finding permanent work, Charlotte preferred walking the northern roads than going back to Warwickshire. Nothing would ever make her go back there. Why her father had to give guardianship to McBride, she'd never understand. Surely there had to have been more suitable friends of his that he could have chosen? All she could think of was that her father never knew the true character of his distant relative.

No, being back in Yorkshire and away from McBride's house was the better option, but still, she had to find long-term work and shelter now summer was over. The responsibility of caring for Hannah with no money or home weighed heavily on her. If she only had to please herself, then she'd happily put up with the harshness of tramping the roads or going into service, but she wouldn't allow being separated from Hannah. She glanced at her sister's unhappy face and another pang of guilt hit her in the chest.

She sighed heavily; sometimes it was as if their former safe and settled life had never existed. Had she dreamed it all: the happy family home she once shared with her parents and grand-parents?

Rounding a high-hedged corner, Charlotte stopped and stared down the length of a village street. Raindrops fell from her hat brim at a constant rate, saturating her brown coat and the skirt beneath, even soaking through to her petticoat. She felt she'd been wet and cold for days instead of hours. Last winter they had managed to survive by her working in a public house in Manchester, until that had all gone horribly wrong...

She gripped her sister's hand. 'There now, Hannah, this must be Belthorpe. It looks a nice enough place.' Glancing at Hannah sent a torrent of water off her hat and onto her coat. She received no reply. Hannah could go for hours without talking if the mood suited her. The cold and wet seemed to have exhausted her completely. Pity filled Charlotte and she injected some eagerness into her voice. 'There are some shops, see? I might be able to get work.'

Hannah obediently stared down the darkening street, her face white and pinched with cold beneath her limp hat, her clothes as wet as Charlotte's.

Continuing, Charlotte looked around. 'I bet there'll be farms about, maybe even a manor somewhere and it's not far from the York Road, so they might get plenty of people calling. There could be work here for both of us.'

'Will we not have to walk to York then?' Hannah asked softly with a shiver.

'Perhaps not.' Charlotte thought fast. She peered through the grey gloom of dusk and downpour to pick out several different shop facades, and an inn, called the Black Hen, further down before the murkiness obliterated the rest of the village. The weather was fast slipping into winter and soon she'd have to take whatever work and accommodation she could get for them both.

If only she could get something better than what they'd experienced so far. Was it too much to ask for a decent position and place to stay? Must they suffer hardship for the rest of their lives? How did people do it day after day, year after year? Again, Charlotte realised how secure she had been as she grew up. She and her sister had never wanted for anything. Were they ever to feel that way again?

Making her decision, she shifted the handle of the battered portmanteau for a better grip, and tugging Hannah behind her, continued down the street. They passed the tobacconists and a haberdashery on one side, and on the other noticed a post office, cobblers and general grocers. Here, Charlotte paused and looked through the rain-streaked window. Inside, lamps glowed, showing the stocked shelves along the walls, the high wooden counter and the numerous items on display.

'We'll go inside and buy some food,' she told Hannah and pushed open the door, making the brass bell tinkle above their heads.

The shop was empty, hardly surprising on such a foul afternoon, but an older woman bustled out from a curtained off doorway behind the counter. She gave them a cool stare, her gaze dropping to the water pooling around their boots. 'You're new. What would you like?'

'Some food, please.' Charlotte placed the portmanteau on the floor, dislodging more drops. The shop was deliciously warm, a small open fire burned in a grate in the corner. From her coat pocket, she pulled out a small leather purse, one of the few things she owned that belonged to her father. Her cold fingers could hardly work the knot to open it. A wave of dizziness made her blink to clear her mind.

'What sort of food? Sweets?' The woman frowned, stepping closer to the counter and her hands sweeping over the glass jars holding colourful hardboiled sweets that lined shelves behind her.

'Yes!' Hannah's eyes widened.

'No.' Charlotte shook her head and then wished she hadn't as another wave of dizziness overcame her. She had to eat. They'd had nothing since yesterday morning. 'Some bread...and cheese... Do you have pickled onions, or boiled eggs?'

The woman stared at her, one eyebrow raised. 'Do you have money?'

'Yes, not much...' The warmth of the shop and lack of food made her head swim. 'I've a shilling here...though I need to find lodgings...' The items in the shop started to move. She blinked repeatedly to steady herself, heard Hannah calling her name, and then all went blank.

Charlotte opened her eyes and focused on her surroundings. She was lying on a dark green sofa in a small sitting room. A blazing fire roared opposite, enveloping the square room like a furnace.

'Here she is. She's coming round now.' The woman from the shop came into view, and patted her hand none too gently.

Charlotte tried to sit up, but was pushed firmly down again. 'Now, steady on. Just rest a minute.' The woman turned to a tall man who came to stand behind her. 'Look, Stan, she's trying to sit up.'

'Aye, my dear, I have eyes, but perhaps we ought to let her sit up and have a sip of tea.' His kind long face broke into a gentle smile, instantly putting Charlotte at ease. Holding her arm, he helped her into a sitting position as his wife pushed plump cushions on either side of her as support. 'How do you feel, lass?'

Apart from a slight headache, she seemed fine. 'I'm better, thank you.'

'Good. Good. I'm Stan Wheeler and this is my wife, Bessie.' Mr Wheeler stepped back and his wife immediately took his place.

'You gave us such a fright. No one has ever fainted in my shop before, well, not a stranger like. Mrs Lawson did last summer, but then that doesn't count as she was expecting. She's a fainter is that one. Ten children she's had and goes out like a light at a drop of a hat. We all say she should wear pillows strapped to her, honest we do.' She gave Charlotte a sharp look. 'You're not expecting, are you?'

'No, absolutely not.'

'Bessie, love...' Mr Wheeler's hand on his wife's shoulder quieted her. 'Go get her a cup of tea and check on the young lass.'

Reminded of Hannah, Charlotte swivelled to the doorway as the woman went out. 'My sister...'

'She's fine and in the kitchen eating her way through a bowl of soup, and no doubt a half loaf of bread, I shouldn't wonder. She has the stomach of a man.' His smile showed his amusement.

'I'm so sorry to have fainted in your shop. Thank you for taking care of us both.'

'Your sister told me your names and that you have no parents, no home.'

Charlotte straightened her shoulders, trying not to feel ashamed of their circumstances. 'That's true. We lost our mother over a year ago in the spring of last year. Our father was killed in an accident some years ago.' She refused to mention McBride's name.

'Are you on your way somewhere, to relatives?'

'No. We have no one. Our grandparents are dead. I'm looking for work and somewhere for us to live.'

He looked surprised. 'Nay, lass, you're not out wandering the roads, are you?'

'We have been, yes, for the last five weeks since we had to leave my previous position. I've been able to work the odd day here and there. We've stayed in different places, renting a bed when we could.' She swallowed, alarmed at how dreadful it sounded. Her parents, such good decent people, would be horrified at what their daughters had become. The image of her mother's sweet smile and the soft touch of her father's hand on her head came to mind and brought with it the sting of long suppressed tears.

'And there's no one you can stay with?' This came from Mrs

Wheeler as she carried a tray into the room and placed it on the small table beside the sofa.

'No. No one.'

'You can stay with us the night. I wouldn't send a dog out in weather like this.' Mrs Wheeler added milk and sugar to all three cups and then poured out the tea before handing them out.

'Thank you, for everything.' As she sipped the refreshing brew, Charlotte looked at the deep red curtains drawn across the window and could hear the rain pelting against the glass. 'I am grateful, truly.'

'I'll make up the bed for you both in the spare room.' Mrs Wheeler replaced her cup on the tray. 'Stan, will you heat some water? I think the girls need a nice bath before supper.'

A bath. Charlotte nearly cried at the thought. It'd been months since she'd had a bath, not since the night before they fled the public house. She'd not had one all summer. Her cheeks flushed hotly at the thought. Glancing down at her filthy dress, boots and coat, she felt the heat deepen in her face. A quick wash in a stream wasn't enough, they must stink. No wonder they'd found it hard to get work. They no longer appeared the decent people they'd been brought up to be.

Mr Wheeler replaced his cup next to his wife's. 'A bath coming right up.'

She was left alone only for a few seconds before Hannah raced into the room and plopped down next to her on the sofa. 'We're staying the night here, Charlotte. In a proper bed!'

'I know. So behave.' She handed her tea to Hannah to finish, a habit she'd got into since they'd been homeless. Whatever food or drink they had Charlotte gave the majority to Hannah to keep her strength up.

'And we're to have a bath.' Childish delight shone from Hannah's lovely deep brown eyes, so like their father's.

'Where is our bag?'

'Over there.' Hannah hurried to bring it back to her and opened it up.

'Check our nightgowns. Are they damp?'

'Yes.' The joy left Hannah's face. 'It's all damp.'

'Here, let's hold them out to the fire for a while until Mr and Mrs Wheeler return.'

'They are nice. I like them.' Hannah knelt in front of the flames, holding her nightdress out. 'They gave me soup and bread and a big glass of milk. I feel so fat!'

'You need to be fattened up.' Charlotte hated seeing her pretty sister so thin, her bones poking out. Though she was just the same now. Their clothes hung off them. They were nothing but skin and bones. She touched her hair, it was lank and matted. Why had the Wheelers given them a second glance? They looked like a pair of ragamuffins from the deepest slums.

'Don't cry, Charlotte, please don't cry.' Hannah dropped her nightgown and rushed to hold Charlotte tight with her reedy little arms. 'We'll be all right, like you said we would be.'

The tears that had built up for months cascaded in a torrent down Charlotte's cheeks. She couldn't stop them and gave up trying. What would happen to them after this night? Tomorrow they'd be on the road again, trudging through all weathers from one place to the next. Was York the right place to go to? Would the city have the jobs and the lodging they needed to survive? Should they have stayed in Warwickshire? But all she had thought about was to get away from McBride and his lusty stares. Should she have put up with him to keep a roof over Hannah's head?

And, in the end, they hadn't been better off by leaving. The last year had been exhausting, frightening and dangerous. Now they were hungry, homeless, poor and dependent on strangers.

Charlotte hugged Hannah to her. 'I'm sorry for doing this to you.'

'We'll be all right.' Hannah held her tighter, causing Charlotte to cry even more. 'I know we will.'

Stan, on his way upstairs with the buckets of hot water, heard the girls talking. He smiled at Hannah's comment of being fat, then his throat constricted at the sound of crying. It was the eldest one, he knew, for he saw in her eyes the heavy weight of responsibility she carried.

Slowly he went up into the spare bedroom where Bess was making up the double bed. Flames of a new fire licked the wood in the grate. He poured both buckets into the tin hip bath.

'I've put a warming pan between the sheets,' Bessie said as she scuttled to the other side of the bed to tidy the pillows. 'They'll be wanting a good night's sleep, I bet. Once they've had a hot meal, they'll be fighting to stay awake, you see if they don't.'

'Lass.'

Bessie turned to him and reading his quiet, serious tone, she stilled. 'Yes?'

'Those girls need us.'

The colour drained from her full round face.

Stan straightened his back, knowing the importance of what he was saying. 'Fate has sent them to us.'

'Fate?'

'Aye.' He took a deep breath. 'Out of all the places in the village, of them even being in this village, something made them choose our shop to walk into.'

'Nay, they wanted food, ya daft beggar. They're not likely to get that at Forster's blacksmith, are they? Of course, they came here. Don't read more into it than there is.' She shook out the pillow, not meeting his eyes.

'You want to send them on their way in the morning, back out onto the roads? Hannah told me in the kitchen that they were robbed by a publican. Charlotte was offered work by some sod who ran a bar, she worked all hours while Hannah sat in the scullery out of the way. Then one night they had to flee, so Hannah says.'

'Why?'

'The man was in their room, Bess, that's what Hannah said, so innocently. Poor child has no idea what was about to happen to her sister, but you and I can guess right well.' He was furious at the injustice of it. 'It was only the next day that Charlotte was looking for their money that she realised the fellow had gone through their bag as well. That's why they were on the road. Charlotte thought to walk to York, and earn money along the way. Walk, mind you, two young lasses!'

Bessie turned away, adjusting the pillowslip. 'I'm sorry to hear of it, I am, but folk do it every day—'

'Then Hannah tells me they worked on a farm for a few weeks, but they weren't paid money, only food. What's the world coming to when people aren't paid a decent wage for a decent day's work?'

'Stan—'

'They had to leave the farm because, not only was the woman's cooking dreadful and not fit for pigs, but without money they couldn't buy shoes or clothes, and what they had wouldn't last forever, not with winter coming on. Since then they've been tramping the roads. God alone knows what could have happened to them.' He took a breath.

'They aren't our responsibility, Stanley Wheeler, as you well know.'

'But they could be.'

'Why?' She faced him now, two spots of heat on her cheeks and her blue eyes wide. 'Why? Answer me that. We're in our late fifties. Why on earth would we take on two strangers?'

'Because they need us. And we need them,' he said very quietly.

'Oh, we do, do we? Isn't the business enough to keep us occupied? Are we now taking in any stray or waif that passes the door?'

'We would have the family we were denied.'

Bessie gripped her hands together and bowed her head. In an instant he was wrapping his arms around her, cradling her into his chest. 'I'm sorry, love.' He was sorry, desperately sorry that their twin boys died within their first year and a little girl had also been born and died before she was three. He knew he wasn't alone suffering in his lingering grief of the children they had cherished and lost. 'No one will replace our John, or Ben, or Mary. And if you are completely against it, then I'll try to understand, but these girls have no one. They need parents, and wouldn't it be nice if we had two lovely girls in our lives?' The idea filled his empty heart.

'But we know nothing about them. They could be thieves or...or...'

'I doubt it, love. They've been brought up properly.'

'I can see that by the way they speak. They have breeding, it's easy to tell even under all that dirt. But I don't know...'

'We don't have to make a decision yet. We can simply allow them to stay with us for a bit. Charlotte can work in the shop, and later, if everyone is happy, we can ask them if they want to stay permanently and become family.'

'Family?' She moved out of his arms a little and looked into his face.

'Would it hurt to have that?'

'Stan.'

He sighed, not understanding why he wanted this so badly, he just did. 'I don't ask for much, Bess.'

'Aye, I know.' A long pause grew before she lifted her chin. 'You're too soft for your own good, Stan Wheeler.'

'Give over, you love me for it, you know you do.' He kissed her swiftly.

'Nay, you daft lump, get that bath filled or it'll be cold.' She slapped him away and turned back to the bed. 'They can stay for a bit and we'll see what happens.'

'Bess?' He hesitated half-way out the door.

'Aye?'

'The girls would be a comfort for you if anything ever happened to me.'

'What's wrong with you tonight? Stop talking daft. Nowt is going to happen to you!'

'In time, lass, when we're older. I don't want you to be alone.'

She nodded, suddenly understanding. 'Go get that water.'

* * *

THE FOLLOWING MORNING, Charlotte woke and slipped out of the warm bed, letting Hannah sleep on. Muted light filled the room and the small carriage clock above the fireplace showed it was just after nine o'clock. Charlotte walked closer to the clock to make certain she read it right. Nine o'clock! They'd been asleep for twelve hours. Looking back at the soft rumpled bed it wasn't any wonder. They hadn't slept in such calm surroundings since leaving home. She pushed away thoughts of home. There was no room in her head for memories, or what ifs. All they had was the future, and she had to make it through each day for Hannah. She couldn't look back, just forward.

Quickly washing her face with the water from the jug on the stand, she then donned her clean, and now dry, petticoat, a faded black skirt and cream blouse, which had a tear in the right cuff. The clothes they had worn yesterday were downstairs as Mrs Wheeler had taken them away to wash.

Charlotte shook out the skirt as she left the bedroom; it was the same one her mother had bought for her to wear to her grandfather's funeral three years ago. The hem was ragged, but it would have to do until her brown one was washed and dry. It was hard to remember a time when she had a wardrobe full of beautiful delicate clothes and changed gowns twice a day.

Downstairs, she peeped into the sitting room, but finding it empty and hearing noise from the back area, she stepped down the dim hallway and into the warm kitchen. A delightful aroma of frying bacon filled the air, along with that of fresh bread. Most of the table surface, and a bench against the wall held trays of bread loaves, currant cakes and an assortment of pastries.

'Ah, it seems someone is up.' Mr Wheeler smiled at Charlotte. 'Sit down, my dear, and have breakfast.'

'I am so sorry it is late. I can't remember the last time I over-slept.' She glanced at Mrs Wheeler, who smiled tentatively and took from the oven a tray of small jam tarts.

'You must have needed the sleep,' Mrs Wheeler said, closing the oven door. 'I'll get you some breakfast.'

'Oh, please don't trouble yourself. I'm sure you have finished your cooking for this morning.'

Mr Wheeler waved her concerns away. 'Nonsense, we don't have our breakfast until this time anyway. As soon as we get up we have to open the shop, which takes us an hour, as the local farmers bring us their produce. Or if it is market day, then I go down early and buy up the fresh stuff for the week. Bessie starts her baking at five o'clock, so it's ready for the morning rush at about eight.' He took a sip of tea. 'Mornings are our busiest times, so breakfast is later than normal people.'

'I see.' Charlotte leaned back as Mrs Wheeler put a plate down before her laden with bacon, kidneys, eggs and toast. Her stomach grumbled loudly and she blushed. 'Thank you.'

'Eat it all up mind.' Mrs Wheeler nodded at the food. 'I've plenty more for young Hannah when she awakes.'

'Shall I go and get her?' Charlotte half rose out of her chair.

'No, lass, leave her be.' Mr Wheeler patted her hand. 'Sit and eat before it gets cold. Besides, we, Bessie and me, want to talk to you about something.'

'Oh?' The pleasure of the food drained from her as she considered his serious face.

'Don't be alarmed, lass. I hope it is good news for you.' He smiled at her and then at his wife. 'Bessie and me have been talking, and we'd like to know if you'd wish to stay here with us.'

'To work.' Mrs Wheeler put in sharply.

Charlotte stared open-mouthed. Stay here? Work? 'I-I don't know what to say.'

'How about yes, then?' Mr Wheeler laughed. 'You and Hannah will sleep here above the shop, in the room you are in now.'

'Mr Wheeler, I would be very happy to accept your offer,' Charlotte gushed, overwhelmed with happiness and gratitude. She didn't even have to consider it. 'Hannah and I will work hard, I promise. We'll be no trouble. We'll do whatever you ask of us. I've never been a maid before, but I've organised a house when my mother was sick, so I know what duties our maids performed.'

'You had maids?' Mrs Wheeler stared at her. 'And you ended up on the roads?'

Charlotte nodded, gripping her knife and fork, desperate to make them keep her and Hannah. 'I will work hard, I promise you. I've been working at any job for over a year now. Although, I don't know how to cook very well. I didn't spend much time with our cook as she was a tyrant for having people in her kitchen, but I'm a quick learner, truly I am, and so is Hannah.'

'Now, lass, calm down.' He patted her hand again, his eyes soft. 'We don't want you to be maids. You'll be—'

'A shop girl,' Mrs Wheeler butted in quickly. 'You'll learn the trade of serving in a shop, which is very respectable, you know.'

'Absolutely.' Charlotte nodded eagerly, willing to do or say anything that wouldn't make the Wheelers regret their offer.

'How old are you both?' he asked, taking a sip of tea.

'I will be nineteen next month. Hannah will be twelve next March.'

'So, Hannah will go to the village school,' Mr Wheeler said, and at the same time the little bell rang over the shop door.

'School?'

He rose from the table and wiped his hands on his linen napkin then shrugged on his jacket. 'She's too young to work in my opinion. And I believe every child should be in school. Do you agree?'

'Yes, of course. Her education has been lacking for a long while.'

'Good. Well, I'll make enquires about it this afternoon. She could start on Monday. During the day you will serve in the shop, or help Bessie out the back here, whatever is needed.' He left the kitchen and went out to the front to serve the customer.

Charlotte looked at Mrs Wheeler. 'I won't let you down.'

'It was Stan's idea. He's a good man, always one to help another. Sometimes, too much in my opinion.' She gave Charlotte a pointed look. 'I won't have his good nature abused, do you hear? You'll work hard and behave decently while under our roof, or you'll be out, back on those roads before you can blink.'

'Yes, Mrs Wheeler. I understand.' She could see who ruled this roost.

'You've been given a chance many around here would cut their right arms off for, and don't you forget it.'

'I won't.'

'Now eat up. You can start being a help today. I've got a few deliveries to pack into baskets, so you can begin with the washing up.'

The amount of baking trays, bowls and utensils piled into the stone sink didn't wipe the smile from Charlotte's face. She wouldn't have cared if the entire house needed scrubbing, she was happy to have a roof over her and Hannah's heads and a position. The fear of McBride, of walking the roads being at the mercy of strangers and the weather, of being homeless and friendless, receded. The future looked brighter than yesterday. She could relax a little.

CHAPTER 2

*H*arry Belmont strode across the flag-stoned yard and through the arch in the wall dividing the house from the service areas. Noise came from the open laundry door to his right as he headed towards the stable block beyond. Maids, coming out of the many buildings that lined the route, bobbed their heads and scuttled away busy with the never-ending chores needed to be done at Belmont Hall.

Glancing up at the sky, it gladdened him to see a streak of pale blue between the pewter grey clouds. A week of rain was annoying for man and beast. Thank the fates that the harvest was in. After turning right at the end of the path, the stable yard opened out before him. Stalls occupied left and right of a large cobbled square. The furthest end contained a double-gated arch leading out to the rear drive and the estate's fields. On either side of the gates, lay the barn and a tack room, above which were the grooms' quarters. Like the main house they were built in the late 1500s from locally quarried stone the colour of butter, but age had weathered to a dull honey hue.

'Good morning, sir.' Hoskins, the head groom, met him in the middle of the square, which was a hive of activity as stable hands mucked out stalls while grooms brushed down the horses standing tied to iron rings on the walls.

'Morning, Hoskins.' Harry nodded, liking this time of the morning when the sun was shining on the backs of the horses, steaming up the piles of manure, and especially after rain had washed the countryside clean. He watched as young Robbie gave the largest horse in the stable a last pat on the nose and brought him over.

Hoskins rocked on his heels. 'I've saddled Mighty, sir, seeing as no orders came for the carriage and the rain has stopped.'

'You did right, Hoskins. I'm sure we both need a good ride to clear our heads after a week of bad weather.'

'He's snappish today, sir,' Robbie, a youth of no more than fifteen added, handing the reins to Harry. 'In a right hurry, he is.'

Checking the tightness of the girth and stirrups, Harry gave a grim smile. 'We'll be testing each other I should expect.' He approached the bay's head and stroked his soft white nose. 'Now then, my good fellow. Behave yourself.' Having watched this horse being foaled and then training him to be one of the best hunter's in Yorkshire, Harry was intensely proud of him, even if he was a trifle too tall to be completely elegant. He had a foot in a stirrup when Fraser, another groom, came through the gates with an empty wheelbarrow and held up his hand.

'Sir, a carriage is coming up the drive, just gone over the bridge.'

'Blast. Another minute and I would have missed it.' Harry gave the reins to Hoskins. 'Did you recognise it, Fraser?'

Scratching his head under his flat cap, he shook his head. 'Hired one, I reckon, sir.'

'Bugger it. Have Mighty walked, Hoskins, will you? I'll try to be as quick as I can.' Returning the way he'd come, Harry hoped the visitor was no one important and quick about their business.

Instead of entering the house through the back entrance, he turned right and went around the side, nodding acknowledgment to both Henshaw, the head gardener, and Albie, the under gardener. Once on the gravel path that snaked through the lush gardens and tree groves, he quickened his stride, determined not to linger a moment more than necessary. He'd spent the last few rainy days cooped up in his study, first with his estate manager tallying up the records of the harvest profits, and then with his mine manager, Nicholas Adams and Mr Shelley, the mine surveyor, as they discussed developing a new coal seam. Now the grey skies were clearing and he was in dire need of fresh air.

Through the ancient oaks and chestnuts, now a riot of colour as their leaves changed to yellow, amber, orange and red, Harry glimpsed the coach bowling along the drive, creating a trailing drift of leaves in its wake.

He met the coach on the gravelled circle in front of the house, but one glance at its occupants sent him up the steps and inside feeling close to rage.

'Master?' Mrs Wynn, his housekeeper, was coming out of the drawing room as he entered the hall. 'I thought you'd gone for a ride, sir?'

'It was my intention, Mrs Wynn.' Harry had the childish urge to kick at something. 'But it seems my errant sister and cousin have returned.'

'They have?' Eyes wide, Mrs Wynn stared through the open doorway. 'But I had no notice, sir. Their rooms aren't ready. I thought they were staying in London until the end of October?'

'So did I, Mrs Wynn, so did I. But please don't stress yourself. My sister and cousin can wait for their rooms until you are ready for them.' In the drawing room he stood before the low fire and shifted a log with the toe of his riding boot.

That Petra and Bertram had come back shocked him, for he had only left them in London three weeks before and the two of them were as thick as thieves, as usual, planning their assault on the capital before coming home for Christmas. Why had they home early? And why couldn't he have a few more weeks of peace without their presence across the dining table? The atmosphere of the house changed when his sister was in residence. Her demands and cutting remarks put everyone on edge, and the fact Bertram followed her around like a devoted puppy made Harry want to knock him to the floor.

Immediately his thoughts became suspicious when Petra flounced through the door, whisking off her floor length black cape to reveal a virginal white outfit beneath, complete with one of the widest hats he's ever seen. Petra never wore white!

'Good morning, brother dear.' Petra gave him a devilish smile and plopped into a chair.

Bertram hastily followed suit and sat on the sofa, his smile weak, like his chin. 'Good morning, Harry.'

'Why have you returned from London?' His doubts grew significantly as Harry looked from one to the other before resting his stare on his sister, who was slipping off her gloves.

'We grew tired of the place, Harry,' Bertram jerked to his feet and walked around behind the sofa, 'you know how it is.'

'If you are going to lie, Bertram, then please do it well. Petra will teach you how. She is a consummate liar, as I've mentioned before.' Harry dismissed his pathetic cousin without a second glance.

Petra sighed dramatically. 'Don't be cruel, Harry. Bertram is correct. We have grown tired of London, of being a part of the same society every day. Everyone who is interesting has gone either abroad or returned to the country. We got bored.'

'Someone must have been left in town, but yet Belmont Hall is less boring than the delights of London?' he scoffed. 'I very much doubt it.' He paused as Winslow knocked on the open door. 'Yes?'

'Would you care for refreshments, sir?' the head butler asked.

'No thank you, Winslow.'

'Very good, sir.' He bowed himself away.

Petra pouted. 'I would have liked some tea, Harry. We've had nothing but dreadful coffee on the train.'

'Do I look like I care, Petra?' Harry raised an inquiring eyebrow at her. 'Now the truth, if you please.'

'Harry, perhaps we could freshen up a little first?' Bertram picked at the material on the top of the cream sofa, not meeting his eyes. 'We've been travelling all night and are rather exhausted.'

'By all means, Bertram, go upstairs, but Petra will stay here and answer my questions.'

'Why are you so suspicious of us, Harry?' Petra stood, her temper making her mouth a thin line. 'We *can* come home if we want to.'

'Your past behaviour makes me distrustful of everything you do. Since a child you have always been at the heart of any unfortunate incident. I left you in London less than a month ago and you were excited and happy to be there and filling your diary with invitations. Now you are suddenly home without warning. And your image of an innocent in white is lost on me. So again, I ask you, what has happened?'

After a quick glance at Bertram, Petra sauntered away towards the window. 'I wanted to escape the gossip.'

'Gossip about what?'

'About me.' She stared out through the lace curtains. 'I'd had enough of being talked about.'

'It isn't the first time you've been the centre of attention. You usually laugh off such things and secretly enjoy it.'

'Not this time.'

'What have you done?' Frustrated, Harry tried to control his anger. She had obviously said or done something to upset some friends or acquaintances of the family. 'From whom should I expect the first letter?'

'Oh...' She waved her hand lazily at him. 'I have no doubt that the old witches of our circle will be inundating you within days. They are likely scribbling away as we speak.'

Harry switched his attention to Bertram, who still stood

behind the sofa, his pale face even more bleached than normal. 'What will their correspondence reveal, cousin?'

Bertram wilted under Harry's glare, as he always did. 'I'm sure I do not know.'

'Try again.'

'Well, that is...it is all nonsense, of course.' Bertram blushed as easily as a young girl given her very first invitation to dance.

'What nonsense should I be aware of then? Speak, man, if you can!'

'That Petra has been involved in a...a liaison.' Bertram's cheeks flared red.

'Traitor!' Petra sneered at him. 'You have no backbone.'

Bertram hung his head. 'He will find out before the week's end, so what does it matter?'

Letting out a breath, Harry nodded his thanks and turned back to his sister. 'Who is he?'

'No one. It's nothing and all done with...'

Harry picked up on her hesitation instantly. 'You don't seem too sure about that. Do I have to make Bertram tell me everything, or will you finally find the courage to do so? I never took you for a coward, Petra.'

His stinging words had the right effect and she spun to him, eyes blazing with hate. 'You don't want to know, believe me!'

'Allow me to be the judge of that.' He tried to think of all the men in their circle she would be interested in. So far none had captured her attention for more than an afternoon. Going through names, he mentally rejected them for being too old, too fat, too boring, too far in debt...

She tossed her head. 'I don't want to talk about it.'

'Tell me!'

'Alastair.'

The name hung in the air between them.

'Alastair who?' Harry wracked his brains for all suitable men called Alastair he knew. The main one was his best friend, but he wasn't even considered, but there were others, such as Alastair Crocker, a banker and—

'Harry, it is Alastair McCoquindale,' Petra said it like a challenge. Her stance was straight, defiant and proud.

For a moment Harry couldn't think, couldn't take in what she had said. His best friend? He gathered his thoughts. 'Society believes you and he to be more than friends?'

'Yes.'

'And are they correct to believe such rumours?'

'Yes.'

'You're lying.'

'Why would I?'

'Because it's what you do. You lie and cheat and torment and bully. You have always done so.' He wondered idly if he would go to hell for hating his own sister, but it was the truth. They had never got along, and Harry had never forgiven her when their brothers Terence and Ray died due to her actions. Now she was dragging his childhood friend into her lies and he wanted to throttle her.

'It is the truth, Harry,' Bertram murmured.

It took an age for Harry to look at him; his neck seemed too stiff to move. 'Alastair and Petra? I don't believe it. Yes, she might have designs on him, but Alastair would not reciprocate. He's married to Susannah. They have a child. He wouldn't look twice at Petra. She's like a sister to him...'

'But he did, Harry,' Petra crowed. 'He loves me and I love him.'

The rage, the denial, burned in Harry like a red-hot poker. He felt sick, disgusted. Yet still his mind refused to accept it. 'Alastair wouldn't. You've invented this to cause trouble. You've never liked Susannah.'

'What is there to like? She's insipid, soft and pliable, always smiling and agreeing with every word out of anyone's mouth as if she's afraid to have her own opinions.'

'The exact opposite of you then!'

Laughing without humour, Petra sashayed across the room, touching the odd ornament as though they were discussing nothing more banal than the weather. 'And that is why Alastair is attracted to me.'

'It's not possible. He's known you since you were in the nursery. You must have flaunted yourself at him, offered yourself to him. Never would he have considered you otherwise.'

'Think that if it helps you.' She shrugged, unconcerned. 'Anyway, we've come home to let the talk die a little. Alastair said he would write to me and we'd see what can be done.'

'Done? Done?' Harry flung himself at her, grabbed her arms and shook her. 'You bitch! I won't let you destroy that family. You'll stay away from him. Do you hear me?'

Her sly grin matched the triumph in her hazel eyes. 'What are you going to do, lock me in my room?'

'It's an idea.'

'And ruin the precious reputation you have in the district? I don't think so. To have people whispering behind their hands would drive you mad. You like being the paragon of local society, the wonderful heir to this estate, the leader of the village, the owner of a thriving coal mine, the man everyone looks up to and admires. You have it all, don't you, Harry? You wouldn't do anything to cast a pall over any of that. The king of all you survey.' She raised her chin and smirked. 'I think you forget that our father is still alive, even if he is on the other side of the world.'

He threw her from him and watched in loathing as Bertram ran to steady her as she stumbled.

She turned to him. 'Oh dear, did I ruffle some feathers, brother? You don't like to be reminded that Father could come home at any time and make you redundant. I feel sorry for you because you actually don't have anything, do you? Not yet, anyway. You spend hours at your desk, for what? You could die before Father and then it's all mine!'

Harry's fists clenched at his side. 'Get out, Petra, get out of my sight.'

Her laughter echoed throughout the house as she went upstairs with Bertram trailing after her.

When he was alone, Harry took a deep breath to calm down. He had to admit his sister knew how to rile him. She knew exactly what words to say to jab at him. But Petra was correct, there were times that he did forget their father was alive and could return home on any given day. After a lifetime of experiencing an absentee parent, he couldn't be blamed that he thought all this was already his.

That aside, the bigger problem was the news about Alastair. Could it be true? Could his best friend, a man he'd known since they met at boarding school aged twelve, be conducting a liaison with Petra? How was it possible though? Alastair loved Susannah, he truly believed that. Was Petra making it up?

Movement at the door made him look up. Bertram stood in the doorway. 'What is it?'

Shuffling in a few steps, Bertram tucked his hands behind his back. 'I'm sorry you're upset with Petra.'

'Of course I'm upset! She's ruining a good man, a family, and what is left of her own reputation.'

'I just wanted to let you know that I insisted we come back home. She wanted to stay in London, but I overheard her and Alastair making plans to run away together, well... I heard Petra making the plans. Alastair was just nodding in agreement. I don't know if he was going to go through with it, but to me, it seemed like he wasn't fully committed. I don't know.'

'How did you persuade her to come home?'

'We went out to the theatre one night. A group of women turned their shoulders on Petra. One even spat at her feet.'

'Good God. Is it widely known, or do just a select group of people know? Who were they?'

'Most were family acquaintances. However, one was your mother's aunt, Mrs Frost-Dunley.'

'Great-Aunt Joan?' Shocked, Harry ran his hand through his hair. 'I don't believe it. Why didn't she help Petra, or advise her?'

'She tried, the week before. Only, Petra sent her away and told her to mind her own business. Anyway, the incident at the theatre shook Petra more than she would let on. I used it as the perfect excuse to leave London and let it all settle.'

'Why wasn't I informed before now?'

'I don't think anyone took it seriously, it was all rumours and Petra and Alastair kept it secret for a while. Even I didn't know. However, last week, they spent every day together in the open, and well, their obvious displays of affection were seen by all.' Bertram glanced away. 'At every social gathering they were together the minute they saw each other. They didn't try to hide their feelings at all. It was embarrassing.'

'Why are you telling me this? You are always on her side. No matter what she does, you are her champion.'

Bertram straightened and for once appeared to have a backbone. 'I'm telling you because I, like you and everyone else, admire Susannah, and I don't think she deserves to be treated in such a way. And also, because I think this is serious, at least on Petra's part. I am afraid she won't give him up. As a family it makes us look rather ghastly.'

Harry rubbed his hands over his face, devastated at Alastair's betrayal and his sister's behaviour. How the devil was he going to fix it?

CHAPTER 3

$\mathcal{H}$arry rode down the village main street, nodding to those who glanced in his direction, and saying good morning to those he knew by name, which were plenty. Dismounting in front of Wheeler's shop, he looked up at the sky and the low clouds that threatened rain. November had blown in cold and wet, matching his dark moods and impatient temper.

The brass bell tinkled over his head as he entered the shop. 'Good morning, Mr Wheeler.'

'Ah, Master Harry, it's good to see you. Wicked weather we're having. Winter's come early.' Wheeler tied up a small sack of sugar and placed it down on top of a much larger sack sitting to the side of the counter.

'Indeed. My gardener believes we'll have snow for Christmas.'

Sweeping grains of sugar off the counter and into a small dustpan, Wheeler tutted. 'Give me summer anytime over the cold. I heard reports you were in London, sir.'

'I arrived home yesterday.' Harry stared around the warm, neat shop. He moved to the fire and put his hands out to the flames, not wanting to think about the disastrous visit to London. 'How's everything in the village?'

'All is well, as far as I know, anyway.' Wheeler held up one of the tall glass jars of boiled sweets. 'For the children?'

'Yes, thank you. A quarter of each that you have, please.'

'Those pit children are fortunate to have such a generous employer as you.' As Wheeler started weighing out the brightly coloured sweets, a young woman walked out from the rear doorway and paused beside him.

Harry stared at her, never having seen her before. His heart gave a jolt, surprising him. A tingle of physical awareness gripped his whole body.

'Master Harry?'

Realising that Stan Wheeler had been speaking to him, Harry gave a little cough and tried to recapture his reeling senses. The young woman before him was a delicate beauty. 'You-you have a new assistant, Mr Wheeler?'

'Indeed, Master Harry, for nearly six weeks now.' Wheeler grinned, his whole demeanour showing his happiness. 'Charlotte, this is Mr Harry Belmont, of Belmont Hall. Master Harry, may I present Miss Charlotte Brookes.'

Harry held out his hand and she tentatively took it for a second before slipping her hands behind her slender back. She wore a huge white apron over a simple black dress. Her hair, the colour of deep chestnut mixed with copper was wound in a tight bun at the back of her head, but a few stray tendrils had escaped and hung over her small ears. Her eyes were a blend of green and dark gold. Colour heightened the unblemished skin on her cheeks. It took him but a moment to notice all these things and wonder at his own astonishment to her appearance. She was attractive, certainly, but he'd seen beautiful women before. So why did this one, a shop girl, rob him of both breath and sensible thought?

'Charlotte and her younger sister, Hannah, are staying with us, you see. They are now without family.' Wheeler gave her a pat on the shoulder in sympathy before regaining his sunny nature once more. 'But they have settled in so well here. Bessie and myself can't think of how it once was without them. Such help they are to us.'

Harry watched Miss Brookes as she smiled softly at Wheeler, the affection between them was mutual it seemed. He wanted to speak to her but didn't know what to say. A first for him.

Wheeler continued to fill up the small brown paper bags of sweets. 'See here now, Charlotte. Master Harry comes in every now and then and buys sweets for the children of the pit rows belonging to his mine. They are the children of the men he employs.' He opened a new jar of humbugs. 'A quarter of each kind from the boiled sweets and a dozen strips of liquorice cut again into smaller pieces. It goes on the Belmont Hall's account.'

'I see, yes.' She watched him intently as he used tongs to separate the black liquorice lengths.

'Are you staying in the village long, Miss Brookes?' Harry finally managed to say, absorbing the way she absently tucked her hair behind her ear.

She looked up at him, startled, her eyes wide as though speaking to him was alarming. 'I hope so, sir.'

He cringed at the 'sir'. He didn't want her to cower before him like a servant. For some reason he sensed she wasn't made that way. He didn't know why he thought so, or what proof he had, but he instinctively believed she was strong, determined and in no way ordinary. The manner in how she stood straight backed and watched Wheeler; the pert thrust of her chin as she helped him to weigh and bag the sweets. Her movements were neat and precise and Harry knew at that instant that he could watch her for the rest of his life.

He jerked at the thought and half stepped to the door, intending to get the hell out of the shop before he made a fool of himself, but his traitorous feet seemed glued to the floor and he continued to stare at her as though he was nothing more than a love-struck youth seeing his first pair of breasts!

'Master Harry?' Wheeler was thrusting out the bags.

'Thank you, Wheeler.' Harry grabbed them, feeling foolish and hot beneath the collar. 'Good day to you, and to you, Miss Brookes.' He spun from them and hurried out of the shop. He was up on Mighty's back and thundering down the street before he knew what he was about.

Once he'd cleared the village and was rising up into the slopes beyond it towards the pit rows and the mine, he slowed Mighty, not wanting to get there yet. The stunning young woman filled his mind and he swore violently. How very inconvenient to be attracted to a shop girl.

The paper bags rustled in his jacket pockets, and suddenly he was laughing. He tried to stop, for really, it was no laughing matter, and after the hellish weeks he'd had in London with Alastair he thought he'd never laugh again, but here he was nearly splitting his sides.

Charlotte Brookes.

Who would have thought it? The woman who finally stole his heart was called Charlotte Brookes and worked in Wheeler's shop. He laughed so hard he nearly fell off Mighty.

He was still smiling, but more under control as he rode into 'The Row', as it was called by the inhabitants and locals, the pit houses he had built ten years ago as an ambitious young man of twenty-one. When he'd had a dream of striking out, or creating something that was his own.

When tests had found that coal was under his land, land that did nothing but graze the odd herd, Harry had immediately known this was meant to be. The family owned mines in other areas, but never thought to have one immediately on their own doorstep. His father, Frank, was aghast. But undeterred, Harry opened a coal mine within three miles of his home, to the great expense and worry to his grandfather, Thomas, but between them they realised it was possible and another way to build on the Belmont wealth. His father had wiped his hands of the whole decision and having no inclination to safeguard the future Belmont generations, he left the country. *He* was too absorbed in his own concerns of botany and exploration in regions across the globe to care where the money came from as long as it supported his interests.

No, Harry had nothing of his father in him. This area, the land his ancestors had owned for centuries, was all that mattered to him. It was his destiny to build upon what they had started, what they had cared for down through the generations. And he would do it, no matter what it cost him. He would leave a legacy for his children, guide his sons to love and honour this land and the people on it. He just wished his grandfather had lived long enough to see the success he'd made of the mine.

Trotting down to The Row, he smiled again as Charlotte Brookes sprang to mind. It would take careful planning, a soft approach, but he would get to know her. Jumping down from Mighty, he greeted the group of children who, on hearing the hoof beats, came running out of doors, whooping out his name.

'Mr Belmont! Mr Belmont.' The air rang with their childish excitement as he handed out the packets to the older siblings for them to share out.

'Good day, Mr Belmont, sir.' An older woman came out onto her doorstep.

'How are you, Annie?'

'Well as could be, sir.'

'Your Albert is better now?' Harry asked of her husband who'd been struck down with the dreaded miner's cough for the last few months. He tried his best to know most of the miners who hauled out his coal.

'Aye, sir, he went back down this morning.'

'Good to hear it.' He nodded to the other wives who now gathered in groups, administering their children the odd slap when they protested someone got more sweets than they did.

Once remounted, Harry gave a last salute and urged Mighty

up the track that ran over the hill and down to the mine itself. Ugly slag heaps created new hills, and on these older girls worked alongside women who sorted through the rubbish slag for missed good pieces of coal.

Harry dismounted at the mine office and gave Mighty's reins to a young lad who took the horse into a small stable near one of the outbuildings. As he climbed the stairs up to the office, Harry was met by Nicholas Adams, his manager and good friend.

'Ah, Harry, I didn't think you were coming in this week.' Nicholas shook his hand and returned inside. 'I thought you were still in London. How did it go?'

'Don't ask.'

'That good, hey?' Nicholas shook his head.

Harry sighed and closed his mind on the unpleasant scenes with Alastair. 'Are you going down?' He went behind his desk, taking in Nicholas's dirty work clothes, which signalled his intentions of going underground.

'Yes, Shelley wants to show me more on the new seam that I wrote to you about.'

'It looks good?'

'It appears to be rather brilliant, Harry.' Excitement shone out of Nicholas's eyes for a moment before he scowled and indicated towards the maps laid out on the desk. 'Only problem is water.'

'How bad is it? Can the pumps handle it?'

'Yes, so far, but well, Shelley seems to think it might be further down where there's a fault.'

Harry drew in a deep breath as a dozen thoughts filled his head. The new seam would keep the miners in work for years, and make him a handsome profit, but the risk of water flooding the levels dimmed his enthusiasm. 'I'll get changed and we'll go down.'

Nicholas nodded and studied the maps again as Harry changed into the old clothes he kept at the mine for wearing underground. 'So, London wasn't a successful trip?'

'No, it wasn't. My sister has caused irreparable damage. And Alastair isn't the man I thought he was.' He tucked his shirt in and pulled on a thick jacket. 'Will you come to dinner tonight? I don't think I can stand another night looking at her and Bertram across the table. The three of us don't speak. It's getting to the stage where I'm losing my appetite, or I'll eat in the study.'

Nicholas laughed. 'Well, I know when I'm being used if nothing else.'

Harry grinned and slapped him on the back. 'With you there I can resist the urge to throttle them both.'

'Petra hates me, Harry. You know she doesn't like sitting at the same table as a mine manager. It's beneath her.'

Donning thick leather boots, Harry shook his head. 'Everything is beneath Petra, including good manners. If you feel uncomfortable then I'll understand if you decline.'

'And miss out on your cook's delicious meal for a solitary and badly cooked something at home? Not a chance.'

'You need to get married, my friend. I don't know how you survive cooking for yourself.' Harry grinned as they made their way down the stairs.

'Funny you should say that.' Nicholas raised his voice over the clanging of activity across the pit top. 'There's a young lady just recently moved to the village. She works at Wheeler's shop, lives with them too, with her sister.'

Harry's step faltered only slightly. 'Is that so?'

'From what I've been able to find out she's originally from Wakefield. Her parents are dead.'

'Indeed?'

They traversed the rail tracks and passed several equipment buildings, from which noise rang out loud enough to almost make their ears bleed, before Nicholas could speak again. 'She's been educated. Went to some private ladies' college. Her father was a solicitor in some firm, his father was a solicitor too, or a barrister, I can't remember exactly. Her other grandfather was a head master at a boy's college.'

'You know a lot, Nicholas.' Harry's chest seemed suddenly tight. 'Has your acquaintance with her developed into something more?'

Nicholas ducked his head shyly. 'No, indeed it has not. But I would like it to. Miss Brookes is beautiful, Harry. A breath of fresh air in the village, she is. Sadly, she doesn't know I exist.'

'Then how did you find out so much?'

'You know how Wheeler likes to talk. We were having an ale in the Black Hen and he told me how pleased he was that the girls are staying with him and his wife. I also overheard most of it from different women in the village. Since she's arrived Miss Brookes has created quite a stir. Many have their noses out of joint because every eligible man in the district is suddenly in Wheeler's shop. His profits must be soaring!' Laughing, Nicholas stopped walking as Christopher Shelley, the mine surveyor, joined them. 'Ah, Shelley. Mr Belmont and I are about to go down. I want to show him what you've surveyed.'

Shelley, tall with a short black beard, shook Harry's hand. 'Welcome home, Mr Belmont. There's been plenty of developments. I think you'll be pleased.'

'I'm very interested in what you've found, Chris.' Harry followed the two men to the main shaft-gate house, but for once his mind wasn't on the task at hand. Images of Charlotte Brookes kept pushing more important matters aside. Damn, was Nicholas right in that every single man in the district was after her? He couldn't waste any more time.

CHAPTER 4

'*B*y heck, it's cold outside.' Stan shivered as he re-entered the shop after scraping snow away from the front door. He passed Charlotte standing at the counter on his way through to the back rooms. 'Fancy a brew, lass?'

'That'd be lovely.' She finished stacking the bottles of ink on a shelf on the far wall, then poked at the fire before adding a shovelful of coal. The bell tinkled above the door and she looked up with a ready smile as a young woman about her own age came in. 'Good morning.'

'Is it?' The girl's eyes narrowed.

'Can I be of assistance?' Charlotte tried again.

'Oh yes, you can help me all right by staying away from my Lenny.'

'Pardon?' Charlotte walked back to the counter, wondering what the girl was talking about.

'I know he's been in here nearly every day, so don't bother to deny it.'

'We have many people in here. Is there—'

The girl gripped the counter and leaned over to peer angrily into Charlotte's face. 'Now listen here, Miss High and Bloody

Mighty. I know what you're about, as do many other girls whose men you're playing about with, and it's not on, do you understand?'

'I'm afraid I don't, I'm sorry.' Charlotte looked over her shoulder, praying for Bessie or Stan to come through the door from the back rooms.

'None of us will let you steal our men. I've told Lenny to not step foot in this shop again until we're married. And now I'm telling you to stay away from him.'

'You are mistaken, I assure you.'

'Don't think your fine ways will work here, miss. We're not having it, I'm telling you. Leave my Lenny alone!'

'Janice Weatherby, what is this nonsense about?' Bessie came through to stand beside Charlotte. 'I can hear you shouting from the kitchen.'

'I'm sorry, Mrs Wheeler, but I'll not stand for it another day.'

'And what is that exactly?'

'Her!' Janice stuck a finger in Charlotte's face. 'She wants my Lenny, and every other man in the village no doubt, the hussy.'

'Claptrap!' Bessie snapped, folding her arms. 'Charlotte would no more look at Lenny Turner than she would look at old Mr Eastley and he's ninety if a day and bedridden.'

'My Lenny—'

'Your Lenny has wandering eyes, Janice, like most men do, but if you keep harping on at him he'll have wandering hands and feet as well. Now think on.'

'I'm not the only one who's upset, Mrs Wheeler. Peggy Saunders said her Horace is forever stopping in here. Why is that then? And Peter Warren and his pals talk of nothing but her. In the Black Hen there's bets on who'll be the first to kiss her and a tally on who she'll marry!' Red in the face, Janice threw her head back indignantly. 'The hide of her, coming here and stealing our men folk.'

Fed up with such stupid talk, and disgusted that there was a tally about her, Charlotte tried not to let her temper show. 'I can assure you, Miss Weatherby, that I have no intentions of stealing anyone's man.'

'Of course she doesn't,' Bessie added.

'I have yet to meet a man within ten miles of this village who would tempt me into marriage,' Charlotte finished. Though it wasn't exactly true, but she'd never tell a living soul how her stomach had trembled when Harry Belmont stared at her.

Janice gasped. 'What do you mean, you stuck up cow! Aren't our boys good enough for you now, is that it? You think you're better than us, don't you? With your nice voice and ladylike manners. It don't make you better than the rest of us, especially since you're nowt but a shop girl now.'

'Oh, good Lord.' Charlotte shook her head in amazement. She couldn't win.

'You're making a spectacle of yourself, Janice, for heaven's sake.' Bessie stormed around to the end of the counter. 'Charlotte can't help it if men with no more brains than a pig come into this shop and gawk at her. She wouldn't have one of them if they offered her all the tea in China. Now leave us to be getting on with our work.'

Janice stomped towards the door. 'Don't think this is the end of it, oh no. There's to be three weddings this spring and *she* ain't going to any one of them!' The door slammed behind her.

Dumbfounded, Charlotte looked at Bessie and they both burst out laughing. 'What was that all about?'

'Nay, lass, some ruffled feathers I should imagine. Haven't you noticed the amount of single men coming in here?'

'I can't say I have. I don't take any notice of them. I simply serve them what they want.'

'Aye, that's the point, lass. They all want you.'

The warmth drained from Charlotte's face. 'I don't want them! I don't encourage any of that. You do believe me, don't you, Bessie?'

'Aye, lass, I do, and so does Stan.'

'Stan knows?' She was mortified.

'There's been talk of nowt else since you arrived, lass.' Bessie gave the counter a wipe over with the ever-present cloth she carried in her apron pocket. 'People get tired of seeing the same faces all their lives. When someone new turns up it causes a sensation through the village. It'll die down eventually.'

'Yes, but by then no one will be speaking to me. The men will be frightened of their sweethearts' ire and the women will be worried I'm trying to steal their men.'

'Only the ones of a certain age. You'll be fine amongst the older ones who wouldn't care if their husbands did wander!' Bessie grinned and turned as a streak of sunshine flooded the shop which was all the more brighter for reflecting off the snow. 'Ah, will you look at that. The clouds have lifted.'

'It's nice to see blue sky after all this bad weather.'

'Why don't you go for a walk, lass?' Bessie suggested. 'I'll see to the shop. You've not been out for over a week because of the snow.'

'Do you mind?' She had a longing to go for a walk and breathe in clear crisp air. It felt like months instead of weeks since she'd had the opportunity to just be alone and not think or talk to anyone.

'Nay, go on and get some fresh air. Stan will walk down to the school and meet Hannah; you know he enjoys doing that. Though the poor girl is quite capable of walking up the street by herself with all the other girls.' Bessie rolled her eyes. 'Still, it gives him pleasure, so why deny him? You go, lass. You've worked hard and deserve a break.'

'All right then, I will.' Filled with anticipation of an hour alone, the first she'd had since arriving two months ago, she untied her apron and walked into the kitchen where Stan was reading the newspaper at the table.

'I'm off for a walk, Stan.'

'What about your tea?'

'I'll have some when I return.'

'Rightio, love. Be careful, it's slippery out.'

'I will.' She hastily wrapped a red scarf around her neck and tucked it into her black coat, before pulling on some black woollen gloves and slipping from the back of the shop. Once clearing the yard, she headed up the incline and away from the village and to the open fields beyond.

Although the snow was thick on the ground in places, she kept to the well-worn track used by people and animals alike, which wound westwards towards the next village four miles away.

Before the snow came, Stan had taken Hannah on such walks and later she'd been told of the pretty views seen from high on the hills surrounding Belthorpe. At the time, Charlotte had been busy learning the shop trade and hadn't the time to go adventuring as Hannah did with Stan, but now, suddenly finding herself free, she felt the need to stretch out her arms and deeply breathe in the cold brisk air.

When she crested the first small hill, she looked back on Belthorpe and the cluster of houses spreading out from the main street like a woman's skirt. Sunlight bathed the whole area, dazzling the snow and making the ice clinging to the trees sparkle like diamonds, not that she had seen that many diamonds to make such a judgement. Her grandmother had a few diamond brooches, which she'd promised to bequeath to Charlotte and Hannah, but they were gone, like everything else had from their old life.

Trudging on, Charlotte refused to think of her family. Yes, she missed them terribly, but it only caused heartache to think of them and today, this hour, wasn't going to be spoilt by being sad.

On the other side of the hill, the track forked and she didn't hesitate to take the right turn and meander beside a small, ice-fringed stream that disappeared into thin woodland. Here, the track grew narrower with snow banking up to several feet in low-lying places.

'Whoa, Mighty.'

Charlotte whirled, alarmed that a horse and rider were right behind her. She'd been so intent on placing her feet that she didn't hear the crunch of hoof beats over the sound of the gurgling stream where the ice had broken. She hastily stepped to one side and into snow that went up mid-calf.

'Please, don't be afraid.' Harry Belmont dismounted. 'I didn't mean to startle you.'

'I was miles away.' She stared at him, willing her silly heart-beat to slow down before she had a seizure at his feet.

'I've not seen you out walking before.' Belmont grabbed his horse's bridle and stood a mere three feet from her.

The coldness of the snow was seeping into her boots, but she couldn't have moved to save her life at that moment. 'I don't get much time to walk.'

'I have often seen Mr Wheeler and your sister though.'

'Yes.' Her tongue felt too big for her mouth as he stared at her. Was he waiting for her to say something else? Her mind went blank.

'Soon the snow will be too thick to walk.' He patted the horse's head as it nudged his shoulder. Charlotte was sure it was the tallest horse she'd ever seen, and not the handsomest either. Unlike its owner. Belmont was a good foot taller than her and she wasn't short, but what made him seem bigger was his air of authority, of purpose. As though this man knew his rightful place in the world and never doubted it for a moment. He was a gentle-man. The owner of much of the district, and so many depended on him to keep them in work.

'I am not sure if you remember me,' he broke the silence. 'I am Harry Belmont.'

'I know who you are, sir.'

'Don't.'

Her eyes widened. 'Pardon?'

'Don't call me, sir. I am not your employer.'

He seemed angry with her and this annoyed her. 'Forgive me, Mr Belmont.' She inclined her head and walked away. In dismay she found him walking beside her.

'I didn't mean to be rude. I apologise.' He sighed heavily. 'It has been an upsetting morning. My housekeeper, Mrs Wynn, died suddenly this morning. Heart failure apparently.'

'Oh dear. I am sorry to hear such news. I have served her in the shop.'

'She was a good woman, loyal to the family, a favourite of my late mother's. Mrs Wynn worked for the house for thirty-five years. She will be sadly missed.'

'Yes, of course. How sad. I will inform Bessie and Stan. Will she be buried in the village?'

'No. If it can be arranged, her family are burying her in Selby, where she is originally from. I shall attend the funeral next week.'

'Life can seem very short sometimes.'

'Yes, I agree. After a morning of talking to the doctor and the reverend and naturally the staff, I was in need of escaping the house even in this weather.'

Not knowing how to answer him, she kept walking.

'Miss Brookes?'

'Yes?' She glanced up at him as the beginning of the wood closed in around them.

'Do you like living here?'

'Yes. There are worse places, believe me.'

He faltered for second. 'Do you...read?'

She gave him a sharp glance. 'I have been educated, Mr Belmont.'

'Of course, I meant do you take pleasure in reading?'

Surprised and a little puzzled at the question, she nodded. 'When I have the time. I used to read a great deal at home.' She suddenly recalled sitting before the parlour fireplace and reading Jane Austen while her mother embroidered on the sofa. It was a sweet memory and one she hadn't thought of in a long time.

'What authors do you prefer?'

'I like reading Charles Dickens, Austen and have enjoyed Anthony Trollope.'

'Ah, I do, too. I'm currently reading a book by Wilkie Collins. Have you read his works?'

'No, I haven't.' She lifted her skirts higher to clear a deep patch of snow.

'Well, we must remedy that. Sadly, Belthorpe doesn't have a bookshop, or a lending library.' He mused.

'No. I read Stan's books though, or the newspaper. He orders books in from York.' The sun's rays speared down between the bare limbed trees. There was only the sound of the snow crunching beneath their boots and the squeak of leather harness.

'Belmont Hall has a fine library. You're welcome to call and select any title you wish, more than one if it pleases you.'

'Thank you-' She nearly called him sir but stopped herself in time. The chances of her borrowing a book from the Hall was non-existent though, he was just being polite.

They walked on without speaking until they cleared the trees and were out in the open again. A bird flew high above them, hovering over an unseen prey.

'A goshawk, I think,' Belmont murmured, looking up. 'My brothers and I used to go hawking.'

'But you don't anymore?'

'They are dead. I didn't have the heart to do it by myself. I sold the birds.'

The soft way he spoke touched her. That he could speak of such a personal subject warmed her to him. She expected a man of wealth and position to be above speaking to a shop girl such as she was now. Even if she still had her parents alive and was living back in their lovely house in Wakefield, she wouldn't have mixed within his society. Her family were town's people and his landed gentry.

She gazed at his profile as he watched the bird. Beneath his hat, his hair was dark, but his eyes were a sharp light blue. They were the first thing she noticed about him. His nose had a slight bump in it, not that it detracted from his good looks, but rather added to them.

He shifted his stance and looked down at her. For a moment they simply stared at each other. Then he smiled, such a warm friendly smile that she couldn't help but smile back. 'I must go. I have company arriving for dinner.'

'Yes, of course.' She stepped back, breaking the spell between them.

'You will come to the Hall, won't you and visit the library?'

'I'm not sure...' How on earth would she tell Bessie and Stan of such an invitation? 'I'm very busy in the shop, but thank you for the offer. Good day.' She turned and walked back the way she'd come.

'Miss Brookes?'

Over her shoulder she looked at him. 'Yes, Mr Belmont?'

'I hope to see you walking again soon.'

Without answering, she quickened her steps and didn't slow down until she was deep in the wood again. Lord above, what on earth was she to think about that!

Throughout the rest of the afternoon and well into the evening, Charlotte replayed in her mind the meeting with Belmont. She still didn't know what to think or feel about it. Was he being a kind gentleman, one who spoke to all like that, or had he singled her out especially, and if so, then why had he?

'You look pensive, my dear,' Stan said, poking the fire in the sitting room. He returned the poker to its stand and gathered Hannah onto his lap as they looked at a detailed picture she had drawn at school. She had a skill for drawing and Stan was eager she make something of it. Their evening meal had been eaten and cleared away and for an hour or two before bedtime they would sit together and read, play cards, talk or work on some menial task not addressed during the day.

Charlotte put down the stocking she was darning, and not doing a successful job of it at that, and watched the sparks shoot up the chimney. 'I was simply thinking.'

'Oh aye? It must have been a sad thought then by the expression on your face.'

'No, not sad. Perhaps intriguing.'

'Intriguing?' Bessie put down her own sewing as she said the word with a frown. 'What was intriguing?'

'When I went for that walk today I met Mr Belmont.'

Bessie and Stan exchanged a telling look between them.

'He invited me to view the library up at the Hall and borrow a book if I wanted to.'

'Go to Belmont Hall?' Bessie gasped as though Charlotte had been offered to sail to the jungles of Africa. She gaped at Stan, but he seemed as astounded as her. 'Harry Belmont invited *you* to go to Belmont Hall?'

'Yes.' She blinked at Bessie's harsh tone. Charlotte knew they would react, and yet telling them seemed the right thing to do. 'I declined the offer.'

'And so you should! Any decent girl would.' Bessie snapped. 'What was he *thinking* of?'

'I believe he *thought* he was being kind and generous.'

'And why would he be that to *you*? You are nothing to him!'

'I am someone respectable and a fellow reader.'

'But he shouldn't be offering you anything at all. Imagine the gossip. You did right to turn him down. I should think he wasn't serious anyway, and probably grateful you have the good manners to not take him up on it.'

'And why wouldn't he be serious?' Charlotte asked, thoroughly irritated now.

'Because you are not of his class.'

'No, I am not now. However, I was raised to be a—'

Bessie jerked to her feet. 'I don't care how you were raised, you aren't gentry.'

'My parents were educated gentle people of good standing, Bessie. As solicitors, my father and grandfather socialised with many of Wakefield's dignitaries.'

'You still aren't landed gentry like the Belmonts, my girl. There's a marked difference. A line you don't cross.'

Stan sat straighter in his chair, hitching Hannah higher on his lap. 'Bess, lass, Mr Belmont and Charlotte were only talking about books. There's no harm in that.'

'No harm in it?' She turned on him, fury colouring her cheeks. 'Are you simple, Stanley Wheeler? He's a gentleman and she's a shop girl. The two only mix for one reason!'

Shocked, Charlotte stood, angry and humiliated. 'How dare you suggest such a thing!'

'Now, now, my dears, let's settle down, shall we?' Stan put Hannah on her feet and attempted to calm the situation, but Charlotte was hurt that Bessie could think so little of her.

'I'll be going up to bed. Come, Hannah.' She grabbed her sister's hand and dragged her from the room.

Alone together, Stan's lips tightened in a livid grimace. 'What is wrong with you, woman!'

Bessie puffed out her chest. 'Now don't you start at me, Stan. I'm only looking out for her!'

'How do you work that out? You all but accused her of seeing Belmont for salacious reasons!' He wiped his hand over his face. 'Charlotte would no more do anything with Belmont than she would with old Mr Eastley!'

'Maybe not, but many a girl's head has been turned by a handsome man, even more so when the fellow in question is someone with position and influence. And what about those gentlemen who simply take what they want? What about that, Stan Wheeler?' In full steam, Bessie didn't pause for breath. 'You remember

Florence Isaacs? She was taken down by Sir Hilliard's son from over Escrick way. He sweetened her with his promises and trinkets and then when he was finished with her she was thrown onto the parish with a child.'

'Mr Belmont is not such a man, and you know it. We've watched him grow from an infant. Yes, there's men like Hilliard, a true blackguard, who abuse their authority over those lesser than them, but again I tell you, Belmont isn't like that. You know how he is kind to everyone, that's the way the man is.'

'Aye, we all know it, but to invite a shop girl to Belmont Hall to read his books? He's never done that before!'

'Charlotte is more than a mere shop girl and you know it. Look how she speaks, her manners, the way she carries herself. She's been brought up in a genteel home. Belmont's probably seen that and knows she's a little out of place in the role she now finds herself, but it's no more than kindness, Bess.'

'Do you care to risk it?'

'We won't need to if you behave like that again. Those two girls will be packed and gone before dawn.' The thought gave him a pain in his chest. 'If you've driven them away by that tongue of yours, Bessie, I'll never forgive you.' He stormed from the room and upstairs.

Outside the girls' bedroom he listened for movement but all was quiet inside. Knowing he'd never sleep now, he returned downstairs and went into the small stock room. Lighting the lamp, he drew his ledgers towards him and prayed Charlotte and Hannah wouldn't leave during the night.

CHAPTER 5

Charlotte lifted the bag of flour onto the counter, smiling as Stan joked about the amount of growing Hannah had done in the three months they'd been living with them. 'She's making up for lost time, that's why.'

'And you're sure she'll like the dress we bought her?' He frowned as he placed one-pound bags of tea on a shelf. 'And the new boots? Perhaps a girl of eleven doesn't want that sort of thing and would prefer something else entirely?'

'She will like what you have bought her. She'll be delighted and grateful. Thank you,' she replied as the door opened and Nicholas Adams came in. Charlotte smiled a welcome. Of all the village men, she preferred Mr Adams, for he was handsome and kind, with an easy manner and soft brown eyes that crinkled when he smiled. He was the sort of man she would like to marry one day. At that thought her heart flipped and Harry Belmont's image swam before her. But he wasn't for her, she knew that. As a gentleman he was not in her sphere anymore and besides that his intensity rather alarmed her.

'Good day, Miss Brookes.' Mr Adams gave her one of his half smiles and Charlotte returned it.

'How are you, Mr Adams?'

'Well, thank you.'

Stan stepped forward, wiping his hands on his apron. 'Your weekly order is it, Nicholas?'

'Yes, thank you.'

While Stan collected items to fill the order, Charlotte continued to weigh the flour, her mind flitting from Adams to Belmont, the only two men who attracted her attention.

'How's things up at the mine?' Stan asked him, while writing down the prices on a sheet of paper. 'A new level has been opened I hear?'

'Yes, that's right. However, it's slow going for the moment. Water is causing problems and Harry…Mr Belmont, is cautious, as he should be, of course.'

'Indeed, yes. Water and gas are no man's friend underground.' Stan handed over the box of goods and told him of the amount.

Nicholas counted coins and placed them on the counter near Charlotte, she smiled again and blushed as he stared at her with interest. 'There's a Christmas dance on at the Belmont's Home Farm, Miss Brookes, did you hear?'

'Yes, I did.'

'It's an annual thing Harry, er…the Belmonts, put on.' He flushed and juggled the box in his arms.

Stan gathered up the coins noisily. 'Aye, that's next week, isn't it? Bessie mentioned it the other day. We're all going, naturally. The whole village always turns out for the annual Christmas dance.'

'Er…yes…' Nicholas took a step backwards. 'Well, let's hope the snow isn't too heavy so we can attend it.' He took a few more steps and then paused. He stared directly at Charlotte. 'May I beg a dance from you, Miss Brookes?'

Not expecting such a request, she hesitated and saw the light die a little in his eyes. 'Yes, of course, Mr Adams. I would like that.'

His smiled returned wider than before and with a farewell he left the shop.

'Well, that's how it is then,' Stan said, turning back to his bags of tea.

'And what do you mean by that?' Charlotte asked, blushing.

'Nicholas Adams.' Stan grunted, a frown reappearing. 'Why is it that every man in this village thinks he can be as free as he likes around you?' Another pound of tea was thudded onto the shelf. 'You know, if you say yes to one man, they'll all be hounding you?'

'It's only a dance, you know.'

His frown deepened. 'No, lass. It's more than just a dance to some of them and you need to be prepared for a flurry of marriage proposals.'

She tried to laugh at the suggestion but couldn't. She didn't want marriage proposals, not even from Nicholas Adams. The thought of marrying any man was beyond her scope of imagination at this time. She was settled here with the Wheelers, she didn't want any more changes in her life, she'd had enough of that already. And then there was Hannah. Her sister had to come first and she needed Charlotte to be around.

* * *

Harry scanned the barn, taking in everything, making sure it was perfect, even though there had been a small army of people preparing for tonight's dance for the last two days. It irked him that he was making such fuss, like a woman. He'd organised these Christmas dances for the last four years, and previously left it to others to arrange it, but this time he wanted to oversee every detail. Why? Well, he knew why, obviously. There was no point denying it. Charlotte Brookes. Her image wouldn't leave his mind. In his head he went over each meeting they'd had, every sentence she uttered to him. It frustrated him that she didn't come to the Hall to borrow books. He'd have to try again, starting tonight. Although he would be polite and dance with a few of the village matrons, he'd make certain he danced with Miss Brookes. He had to gain her confidence, show her his intent, but for the first time in his life he was unsure how to go about getting something he really wanted.

Normally he'd talk over this predicament with Alastair, but since his friend had lost his mind over Petra, their friendship had faltered, splintered, and he was distraught to have lost such an important person from his life. He doubted they would ever be as easy as they once were and he felt the loss keenly. Perhaps it was fate's way of telling him it was time to find a new person to fill his life. Someone to become his mate, his best friend, the one he could turn to no matter what. He'd lost his brothers, and now Alastair. Could that person be Charlotte? Instinct told him she could be all these things.

Daylight had gone by the time the first of the villagers filtered into the barn. Harry greeted them one by one, cursing Petra for delaying her appearance to miss this duty. He knew she felt it beneath her to mix with the people of the village, and in previous years she'd only stayed a minimum of half an hour to show her face before disappearing back to the Hall, dragging Bertram behind her. She did exactly the same at the staff's Christmas party on Christmas Eve. Their mother had never been so rude, and treated staff like the important people they were. Without them, the estate would not thrive. Their father, although not rude, was always in his own world and the people who ran his home never really entered his consciousness. Perhaps, that was why he happily handed the whole lot over to Harry when Grandfather died, and quickly made his escape to some jungle in Africa.

Harry shook hands with Mr Stevens, the vicar, and Mr Groates, the school-master. Both men fell into conversation and moved away, leaving Harry to shake the hands of Mrs Kilmore, the owner of the haberdashery shop, and her niece. The surveyor,

Mr Shelley, entered with his pretty wife, followed by Mr Richard Clarke, one of the mine's engineers and his wife. Harry greeted them warmly. More people filed into the barn, and after another ten minutes of greeting people, Harry was ready for a drink.

He smiled widely as Nicholas came through the doors, and feeling he'd done his duty enough, he slapped Nicholas on the back and turned them towards the tapped barrels of ale in the corner. Hall staff manned the refreshment tables, and made sure people were fed and watered, but the atmosphere was relaxed and friendly. With nearly the whole of the village attending and since most of the staff were originally from the village, it made it an evening of families reuniting and friends having the opportunity to be together.

A musical band made up of local men, were set up on top of one of the farm wagons and their noisy tuning of instruments suddenly became a foot tapping song and a few couples got up to dance.

Nicholas passed him a pint of ale. 'It's a good turn out again, Harry.'

'Indeed. I thought the threat of more snow might deter some, but it's a long time until the summer dance and this gives everyone an enjoyable night in the meantime.'

'My favourite time of year is spring,' Nicholas said, nodding to a passing couple. 'Don't you find...' Nicholas stopped talking, his pint half way to his mouth.

Harry turned to glance at what had caught Nicholas's attention. The Wheelers had arrived, and alongside them, Miss Brookes and her sister. Harry's stomach did a flip as he watched her smile at someone and shed her cloak. The cream lace dress she wore showed off her slim figure. It was the first time he'd seen her wearing something other than the dark clothes she wore in the shop. Her thick chestnut hair shone and was gathered up and secured with pearl combs. Little copper tendrils framed her heart-shaped face. He sucked in a breath. Within the golden globes shinning from the hanging lamps she appeared a fragile beauty. And he wanted her. Desperately.

'There is no one her equal within fifty miles,' Nicholas breathed.

Startled by the confession, Harry stared at his friend. Before he chanced to respond, Stan Wheeler brought his family over.

'Master Harry, Nicholas.' Stan shook hands with them both.

Harry went through the greetings without thought, his gaze barely leaving Miss Brookes. Up close she was stunning, her amber-green eyes bright, and her lips... Lord, he ached to kiss her lips. He wanted to taste them until he lost the ability to stand.

'A dance, Miss Brookes?' Nicholas held out an arm, which she took, and he guided her to the middle of the barn to dance among the other couples.

'They make a fine pair, do they not, Master Harry?' Bessie smiled at him. 'What a match that would be for Charlotte. Such a good man is Mr Adams.'

'Indeed,' Harry managed to utter. 'If you'll excuse me, I see my sister has arrived.' He gave a last look in Charlotte's direction, disliking the way Nicholas had taken the opportunity to get the first dance with her.

Petra stood just inside the barn's entrance, a look of boredom on her face, and her manner aloof. Bertram hovered behind her, but at least he acknowledged those around them with a slight nod.

'You're late.' Harry gripped his sister's arm to draw her further into the barn. 'Smile, Goddammit. You'll do this duty and enjoy it. They are good people, not lepers.'

'This is your party, Harry, not mine. I have no wish to be here,' Petra said, through gritted teeth. 'It's bad enough I have to attend the staff Christmas party every year, never mind this charade.' She sighed heavily.

'Let us dance.' Not allowing any protests, he moved her swiftly into the middle of the dancing.

'You're becoming more of a bully with every passing day,' she whispered harshly, tossing her head making the diamonds she wore sparkle in the light.

He raised a sarcastic eyebrow as he swung them around. 'It runs in the family doesn't it, dearest sister?'

'No wonder you aren't married yet. No one will have you.'

'Whereas you have gentlemen queuing down the drive?'

'I only want a certain one!'

He faltered. 'That is done with. Put it from your mind.'

'Easier said than done. You don't know how difficult it is, as you've never felt such passion in your life.'

His gaze flicked to Miss Brookes, who was smiling widely at something Nicholas was saying. Jealousy speared through Harry like a knife. Despite being in the middle of a throng of people, he felt alone. Lonely.

The music ended and Petra slipped away from him. He turned away and at that moment he wanted nothing more than to take Miss Brookes's hand and run from the barn, from everyone and everything and just talk to her, look at her, make love to her.

When the music started again, he found that Mr Shelley had taken his turn to dance with her. Frustrated, Harry took a pint of ale from the lad at the barrel and drank most of it down. He was being stupid, he knew. Acting like a child denied its favourite toy. Determined to enjoy the night, he took a deep breath and stepped to where Doctor Neville and his wife were standing. They were often guests at the Hall and good friends. Easy conversation was what he needed. Then, when he'd got himself under control, he'd ask her to dance.

'Who is that?' Petra spoke right behind him as he chatted to the Nevilles. Her rudeness was disgusting.

'Good evening, Miss Belmont,' Doctor Neville inclined his head to her.

Petra finally had the good manners to flash a small smile to him and his wife. 'Good evening to you both. Now can someone tell me who that is?' She pointed straight at Miss Brookes.

Harry's heart sank. 'That is Miss Charlotte Brookes. She and her sister live with the Wheelers.' He watched as Petra studied her with narrowed eyes.

'She is very lovely,' Mrs Neville commented. 'I've had a many a nice chat with her in the shop.'

'So, she is a shop girl.' Petra's shoulders relaxed a little.

'Hardly that, really.' Mrs Neville frowned. 'She's not had it easy lately, but she comes from a very respectable family in Wakefield. Solicitors, I believe.'

'Then why is she here?'

'Her family are all dead. The Wheelers took them in.'

'Like waifs?' Petra snorted. 'There is no family money? Nicholas should think hard on spending too much time with her. All she will give him is a pretty face.'

'Petra!' Harry snapped. His sister was impossible, and it didn't help his mood to find Nicholas once more standing next to Miss Brookes and them deep in conversation.

Doctor Neville coughed a little. 'Sometimes, a pretty face and a pleasing manner is all a man wants. Family and fortune are all well and good, but the person inside counts for more, in my humble opinion. Life can be very long when you're unhappy with someone. Money doesn't always compensate.'

Petra sniggered. 'Oh, Doctor Neville, you are so innocent.'

It seemed as though the doctor was going to say something more, but instead he inclined his head to her, before taking his wife's hand and leading her into a dance.

'Go home, Petra.' Harry sighed and walked away from her. Determined, he went straight to the one person who mattered in the room and held out his hand. 'A dance, Miss Brookes?'

Her eyes widened fractionally, she excused herself from talking to Nicholas and Mr Shelley, and stepped into his hold. Harry thought his heart might actually jump out of his chest as he felt one of her hands rest on his shoulder, and the other nestle within his fingers. What the hell was the matter with him? He concentrated on making normal conversation. 'You aren't wearing any gloves now, Miss Brookes.'

She looked up at him. 'No, Hannah, in her excitement just bumped into me and spilled my port over them. I thought it best to remove them altogether than to wear red stained gloves. I looked like I had gutted a pig.' She laughed.

'Sisters.' He smiled in response.

'Indeed.' Her gazed flickered to where Petra stood with Bertram, but he said nothing. He didn't want to talk about Petra.

'You still haven't investigated the Hall's library,' he said quietly, bringing her a little closer to him, liking the supple way she moved with him.

'No.'

'I wish you would. Such collections should be read and admired, not ignored for years on end.'

'I do wish to see your library, but...' Her cheeks flushed. 'It wouldn't be correct.'

'Why not? I've invited you.'

'People would talk.'

'Nonsense.' Though he didn't believe that. He knew they would. Village gossip spread faster than disease. 'I would not be ashamed should they talk about us. I'd be honoured, in fact.'

'That's because you're a gentleman and such things are accepted. Whereas I am—'

'A fine woman,' he spoke instead.

'Mr Belmont, please.'

'I've embarrassed you. I apologise.' He smiled down at her and led their steps across the floor.

'It seems forever since I last danced before tonight,' she murmured.

Harry gazed at her downcast face. She was delicately beautiful. A soft tendril of hair had slipped from her combs and curled around her ear. He itched to touch it, to nuzzle his nose behind her ear and kiss the tender skin of her throat. Lost to the moment, he suddenly straightened when she pulled away a little.

'Thank you, Mr Belmont.' She stepped out of his hold.

He blinked, realising the music had stopped, and gathered his scattered wits.

'Harry, I do believe it's time we left.' Petra came from nowhere, her expression as hard as granite.

'Miss Brookes, may I introduce you to my sister, Miss Petra Belmont. Petra, Miss Charlotte Brookes.'

With an expression on her face as though she'd just sucked a lemon, Petra held out the tips of her fingers for Charlotte to touch. 'I believe you work in a shop, Miss Brookes?'

'You are correct, Miss Belmont.'

'And you are without family?'

'True again.'

'Is it also true you and your sister were beggars on the street?' Petra's voice carried to those around them.

Charlotte straightened. 'You seem well informed about me, Miss Belmont.'

'I wasn't certain as to whether such tales were falsehoods, Miss Brookes, after all, it's not every day we mix with actual people who have walked the roads homeless.' Petra turned a triumphant gaze to Harry. 'Isn't that correct, brother?'

'I think it is time I took my sister home. Excuse me.' Charlotte turned away before Harry could say another word, but he saw the wounded look in her eyes.

'Harry! Harry stop gazing after her like a love-struck fool!' Petra hissed like a disturbed snake. 'You're making a spectacle of yourself. Are you drunk? I'm all for having fun flirtations, but you're making it obvious and she is not worthy of such an open display.'

'What are you talking about?'

Petra discreetly pulled him away from the new sets of dancing couples and towards the doors. 'I'm talking about you and the shop girl, for heaven's sake. Have her, by all means, I know you men like to sample a bit of rough from time to time, but don't do it noticeably. Anyone with eyes could see the way you were looking at her just now. It was disgusting. Pathetic.'

'Stop.' Harry's fists curled at his sides. 'You're being ridiculous.'

'I saw the way you were staring at her. I'm sure I wasn't the only one.'

'You are mistaken.'

'No, you are.' She leant in closer to whisper, 'She is a *nobody*. A *homeless* nobody. Have her in a barn at some point, if you must and get her out of your system, then let that be an end to it.'

'You are vulgar.'

She lifted her head, defiant. 'I'm not naive. I—'

Harry raised his hand, stopping her mid-sentence. 'Enough. Miss Brookes is decent and pleasant and I'll—'

'Listen to yourself, Harry.' Petra flicked a cold glare to where Charlotte stood next to the Wheelers. 'She has claim to some looks, in a farmer's daughter kind of way.'

Harry grinned at her absurd description. 'Petra, she looks nothing like any farmer's daughter I've ever seen. Her family weren't without substance, you know. She's educated and—'

'What does any of that matter?'

'Will you let me finish a sentence, please?'

'No, I will not. Especially when you're talking drivel. She's not one of our sort, is she? So, leave her alone. Besides, Nicholas seems besotted with her, Lord knows why. She's done well for herself to have you both after her. Anyway, he's far more suited to her than you. Stop making a fool of yourself and let Nicholas have her.'

Let Nicholas have her...

Petra's words lingered in his mind for days and weeks after the party. He found it difficult to concentrate on anything important. He made excuses to call in at the Wheeler's shop, just so he could catch a glimpse of Charlotte or at best exchange a few words.

But as winter took a strangle-hold on the country, creating havoc with travel when snow storms hit the area after Christmas, Harry was forced to stay indoors at the Hall. The roads to the village and mine were blocked with snow and then weeks of freezing winds turned everything to ice. He paced the rooms like a caged animal, snapping at every word Petra and Bertram uttered, and longing for the thaw and spring so he could ride off his frustrations.

CHAPTER 6

March 1914

Charlotte hurried along the bustling streets of York, not wanting to get too wet from the slight drizzle of rain falling. The majority of the winter snow had thawed, only remaining high on the hilltops, and there had been a few bright days of early spring, but the weather today was dull and grey. However, it didn't deter her when Stan had offered to take her shopping in York for a present for Hannah's birthday.

They had planned a small tea party tomorrow for Hannah after she came home from school, and invited a few of her new friends as well. Charlotte hoped that the weather would turn and the sun would shine.

She paused in front of a toy-shop window and looked at the goods on display. Wooden hoops, spinning tops, dolls and games, so many things that she knew Hannah would adore. Going inside, Charlotte took her time to view everything on the shelves. With her limited money, saved from her wages she received from working for Bessie and Stan, she had enough to buy a few small gifts. Besides, she felt guilty that Hannah was forced to leave behind all her possessions when they fled from McBride.

After fifteen minutes of making choices, she settled on a yellow paper kite, a book, *Alice's Adventures in Wonderland* and a small stuffed rabbit wearing a red bow. Next, she stopped at a sweet shop and bought four small bags of sugared almonds, something they didn't sell in Wheeler's shop.

With her money spent and arms full, Charlotte, thirsty and late to meet Stan, hurried along Market Street towards the tea shop where they had arranged to meet after her shopping and his business was completed.

Side-stepping an elegant tall woman instructing her driver to load her parcels into her sleek automobile, Charlotte wasn't really watching where she was going and suddenly she collided with a man emerging from an alley.

'Forgive me, miss!'

'I'm so sorry.' Juggling her packages, Charlotte shot an apologetic glance at the stranger then froze on recognition. Neil Featherstone. Her heart flipped and she instantly stared around looking for McBride, for the two men were thick as thieves and just as dangerous as she knew to her cost.

'Well, well, well.' Featherstone smirked. 'The little lost sheep has been found! What luck.'

Shaking, Charlotte tried not to show her fear. 'Leave me alone!' She barged past him, but he grabbed her elbow and pulled her closer to his side.

'Not so fast, little chicken. We have much to discuss.'

'Let me go.' Her heart felt like it would clearly jump from her chest as she looked into Featherstone's granite grey eyes.

'You're coming with me. McBride is only a few streets away, and he's going to be beside himself to have you back.'

'I'm not going back to him. I'm going nowhere with you.'

He chuckled. 'McBride said you were a feisty little thing.

Apparently, you gave him a right fight the night you left. Gave him a good lump on his head.'

'Let me go, please.' She tried to tug her arm free, but he held on tighter, squeezing viciously.

'Enough of that!' He sneered close to her face, lowering his voice. 'I'll be forever in McBride's good books if I hand you over to him. All the plans he had made can come true now.'

'What plans?'

Featherstone straightened. 'You know, he'd have made you a good husband if you'd stayed. I truly believe that. I think he would have spoilt you rotten, especially if you'd given him a son. Now, if that had come about you'd have been his queen and never wanted for anything for the rest of your life.'

'I didn't want him.' Her mind reeled. He wanted to marry her? She shivered at the thought.

'He won't rest until he has you, do you not realise that? He's spent good money on hiring people to find you.'

'Just to marry me? That's insane.'

'It's more than just wedding you.' Laughing, Featherstone turned about and started walking, pulling her along with him. 'I think you've driven him senseless since you scarpered. He talks of nothing but of getting you back. I do think he's gone quite mad.' Featherstone's face grew serious. 'He *is* very dangerous.'

'I would never have married him.' Charlotte jerked back as he marched her along. 'Stop! I'm not going with you!'

'You've no choice. He'll be forever in my debt if I deliver you to him and I like the sound of that.' He pulled her again. 'He wants that money and—'

'What money?' She dug her heels in, forcing him to stop.

'Your inheritance.' At Charlotte's shocked face, he snorted. 'You had no idea, did you? When you're twenty-one you'll inherent your share of your grandfather's will. McBride wants it. He can get it if you marry him. He'll not rest until that happens.'

'I'll never agree.'

Featherstone snorted. 'You stupid wench. If you didn't agree to marry him, he'd simply have you tied up and bed you until you swell with his child, then you'll have to marry him or be disgraced and back running for your life. That would be the worst case, or you could simply agree to marry him and have a good life. Either way, he will get you and the money, and McBride always gets what he wants. Did you really think Deirdre's death was an accident?'

'What do you mean?' His words buzzed around her head like bees.

'He got rid of her to free himself for you. He's *obsessed*.'

'Charlotte! Charlotte!'

She whirled around to see Stan running across the street. 'Stan!' Catching Featherstone off guard, she yanked her arm free and fled to Stan.

'Who was that?' Stan held her to him. 'Where was he taking you?'

'We have to leave, please.' She couldn't stop shaking now she was safe.

Still staring in the direction of where Featherstone had slipped down a side street, Stan's voice was tight with anger. 'Come, I'm taking you home, and you're going to tell me everything.'

Much later, sitting in the warmth of the kitchen, Charlotte waited for Bessie to pour out the cups of tea and settle herself at the table with Stan. Hannah was in bed and the only sound was the crackle of the low fire and the ticking of the clock on the mantelpiece.

'Right, we're ready,' Bessie said. 'Let's hear it then.'

Charlotte took a deep breath and tried to relax, but thinking and speaking of the past always affected her. 'McBride took us in when my mother died. We had nowhere else to go. He was a distant cousin of my father's. I don't believe my family expected to all go so soon after my father died. Father's instructions for

McBride to be our guardian was never taken seriously. After all, my mother was in good health and so were my grandparents, but within four years they were all dead.' Charlotte took a sip of tea, remembering the warmth and love of her family, and the beautiful old house they lived in in the centre of Wakefield.

'Wasn't there anyone else you could go to?' Stan asked.

'McBride and his wife came to collect us after my mother's funeral. He arranged the closing and selling of my grandparents' house, everything.' She shrugged. 'I didn't pay much attention to any of it as I was only concerned about helping Hannah adjust to not only living without our mother, but also moving to Warwickshire, away from everything familiar. She needed me.'

'What happened then?' Bessie asked.

'The first few weeks were fine. McBride went out of his way to be kind and courteous, making sure Hannah and I had everything we wanted. Sometimes, I thought...I thought he was overly familiar towards me. Only at the time I ignored my instincts, wondering if it was just me being too sensitive. His wife wasn't as nice, she made it quite clear that she hosted us under sufferance. Then suddenly she was dead. An accident. Her carriage overturned off a bridge.'

Charlotte stared into the fire. 'I tried to step into her place, run the house for McBride and he was thankful for my help, but then he seemed to become deeply interested in me. I couldn't leave a room without telling him my intentions. He insisted I sit with him after the evening meal and Hannah and I couldn't go out walking without him. He watched my every move. Then... then he began to stand too close, or touch me in passing. His hands would linger on my body, he started kissing me goodnight. He would look at me strangely. I felt uncomfortable being near him. I dreaded each evening when he'd come back to the house.'

Charlotte shivered at the dark memories of Vernon McBride, all clammy hands and hot breath trying to touch her under the table, or catching her in the hallway. After Deirdre's accident he became a changed man. Gone was the kindness, the concern for her welfare. Instead, he became short-tempered, demanding, threatening and his actions ungentlemanly. No, they couldn't have stayed there another day.

'There was no one at all you could go to, lass?' Stan asked softly.

'No. Friends were left back in Wakefield, and they were my mother's or grandparents' friends, not people we could impose on. I had no money, just a few pieces of jewellery.'

He nodded in understanding. 'How did you get away?'

'One night, McBride came home a little drunk. He was excessively attentive to me again, and I was growing tired of it. I just wanted him to leave me alone. The night before he had cornered me upstairs on the landing, trapping my way to my bedroom. He'd kissed me, his hands touched my...my chest...'

Stan murmured something angrily under his breath.

Charlotte sighed. 'When he came home drunk, I knew I'd have to quickly escape up to my room, and I did. He wasn't pleased, and after a while I heard him come upstairs. He came into my room. I didn't lock the door in case Hannah wanted to come in during the night. She sometimes did that when she'd had a bad dream.'

'What did he do, lass?' Bessie whispered.

'I asked him to leave my room. He ignored me. In fact, he laughed at me, but the look of fear on my face must have sobered him a bit because suddenly he was sitting on my bed, holding my hand and saying he loved me. His greatest wish was for me to love him back.' Charlotte stared at Bessie. 'But I couldn't, Bessie, I really couldn't. I wish I could because my life and Hannah's would have been so much better off, but the thought of him touching me repulsed me. I tried to be his friend, but he wanted more, and I couldn't do it.'

'Nay, lass, don't fret.' Bessie placed her teacup on the table and took Charlotte's tea out of her hands too, before gripping them into her strong hold. 'Don't be blaming yourself. He is older and should have not put you in such a position.'

'I tried talking to him, telling him we weren't suited. But he wouldn't listen, then he kissed me to shut me up. I tried to get away…he held me down on the bed, tore at my nightdress…' She shivered at the painful memory. 'I fought. He kept saying that once he'd bedded me I'd have to marry him. I kept fighting him. His hands were hurting me, and he bit me. I screamed and Hannah came running into the room. She was crying and I managed to grab a small lamp from the bedside table and I smashed it over his head.'

'Good girl.' Stan nodded in agreement.

'I told Hannah to get dressed. I packed a few bits of clothes and we fled into the night.' She took a deep breath and let it out slowly. 'I've never been more frightened in my life than I was that night. First with McBride and then walking the streets until dawn. I had a little money and my grandmother's jewellery, which I managed to pawn.'

'He seems a right evil swine!' Bessie snapped. 'You did well to get away from him.'

'You couldn't have stayed there, lass,' Stan said more gently.

'No, but for over a year I doubted if I had done the correct thing. My decision put us in harm's way repeatedly. We lived rough and Hannah had to work just as hard as me when I did find work. Men tried to have their way with me so many times, like I was a piece of meat at a market, free for them to touch. Sometimes I thought that if I'd stayed I could maybe have put up with McBride, and at least Hannah would have been cared for properly and had the chance to marry well. McBride did mix in a similar society to us.'

Stan shook his head. 'You had no choice but to leave. I know it was hard looking for work, especially a beautiful young lass like

THE PROMISE OF TOMORROW

yourself, you're bound to get attention from men wherever you go.'

'If we hadn't arrived here and you hadn't taken us in, I don't know what we'd have done.' Charlotte felt the sting of tears prick her eyes at the kindness this couple had shown her and Hannah over the last six months.

'Well, you're safe here with us.' Bessie stood and refilled the kettle to replenish their cold teas.

'But Featherstone has seen me. He's seen Stan.' She couldn't stop worrying at that, no matter what they said, it was a concern.

'This money Featherstone talked about, do you think it is true?' Stan asked as he added more coal to the fire, sending sparks up the chimney.

'I think it could be true, yes. My grandfather was wealthy. I believe he would leave all his estate to Hannah and myself as we were his only grandchildren.'

'Good God, you're an heiress then?' Bessie mashed the tea in the teapot and brought it over to the table.

'I'm nothing until I'm twenty-one, when I'm legally able to access my inheritance. Until then, McBride will hunt me. He'll not stop until I'm his wife.'

Bessie frowned, annoyed. 'Nay, he has to find you first. He'll never look in this little village, will he?'

Charlotte rubbed her face tiredly. 'I don't know. He's hired people to search for me so Featherstone said. I know from when we lived with him that he has many, many friends, and not all of them are good people. He did business with all classes, I know as I heard the house staff talking one time about his dealings with felons.'

'You need to stay away from York.' Bessie looked at Stan. 'She needs to stay close to home.'

'I agree.'

'And Stan needs to stay close to home too.' Charlotte gave him an apologetic smile. 'Featherstone can give a description of Stan now. They'll be looking for him and asking questions.'

Bessie and Stan exchanged glances. 'It'll be all right, lass, we'll make sure we're careful,' Stan said.

'I'll be twenty-one next year, then I can go to my grandfather's solicitor and deal with my inheritance.' She stood and kissed them both on the cheek. Tiredness drained her body. 'Thank you for helping us. I'll see you in the morning. Goodnight.'

After she left, Stan sipped his tea, thoughtful. 'Can we keep her safe for over a year?'

'We have to. What choice do we have?' Bessie answered, her mind whirling. 'We've no one we can send them to, nor know of a place that is safe. They'd be on their own again. We know nothing of this McBride fellow, or how long his reach is. He might have police in his pocket. How would we know that they were safe if we sent them away? At least here, we can watch over them.'

'A man as dangerous as McBride sounds is not going to give up easily if he thinks he can get his hands on loads of money.' Stan stood and checked the locks on the back door. 'He wants the money and he wants Charlotte.'

'Greedy evil men like him will stop at nothing. You're known in York, Stan, you grew up there, you go there every week. I'm worried he'll soon find out who you are and come here.'

'I know. I'll stop going to York, and anything we need for the shop I'll source from Leeds. I'll send a letter to Marty, ask him to keep an ear out for anyone asking after me.'

'Yes, good idea. Your cousin knows most of the people in York, good and bad.' Bess banked down the fire and placed the guard around it.

Pausing from emptying the teapot into a bucket, Stan glanced at his wife. 'I love those girls, Bess, like they were my own daughters. I'd do anything for them. I'll not let McBride have them. I'll kill him first.'

CHAPTER 7

*H*arry dashed up the stone steps leading to the front entrance of the gentleman's club in Mayfair. He'd been a member since he was eighteen and introduced and sponsored by his grandfather.

'Good day to you, Mr Belmont.' Gerard, the manager of the club, and who knew everyone worth knowing, walked up to him, took his hat and coat and gave them to another man to put away. 'It has been a while since you visited us.'

'I'm a busy man, Gerard, and I don't come to London as often as I would like.'

'Indeed, all men are busy, but we must also find the time to relax.' His black hair slicked flat against his head and his small dark eyes gave him a sly appearance but Harry had learnt that Gerard, although he missed nothing, was also the soul of secrecy and whatever happened within the walls of the club went no further.

'Can you tell me where I may find Alastair? I assume he is here as he is not at home.' Harry didn't have to say anything else, for Gerard knew which Alastair was Harry's closest friend. Gerard knew everything about his members.

'In the billiard room, sir. He's been here for over two hours.'

'Drinking?'

Gerard nodded slightly, and leaned closer to Harry so no one overheard him. 'He arrived inebriated and has continued drinking.' Gerard straightened. 'I shall send in coffee.'

'Thank you.' Harry sighed. He walked up the red-carpeted staircase, nodding to a few men he knew as he passed them, but not wanting to stop and chat, he moved purposely for the billiard room. A few days ago, he'd received word that Alastair had returned to London from Paris where he had gone after their last argument over Petra.

Opening the door, he saw Alastair bent over the table ready to take his shot, he looked up at Harry at the same time and the cue missed the ball, making his opponent laugh.

Harry closed the door behind him and stared at the younger man by the window. He didn't know, nor cared who he was. 'Forgive my intrusion, but I must speak to Mr McCoquindale alone on an important matter.'

'We've not finished our game!' The impudent youth couldn't have been more than nineteen and full of self-importance.

Harry strolled up to the table and with a swipe of his hand sent the remaining balls scattering across the table. 'You have now. Leave.'

Affronted, the younger man gaped, then reddened. 'Do you know to whom you are addressing?'

'You could be the Prince of Wales for all I care.' From somewhere deep inside a rage was building in Harry and he took a deep breath to control it.

Alastair staggered only a little as he smiled to the other man. 'Reginald, forgive my friend.'

'I am not your friend anymore,' Harry butted in.

Reginald stared from one to the other, recognising the controlled menace in Harry. 'Shall I get Gerard's men to come up?'

Alastair shook his head, straightening his shoulders. 'Thank you, but no. I'll see you later.'

Once Reginald had finally left the room, Alastair replaced the cues in their stand. 'If you've come to discuss Petra, I'm afraid you've wasted your journey. I shall not talk about her.'

Harry studied his former best friend. Alastair was a good-looking man, the women swooned over his light brown hair and hazel eyes. As boys growing up into men, they'd laughed at the ease in which women would flock to them both. Besides looks, Alastair was wealthy, well born, and best of all, he was kind and good fun to be with. To Harry he'd been his instant friend since school, and now that friendship was shattered beyond repair.

'You've taken my sister to bed. I believe there is much to discuss about the subject. Since the last dismal time I came here to try and reason with you and you refused to listen to me. I want this resolved. I want to leave London this time with this incident finished with.'

'Harry—' Alastair broke off as a knock preceded a waiter carrying a tray of coffee. He placed it on the table by the wall and disappeared as quickly as he came.

Silence descended in the room.

Harry poured two cups of coffee but didn't touch them. He glanced over at Alastair. 'Do you intend to divorce Susannah? Marry Petra?'

'No!'

'No?' The anger built higher. Harry spoke through gritted teeth. 'You mean to say you used Petra, like some sport, a bit of fun?'

'No!' Alastair paled. 'I would never treat her so abominably.'

'Then please explain to me the situation, as I am struggling to understand it all. Is my sister your mistress?'

'Harry...'

'Answer the question, damn it! Do you realise just how much I want to smash your face in right now?'

'Yes.'

'I'm using every ounce of my willpower to not throw you through that window, only because once we were the best of friends, and I'm trying to respect that, more than you did.'

'We didn't mean for it to happen, of course. I told you that the last time you confronted me! We fell in love.' Alastair ran his fingers through his hair. 'I don't know how it began really. I never even liked her when I stayed at Belmont Hall. All those years of her irritating me and then suddenly, wham!' He picked up a billiard ball and rolled it between his hands. 'One night after the opera we all went out as a group and got a bit drunk and we sort of fell into it.'

'Did you not think the next day that perhaps you should have decided to never see her again? Considering our friendship, and more importantly, your wife?'

Alastair hung his head in shame. 'Naturally I did. But I found I couldn't stop myself. At the time Susannah was heavily pregnant and then she had the baby and it was all she talked about. Being a mother consumed her. She had no time for me and stopped accompanying me to various events. Petra was there.'

'My sister would have taken advantage of Susannah's non-appearance because she's calculating and selfish, and will do anything to get what she wants. But you! From you I expected more. I expected loyalty.'

'I am truly sorry, Harry. More than you know. I have ruined everything. Susannah has found out and has taken the baby to her parents in Kent. Her father, the old Colonel, wants to run me through. The gossip is all over town. I thought going to Paris for the winter would help, but it hasn't.'

'Do you want my sympathy?' Harry mocked.

'No, of course not.'

'You will not see or contact Petra again in any way.'

'I do love her, Harry,' Alastair murmured.

'Then divorce Susannah and marry her.'

'I cannot. I simply cannot do that to Susannah. She doesn't deserve that.'

'No, nor does she deserve a cheating husband who has shamed her.'

'True. It's a mess and I don't know how to fix it.'

'Go and beg your wife's forgiveness. You may be able to save your marriage, since you have lost our friendship and my sister.'

'I will make it up to you, Harry, I promise.'

'No, you won't. Petra's reputation is completely ruined. You gave no thought to her, Susannah, your child, or to me. When I look at you now I don't see my friend, I see a pathetic man who cheated on his wife with my sister.' Harry shook his head in amazement. 'I still find it inconceivable. You and Petra!'

'She can be nice, Harry. You just don't give her a chance because you're still blaming her for your brothers' deaths. No wonder she behaves as she does. She's looking for someone to love her, Harry. Like we all do. Have you ever wondered what it's like to have someone totally grip your heart and mind and nothing else exists but them?' Alastair scoffed at his own question. 'No, of course you haven't. You're too wrapped up in your mine to even consider a woman.'

Harry thought of Charlotte, but remained silent. She was becoming an obsession with him, but he'd not tell Alastair that.

'I am sorry I caused this misery. If I could turn back time I would.' Alastair looked hopelessly at Harry. 'I would wish for your forgiveness.'

'You can wish all you want, but you'll never have it.' Harry turned his back on the friendship that sustained him through his brothers' and mother's deaths. He turned his back on the one man he had always confided in, the man he'd laughed with, drank with, the one man he'd trusted.

* * *

As the village basked in the mild warmth of a bright sunny day, Harry walked into Wheeler's shop, instantly looking for Charlotte. He had thought constantly of her while away and it had been too long since he'd seen her. However, business had kept him in London for weeks longer than he expected. Good returns on investments had meant him looking to expand his interests in other areas of business. He bought land on the outskirts of London, as well as a few properties going cheap on the south bank of the Thames. As yet he wasn't sure what he intended to do with them but even renting them out would generate a considerable return. He'd spent most of March in the capital and now here it was mid-April, his thirty-second birthday had been and gone, and he'd not even bothered to celebrate it. Not that celebrating it would have done much good while in London. Friends and acquaintances seemed to only want to discuss the budding tensions in Europe and politics was something he couldn't focus on right now.

'Master Harry, it's been a long while since we've seen you,' Stan said, coming out of the back room. 'Are you well, sir?'

'I am indeed, Stan, thank you, and you and your family?'

'All in good health, yes...'

Harry paused in idly picking up a shoe horn and stared at Wheeler. The older man seemed thinner, tense. The usual laughing expression he wore gone and replaced by a wariness in his eyes. 'Is something amiss, Stan?'

Startled, Stan took half a step back. 'No...er...everything is fine. What can I get you, sweets for the children?'

The doorbell jingled as someone else come into the shop and Stan jumped. Harry frowned, something was wrong. He strolled around to the other side of the shop and let Stan deal with the woman who bought a few items and talked about the weather. Harry nodded to her politely as she left and waited for the bell to stop jingling before turning back to Stan. 'Care to tell me why you are as jumpy and tense as a rabbit caught in a snare?'

Stan glanced behind him, checking the doorway leading into the back. 'I shouldn't really, but to be honest I'm at my wits end if I don't discuss it with someone besides Bessie.'

Harry folded his arms. 'Sounds serious. I hope I can help.'

'I don't know what to do. I feel like a man awaiting the gallows.'

'Tell me, it might ease your mind.'

'It's about Charlotte.'

Harry's stomach flipped. 'Oh? She isn't ill, is she?'

'No, no. She's in perfect health, though worried, as I am.'

'About what?'

'Her guardian, an evil man named McBride, who has been trying to find her since she ran away from him. He wants her inheritance and to do that he has to force her to marry him.'

'What?' For a minute Harry couldn't take in what he'd said. Charlotte was being pursued? She had an inheritance? Marriage?

'One of his henchmen saw Charlotte in York and he grabbed her but I came along in time. But I'm known there, they could and probably will find out about me and where I live, if they haven't already. In fact, I thought I was being followed one night last week when I left the Black Hen. I can't tell for certain, it was just a feeling. It nearly gave me heart failure, I tell you. I jump at every shadow. I've not been out since. I could lead them straight back to Charlotte, if I haven't done already.'

The doorbell jingled again as two more women entered, chatting loudly, one held a crying baby.

Annoyed at the interruption, Harry leaned closer to Stan. 'Come up to the Hall when you close the shop, bring Charlotte.'

'Are you sure?' Stan looked behind him again, obviously expecting Bessie to come out at any moment. 'It's a family matter. We've told no one,' he whispered.

'I can help.' At that moment Harry didn't know how he was going to help, but he would do something. He nodded to the woman who asked after his health and with a last look at Stan strode from the shop.

His thoughts whirling, Harry let Mighty pick his own pace back to the Hall. Although there was work to do at the mine, Harry couldn't face it, knowing he'd not concentrate now on anything but Charlotte. That she had an inheritance surprised him, however, it did gladden his heart that she wasn't totally without substance in her life. But this information about her guardian, McBride, was it, how could he possibly hope to marry her if she wasn't willing? And his henchman grabbing Charlotte off the street in York? His heart lurched at the thought. It was all madness.

He needed to think, to plan. He needed more information. Charlotte needed protecting and Stan couldn't do it by himself.

* * *

IN THE TWILIGHT golds of late evening, Charlotte stood on the doorstep of Belmont Hall. Beside her, Stan tugged on the bell pull beside the large oak door, before nervously tightening his tie.

'Your tie is fine, Stan.' She smiled, then looked over her shoulder at the splendid gardens that curved around the edge of the gravelled drive. Parkland stretched for several acres before woodland etched the horizon. From the outside Belmont Hall was beautiful, its elegance softened by age but enhanced by the well-tended lawns and spring flowering plants. It was quiet, peaceful, just the night song of a bird in the tall trees somewhere to the side of the house. She sighed deeply at the tranquillity of it.

She turned back to the butler, who'd opened the door and stood aside for them to enter.

'Mr Wheeler and Miss Brookes?' inquired the butler, a thin tall man with kind eyes and a shock of silver white hair though he didn't seem so very old.

'Yes. We have an appointment with Mr Belmont.' She smiled and stepped into the wide spacious hall with a polished wooden floor and the odd occasional chair and table. Her gaze was taken by a deep red carpeted curving staircase sweeping up to the next floor. Large portraits hung on green and silver papered walls.

'I'm Winslow, Mr Belmont's butler. If you'd care to come into the drawing room?' He led the way across the hall and into a generous-sized square room, where the inviting décor was of subtle creams and greens.

Charlotte nervously perched on the sofa, while Stan lingered near the fireplace, holding his hands out to the low heat. The butler vanished silently, and she took the opportunity to gaze at the numerous paintings on display.

'Stan. Miss Brookes.' Harry Belmont strode in, his hand held out to shake Stan's. 'Welcome to Belmont. Please, will you follow me? I thought my study would be a little more private for our discussion.' He preceded them out into the hall and then they turned and went down beside the staircase where large, wood-panelled rooms went off to the left and right. At the second door on the right, he stopped and allowed her and Stan to enter, and he closed the door behind him. The room was painted in a dark blue with a large mahogany desk placed in front of a wide high window and at angle to the fireplace. Farming and pastoral paintings dominated the room, as well as extra chairs, and a thick red patterned Oriental rug covered most of the wooden floor. It was very much a man's room.

Charlotte and Stan sat on soft leather chairs opposite the desk. She folded her hands in her lap and looked at the man who had the ability to stir her mind and body. She really wished it didn't happen and she tried hard to fight it, but it was impossible. He came into her mind when she least expected or wanted him to. Mundane chores in the shop would find her thoughts wondering to him. Where was he? What was he doing? She'd picture his smile, his eyes, the way he held her when they were dancing last Christmas. And now she was sitting in his house, and he was offering to help her in some way against McBride. It didn't make sense. Why would he help her? She was nothing to him.

Winslow brought in a tray of tea, a maid accompanying him with another tray of small cakes. He poured them all a cup of tea and after he and the maid had left, Charlotte gave in to temptation and looked at Harry.

'Shall we begin?' he asked, a gentleness in his eyes as he smiled at her.

Holding his stare, Charlotte took a deep breath. 'What do you want to know?'

'If you want my help, then all of it, every detail,' he said tenderly. 'You can trust me.'

And she did. For some unknown reason she trusted this man. The cup rattled on its saucer in her hands, and Stan lightly touched her arm in support. She smiled in thanks and straightening her shoulders, she told Harry everything, from the moment her mother died until the evening she and Hannah walked into Wheeler's shop and then the run in with Featherstone. She left nothing out. The months of unwanted attentions from McBride, then horror of McBride coming into her bedroom, fleeing into the night with Hannah, the struggles of finding work, walking the roads, the hunger, the fear, the lecherous men in places she worked, the humiliating lowly tasks she did for food. The words poured from her, the memories making her shiver. Her gaze grew vacant as she remembered and her tea went cold.

After she had finished there was silence for a moment. Stan patted her arm again. She had mentioned things even he and Bessie didn't know.

Charlotte looked at Harry, as that's how she thought of him now, Harry, not Mr Belmont, though she'd never say that to a soul. He wasn't looking at her, but down at his desk, he seemed deep in thought. Had she said too much? Her chest tightened, she felt heat flush her cheeks. How foolish was she to tell him everything? What did he care? He'd been doing his duty as leader of this village to listen to her, but none of it was his problem.

She fiddled with her gloves. Why had they come here anyway? She should have told Stan not to, it was none of Harry's business. She half rose from her chair, needing to leave, to go anywhere but stay in this room. Harry raised his gaze to her, stopping her from standing and fleeing. In his blue eyes was sadness, perhaps pity, and that annoyed her even more. She wanted no one's pity, least of all his!

'How brave you are, Miss Brookes.' Harry stood and walked to the window, only to turn back again. 'This money Featherstone mentioned, your inheritance? You know nothing at all about it?'

'If there was something then McBride would know, but he told me nothing, and I didn't think to ask questions concerning my grandfather's house, or anything.'

'Your mother didn't mention it to you after her parents' died?'

'No, not really. I was much younger then, I assume Mother didn't want me to worry. All she said was we'd remain in the house. Grandfather had looked after us.'

Harry nodded, deep in thought. 'And then when your mother died, McBride came and took over, but mentioned nothing.'

'That is correct.' She rubbed her forehead, trying to think. 'I feel foolish now. I should have paid more attention to such things. Only, my sole focus was settling Hannah at McBride's house in Warwickshire. Everything was new and different. We were mourning our mother and it was easier to just get through each day without thinking too much. It is my fault entirely.'

'Nonsense, lass.' Stan shook his head. 'I've told you, McBride took advantage.'

Harry sat back down behind his desk. 'Stan is right. As your guardian, McBride knew he could oversee everything that belonged to you. And I have a feeling your inheritance is a substantial amount for him to go to such lengths to marry you. Do you think it is possible he killed his wife?'

Charlotte nodded. 'I think he's capable of doing anything. Deirdre was in a carriage accident, but he could have made that happen, tampered with the carriage…I don't know. Featherstone said he had. Why would he lie?'

There was a knock at the door and Winslow entered, his face controlled but a worried look in his eyes. 'Forgive me, sir, but Mrs Wheeler and a child are in the hallway. She says it is very important she sees her husband and Miss Brookes.'

'Bessie? Here?' Stan launched to his feet.

'Send them in, please.' Harry stood also.

Bessie hurried in, holding tight onto Hannah's hand. She stopped beside Stan, the colour had drained from her face and she was visibly shaking. She stared at them all, then down at Hannah. 'I'm sorry, Mr Belmont, I had to come.'

'Of course, Mrs Wheeler, please sit down.' Harry brought another chair from near the door and placed it beside Stan's.

'What's happened, lass?' Stan asked Bessie, and automatically taking Hannah's hand and pulling her closer to him.

Bessie looked at Charlotte. 'We had a visitor, who brought a letter.' She took it out of her pocket and passed it to Charlotte.

Shakily, Charlotte read the note.

Dearest Charlotte,

Please don't be afraid. I simply wish to talk to you. There are things to discuss. I only have yours and Hannah's best interests at heart.

I ask you and Hannah to meet me, so we can talk, as family. I am yours and Hannah's legal guardian. We need to be together. I know what is best for you and can give you the life you deserve. Your family would be horrified to know you live and work in a grocer's shop. I promised your father I'd take care of you. Think of his wishes, and of your dear mother's memory. She would want you to put Hannah first and make certain her life is what it always should have been. I can provide that.

I have made mistakes, for which I sincerely apologise and I would like to make amends, please allow me to do so. It is of the utmost importance to me to see you and Hannah and make sure you are both well.

I beg of you to meet me next Saturday at the address below.

Yours sincerely, Vernon McBride.

He knew where she lived. It was all she could think about. Her shaking increased as she gave the note to Stan to read and gazed at Hannah, who innocently smiled back. The monster wanted to meet her and Hannah. The thought of being in that man's presence made her breath shorten.

'He's insane, obviously,' Stan muttered, passing the note to Harry, who quickly read it.

Harry strode to the bell pull by the fireplace. He turned to Hannah. 'Do you like horses and kittens? We have a new litter of kittens in the stables, would you like to see them?'

Hannah nodded. 'Yes, please.'

Within moments, Winslow entered. 'Winslow, will you be kind enough to take young Hannah here over to the stables to see the kittens.'

'I'll go too.' Bessie stood.

'She'll be safe, Mrs Wheeler. Winslow won't let her out of his sight,' Harry said.

'All the same, I'd prefer it if I was with her.' She turned to Hannah. 'You go on, sweet, I'll be right behind but I just need to speak to Stan for a minute.' Once Hannah had left with Winslow and the door closed, Bessie's expression changed. 'Never in my life have I been so frightened as when those two fellows turned up at the shop. I knew straight away something wasn't right. One fellow, a tall ugly low life, he was, he started asking questions about us all, and then Hannah came out to me and the other fellow started talking to her. Asked if she had a sister, and so on. The ugly one gave me that letter and said it was from McBride. I asked them to leave, and as they did they took some fruit on their way out, and at the door, the ugly one said that we had to think real hard on what we do next, because they would be watching.'

'Good God,' Stan whispered.

Charlotte felt the blood drain from her face. Hannah had spoken to them. They had seen her!

Bessie twisted her hands together, a sign of her distress. 'I locked the door then we left out the back way. We went down behind the High Street until I saw John Booth from the pit, he had his little dog cart and I begged him to bring us here. I couldn't wait until you got home in case they did something when they saw Charlotte. I didn't tell Hannah anything, only that we were visiting the Hall.'

'You did the right thing, Mrs Wheeler.' Harry gave her a tight smile.

Her shoulders relaxed a little. 'Thank you. I'll go to Hannah now.' She paused by the door. 'I can't live like this, frightened in my own home. It needs sorting, Stan, and quickly.'

'Yes,' Harry agreed, when the door closed behind her, 'and Miss Brookes and her sister aren't safe there.'

'Hannah?' Charlotte stared at him, shocked and fearful. 'He wants me, not her.'

'Yes, and if he can't get you, he can do it through Hannah. McBride could take her to make you come to him. Or, worse case is that he'd hide Hannah away until she came of age so he'd marry her instead. Remember, you and she share the inheritance. If McBride has lost his reasoning, then that is something he could do. He could use Hannah to blackmail you. He knows you'll do anything for your sister and if that means you marrying him as a sacrifice then you would, or he waits several years and marries Hannah. He's already sent two henchmen here to Belthorpe. He could have her abducted and out of the country before the police have even come to interview you. Men like him would have some crooked police in their pocket, so you can't rely on them to help you. A missing village girl would be low on their priority list.'

'No!' Stan jerked in his chair. He looked ready to fight someone. 'I'll not have Hannah in danger. He has to be stopped. I'll kill him first.'

Her sister in McBride's clutches sent shivers down Charlotte's back. 'Then we'll go away again. Leave the country if we have to.'

'What?' Stan stood. 'How can that be the best thing to do? You two on your own again with no one to help you or protect you? What happens when your money runs out? You'll spend the rest of your life looking over your shoulder. I'll not have it, do you hear?'

'Calm down, Stan.' Harry picked up a pen. 'But he is right, running away without a good deal of money will not help you.'

'I'll be twenty-one next year. We can hide until then.'

Harry looked at her. 'Yes, you'll be of age, but your sister will not. There might be a way of securing Hannah's share by making you her guardian, but then who's to say he can still come after her as punishment. Can he be trusted to leave you alone once you have turned twenty-one? It seems he has lost his mind where you are concerned. That is what is so dangerous. I have read about such things before, where people become so infatuated that they lose their minds over someone.'

'I can't believe this.' Overwhelmed, Charlotte didn't know what to think. Then suddenly a thought grew. 'Can I not just give him the money? If that's what he wants, then he can have it. Hannah and I are fine with you and Bessie, aren't we, Stan?'

'Aye, lass, of course. You've a home with us forever.' Stan quickly sat beside her. 'That's what we can do, give it all to him.'

Harry sighed. 'I'm sorry to say this, but you can't give anything away until it is yours, and that's not for over a year. Besides, why should you do that? It's yours and Hannah's inheritance, so that you may live in comfort. It is yours by right. Do you think your grandfather would want his estate to go into some fortune hunter's grasp?'

'But if it saves us from being in McBride's clutches?'

'Would it though?' Harry tapped his pen on the desk. 'It sounds to me as though this man is delusional and bent on getting what he wants. And, from what I can gather, he doesn't need your money; it's no longer about the money. It's about you. He wants you. He obviously will not stop and if you went into hiding, he'd still come looking for you. I could set you up in a house in London or somewhere. However, all it would take is one mistake, one wrong word, or for someone to spot you and a good detective would find you and Hannah.'

Stan swore under his breath. 'What's the answer then?'

Harry shook his head, perplexed. 'Ideally, if Miss Brookes was married, then McBride couldn't touch her, and her inheritance would be under her husband's control. McBride would no longer be Miss Brookes' guardian. It would have to be known that her new husband was able to take care of Hannah's share as well. A husband could protect you physically as well. That might scare him off. I do not know. Without knowing the details of the will, it is hard to say. Miss Brookes do you know the name of your grandfather's partners at his office?'

'Yes. Leeming and Bottomley. Mr Smithfield was Grandfather's primary partner but I'm sure he retired a year after Grandfather died. Mr Bottomley was younger. I believe he took over the whole business.'

'Well, I'll contact him. I doubt if it will help as he will not be able to discuss client details with me, but it's worth a try, I suppose.'

'Thank you,' Charlotte murmured, unable to offer him a smile of gratitude. She felt deflated and overwhelmed, and as though she'd never smile again.

Harry turned to Stan. 'I do believe that both Hannah and Miss Brookes are not safe at the shop. I propose they stay here at

Belmont Hall. No one would dare try to enter my home. They'd be safe.'

'We couldn't possibly impose on you,' Charlotte blurted out. She couldn't live under the same roof as this man. She thought about him more than enough as it was without seeing him every day, too.

Frowning, Harry appeared annoyed at her outburst. 'It is no imposition, Miss Brookes. You and Hannah are very welcome to come here for a few weeks until I hear back from the solicitors in Wakefield and we come up with some sort of plan. I would have thought you'd want your sister safe? Forgive me if I have made an unwelcome proposition.'

'Nay, lass, Master Harry is right. You'd be safer here than at the shop. I'd sleep better knowing you were here.'

'The house is large, there's plenty for you both to explore and keep yourselves occupied.' Harry rose and walked around from behind the desk. 'There are the gardens, and if you keep close to the house, you'll be safe.'

'Yes, but it's hardly fair to you...' Charlotte's words dwindled on the argument.

'Why?' The smile returned to Harry's face. 'You are both very welcome.'

'Thank you.' Stan stood also and shook his hand. 'We appreciate your kindness.'

Charlotte dragged her gaze away from Harry's warm smile to stare at Stan. 'Stan, I—'

'No, Charlotte,' he rebuked her. 'Master Harry is right. Here, for now, is the best place.'

Before she could reply, the door opened and Hannah skipped in with Bessie behind her. 'Charlotte, the kittens are so adorable. Black and white they are. There's five of them. I named them!'

Harry stepped forward and smiled down at her. 'Would you like to see them every day, Hannah? I've asked your sister if you'd both like to come and stay here for a little while. Would you like that?'

Confused, Hannah stared from him to Charlotte, but her hand reached out to Stan's. 'Leave the shop, Charlotte?'

'Only for a short time, and Stan and Bessie will come up and see us.'

'We'll come every Sunday, poppet.' Stan pulled her to him and kissed the top of her head. 'But think of the fun you'll have here. Mr Belmont has the kittens and this nice big house for you to explore with Charlotte. Then, when the holiday is over, you'll come back to the shop.'

'Could we just not come during the day?'

Stan blinked rapidly, he glanced at Bessie, and she touched Hannah's back gently. 'Well, I was thinking that while you stay here with Charlotte, Stan will wallpaper your room in that nice flower pattern you saw last week. How about that? It'll be a surprise for when you return.'

Hannah nodded, but still wasn't convinced. 'It wouldn't be for long, would it?'

Stan knelt in front of her. 'How about if you are a really good girl while you're staying here, perhaps we could ask Mr Belmont if you can take a kitten home to keep?'

Eyes wide, Hannah clapped her hands together. 'Could I?'

Stan grinned at her. 'While you're here you can play with them all, and then see which one you want to take home. Good idea?'

Nodding, Hannah grinned. 'Could it sleep on my bed, too?'

'Of course.'

Harry came to Charlotte's side. 'Are you in agreement then?'

What choice did she have? She had to keep Hannah and herself somewhere McBride couldn't get to them, but Lord, to spend every day with Harry would test her. Why he would be so kind as to do this for them, she didn't know. He was going beyond the call of a gentleman. It didn't make any sense to her why he was being so compassionate. This was taking two strangers into his home. And how would she cope living in such splendour? To have servants again? To experience this golden life again, only to eventually have to go back to living at the shop when this was all over. How would she bear it?

She sighed and nodded. 'Thank you. You're very generous.'

CHAPTER 8

*H*arry spurred Mighty on towards home, leaving the noise and dust of the pit behind. All week he'd gone to the mine in the morning, and not come home until evening, and even then, he'd coop himself up in his study and work, or try to pretend to work. The joy he felt at having Charlotte under his roof had soon evaporated by her reserved manner. She made it plain to him that his company wasn't wanted or needed, and he'd taken offence and thrown himself into working. He knew she ate her meals with Hannah upstairs in the suite of rooms he'd allocated to them, those that used to be his mothers. He had reports from Winslow that she and Hannah were discreet and respectful. They had spent most of this first week in the stables with the kittens, or sitting quietly on the lawn drawing or reading when the weather was fine. They asked for nothing and only ate when Winslow instructed one of the maids to take them a tray of food.

He didn't know what he expected when he compulsively asked Charlotte to stay. Yes, he thought it would keep them out of McBride's clutches, but selfishly he also wanted her here to get to know her. Petra and Bertram were staying with friends in Cornwall, and it was the perfect opportunity to have her all to himself. Yet, from the start she had distanced herself from him; keeping to her rooms and not venturing into any other parts of the house. He had to arrest the situation and make the effort for them to be in each other's company. Hence the reason he had left the pit office at midday and was now urging Mighty to get a move on. He wasn't prepared to let her live like a hermit in his own home. He wanted her to notice him and like him.

She was in the stable yard when he rode in. He dismounted and threw the reins to a stable lad. He smiled inwardly at her surprise at seeing him. 'Kitten duty again, Miss Brookes?' he joked, wanting them to be friends.

'Yes, it's all I seem to do at the moment.' The small smile she gave him didn't reach her eyes.

He took off his riding gloves. 'Do you have everything you require? Are you comfortable?'

'Oh yes, indeed. Thank you.' She turned to the stable door. 'Hannah, I'm going back, are you coming?'

'Can I stay a bit longer, please?' the answer came from within the shadowy doorway.

'Very well, but you are to come straight back into the house.'

Harry saw Hoskins exit a stable door further down. 'Hoskins, keep an eye on Miss Hannah please, and see she is escorted back to the house when she is ready.'

'Aye, sir.'

Pleased when she fell into step beside him, Harry felt the need to break the silence, but didn't want to say the wrong thing to send her scuttling inside. 'Do you ride, Miss Brookes?'

'No, Mr Belmont, I don't.'

'Perhaps you'd like to learn?'

'I doubt I'll have need of it, do you? A shop girl doesn't have the time or the finances to own a horse.' She glanced at him then away. 'Besides, aren't automobiles going to change everything soon anyway? The horse will be redundant in ten years, or so I read from one report on it in the newspaper. All it'll take is mass production, I believe, to make them more achievable in price for people.'

He was shocked at her knowing about such things, yet liked it. 'There is a great possibility of that, yes. While I was last in London I visited one of the manufacturers as I'm thinking of investing in one of these companies. I have recently ordered my own automobile. I'm behind the times a little in doing so. Many of my friends have several motor cars in their stables already. But I couldn't give up Mighty completely.'

'The cities are full of those things now, aren't they? I noticed when we were in York how many rumbled along the cobbles. They nearly out-number horse drawn vehicles.' Charlotte paused to sniff a flower, and it pleased him she felt comfortable enough to do that in his presence. She glanced at him again, as though unsure whether making eye contact was allowed. 'I think I would enjoy learning how to drive one of those automobiles more than learning how to ride a horse. A horse has a mind of its own.'

'Really?' Astonishment made his voice high, and he laughed. 'Well then, I propose the idea of you learning to drive mine when it arrives. We can learn together. Yes?'

'All right.' She smiled properly at him for the first time since they'd met last year and her face transformed into such beauty that he found himself staring. Her eyes, a mixture of green and gold, shined, and a small dimple appeared near the corner of her mouth. He ached to kiss it, to kiss *her*, to enfold her in his arms and kiss her until they couldn't breathe. She was all he thought about. At night knowing she was just along the corridor wearing only a nightdress made him hot with want.

She strolled on, touching the odd bush and flower as she went by. He focused on her movements, the slender shape of her back, the sun highlighting the copper in her hair. He longed to pull out the pins holding it up and watch it fall down her back.

'Mr Belmont?'

Startled, he hurried to her side, embarrassed he'd been daydreaming about her like a lovesick boy. 'Excuse me, I was miles away.'

'I asked if you would mind terribly if I took advantage of your library this afternoon?'

'I insist that you do. Did I not invite you to do just that last year?' He smiled, as he opened the Hall's rear entrance door leading into a wide corridor. 'I'm surprised you've not had a rummage before now. You've been here seven days.'

'I didn't want to be presumptuous. You've been so kind to my sister and I, and I felt we'd be better staying out of everyone's way. However, I've read everything I asked Stan to bring for us.' She shrugged, as though in apology.

Winslow met them as they turned onto the main hallway. 'Ah, sir. I wasn't expecting you. Have you eaten at the mine?'

'No, I haven't. If it's not too much trouble for Mrs Morrissey, could you ask her to create a light lunch for Miss Brookes and myself?'

'Very good, sir.' Winslow carried on down the hall and turned out of sight.

Harry led the way into the library opposite. 'You do not mind eating with me, do you? I get so tired of dining alone.'

'I am not dressed for the dining room.'

'I'm very informal, Miss Brookes. What you are wearing is fine to me.' He saw no problem with her cream blouse and dark brown skirt. Was that the reason why she stayed in her rooms because of her lack of correct attire? It upset him that such a menial thing could be the cause, but then he realised if Petra had been home she would have made such a reason insufferable.

'Thank you, I will then.' Charlotte paused in the doorway and gazed at the book laden shelves covering each wall from floor to ceiling, breaking only for the two large windows and the fireplace on the far side. 'What a collection.'

Harry, who'd grown up knowing nothing else, tried to see it through her eyes. The oak shelves had aged and darkened over time. The books, though familiar, were largely unread by him or anyone in his family except his grandfather and later his father. 'My grandfather was the collector. A great reader. I sadly am not. It's a flaw I know.' He chuckled. 'One of many I can claim to.'

He watched Charlotte slowly run her fingertips across the spines like a caress and wished she was doing it to him instead. She stopped and pulled one book out and flipped through the first few pages. 'My grandmother was an avid reader, but her collection was small. She used our local town's library mainly, even became a patron of it. I think I get my love of reading from her.'

'It would make me very happy if you used this library,' he said softly.

'I will, thank you.' Again, she wouldn't meet his eyes. He desperately wanted her to look at him like she did in the garden. He wanted to see her smile, and hear her laugh.

A tall man in the black uniform of a footman tapped on the open door. 'Excuse me, sir.'

'Kemp. You're back I see. How was Leeds, and your family?' Harry asked him, having always liked the young man who had come to him from a personal recommendation.

'My father has recovered from his accident, thank you, sir. My mother wishes me to convey her regards to you for allowing me these last two weeks to be with them.'

'You're welcome.' Harry turned to Charlotte. 'This is Kemp, Miss Brookes, our footman and my valet, and I don't know how we coped before he arrived here two years ago. He's been away since you've been staying.'

'Pleased to meet you.' Charlotte smiled. She recognised him from serving him in the shop, as she had with most of the servants.

'Miss Brookes and her sister Hannah are staying at the Hall for a while. They are in the Rose rooms.'

THE PROMISE OF TOMORROW

'Very good, sir. Mr Winslow asked me to convey that lunch is served.'

'Good, I'm ravenous.' Harry indicated for Charlotte to precede him.

They crossed the hall and walked into the dining room. As he helped her to be seated, Harry nodded to Winslow, who stood beside the serving tables, which held various bowls of salads, plates of cold meats and stands of delicate pastries and sandwiches. 'A cup of tea for me, please, Winslow. Miss Brookes?'

'Tea also, please.'

Winslow brought them their tea and addressed Charlotte. 'Miss Hannah is in the kitchen, happily eating and telling all who'll listen that the kittens are growing by the minute.'

'In the kitchen?' Charlotte half rose from her chair. 'I do apologise, Mr Winslow. I'll get her at once. I'd hate for her to be a nuisance.'

'Please, Miss Brookes, do not worry.' Winslow looked affronted. 'I merely told you so you knew her whereabouts. She is perfectly content in the kitchen and Mrs Morrissey is more than happy to have her there, chatting away. She keeps her and the staff entertained.'

'Are you sure?'

'I would not lie to you, Miss Brookes.' Winslow went back to the serving table and Charlotte sighed.

'Your sister will be in no one's way.' Harry left the table and went to help himself to the food. 'Come, eat,' he called over his shoulder.

For over an hour they ate and talked, discussing general subjects such as the situation in Ireland and women's votes. Harry enjoyed listening to her as she was well read on many topics that he knew Petra would have trouble understanding. It also gave him the opportunity to watch her, to take mental notes of her features, her expressions and gestures. Charlotte asked him questions about the estate, his family and the mine. Winslow was dismissed, and Harry collected the teapot and stand of pastries and brought them to the table so they could nibble as they chatted.

As they were finishing the last dregs of the teapot, Hannah came in for a short time and spoke of the delights of the stables, then left to go play upstairs.

'Shall we head back to the books?' Harry asked Charlotte, and at her nod, they went back to the library.

Selecting a book randomly, Harry barely glanced at it as he watched Charlotte studying a tome about wildflowers. 'That is one of my father's favourites. He bought two copies, one to stay here and the other he took with him on his travels.'

'It has such beautiful illustrations.' She turned a page. 'Do you never wish to accompany him on his journeys?'

'No, never. I've been to several countries in Europe, that's enough for now. I have too much to do here.'

Sunlight streamed through the window, falling on Charlotte where she stood, catching the copper in her hair, turning it nearly red. He desperately wanted to touch it. The colours in her hair fascinated him. 'Will you dine with me this evening, Miss Brookes? I have enjoyed your company very much.'

'I'm afraid I have no suitable clothes to dine in, Mr Belmont. My evening wear was left behind at…McBride's house.' A shadow passed over her face at the mention of his name.

'You could borrow something of Petra's.'

Charlotte gave a tinkling laugh. 'Your sister towers over me and I'm afraid she would not be thrilled at the knowledge I wore something of hers.'

'Your own clothes will be fine then. I do not mind what you wear. Please. Indulge me.'

She sighed deeply. 'What of Hannah? I cannot leave her by herself most of the night.'

'I'll have Lucy or one of the other girls sit with her.' He smiled when she nodded in agreement.

A knock on the door preceded Winslow. 'Excuse me, sir, Mr Adams is here. Shall I show him in?'

'Thank you, yes.' Harry cursed under his breath. He didn't want Nicholas here, not when he'd spent such a lovely couple of hours with Charlotte and had the prospect of more.

'Good afternoon, Harry.' Nicholas strode in full of happy smiles and a yearning in his eyes as he gazed at Charlotte. 'I am delighted to see you, Miss Brookes. I'd heard from Stan that you were here.'

'How are you, Mr Adams?' Charlotte held out her hand for Nicholas and it irked Harry that he got to touch her.

Nicholas stood beside her. 'I'm very well, thank you. Are you enjoying your stay at the Hall?'

'I am. It is a beautiful home.'

Harry hadn't spoken to Nicholas about Charlotte's stay and knew he'd be curious. How much had the Wheelers told him? Well, let him ponder. It was none of his damn business.

'Do you have something we need to discuss, Nicholas? Shall we go to the study and leave Miss Brookes in peace?'

'Er...nothing of importance, Harry. Just that it's Friday and I wondered if you wanted to meet later in the Black Hen for a pint?'

'Not tonight, but thank you.' Harry saw through him, knowing full well Nicholas had come in the hopes of seeing Charlotte. The odd occasions he went to the Black Hen was usually a Saturday night, besides he could have asked that question this morning at the mine office.

Nicholas seemed about to speak again, but stared at the window. Harry turned to see what he looked at just as glass shattered into the room. Charlotte screamed, the heavy missile thrown missed her head by inches. Harry dived towards Charlotte, taking her to the ground in a hard thump that knocked the breath from his lungs.

For a moment it was mayhem as Winslow and Kemp rushed into the room, and everyone talked at once.

Harry held Charlotte to him, her face white with shock. 'Are you hurt?' he asked gently.

She shook her head, her fingers gripping into the material of his jacket.

'Miss Brookes, Harry.' Nicholas helped them up before handing to Harry the paper covered rock that had landed on the carpet at their feet.

Untying the string, anger made his voice harsher than usual. 'Winslow, I want every man to check the grounds, and then the village. I'll have the culprit found!'

'Yes, sir.'

Harry read the note.

My dear Charlotte,

You missed our meeting. I'm terribly disappointed.

I was also saddened to learn that a man I do not even know, a Mr Henry Belmont, had contacted your grandfather's solicitors. They wrote to me and asked for advice on their reply to him. I do not appreciate being threatened by him on how to conduct my relationship with you.

Why have you involved people outside of our family? Your inheritance concerns only yourself, Hannah and me. Yet I am told by this Mr Belmont to stay away from you, and that once you've come of age, you will be responsible for your own and Hannah's welfare. My dear girl, you need to understand I will never stop wanting to help you. You are my responsibility alone. I will not have anyone interfere with my plans!

I have sacrificed too much to walk away now.

Why did you run from me? You have angered me. Did you think leaving the shop would keep you safe? Do you think I will give up? You are mine Charlotte. Accept that and we will be so very happy. Harry peered at the messy writing that had been crossed out.

I'll take care of you and Hannah and we'll be very happy, I promise you.

I'll contact you again soon, my dearest girl.

With fondness,
Vernon.

Harry passed the letter to Charlotte, whose hands shook as she took it. She read in silence and then looked up at Harry with such misery in her eyes that he reached out to hold her, but remembered in time that he had no right and instead lightly touched her arm.

'A drink, Miss Brookes.' Nicholas had poured her a shot of brandy. 'It'll steady your nerves.'

'I think he is insane. You must think that too, don't you?' Harry said, watching her take a small sip and grimace at the taste. 'You can tell by the state of the writing. It starts neatly, but towards the end it is badly written, words crossed out, and then it becomes clear again. He wrote that in a rage.'

'Was he here? Was it him who threw the rock?' Her voice trembled.

'No, he has men to do his dirty business for him.'

'What is this all about Harry?' Nicholas stood aside as two maids came in to sweep up the broken glass. 'Can I help?'

'No, Nicholas, not really, but thank you, and sorry about all of this. I'll see you tomorrow.'

'I can stay...'

'No, there's no need to involve you, too.'

'I'm your friend, and Miss Brookes, too.'

Harry patted Nicholas on the back. 'Yes, we know and are grateful, but I can handle this.'

Nicholas hesitated. 'As long as you're sure.'

'Very sure.'

'Thank you for your concern.' Charlotte gave him a wobbly smile. 'Good day to you, Mr Adams.'

'I'll see you at the mine on Monday, Nicholas.' Harry took Charlotte by the elbow and led her out to into the hall. 'Come and sit down in the drawing room for a moment.'

'Hannah?' Charlotte balked.

'She'll be fine, and unlikely to even be aware of what just happened. I'll get Winslow to send someone up to check on her.' Harry persisted in her sitting on the sofa in the drawing room. His anger simmered like a pan of hot water. How dare someone violate his home! The danger to Charlotte was very real. 'I'll have McBride strung up from the nearest tree if I catch him,' he muttered under his breath.

'He's too clever to be caught,' Charlotte murmured.

'I'll send for the police. We have evidence of his corruptness. He's deranged, threatening you.'

'Will it be enough to put him in prison? I doubt it. You said yourself that the police might be in his pocket.' Charlotte's voice rose in panic. 'No. I need to get away, both of us, where he can't find us.'

'We have discussed this. You cannot run for months.'

'We aren't safe here, or anywhere in the village.' She paced the room, unable to sit still. 'I'm giving him the money, all of it. I don't care about it. I need to protect Hannah.'

'That is ridiculous, and no guarantee that it will be enough to stop him. He wants *you*!'

'It might be enough!' she snapped.

'And what of Hannah? Are you willing to give away her future security too? Have you thought of that? What if, when she grows up she resents you for giving away what is hers? If she doesn't marry well, you are basically surrendering her to a life far below what she's entitled too. How would that be honouring your family's wishes?'

'I don't know!' She put her head in her hands in despair and Harry's heart melted at the forlorn sight.

'I am sorry. I should not be so harsh.' He stepped closer to her, laying a hand gently on her shoulder. 'I am merely thinking of you and Hannah and your futures.'

She nodded and sighed. 'Thank you, but at this minute I don't feel like we have a future.'

'We will sort it out, I promise.'

'This doesn't concern you, Mr Belmont. I am very sorry you have become involved. I'm dreadfully sorry that this has landed at your door. Hannah and I will return to Stan and Bessie's. We cannot inconvenience you any further.'

'I want to be involved. I want to help you. Do not leave yet. You are safer here than at the shop. No one will get into the Hall, I promise you. I'll have men patrolling the grounds if need be.'

'I cannot have you doing all this for me.'

'Why? I am offering— no, I am insisting.'

'But why?' Confusion filled her eyes.

'Because I like to think of you as my friend, and I always help my friends.' He hoped his smile was warm enough to squash her doubts.

'Thank you. I'll go up and spend some time with Hannah.'

He dropped his hand to let her leave. 'Very well. Try not to worry.'

Stopping at the door, she paused. 'I'm sorry about your window.'

'It is not your fault. I will see you at dinner.' He stood in the middle of the room long after she'd gone. His mind a whirl of thoughts, most dismissed immediately, yet some took root and grew. One thought and one feeling was uppermost. He cared for Charlotte Brookes. He wanted to protect her, keep her safe. Equal to that he wanted her with him, he liked her company. When she smiled his heart soared. Deep in his gut was the urge to make love to her, to make her his, and only his. The seed of a plan grew some more and he took a breath to calm down his excitement.

CHAPTER 9

With the curtains drawn, and the lamps turned down to create a nice cosy glow, Charlotte left Hannah changing into her nightdress while chatting like a monkey to the maid, Lucy. Slipping from the room, she smoothed down the dark green skirt she wore with a pale lemon blouse that had tight sleeves and a double row of small ruffles down the front to hide the buttons. It was a suitable outfit, but sorely lacking in what normally she would have worn had she been still living in Wakefield. Durable cotton, linen and wool had replaced the sateen, silk and muslin she used to wear.

As she had done often in the last week, she meandered down the corridor gazing at the family portraits hung between windows and doors. The Belmonts were a handsome family. Harry's dead brothers remained youthful, sharing a distinct like-ness to Harry with the same light blue laughing eyes. Whereas Petra's portrait showed her cold beauty. It pleased Charlotte immensely that Harry's sister wasn't at home.

With each step she took going down the wide stairs, she thought of the evening ahead. Spending the afternoon with Harry had delighted, yet confused her. Why had he sought her out? Surely a man in his position had much more to do than sitting with her, showing her books. However, he seemed to enjoy her company as much as she did his. Whenever he looked at her, fluttering would start in her stomach. His concerns for her and Hannah's welfare touched her deeply. Her thoughts changed from Harry to McBride and she shuddered. She had to be free of him somehow. Something had to be done, but what?

At the bottom of the staircase she stopped and glanced about the hall. It was a lovely home and she felt comfortable here, strangely. It concerned her how much she liked this house. It would do no good to get too relaxed here or anywhere, for McBride would never leave her in peace. No, she had to start thinking sensibly, and her only option to escape his clutches was to disappear. She must take Hannah and go far away. If she borrowed money from Stan and Bessie, enough to buy a ticket to New York, then McBride would never find them. He'd not expect her to travel so far without help. She could do it though. Although daunted by the idea, now that she had a plan in place she felt better, easier of spirit.

Head held high, she walked into the drawing room. Harry stood reading the paper, leaning against the mantelpiece. On her appearance he folded it away and smiled at her.

He had such a lovely smile. She liked the tender way he looked at her. She was privileged to have a friend such as him. Sitting down on the sofa, she returned his smile.

'Is your sister unaware of what happened?' he asked.

'Thankfully, she heard nothing.'

'The walls are rather thick in this house.'

'I'm glad of it. I'd hate her to be alarmed.'

'She is safe and happy. So, you can unwind a little.' He headed over to the trolley by the window filled with bottles of alcohol. 'Drink? Sherry? Madeira?'

'A small sherry, please.' She watched him pour the drinks, feeling comfortable in his presence. 'Kemp and Lucy have shown

Hannah the old nursery on the top floor, and she's making it her mission to tidy it up and see what hidden treasures she can find. Lucy gave her an apron. The two of them are best of friends.'

Harry handed her a small glass of sherry. 'I'm pleased to hear it. I've not been up there in years. I imagine it's full of things to delight her. My brothers, Petra and myself had hours of fun in the nursery.'

'I think it reminds her of the one we had at my grandfather's house.'

'Happy memories?'

'Yes, a great many.' Charlotte allowed herself a moment to reflect on her old home and the love that was in that house.

Winslow silently entered the room. 'Dinner is served, sir.'

They followed him down the hall and into the dining room. Harry helped Charlotte to her seat to the right of him and Winslow offered her wine, which she accepted.

'Parsnip soup, sir, followed by roast lamb.' Winslow, with Kemp as his helper, served them.

For a few minutes they ate in silence, delighting in the smooth taste of the soup. As Winslow instructed Kemp to bring in the covered platters and adjusted the heat on the warmers, Charlotte let her gaze wander to Harry. Tonight, he wore black trousers and jacket with a snow-white shirt, and no tie, to match her own informal style of dress. He'd bathed as she could smell soap. How was such a handsome and kind man as him not yet married?

'Do I have something on my mouth?' Harry laughed.

Startled out of her day dream, her cheeks flushed with embarrassment. 'I'm sorry for staring.'

'May I ask why you were staring at me?'

More heat raced up her neck. 'I was wondering why you weren't married. You must be the most eligible bachelor in the whole district?'

'Not quite. Sir Houghton-Fielding who lives a few miles away has recently buried his fourth wife. He owns a great deal of land, more than this estate. Plus, he has shares in a diamond mine in Africa. He is the man any woman in the area would want to marry.' He chuckled. 'My dirty coal is no match for diamonds.'

'Four wives dead? I think he is the last man a woman would want to marry!' she joked.

Harry grinned. 'True. I have not married simply because in the past I have not met any woman who has tempted me enough to take such a step.' He sipped his wine and pushed his empty bowl away a little. 'But I have changed my mind on that subject recently and I hope to marry quite soon.'

Charlotte jerked back as though ice water had been thrown over her. Her heart plummeted to the soles of her shoes. 'I see.' She didn't. Not once had it been mentioned he had a prospective bride somewhere, and she felt unreasonably hurt that no one had told her. 'She is a lucky woman indeed.'

'I hope I am the lucky one.'

'Of course.' Charlotte gulped her wine, and Winslow immediately filled her glass again.

'Would you like to know who she is?'

'I doubt I would know anyone you are associated with. We move in very different circles.'

'Well, not for much longer because I'm hoping it will be you.'

'What?' Charlotte's astonishment was paired with Winslow's who dropped a serving spoon at the same time as they both stared at Harry.

'Does the idea disgust you?'

Charlotte blinked. Had she heard correctly? Was he joking? 'I fail to understand your meaning.'

'I think we get along rather well, and it would stop McBride in his tracks if we were to marry.'

'That's not a good enough reason to marry!' Her treacherous heart jumped at the thought, but her mind recoiled. To marry Harry? It was absurd. She would only marry for love, not to spite McBride.

'Think about it, please? It's bound to have shocked you, and I apologise for my clumsiness. But I think it is a very suitable plan. I like you. You are caring and considerate, intelligent and from a good family. You would be a wonderful asset to this family, and I believe you could be an excellent mistress to this house.'

'But—'

'And you would gain security, a permanent home, a husband to provide and care for you and Hannah. As a married woman, McBride is no longer your guardian, he has no hold over you. I would transfer your inheritance into your own name and control, along with Hannah's. You would never have to worry about it again. You would be returned to the status you once held in Wakefield.'

Her mind felt like a thousand butterflies flapped inside it, her thoughts swirled around madly and not one coherent. He had offered to marry her. Like it was a business transaction. It was ridiculous. She felt the sting of tears prickle the back of her eyes. Was that all she was ever to have, a business proposal? Would no one love her? Oh, she knew life wasn't like the books she read. There was no certainty to a happy ever after, but she at least wanted to try and see if it was possible. Her parents were deeply in love throughout their marriage, and her grandparents too. Could she not have that? Bizarrely, Nicholas Adams came into her mind and she knew without doubt he'd never ask her to marry her in such a calculated way.

Charlotte rose from her chair and Harry instantly stood to pull it out for her. 'Excuse me, please. I think I'll retire.'

'Charlotte, Miss Brookes, forgive me. Stay and dine, please.'

She shook her head, not trusting herself to speak as she saw the suffering in his eyes that he'd upset her. She fled the room and hurried upstairs, only to stop at the rooms she and Hannah shared, as she couldn't face her sister's chatter now. Turning blindly, she ran to the end of the corridor and up the small flight of stairs to the nursery above. Here, she closed the door and leant against it in the dark. The tears fell. Stupid, wasteful tears that had no meaning or reason. What had she expected from him?

She ran to the first narrow bed and threw herself on it and cried out her pain, her loneliness, and the heartache of being strong for so long. She cried for her mother and for her old life that had been so simple and happy.

When at last she could cry no more, she rolled onto her back and stared unseeing at the ceiling. Moonlight turned everything grey. As her eyes adjusted, she picked out the old rocking horse in the corner, the doll's house Hannah had loved the moment she saw it, the wooden shelves stacked with books, games and an odd assortment of toys. A doll's cradle sat beneath one of the dormer windows, and next to it a small puppet theatre. A pile of dust-sheets were near the door, taken off by Lucy as she and Hannah tidied and explored. Only the bed Charlotte laid on had the last remaining dustcover and she pulled the end of it over her, finally noticing the chill in the air. Dust tickled her nose, but she didn't care. It was silent, peaceful in here...

'Miss Brookes, wake up.'

Charlotte woke to her shoulder being shaken and Winslow looking down at her. 'Oh!'

'Tell me you didn't sleep in here all night, Miss Brookes?' Winslow admonished.

'I'm so sorry.' She sat up and sneezed.

'Miss Hannah has been looking for you, and I said you'd gone out for a walk so she wouldn't be worried, then I came looking for you.'

'Thank you, Winslow, you are very kind.' She stood and shook out the creases in her skirt, unsuccessfully.

'I may be speaking out of turn, Miss Brookes, but naturally I overhead Master Harry's conversation with you last night.' He held up his hand when she went to speak. 'No, hear me out, this will go no further, I promise you. I'm a man of discretion, I assure you.'

Walking to the window, Charlotte stared out at the fields in the distance. The sun was shining. It would be a beautiful day.

'Master Harry is one of the best men I have ever known, and I should know as I've met a few in my time. This house used to be a hive of activity in his grandfather's time. Every weekend some event would be happening, and when his brothers were alive the house rang with noise, laughter and bantering. It was a joy to work here. It still is, but something has died over the last few years. Master Harry works every hour, pushing himself constantly. His father has been travelling for years and Miss Petra, well, she comes and goes like a flighty bird. Neither of them can settle down. Something is missing in their lives. Too many deaths, their mother, their brothers, their grandparents. They, Master Harry and Miss Petra, are both so unhappy yet neither will ever admit to it.'

Out of the corner of her eye, Charlotte saw Winslow come to stand just to the side of her and he too looked out of the window. 'How Master Harry proposed was...disappointing. He knows this. He tormented himself all night until drink allowed him to fall into oblivion around three this morning. I waited up for him even though he sent me to my bed. But he's not a drinker and I knew he'd need help up to his room, but in the end, I let him sleep in his study.' Winslow sighed deeply. 'He needs you and, I believe, knowing only the few facts I have been privy to, that you need him. You may not think it is enough to base a marriage on, and you may be correct in that. But many have married with less.'

'And what of love, Winslow?' she whispered, her voice hoarse from dryness. 'I could easily fall in love with him, but would he feel the same for me? I am not of his class. His sister and friends might not take to me. They may disagree with his choice and shun him. I would hate to do that to him, to be a cause of misery to him.'

'Who is to say love won't come? You are both handsome people. I see the way you both look at each other when the other person isn't looking. Master Harry is loyal. He will protect you until his dying breath if you give him just a little of yourself. Be his friend, his companion. Love will grow for you both. And as to his sister and friends…well, Master Harry does what he wants. However, he has always carefully considered the consequences. I believe he would not have offered marriage if he hadn't thought it through and sincerely wanted it.'

'And what if it doesn't work out, the marriage? What if he or I come to realise in a year or two that we have made a terrible mistake?'

'Then, you will go your separate ways, just as his mother and father did. His mother filled her life with her children and friends, while his father enjoyed his travels and his writings. Master Harry does not want a repeat of his parents' marriage. He will not want failure. I trust that's why he's held off from it for so long. He's had plenty of opportunity to select a bride.' Winslow adjusted his cuffs, as though to let that information sink in. 'A positive attitude helps though. Wouldn't you agree?'

She nodded, a slight headache pulsing behind her eyes. 'Is it too late for a cup of tea?'

Straightening his shoulders, and once more the efficient butler he was known to be, Winslow led the way to the door. 'Mrs Morrissey has a full breakfast waiting for you. She'll be cross if you don't clear your plate.'

Charlotte paused by him and smiled warmly. 'Thank you, Winslow.'

After eating Mrs Morrissey's delicious breakfast, then grabbing a quick wash and changing her clothes, Charlotte spent the morning with Hannah. They played with the kittens for an hour in the stable, then Charlotte listened to Hannah read for a while before they explored the books in the library and delighted in spending a few hours studying a large atlas, with Charlotte teaching Hannah about different countries in the world.

The day was dry and fine so later they strolled about the

garden, trying to name as many flowers as they could until Lucy came to find them to say dinner would soon be ready.

Although she didn't see Harry at all that day, he was never far from her mind, despite her best efforts to keep him at bay. She asked Lucy if she and Hannah could eat in the dining room instead of their room, so that Charlotte could get Hannah used to the correct dining etiquette as she had been taught by their mother.

'Why can we not eat upstairs in our room?' Hannah sighed, tugging the cuffs of her best dress as they entered the dining room.

'Because we are living here and it's time we behaved accordingly. There is no need for us to be closeted away. You need to start learning the correct way to behave at the table and learn the correct use of the dinner service.' Charlotte waited for Winslow to pull out her chair, and then he did the same for Hannah.

'I know how to use a knife and fork, and which is a dessert spoon to a soup spoon. I knew that before Mamma died.'

'I know, but since then we've not had the opportunity to dine as we can do here at the Hall. It's an important part of your education that you learn everything about being a young lady.'

Hannah opened her napkin. 'But why? At the shop we just sit at the table in the back room.'

'You won't always be living at the shop.' Charlotte nodded to Winslow's offer of wine.

'Why?'

'Because one day you will marry and be the lady of the house, and as such you will need to know, amongst other things, the correct way to behave and dine.' She turned to Winslow. 'Is Mr Belmont joining us?'

'No, miss. He sent a message saying that he'll be late.'

'Even if I marry a pit lad?' Hannah suddenly announced.

'What?' Shocked, Charlotte stared at her.

'I don't need to be a lady if I marry a pit lad.'

'You'll not be marrying a pit lad. I think our parents would want us to strive for better than living in a pit house.'

Hannah played with her fork. 'I go to school with children who live in the pit houses. Susie is one of my best friends and her father and brothers work in Mr Belmont's mine.'

Charlotte looked to Winslow for help as he served them a small plate of duck pâté and slivers of toast.

'Well, Miss Hannah, your parents would have only wanted what is best for you, and although you may currently go to the village school, you will in time be an educated and smart young lady, who will be able to set her sights higher than a pit man to wed. Your aim would be to live in a nice house, would it not? Have nice clothes and a carriage?'

'Yes, Mr Winslow.'

'Do any of the pit families have that?'

'No, Mr Winslow.'

'So then, listen to your sister's instructions and follow her advice and you will emerge into a beautiful young lady to make your family proud and gentlemen will flock to your side offering diamonds and pearls.'

Hannah giggled. 'You are funny, Mr Winslow.'

'I aim to please, Miss Hannah.'

Once they'd finished their pâté and their plates had been removed and replaced with salmon and salad, Charlotte took the opportunity of Kemp talking to Mr Winslow to lean in closer to Hannah. 'I want to ask your opinion about something very important.'

'Really?' Hannah sat taller and grew serious, suddenly appearing older than her twelve years. 'Is it bad?'

Charlotte touched her hand, seeing the shadow of the last few years change her expression. She realised that despite the happiness Hannah basked in now it didn't take much to remind her of the hardships they have suffered. 'No dearest, not bad. How would you like to live here at the Hall permanently?'

'You mean not to go back to live with Stan and Bessie?'

'Yes. Mr Belmont has asked me to marry him and if I said yes it means we would live here and become a part of Mr Belmont's family.'

'Would we still visit the shop though, and see Stan and Bessie?'

'Of course, every week.' Charlotte hoped Harry still wished to marry her after her spending all day of thinking about nothing else. It would be the biggest decision of her life and she needed to know Hannah's thoughts. If her sister was totally against it then she would decline and think no more of it, but if Hannah was in agreement then perhaps there was a chance that marrying Harry would solve most of the financial and security problems. Her own personal happiness would have to be content with seeing Hannah live the life she was meant to, one that her parents and grandparents would want for them both.

Hannah picked at her salmon, deep in thought. She gazed around the dining room. 'It is nice here.'

'It is, very nice.' Charlotte finished her salmon. 'For one thing Mrs Morrissey is an excellent cook.'

'She makes the best puddings.' Hannah grinned. 'The Hall is bigger than Grandpapa's house in Wakefield, isn't it?'

'Well, yes. Grandpapa's house was in the town, and townhouses are designed and built differently to the houses in the country because of space.'

'Would I be able to have a pony, do you think? Just a little one, not a big horse like Mighty.'

Charlotte hesitated, wondering if Harry would agree, but then she would have her own inheritance next year and could buy Hannah a pony. 'Yes, I think you could have a pony, and learn to ride.'

'And keep all the kittens?'

'Do you need them all?' Charlotte reprimanded, she wasn't going to spoil Hannah just because she'd have the means to. 'I think the kittens will need to go to new homes, but Mr Belmont said you could keep one.'

'A puppy then?' Hannah persisted.

'Finish your dinner, please.'

'What room could I sleep in?'

'I don't know yet. There are many things I need to discuss with Mr Belmont first. One change I plan to make is to employ a governess for you. You'll not be attending the village school anymore.'

Hannah pouted. 'What about my friends?'

'You can still see them in the village. However, it is important you receive a proper education befitting your new status of living here at the Hall. It is what Mama would have wanted.'

'I miss her so much.' Hannah took another mouthful. 'Well, if Mama would have wanted it, then I think it is a good idea.'

Surprised at the easy acceptance, Charlotte let out a deep breath. 'I'm pleased you do. It will be the best thing for our future, I'm sure of it.' She might have said that more to convince herself than Hannah.

Winslow re-entered the room with a tray containing their desserts; apple and rhubarb crumble and a jug a steaming vanilla custard, which he placed on the serving table

Hannah sat back in her chair. 'Mr Winslow, Charlotte is going to marry Mr Belmont and we will live here.'

'Is that so, Miss Hannah? That is happy news indeed.' He gave Charlotte a small smile, as he cleared their plates away. 'Mr Belmont has just ridden in.'

Charlotte's heart skipped a beat. 'Will he be joining us?'

'I believe he has already eaten, miss, but you'll find him in the study, no doubt.'

Hannah chatted about going butterfly hunting tomorrow if the weather was fine and Charlotte, only half listening, nodded as they ate their dessert. With each mouthful, she found it harder to swallow, her stomach in knots at the prospect of speaking with

Harry. It was silly really, she'd have to learn to behave naturally in front of him if they were to be married, but the mere thought of what that decision entailed was starting to make an impact on her mind.

She'd be his wife... They'd be intimate...

The contents of her stomach surged.

'Miss Brookes.' Winslow came to her side. 'Shall I summon Lucy for Miss Hannah?'

Charlotte stood, feeling ill. 'Yes, please... Although...'

'All will be well, I promise you,' he whispered.

She sucked in a deep breath and forced a smile at Hannah. 'I'll join you upstairs shortly. I just need to speak with Mr Belmont for a moment.'

Before her courage deserted her completely, she strode across to the study and tapped on the door. His curt, 'Enter' did nothing for the state of her nerves.

He sat behind his desk, head resting against the chair, his hands loose in his lap and it seemed the weight of the world on his shoulders. Slowly, he brought his head forward and stared at her. 'Miss Brookes.'

'Mr Belmont...' She faltered, seeing the dark shadows under his eyes.

'Winslow has told me that there have been no unpleasant instances today.'

Her chest tightened. 'No, though I suspect it won't be long before I hear from McBride again in some form.'

He stood abruptly, dithered for a moment before walking to the cabinet against the wall that held a silver tray containing two glasses and a few crystal decanters of spirits. His hand hesitated on pouring the drink. He seemed upset and Charlotte wanted to ease that from him somehow.

'I will marry you, if you still wish it,' she blurted.

Harry slowly turned to her. 'If I wish it? What do you wish,

Miss Brookes? Would it be a great sacrifice of your freedom to shackle yourself to me?' he snapped.

'Of course it is! I barely know you!'

'Yet, I am willing to take the risk.'

Puzzled at his anger, she lifted her chin in defiance. 'You have to allow me some hesitation regarding an important decision such as this. Much depends on me not making a mistake.'

'How nice to be thought of a possible mistake.' He sneered. 'I'm giving you my name, my protection, my family home, but *I* could be considered a mistake, for *you?*'

'If you're going to act this way, then I'll reconsider!' She wanted to slap his arrogant face. 'What did you expect? That I would fall gratefully at your feet, sobbing out my thanks? That I would be forever in your debt and because of it I would be a biddable, humble wife, constantly bowing and scraping to your every whim?'

He laughed harshly. 'I can see I would be misguided if I thought that!'

'I have survived on my own, I don't need you!'

'Really, then why are you marrying me?'

She didn't know how to answer that. What possible explanation could she give him? I want to marry you because you're all I think about? He'd laugh at her. She struggled to find the right words and felt foolish. 'I…I have thought about this all day until my head hurts. I have spent hours going over all the reasons, good and bad…I…it seems…what I mean is…'

In an instant he was inches from her, grabbing her by the upper arms and crushing her into him. He kissed her hard, pushing her lips back against her teeth for a moment, and then suddenly his grip loosened, and his hands slipped down her back and his hold softened. His mouth moved over hers gently and she melted against him like butter on toast. He sighed her name and without her being fully aware, her mouth opened, and his tongue plunged inside, thrilling her. She grasped his shoulders, needing to hold on as the kiss depended and grew sensual. The pit of her loins tightened and tingled, and she was light-headed in amazement of the sensation.

'Marry me because you want this, you want me, I beg you, please,' he whispered against her cheek, kissing her eyes, before plundering her mouth again.

Charlotte tried to gain focus, tried to think straight, but all she wanted was for this kiss to never end and for this man to be hers. Surely to have this fire between would be a good start to marriage? 'Yes, yes I do.'

He pulled away slightly to gaze down into her eyes. 'Come with me in the morning to church, we'll have the banns called. In three weeks we'll be married.'

She nodded, not caring, just wanting him to kiss her again.

CHAPTER 10

*A*s Harry predicted, they were married on a sunny May day, three Sundays later, a quiet ceremony with only Hannah, the Wheelers, Nicholas, and the Hall staff in attendance. Petra and Bertram had stayed away. His sister wrote him furious letters on the subject of him being a complete fool to marry a penniless nobody. He burnt every one of them without showing them to Charlotte. From McBride Charlotte received a letter each week leading up to the wedding. Each letter started with him imploring her to meet with him, but by the end he was raging, threatening and delusional. Harry sent these letters on to his solicitor, with the instructions that on the day they marry, he was to send copies to the police and to Mr Bottomley, Charlotte's family's solicitor in Wakefield.

A week before they married, Harry had taken Charlotte to Wakefield and they'd seen her grandfather's partner to arrange everything. At last Charlotte was able to read her grandfather's will and learn of what he'd provided for her and Hannah. It had come as a shock to see just how much the will revealed. Shares in stocks and bonds, both in the United Kingdom and the United States of America. There were houses and businesses in various cities around the country, as well as several bank accounts with sizeable amounts of money in them.

Charlotte had been dumbfounded, Harry also. Neither expected it to be so much, especially since Charlotte mentioned that her grandparents' house was large, but not a castle or even a manor such as Belmont Hall, and they didn't live an extravagant lifestyle. It was no wonder McBride was so eager to make Charlotte his bride one way or another.

Before going on their honeymoon tomorrow, Harry and Charlotte were to travel to Wakefield for her to sign the necessary papers so that her inheritance could be signed over to Harry.

Harry was suspicious that McBride had been milking money off the estate, but had no positive proof, and now it no longer mattered. McBride would be in the past. Finished.

Now, as everyone gathered in the drawing room, celebrating at the wedding breakfast, Harry allowed himself to be at ease. Happiness spread through him as he watched Charlotte, looking beautiful in a long cream lace dress, chat with the Wheelers. He still didn't believe his luck that he had her, that this magnificent woman was his.

They hadn't spoken about the wedding night, or whether she'd sleep in his room or stay in another room, perhaps they should have done, but he couldn't face her refusal to share his bed, so he'd remained tight-lipped on the subject, but he hoped she would be his wife in every way and decide that his bed was where she belonged.

In the last three weeks they had been so busy with organising the wedding that he'd only briefly seen her at dinner each night. A chaste kiss before bed had been all she'd allowed him to do, but he knew of the fire inside her from that one passionate kiss in the study.

'I'd be grinning too, if I'd just bagged such a prize.' Nicholas clinked his glass against Harry's. 'I'm happy for you, my friend, but also furious with myself for not claiming her first. I was too slow.' He shook his head in disbelief.

Harry patted him on the back. 'I am sorry, truly, I am, but I wanted her too, and well…'

'You don't have to explain.' For a moment regret filled Nicholas's eyes. 'It's done now. I have to learn to live with it.'

'You'll still be a regular dinner guest though, won't you. You'll not allow this to interfere with the friendship we have?'

'Not at all, and of course I'll still come once a week for dinner. It's the only decent meal I get.' He laughed.

Hannah, looking very grown up in her pale lilac dress, sidled over to them and smiled up at Harry. 'Charlotte said you are my brother now.'

Harry chuckled. 'Yes, I am, and I have a new sister in you now.'

'In the church the vicar said your name was Henry. Did he make a mistake?'

'No, he didn't. My name is Henry, but from a small boy I was called Harry.'

'I can call you Harry?'

'That you can, Hannah.'

'I'm pleased.' She walked away back to Stan who immediately gave her all his attention.

They were interrupted by Mr Ardent, a photographer Harry had hired for the day. 'Mr Belmont, I am ready for you and your bride outside.'

Gathering everyone out into the gardens, where the May sun shone gloriously on them, Harry watched while Ardent fussed around Charlotte as she stood on the lawns for a formal photograph. Harry had plans that from the photograph he'd commission an artist to paint a life size portrait of Charlotte so it could be hung in the Hall.

'Everyone, everyone, please.' Ardent ushered Harry and the guests to stand around Charlotte and took a group shot. He took one of the bride and groom. After a few more takes, he let them go back inside, as Harry had also instructed him to take photographs of the estate, and the staff, and then he was to go along to the mine and the village.

'What a great way to record the day,' Stan said as they entered the Hall once more. 'A very good idea that is.'

'I'm glad you approve, Stan.' Harry grinned. 'I'm not sure why I insisted on it, but I was compelled to have it done for some reason and Mr Ardent has a good reputation.'

'He'll have some refreshments, Harry?' Charlotte asked, sitting on the sofa and taking a cup of tea that Winslow handed to her.

'I'll see to it, madam,' Winslow said before Harry had a chance to reply.

'Madam?' Charlotte gave a tinkling laugh. 'Yes, I suppose I shall have to get used to being called madam now.'

'And Mrs Belmont.' Harry raised a questioning eyebrow at her. 'You have many new titles now. Wife. Sister-in-law. Daughter-in-law. Mistress of Belmont Hall.'

'And mother one day, hopefully.' Bessie sat down next to Charlotte. 'What a beautiful day it has been.'

Charlotte turned to talk to her, and Harry saw the blush creep up her neck at the thought of what act it takes to become a mother. His own body responded to such thoughts. He was eager for the night to come, but was Charlotte?

A commotion at the doorway caused everyone to turn and stare. Harry stifled an oath as Petra stormed into the room, with Bertram not far behind her. 'This is a surprise, sister.' Harry tried to instil some warmth into his voice.

'It shouldn't be.' She snapped, her eyes as sharp as a hawk's as she glared at each person in the room. 'I see it is too late.'

'Too late for food? Not at all. We have eaten. However, Winslow will kindly arrange for more.'

'I don't want food.' Her anger was palpable. 'Too late to stop this farce of a marriage.'

'This is no farce.' Harry's teeth clenched in rising fury. He'd not let her spoil today. 'If you are not happy for us then you can turn around and leave now.'

'This is my home!'

'Only while I allow it. I provide for this house and only I say who resides in it.'

'You mean you'd ask your own sister to leave and yet willingly have riffraff here instead? Have you lost your mind?'

Harry grabbed her arm and marched her out of the room, along the hall to his study. There, none too gently, he threw her away from him. 'You disgust me. Your bad manners are an embarrassment to me and this family. How dare you behave in such a way?'

'How dare I? What about you?' She jeered at him. 'You marry a shop girl and I'm supposed to be happy about it. You could have had anyone, any woman in this district or London from a good family and with connections, but you had to flout the rules of society and think it clever to slum it. She won't be accepted, you know. You'll be talked about the pair of you.'

'Then I'll be joining your ranks then, won't I? Since you seem intent on bringing down the family's reputation all by yourself.'

She pouted. 'I love Alastair. Ours is a tragic situation. You don't love her. I can see why you would lust after her, but why marriage?'

'My feelings for Charlotte are none of your concern.'

'There, you admit it, you don't love her.'

'I admit to nothing.'

'How could you possibly love a girl with no family or breeding?'

Harry laughed, releasing the tension and anger out of him. He walked around to his desk and opened a drawer and took out a letter, which he tossed onto the desk. 'This is a letter from a solicitor in Wakefield. Charlotte's grandfather's solicitor. Read it.'

Her expression was all revulsion. 'I think not.'

'Your new sister-in-law is wealthier than you, my dear sister. Charlotte is an heiress. So perhaps you should think of that next time you have the urge to call her a shop girl.' He strode from the room, secretly delighting in her shocked face.

He came to an abrupt halt in the hall as Charlotte stood there very still, obviously having heard their argument. 'Charlotte. Don't listen to her. She speaks with a poisoned tongue.'

At that moment Petra exited the study and faltered on seeing them standing there.

Harry stiffened. 'What have you decided, sister?'

'This is my home. I wish to remain here.'

'Then you'll be civil to my wife.'

'Naturally.' Petra's false smile twisted her handsome face.

* * *

LATER THAT EVENING, after all their guests had gone and Lucy had come to take Hannah upstairs to bed, Charlotte reclined back on the sofa and closed her eyes. Petra and Bertram had also retired to their rooms while Harry had disappeared for a moment. Charlotte ached to slip off her shoes, but dared not. Walking around in stocking feet would not be the done thing. There was a small stool nearby and she pulled it closer to her and rested her feet on it. Stifling a large yawn, she grinned to herself at the thought of taking a little nap. In fact, she would be happy to sleep here all night. Her mind drifted to the other prospect of the night. Sleeping in the same bed as her husband, being intimate with him. There, her thoughts scattered and swirled, making no sense and scaring her a little. Nerves butterflied in her stomach. She had drunk rather too much champagne and she felt a little light–headed.

'Charlotte?' She woke to Harry leaning over her, his hand resting on her shoulder.

'Shall we retire?' He smiled kindly, with a twinkle of humour in his eyes.

'I'm so sorry. I didn't mean to fall asleep. How rude of me.'

'Nonsense, you've had a very tiring and hopefully exciting day.' He tucked her hand through his arm and they went upstairs, saying good night to Winslow as they passed him in the hall.

'I had a wonderful day, did you?' she asked Harry as they entered his, and now their bedroom.

'I did.'

She stopped and stared in wonder. The thick heavy brocade curtains were closed and the room was lit with dozens of candles, a low fire burnt in the grate even though it wasn't cold. Vases of flowers stood on every flat surface, a bottle of wine, with two glasses poured and a box of chocolates were placed on a small table by the window. 'Harry, it looks wonderful.'

'I'm pleased you like it. I wanted our first night to be special, comfortable...' He gave her one of the wine glasses, which she sipped. He selected a chocolate and his gaze never leaving hers, he popped it into her mouth, his fingers lingering on her lips. 'I promise I will try my best to make you happy.'

The soft centred chocolate melted in her mouth. Feeling embolden by his sincerity, she reached up and placed her hand against his cheek. 'I promise to do the same.'

Harry drew her into his arms and kissed her. 'You taste of chocolate. I like it.'

She chuckled, her nerves settling as excitement surged. She felt a little tipsy. She'd had far too much alcohol today and put her glass back on the table. As he kissed her again, she responded, knowing that whatever the night brought she would try so hard to make it a success, for both their sakes. She had read enough books and made her own conclusions that the marriage bed couldn't be too horrible otherwise no one would ever be happy.

Such sensible thoughts flew from her head as Harry gathered her into his arms tighter, his mouth leaving hers to kiss down her neck until the lace of her dress stopped him. He turned her around so he could undo the pearl buttons down her back, his fingers pulled away the material and the dress fell to the floor. Her corset soon followed and then standing only in her shift and bloomers, he traced the outline of her curves with his hands. 'You are beautiful, Charlotte.'

She didn't know what to say, and remained silent as he gently turned her to face him. The pins were soon pulled out of her hair, and he shook out its length.

Harry kissed her tenderly and guided her hands to his chest.

Her heart in her throat, she began to unbutton his shirt enough so he could pull it over his head. Her fingers traced the muscles of his chest and down to his stomach to the waistband of his trousers where she hesitated.

'Go on,' he urged.

Biting her lip in concentration, she spent the next few moments undressing him until he was completely naked. She stared at his body, amazed and curious.

He laughed and picked her up, and in a leap, they both landed on the bed in a fit of giggles.

'This is going to be a good night, my love.' He rained kisses over her face, his hands cupping her bottom and pulling her against him. Then abruptly he rolled away on to his back and grinned at her. 'I'm not doing all the work!'

Surprised she sat up. 'What do you mean?'

He squirmed more comfortably on the bed. 'You, my dear wife, are going to touch me until I lose my mind and then I'm going to do the same to you.'

'But Harry—'

'No buts.' His fingertips brushed over her thigh. 'Let us explore.'

CHAPTER 11

August 1914

Charlotte scanned the week's menu created by the cook, Mrs Morrissey, and nodded to Winslow. 'I'm very happy with those choices.'

Winslow, sitting to the side of her desk, frowned. 'Madam doesn't wish to suggest any changes? Mrs Morrissey is only too happy to change anything you wish.'

'None at all. They are perfectly acceptable.' She read them again quickly just to double-check. 'We'll not be home on Friday evening as we've been invited to Forrester Court for dinner.'

He inclined his head. 'Yes, madam, I have it noted.'

She glanced at her diary. 'We must return their invitation next month, Winslow. I mustn't forget.'

'No, madam. I'm certain there is a date free at the end of the month.'

'Yes...' Charlotte marked the twentieth as a possibility.

Playing hostess was still something she was getting used to. 'Is Mrs Morrissey feeling better?'

'On the mend, madam. She assured me she will be back on her feet this afternoon.'

'If she needs more time then I'm sure a light meal tonight will be sufficient for us. I'd not like her to be working when she's not in full health.'

'I'll talk to Mrs Morrissey and let her decide, madam.'

'Very well.' Charlotte closed the household ledgers she'd been working on after breakfast. Rising from her desk in the morning room, a small room situated next to the dining room and entirely for her personal use, Charlotte looked out of the window that gave a lovely view of the rose gardens to the side of the house and beyond those the path that led to the stables.

'Do you have any further instructions for me, madam?' He rose also and replaced his chair back against the wall.

'I don't believe so.'

'I thought we would discuss the linens. Without a house-keeper, there have been some aspects of the house that are lacking. I do try...'

Charlotte tidied her desk. 'You have done very well. I shall consider employing a housekeeper soon, or we can promote one of the senior maids?'

'That could be possible. Edith is very sensible. She has stepped into the breach since Mrs Wynn died, and she is getting married next month so it'd be all very respectable. Would you like to have an interview with her? I can fetch her, madam?'

'Not today, Winslow. Tomorrow, perhaps, if that is convenient to you? You've taught me so much since my return from my honeymoon.'

'Madam did want to learn the running of the house...' Winslow looked affronted.

'Oh yes, indeed I do, all of it, as I said last week, and I thank you most sincerely for your time. But today...today I feel the need to walk, and feel the sun on my face.' She smiled at him and he gave a ghost of a smile back, the most he ever revealed.

'Of course, madam, and rightly so.'

They walked out of the room together. 'What time will my husband be home, did he say?'

'Mondays are his busiest days at the mine, madam, and he's missed a few months while you've been on your honeymoon. I imagine there would be a lot that Mr Adams will want to discuss with him.'

'In that case, I'll take a short walk while Miss Hannah is having her lessons.' She turned right at the end of the corridor and left the house via the back entrance.

The gardens were in full bloom, fragrance filled the still summer air. The sun baked down on her and she should have put on a hat, but not wanting to return inside, she headed to the sunken garden that had a large pond in the middle of it. Ornamental trees from Japan bordered the four sides of the garden, large enough to provide some dabbled shade but not tall enough to block out the sun from the pond or the flowering beds surrounding it. This was her favourite garden of all the ones created around the Hall. The red and white carp broke the surface of the water, expecting food, but again she'd not thought, and her pockets were empty of bread for them.

Impulsively, she lay on the lush grass between the pond and the garden beds and closed her eyes, enjoying the warmth on her face. The heat of early August reminded her of the little Italian villa Harry had rented for a few weeks at the end of their honeymoon. She sighed happily at the memories of their time away. Harry had spoiled her, taking her to France and Italy, before hiring a friend's yacht to bring them home. It had been the most joyous time of her life, and although she missed Hannah, she had delighted in spending every day with Harry, and learning about her husband.

For two months they travelled, visiting galleries, museums,

cathedrals, cities and small villages. They ate fine food, walked crowded streets and quiet lanes. They danced in ballrooms and laughed at comedy concerts. They spent time alone and also met new friends. They talked for hours, or laid in blissful sleepy silence in the sun, and did their best to ignore the budding tension of war rumours sweeping through Europe.

They made love so much that Charlotte no longer knew where she finished and Harry began. They became best friends, as well as lovers.

Although she had married him to secure her inheritance from McBride and a home for Hannah, he claimed her heart from the first night of their marriage and she knew it would never belong to another.

And now her days were to be filled with other things, in other ways. She had to get used to being the mistress of the Hall. The running of the house with Winslow, the calls from neighbouring estates, the requests to be patron of various charities, attending or hosting events and organisations within the district were all her responsibility now. However, she would always have the memories of her magical honeymoon, and despite missing Harry during the day, she knew that come night time, he was hers alone.

Shadow blocked the sun on her face, and she squinted up to see the cause of it. 'Harry!'

He reached down to help her to her feet. 'The lady of the house lying on the grass like a village lass.' He kissed her tenderly.

She smiled. 'I was hidden. No one is about.' She paused at the worried look on his face as he sat on the wall of the pond. 'You're home early. What is wrong?'

'It is what we all feared would happen. England has declared war on Germany.'

'Oh no.'

'Naturally, the hope is that it is a situation that lasts mere months...'

'But you don't think it will?' She sat beside him, ignoring the carp that popped open-mouthed to the surface.

'It is a feeling I have. Remember when we were in Paris, and after the opera we went to that little restaurant, Pierre's? Remember that German couple we talked to? The gentleman was extremely bold in his political opinions.'

'Yes, I remember. It was when news had broken of Franz Ferdinand being shot in Sarajevo. I also remember that I preferred talking to his wife than to listening to him. He was very full of himself, unlike his quiet wife.'

Harry looked up into the trees, his gaze distant. 'That German worked in the government. He held total belief in the idea of war, as their right. There was no doubt in his mind it would come, and what's more, he said it would not go away for some time.'

She took his hand in hers. 'And you believe him?'

'I do. He was convinced the time had come for his nation to rise and make a stand. For too long the close proximity of countries in Europe has been a smouldering hot bed of discontent. Each one wanting more than they could have.'

'The Kaiser is our King's own cousin. Surely he would not want war with us?'

'I believe he hesitated, but his advisors want it.'

'Will it affect us?'

'Yes. Only I'm not sure in what way just yet.' He squeezed her hand. 'I don't want to frighten you, but I think we should be prepared.'

'Our army will handle it though, won't they?'

'Let's hope so.' He kissed her, and then linking arms they strolled back to the house.

'But you aren't convinced?' she asked.

'Our army isn't as great as France's, or Germany's.' He paused at the door leading into the house. 'I have a feeling we, as a country, just might be on the back foot in this situation.'

'What do you mean?'

'If this war goes on for a good length of time, our army will need to be increased. If ordinary men, outside of the military, decide to join and go to war the country could and possibly will be compromised in services and industry.' He opened the door for her and followed her inside, exchanging the heat of outside for the coolness of the corridor.

'You're worried about the mine and not having enough workers?'

He nodded. 'Yes, but also the estate, Home Farm and the village.' At the doorway of his study he stopped. 'We have to anticipate changes. It's obviously too soon to tell, but I want you to be prepared in advance.'

'In what way?'

'The call to arms.' His gaze didn't meet hers.

They were interrupted by Hannah and trailing behind her was Miss Newton, her new governess. 'Charlotte, Harry, are you busy? Would you like to come out for a walk with Miss Newton and me?'

'Miss Newton and I,' the tall, thin governess corrected gently.

'Not at the moment, Monkey,' Harry called her by the nickname he'd given her and tweaked her ribbon, 'but maybe later we can watch you ride on your pony?'

'Oh yes, that would be wonderful.' Hannah turned to Miss Newton. 'A riding lesson is far more important than a painting lesson.'

Charlotte gave her a pointed look. 'Both are equally important. Go along now and we'll find you shortly.'

Entering the study with Harry, Charlotte closed the door. 'I'm very pleased with Miss Newton. She is far more suitable than Hannah attending the village school. I know it's only been a few months, but I believe Hannah respects her and they get on well. She is quiet and very intelligent. She'll be a good influence on Hannah.'

Harry grinned. 'Monkey would like most people. She has that sort of character.'

Charlotte sighed. 'Hannah will need an excellent education if she is to manage her own substantial inheritance when she comes of age. She will learn that better with Miss Newton than at the local school, sadly. I know she misses her friends there, but a governess is the best solution.'

'I agree. You don't need to convince me. It will work out for the best. Miss Newtown seems an ideal governess.' Harry looked at the ledgers and papers on his desk and sighed. 'Give me an hour or two to sort through this lot and then we'll take the Rolls out and I will give you another driving lesson.'

Charlotte laughed. '*You* will give me a lesson? I can drive better than you can! Patterson gives me lessons every day while you're at the mine.' She couldn't help but grin at him. It irritated him that she had more time to practise driving the silver Rolls Royce that had been delivered while they were on their honeymoon. Patterson, a charming young chauffeur, was hired as soon as they returned.

'Yes, and Patterson is very keen on showing you the driving skills he has.' Harry raised a sardonic eyebrow at her.

Charlotte slipped her arms around his waist. 'Are you jealous of him, husband?'

'Of course! A good-looking young man spending time with my very attractive wife is very good cause for jealousy.' He kissed the tip of her nose.

She kissed him and laughed again. 'He is young and handsome...' She kissed him again. 'But not a patch on the man I married.'

CHAPTER 12

*B*y the New Year, the country was gripped by war. Devastating battles such as in Aisne and Ypres had wounded thousands, bringing home the reality that over the Channel men were getting slaughtered and the 'over by Christmas' saying had long died on people's lips as the men died on foreign soil.

Bombs had been dropped on British soil for the first time from German bi-planes, scaring the nation to the core. Patriotic fever flowed through the population and Charlotte couldn't help but wonder when Harry would announce he could sit by no longer and watch from afar.

Their Christmas had been quiet, but despite the ongoing war news in every newspaper, Charlotte wanted their first Christmas as a new family to be special. Harry complied, and did his best to act happy and carefree but she knew him well enough by now to know that it was all false. Constantly preoccupied, he made a good show of enjoying unwrapping presents and eating a lovely meal with Stan and Bessie and Nicholas. They went to church on Christmas Eve, and visited neighbouring estates for drinks, they attended the village play and gave out presents to staff. Yet, underneath it all, Charlotte watched him and knew something was on his mind.

'Are we to have a New Year's party tomorrow, Charlotte?' Hannah asked, putting down the book she was reading.

'No, dearest. It doesn't seem fitting with the war on.' Charlotte sipped her tea that Winslow had just brought in for her. Outside snow fell lightly from thick grey clouds, and she hoped it wouldn't stay on the ground for Harry was at the mine and Patterson had left to collect him before the weather became worse.

Winslow, pretending to straighten the curtains, was actually watching out for the Rolls coming down the drive. He turned to Charlotte, his shoulders relaxing. 'An automobile, madam. The master is home.'

Charlotte smiled, relieved, but the smile froze on her face as Winslow peered closer to the window. 'No, not Master Harry. I don't recognise the vehicle.'

'Visitors? In this weather?' Charlotte rose, putting a hand to her hair and adjusting the lace cuffs of the sleeves of her soft blue woollen dress.

'Shall I go up, Charlotte?' Hannah asked with a sigh. 'Miss Newton isn't back yet, but I can read in my room.'

'If you want to, but it wouldn't hurt for you to participate in conversations with our neighbours when they call.'

'It is boring listening to you talking to people I don't even know.'

'I don't know them all that well myself, but it's a duty I must perform as Harry's wife.'

'Can I go upstairs, please?'

'Yes, very well. Miss Newton shouldn't be too much longer. Her train is to arrive at three. I believe Patterson is going to try and collect her from the station on his way back from the mine, if Harry isn't late.'

'I do hope Miss Newton's grandmother isn't too sick,' Hannah said, walking to the door with her book. She stopped as the door opened and Petra strode in with Bertram behind her.

Charlotte stiffened, wishing it was a neighbour calling to gossip rather than them. She'd not seen her sister-in-law since her wedding. 'Petra. Bertram. This is a surprise.'

'Unfortunately, London has become tediously boring with all this war nonsense. How dare the Germans drop bombs on London? We've decided to come north and see if people are cheerier here.' Petra sat on the sofa Hannah had just vacated.

Bertram smiled and said hello to Hannah before the girl slipped quietly out of the room. Petra had ignored her, and Charlotte's hackles rose.

Sitting back down, Charlotte nodded a welcome to Bertram before picking up her cup and saucer again. 'Harry and I thought you both to be in Cornwall.'

'We were for a couple of months, but we expected London would be exciting with all the soldiers. However, the parties soon dwindled down, and everyone became deeply serious.'

'War is serious.'

'Oh no, not you too?' Petra pouted. 'All this will stop soon enough. The Kaiser is our royal family's cousin. He cannot seriously think our two nations will continue to fight. It is nothing more than a spat that has got out of hand.'

'I don't think that is quite true. The newspapers tell a different story. Would you like some tea?'

'I have ordered Winslow to bring some in as he took our coats.' Petra yawned. 'How tiresome trains are, especially now they are full of soldiers in every carriage. London is teeming with them. So many of our friends have died in stupid battles. Did you know that half of Bertram's class at Eton have perished?'

'Yes, Harry did mention it.' Charlotte smiled sadly at Bertram. 'I'm sorry to hear it. Were any of them good friends of yours?'

'A few, yes. I—'

'Are we having a New Year's party?' Petra butted in.

'No, I just explained the same to Hannah. It's hardly considered appropriate, celebrating while men are dying across the Channel.'

'My, you *are* as dreary as those in London.'

Charlotte ignored her insult and looked at Bertram. 'Has it been snowing in London?'

'No, nothing,' Petra answered for him, and Charlotte gritted her teeth at her rudeness. 'I did meet a man in London called McBride. He was very interested in you, said he was distant family to you?'

Charlotte stilled. 'I have nothing to do with him. He is not a decent person to be acquainted with.'

'Oh, don't worry on that score. I saw he was not of the same class as us and ignored him. But he was insistent on talking about you. Extremely rude, wasn't he, Bertram? I turned my back on him, obviously.'

Winslow and Lucy brought in the tea service and a stand of dainty pastries, which Petra and Bertram rapidly ate as though they'd not eaten in days instead of hours.

'Is my brother at the mine?' Petra asked, reaching for another raspberry tartlet.

'Yes, but he's due home any moment,' Charlotte answered, her thoughts on McBride. He'd have hated how Petra treated him. Was the man never going to leave her in peace?

'Good, I need to discuss with him my need to engage a new maid. I had to let go of Flora in London. She was a gossip and idle.'

'That is sad news.'

Petra waved her hand lazily in the air. 'London maids are too full of themselves. I think I shall engage a country girl, someone who can work hard and keep her mouth shut.'

Sipping her tea to hide her thoughts, Charlotte was thankful when the door opened, and Harry appeared. Winslow must have warned him of the new arrivals for he wasn't shocked on seeing them.

'Brother.'

'Sister. Cousin.' He gave them the merest of niceties and bent to give Charlotte a kiss.

'I didn't hear you arrive.' She gazed up at him.

'The snow muffles everything now. It is rather thick and not finished yet.'

'Tea?' Charlotte motioned to Winslow standing by the door.

'No, darling. I would instead rather we talked in private when you are ready.'

Charlotte rose. 'I'm ready now.'

Petra frowned. 'Aren't you going to talk to us? We've not seen you for months.'

Harry sighed. 'I will, Petra, later, but first I must speak with my wife.'

The seriousness of Harry's manner worried Charlotte, but she remained silent as they went upstairs to their bedroom, the one room in the whole house where they wouldn't be disturbed. Sitting on the edge of their bed, she waited for him to speak.

He sat down suddenly and took her hand. 'I want to discuss something with you.' His gaze locked with hers. 'I want to join the war.'

'Join the war?' Her heart gave a thump.

'I can buy a commission. I will be an officer in the army.'

She stared at him. 'You mean to go to the War Office in London to help...' Even as she said it she knew it was ridiculous. Harry wouldn't want an office position. No, he'd want to be in the thick of things, that was who he was.

'I am losing men every day who are joining up to fight. Nicholas and I thought that we should create our own unit of Belmont men, if possible.'

'But why?' she whispered, trying to ignore the emotions that were starting to fill her head and tighten her chest.

'I have felt for some time, that the more men who fight, the sooner it will be over. From everything I have read, and the letters I receive from friends, we are floundering at the moment. You've read the accounts of the battles so far and the huge loses we have suffered.'

'But there are true soldiers, career soldiers, who are there to fight. That is what they do. They don't need ordinary men.'

'They do, my love, more now than ever.' His earnest expression failed to move her. 'Listen to me, bombs were dropped on London, and just a few weeks ago we had German ships firing at Scarborough, Whitby and Hartlepool. People were killed on our soil, and not too far from our home!'

'I know this. I read the newspapers too!' She jerked to her feet and walked to the window to look out on the pristine white world. She'd been upset by the German attacks, and the reports of thousands of casualties in the many battles being fought on the different war fronts. Yet, and perhaps naively, she never thought Harry would want to go, would want to leave her. They were happy. Against the odds, of being near strangers when they married, they had found a passion and quickly formed a close friendship. They loved each other. Why was he willing to put that in jeopardy?

'Charlotte look at me.' He'd come to stand by her side.

She kept staring out at the snow falling, not trusting herself to face him or she'd give into the tears threatening to escape. 'Why do you have to go? The mine is important. The government has said they need the country to keep working, that we need our miners and farmers and fishermen. Let other men go, those with no jobs or families.'

'I want to do my bit, Charlotte.'

She glared at him, fist clenched. 'You are doing your bit! You are producing coal. We have land to grow food. You are the leader of our community. That *is* you doing your bit!' She wanted to slap some sense into him. 'You are needed here!'

'Please try to understand. I cannot sit by and watch from the comfort of my home when our country is in danger. I couldn't respect myself. I must do this. It is my duty. I need you to support me in this, please.'

She felt wounded. He had never asked her to do anything for him. He gave her everything, security, a home for herself and Hannah, his name, and his love. She had to put her selfishness aside, but it was so hard. He was her husband and she wanted him at home safe with her. She'd only just got used to relying on him, on feeling like she was safe and could enjoy her life now that McBride was no real threat. Stupidly she believed she could be happy now, at last. But this, this changed everything. Now she would be worrying day and night about Harry surviving battles.

He put his hands on her waist. 'I'm sorry this is so difficult for you. Believe me when I say nothing else would take me away from being with you. I wish I could be the kind of man who could sit at home and do nothing, but I can't.'

She saw the anguish in his eyes. He was torn just as much as she was, but for different reasons. Placing her hand on his cheek, she reached up to kiss him softly. 'Do what you must. I will support you.'

He crushed her to him and kissed her deeply before picking her up and laying her on the bed. 'I love you.'

She let the tears fall as they made love and he kissed them away tenderly. She cherished every touch and every look they shared. She had to show him how much he meant to her. Each moment was a sigh, a memory to be stored away for another time when distance would separate them.

Much later, they lay cuddled in bed, not wanting to break this precious time together.

Harry ran his fingers down Charlotte's spine while she laid with her head on his chest listening to his heartbeat. 'What will happen at the mine? And this estate?' she asked him.

'Nicholas wants to go with me, as do Mr Shelley, Mr Clarke and a dozen others from the mine and in the village. I'm going to put a manager in at the mine, one of the older men, a foreman by the name of Tom Blaneley, who is ready to retire, but I know he's very capable as he's been a miner since he was a small child. He can read and write and has been a natural leader of the men underground for decades. I hired him when I opened the mine and he's never let me down. I trust him completely. I will have others promoted to assist him.'

'And the estate?'

'You.'

She raised up on her arms and stared at him. 'Me?'

He nodded. 'I trust no one more than you. Home Farm is run by Mr Tyler, as you know, and he is a good man, and for the house you have Winslow inside and the men outside will listen to you. You are the mistress of Belmont Hall. Who else would oversee the running of it?'

'But I'm only just learning.'

'And there are plenty of people to help you. Winslow is like your shadow, and respects you greatly. When I inform him of my plans he will be everything you need.'

'Except my husband.' She couldn't resist sending that barb home.

Harry grabbed her and rolled her beneath him. 'Please don't make me feel guiltier than I already do.'

She ran her fingers through his hair, and looked into his eyes. 'I will miss you dreadfully.'

'And I you, but hopefully by the end of this new year or even sooner, we will have won and peace declared.'

'Kiss me,' she murmured, hoping what he said would come true.

CHAPTER 13

France, July 1915

*H*arry pushed aside his empty tin plate. Bread and jam had been supper with a lukewarm cup of watery sugarless black tea. At least it was quiet, the only noise was the odd scurrying of rats in the corners of the dugout, and in response Nicholas throwing boots at them. The bombs had stopped an hour ago as dusk fell, giving the men on both sides of the trenches respite from the ceaseless noise of war.

Harry looked around the cramped dugout, home for the last few weeks. He was fortunate to have connections in the War Department, old boys that were friends of his grandfather and father, and they pulled strings to allow him to buy his commission to be a Captain, and keep the Belmont men with him. Nicholas, Mr Shelley, Mr Clarke were Sergeants of various roles, and the miners and village men who enlisted with him were Corporals or Privates. There was a lot to be said for keeping people together from the same area. Those faces you knew were a comfort when you were in danger.

He glanced up as Private Simmons, one of his miners, knocked on the wooden post and flipped the curtain back to enter the dugout. 'Sir.' He saluted and Harry returned it before taking the mailbag from him.

Dispatches and their orders sent from command, plus letters from home for the men. Harry passed the bundle to Nicholas to sort out, while he read the orders. Another attack at dawn. Over the top and into no man's land again to charge a well-protected enemy. Stupid. Harry's teeth clenched. Nothing would ever get solved at this rate. Just more useless slaughter. More blood spilt on French soil. Nothing in the months of training prepared them for the reality of the war.

'For you, Harry.' Nicholas passed him a small pile of letters.

His spirits lifted as he recognised Charlotte's writing, beneath her letter was one from Winslow, as he had secretly instructed the man to send him reports on how Charlotte was coping without her knowing, for she would never send a letter which would cause him concern when he was so far away. Another letter from his solicitor, no doubt to do with his businesses, and lastly a letter from Bertram, which surprised him. He'd not seen or heard from Bertram since he left Belmont Hall in the New Year.

He opened Charlotte's letter first and seeing her writing gave him an overwhelming sense of love towards her. He had under-estimated just how much he would miss her. The nights were the worst when his brain wouldn't shut down for sleep and he'd lay in his cot and think of her in their bed. Those times were diffi-cult, especially when his body wanted to feel hers against him, but instead all he had was lice and rats and the ever threat of attack.

My darling,

I hope this letter finds you safe and well. I'm so pleased that your letters are frequent and full of what you are doing, please don't hide from me what you are experiencing. I want to know it all, or what the censors allow. Bessie tells me that many of the village women hear nothing from their loved ones, and when something does arrive it is merely a few lines. I would be most unhappy if you did that to me!

We are all well here, as are Bessie and Stan, though Stan had a terrible cough a few days ago, but he seems to be recovering now. The days are warm and so Hannah is on her pony as much as Miss Newton allows her, but she is pleased with her progress and aptitude in regard to her lessons, for which I'm thankful. Hannah wishes me to give you her love. She will write to you tonight apparently, I'm told.

The Hall and estate are completely fine. You must not worry about us. I am managing well, though we lost a few more men to the war effort from the mine, Mr Blaneley told me on my visit there last week, but he is managing brilliantly despite it all. And yes, don't be annoyed with me, but I have been going to the mine office once a week to check up on things, and to speak with Mr Blaneley. It's only prudent that I am aware of what is happening so I can tell you, since Mr Blaneley says he's not one for writing letters. Orders for coal have risen sharply, naturally, for the factories are producing so much for the war. We won't be able to keep up the demand if more young men leave us. I did hear some of the women from the pit rows saying that they'd go down the mine if need be to keep a place open for their own men when they return. I did assure them that you promised all men would have jobs to come home to, though I'm not sure they believed me.

Harry paused in reading to smile. What a woman he had married. Any other lady of his class would have no more considered venturing to the mine than going to a ball in their nightgown! Yet, Charlotte was made of stronger stuff and he couldn't be more proud.

Sadly, I heard the news that the Nesbits from near Deighton — do you remember them from the ball in York we attended last year? Mr Nesbit knows your father from school. Well, they've lost both their sons in two separate battles last week. I sent my condolences to Mrs Nesbit, she'll be heartbroken at losing her only children.

I must sign off now, my love, for Winslow is at the door talking to the postman and I want this to go out to you today. I can't put into words how much I miss you. Months without you has been difficult. Forgive me, I'm being selfish. But I want you home. Our bed is too big without you in it.

Oh dear, Winslow has coughed discreetly in the doorway, my summons to hurry! Take care of yourself, and write to me as often as you can.

> With all my heart,
> Your loving wife,
> Charlotte.
> July 1915
> Belmont Hall

Harry jumped as a bomb exploded somewhere along the trench. Dirt and dust showered them from between the crude slats serving as their roof under the ground where they had dug their sleeping quarters into the earth. Shouts and boots running on the duckboards sounded outside. He shook Charlotte's letter free of dust and folded it away into his breast pocket. The German trench was only a hundred yards away from theirs at its narrowest point. He stood with a sigh. Another night of broken sleep for them all it seemed. 'Right, men, let's go and give them a taste of their own medicine for an hour or two before bed, shall we?'

* * *

CHARLOTTE INSPECTED the column on the ledger. Outside the mine office, the air rang with noise as a train full of coal pulled away, heading towards Manchester and its hive of industry.

'They are correct, Mrs Belmont?' Mr Blaneley asked nervously. 'I double-checked myself, but fresh eyes are a blessing.'

'It's correct, Mr Blaneley.' She smiled at him. 'You're doing brilliantly, as I tell my husband each time I write to him.'

'Thank you, madam.' His chest swelled with pride and his eyes twinkled.

They were interrupted by a knock, and a boy no more than fourteen opened the door. 'Excuse me, Mr Blaneley, ma'am,' he doffed his cap at Charlotte, 'but you're wanted Mr Blaneley.'

'Aye?'

'There's been an incident, cave in, in D level, the north vein.'

Mr Blaneley grabbed his hat from the peg by the door. 'Anyone hurt?'

'No, sir, all got out of the way at the first crack.'

Pausing at the door, Mr Blaneley turned back to Charlotte. 'I do apologise, madam, but I must go.'

'Of course.' Charlotte looked at the boy. 'You are sure no one was injured?'

'No, ma'am.'

She hesitated a moment. 'I'm going down with you.'

Mr Blaneley paled. 'No! What I mean is, Mrs Belmont, the mine is no place for a lady such as yourself. It's far too dangerous underground.'

'Stuff and nonsense, Mr Blaneley. You've no idea what dangers I've faced in the past.' She swept past them and headed down the stairs to the few men waiting for Mr Blaneley. 'Good day, gentlemen. I'll be accompanying you. It is my mine and I want to inspect it.'

A general rumble of comments greeted her statement.

'Your clothes, madam,' Mr Blaneley said, coming to stand beside her. 'They'll be ruined.'

Charlotte glanced down at her dark brown skirt edged with black embroidery. She smiled at him. 'It'll be worth it to see what you all do and the conditions. My husband would have gone down to assess the damage, would he not?'

'Aye, but he's a man.'

She laughed, not at all frightened and felt excited to be doing something out of the ordinary in her everyday life that was filled with social calls, housekeeping accounts and estate business. 'Mr Blaneley, I will go with you and you will show me the damage and perhaps take me on a small tour. No arguments. Then I can report to my husband exactly what is happening. I want to learn.'

'But Mrs Belmont, there's been a cave in, it's not safe—'

'Come, Mr Blaneley, we are wasting time.' She led the way through the small gathering of men and was pleased when they hurried up to walk beside her as she didn't really know which way to go. However, turning a corner behind a long building and walking down beside the railway, she saw more men and boys working and then opening out before her was the black hole – the mouth, the men called it. The beginning of the wide tunnel that went into the mine. She was secretly glad they didn't have to enter a cage and be dropped down to the levels as she knew happened in other pits.

Lanterns were lit and passed around. Mr Blaneley told Charlotte to stay close to his side and he was relieved to see she had stout walking boots on under her skirts. To protect her clothes, he handed her a waterproof coat made from seal skin or something leatherish, which smelt dank. 'If you're frightened at any time, madam, we can have you taken out straight away.'

'I'll be fine, Mr Blaneley.' She stared ahead as they walked into the mouth. Five men, all who had various selected roles within the mine, joined them. She listened to them explain what happened. She could sense they were hesitant speaking at first with her in their company, but she remained silent and gradually as the minutes passed they relaxed a little and started joking amongst each other.

To Charlotte it seemed like they had walked for many hours,

when in fact it was only just over an hour, but the tunnel was constantly sloping sharply downwards, so she couldn't walk normally but had to lean back a little. Her feet were aching but she dared not utter a complaint. Intense darkness rimmed the edges of the lantern's light and she knew that without the lanterns and candles stuck at intervals in the walls, the blackness would be complete. At one point they had to quickly step aside as a boy led a pit pony that had gone lame and the pony, knowing that fields of grass soon awaited him, was eager to get out into the sunlight.

At first it was cold but the deeper they went into the ground the warmer it became, and also wetter. Water ran down the sides of the tunnel, puddled and soaked everything through. The tunnel and its roof was propped up by thick wooden posts, called props, so the youth told her. Their girths so wide she doubted she could get her arms around them. She was aware of the noise too, and expecting it to be quiet underground, it surprised her that the earth was noisy, full of creaks and cracking sounds.

'She's talking to us, ma'am,' the youth told her when she mentioned it. 'We have to listen to her, and we watch, then we know if she's happy or angry.'

'Listen and watch?'

'Aye. We listen to the type of cracking noise. The odd creaking is normal, but we have to listen for the deeper louder booms, and that not always easy when there's so much banging going on.'

'Of course.'

'And we watch. We watch the props to see if the timber starts to break. We watch the walls to see if cracks appear and we watch the roof to see if water seeps through fast or slow.'

'I never imagined…' She was fascinated by his little talk.

'A pit is always a she, too. A woman. And she can be happy or angry. Moans and groans means she's happy.' He grinned white teeth in a coal-blackened face. 'And when she's angry, then we hear her thunder until she roars and then we run like hell!'

'Smith! Language!' Mr Blaneley cuffed him across the head.

Smith grinned even wider, not at all chastised. 'Sorry, Mrs Belmont.'

'No harm done.' She winked at him when the others weren't looking.

After an age of walking, turning left and right into different tunnels, waiting for skips to pass, or air flow doors to be opened or closed, they made it into D level and the site of the incident. Before them, standing in a pool of light blazing from dozens of lanterns and candles, were a group of half-naked men, clearing a wall of rubble by hand.

'Shirts on, lads, Mrs Belmont has joined us.' Mr Blaneley stepped in front of Charlotte to block her view as the men hurriedly grabbed their shirts and pulled them on. He spoke to the large man who seemed to be in charge of this section. 'How deep do you think it goes, Jim?'

'A good twenty yards to the wall face, I'd say.' He turned to point into the darkness behind them. 'The fifty-yard marker is back there.'

'Was it a clear fault you hit?'

'Nay, it broke apart behind us. Not much of a warning. The prop nearest to me splintered like a toothpick.' He held up a bleeding elbow. 'It was like arrows were being shot at us. If we hadn't have run, we'd be buried under this lot.' He gestured to the rubble that went from floor to ceiling.

Mr Blaneley raised his lantern high and gazed up, Charlotte did too, and gasped at the huge dome above their heads, exposed from the roof collapsing. 'Well,' he said, 'we should be grateful no one was injured and that there isn't an underground river above us.'

'An underground river?' Charlotte asked.

'Yes, madam. As you know water is a big problem in mines. Sometimes we can break into a new seam and tap straight into a hidden river and flood the level.'

'I see.' She'd heard Harry and Nicholas discuss water problems many times at the dinner table. She had assumed they meant small trickles of water seeping out of cracks in the rock. Never did she think a whole submerged river could smash through the walls and drown the men working and fill up a level within minutes. A shiver of fear ran down her back, but she raised her chin and straightened her shoulders so the men would never guess.

'I'll have more props and men sent down to you, Jim. We need to get this lot shifted as quick as possible, that seam is a good one. I don't want to lose it.'

'Aye…'

'You're not in agreement, Jim?'

Big Jim, as young Smith told Charlotte he was called, shook his head. 'I don't like this level. I've told you that before.'

'But the yield potential is greater than any of the other levels. You know I'll have to close down Level E soon as we can't deal with the water down there.'

'Aye, I know.' Big Jim shuffled the tip of his boot against a rock the size of a horse's rump.

'Listen, after clearing all this up, we'll secure it well and assess it again.'

'We'll need to prop every few yards. This level might not have water, but it's flaky.'

'Aye.' Mr Blaneley nodded. 'We'll secure the roof best we can. You'll need air down here. I'll get it sorted.'

'Air?' Charlotte whispered to the youth called Smith.

'When there's been a fall, there can be a build-up of gas. We need clean air to be pushed down here through the opening of air doors further up to direct the wind down this level. Sometimes, we can dig shafts straight up and break through the ground above.'

'I understand.' She'd seen the shafts while walking the moors around the village. Every man, woman and child living in the country knew to keep a sharp eye out for mine shafts in the ground when they went walking the moors.

After few more minutes of talking, Mr Blaneley led Charlotte back along the tunnel. The rest of the men stayed to help clear the rubble.

'We should dig a shaft, Mr Blaneley, for clean air,' Charlotte said, very aware that with only two lanterns the darkness was ink black around them.

'It isn't a simple thing, Mrs Belmont. It's expensive. We need to have it surveyed, we need an engineer, the men to build it, all of that takes time and money.'

'The mine is doing well. We have the money, surely?'

'Yes, madam, it's not that, it is the man power. With the war on and every day more men leaving us to join up, we simply do not have enough men to do it. Mr Shelley, our surveyor, and Mr Clarke, our engineer, are both serving with Mr Belmont. There is no one here to replace them. I'd have to advertise.'

'Then we advertise.'

They talked about mine issues all the way back to the pit top. Charlotte blinked in the bright sunshine and sympathised with the poor pit ponies in their eagerness to get out into open fields after being in that black hole for days on end. She took a deep breath of fresh air. Her dress was ruined, a good six inches of her hem was covered in wet coal grime and her gloves the same. She took her gloves off and threw them into the nearest barrel full of waste.

After saying farewell to Mr Blaneley, she drove the motor car out of the mine site and headed along the track leading to the village. With Patterson gone to the army with Harry, she drove herself and enjoyed the freedom of it. Though she felt the Rolls was too big for her and decided she'd buy herself a smaller car, something she could whizz around in. Then she thought realistically, car manufacturers would not be too concerned with making little cars for women, and instead would be putting their resources to better use for the war.

Sweeping down from the pit site, Charlotte followed the road winding through the fields towards the village. Ahead on a bend in the road and just before the large wood that covered the hill behind the Wheeler's shop, a large black car had stopped, blocking her. Charlotte slowed the car, looking for the driver. Not seeing anyone, she pulled to a halt and climbed out. She'd only got a few yards before the other car door opened and a big man got out and faced her.

'Do you have a problem?' She skirted a hole in the road, noting that the man's driver stayed in the vehicle.

'Yes, I do.' His hat brim shadowed his face.

'If we move your car over so I can get passed, I'll go into the village and bring someone…' The words dried in her mouth as the man lifted his face. She stared at McBride.

'You don't need anyone, Charlotte.' His voice was deadly low.

She shivered despite the warmth of the sun and took a step backwards. 'Go away.'

'It's been too long, my dear. There are things we need to discuss.'

'There is nothing we need to talk about. I'm married now. You have no claim over me or what is mine.'

His grim smile made his eyes look colder. 'You think you got one over me, didn't you? Belmont took what was mine.' He shrugged as though it no longer was important. 'I was very disappointed in you, my dear. I wondered how I could get my revenge on you both, but then the war erupted and altered things.'

'You have no business with me any more.'

'I beg to differ.' McBride's eyes narrowed.

'My husband—'

'Your husband? What *exactly* is your husband going to do, Charlotte? I was made aware that your stupid husband has joined up. A German bullet just might do the job for me. And if the

German's fail, well, I have other ways of getting rid of him. After all, it's all so confusing in battle, isn't it? There's plenty a man who, for the right price, would happily become muddled in battle. Such a man might not know his allies from his enemies.'

Charlotte stared in horror at him, his deathly meaning all too clear. 'I'll go to the police if you don't leave me and my family alone.' Her words sounded pathetic even to her.

McBride chuckled. 'I'll never leave you alone, Charlotte. And if I can't have you then I'll have your sister.'

She gasped, and took a step back.

'Ah, you see now, don't you? I will always be around. You think you got rid of me by marrying Belmont in such haste, but that won't stop me. I will have what I deserve, one way or another.' He grinned evilly. 'The whole country is in chaos at the minute, and what happens in a little village far from anywhere isn't going to be of any concern to anyone when we might be invaded by Germans. If I happened to take you, or more importantly, your sister, who will care? Not the police, some of whom I pay, that I can assure you.'

'If...if you want money I'll give it to you.' She was shaking so hard her teeth rattled.

'I don't want or need your money. For the last six months the war has provided most generously.' He laughed. 'War profiteering, my dear, is a wonderful thing.'

'Then what do you want?'

'To teach you a lesson, my dear. I helped you, I was willing to give you everything and you threw it all back in my face. I will never forgive you for that. You made a fool out of me, a laughing-stock.' He tugged down the sleeves of his suit and then turned towards his motor car. He opened the door and looked back at her. 'You will never know another restful day, Charlotte. I'll make sure of that.'

She didn't know how long she stood there once his car had disappeared down the road. She didn't really remember driving home. Somehow, she walked inside the Hall and stared at Winslow, who acted immediately, and by breaking all protocol, took her arm and led her to the sofa in the drawing room.

'I'm fine. Please don't fuss.' She took the teacup from him that seemingly appeared from nowhere, but it rattled badly on the saucer, and Winslow took it from her.

A maid hovered in the background and Winslow muttered something to her before coming back to bend low next to Charlotte. 'Madam, can you not tell me what has happened? Is it Master Harry?'

'Master Harry?' Her lip trembled in the effort not to cry at the mention of his name. 'No. I've heard nothing.'

Winslow sagged in relief. 'Then something else? Are you hurt, madam?'

She looked at him, trying to calm down. Her insides felt like jelly, her knees shook. 'I saw McBride, Winslow.'

He jerked upright and stared around as though McBride would materialise through the walls. 'McBride? Here? Where, madam? I'll call the police.'

'On the road from the mine to here.'

'The scoundrel.' Winslow headed for the door. 'I'll summon the police, madam.'

'To what end?' she said dully. 'They'll do nothing. He didn't touch me, just threatened me.'

'They have to act!' Red spots of anger coloured his cheeks. 'He needs locking up!'

'Where is my sister?'

'Upstairs, madam. Miss Newtown just ordered a tea tray for them both. They've been practising the waltz. Lucy was doing the counting for them. She is very good at counting them in apparently. I—' He stopped abruptly, realising he was rambling.

'She must never be alone, Winslow, at least not alone outside. We must have a member of staff watching over her at all times.'

'I'll see to it, madam.'

A noise came from somewhere in the house. Charlotte jerked to stare at the doorway. Two maids passed carrying heavy rugs. Letting out a breath, she glanced at Winslow and saw he'd done the same.

'So, this is how it will be. Jumping at every noise and shadow.'

'No, madam. I'll not allow it.'

'Has Miss Petra and Mr Bertram returned?'

'No, they sent a telegram saying they are staying another night in York.'

Relieved that she'd not have to deal with Petra as well, Charlotte fought back tears while Winslow left her to answer the doorbell. She was annoyed at herself for being so weak. Crying solved nothing.

Flustered and out of breath as though they had run the entire two miles from the village to the Hall, Bessie and Stan hurried into the room. Bessie enfolded her into her arms and hugged her to her ample breast while Stan questioned Winslow like he was a member of the Spanish Inquisition.

'How did you know?' Charlotte asked, grateful for their support.

'Mr Winslow sent the gardening boy to tell us.' Bessie nodding to him in thanks. 'But we were on our way here anyway to see you, and met the boy on the path through the woods. Now, tell us what happened.'

As Charlotte told them the events, an anger built up inside her. Her tears evaporated with every sentence.

'I'll not have this madman running about threatening my girls.' Stan stormed around the room. 'I'll not have it.'

'There is nothing we can do.' Charlotte tried to speak reason, but her mind was spinning, trying to find ways to be rid of McBride.

'There has to be!' Bessie huffed. 'The disgusting beast.'

Charlotte squeezed Bessie's hand, feeling calmer now they

were here. 'He's gone now. He'll leave us in peace until next time he fancies causing me upset.'

'So, we just have to put up with him turning up whenever he wants and scaring you?' Stan looked at each one of them in astonishment. 'Master Harry wouldn't calmly accept this.'

'Harry isn't here though, is he?' she said harshly. She wanted her husband with her, not God knows where in France being shot at! Marriage was supposed to save her from this kind of thing. Harry was meant to be here to support her when she was frightened, that's what he promised.

'It's hardly his fault, lass.' Bessie rubbed her arm compassionately. 'He's fighting for his country.'

'I want him to be here and fight for me! For mine and Hannah's safety! Our enemy is here not in France!' She slapped her hand over her mouth, ashamed of her words. 'I'm sorry. That was unforgivable.'

'We know you don't mean it, lass.' Stan smiled gently. 'You're upset.'

Charlotte sighed. 'I naively thought it was all over. That McBride would just disappear after I got married. So senseless of me.'

'Lass...' Bessie shook her head.

'It's true, Bessie. I stood there and allowed him to scare me witless. Again. He always has the ability to scare me. I must change that. Until I do, he will always be in control.'

'You're a bit of a lass, of course he would scare you,' Bessie argued.

'No, I'm not, Bessie, not anymore. I'm a married woman. I'm mistress of this estate. I'm an owner of businesses. People depend on me. Harry depends on me. Hannah depends on me. My responsibilities are endless. I have to stand up and be the person I have to be to take care of all of that.'

'You already do, madam,' Winslow murmured.

'Not enough, Winslow. Not nearly enough. How can I cope with all of this if I go mindless with fear at the mere thought of McBride?' She stared at each of them for confirmation, but continued before they could reply. 'On the pit road I was rigid with fear. I couldn't move or talk properly. I couldn't function. I hate that I was reduced to such a state. That *he* could do that to me.' She stood and walked to the window. 'Ever since we escaped from his house I've been scared. I've always been peering over my shoulder, petrified of him looming out of the darkness, or out from behind a building to snatch me back. Not until I was on my honeymoon in another country did I feel safe. I was with Harry...'

'You will again, lass,' Stan said, coming to stand beside her. 'I promise you, you will feel safe again.'

She took a deep breath, but didn't say what she was thinking. She *would* feel safe again. She'd make sure of it. No more would she feel as frightened as she did on that road, or that night he snuck into her room. Enough was enough. No one could help her. It had to be something she conquered herself.

Forcing a smile, she turned to Stan and Bessie. 'You'll stay for dinner? Hannah will want to spend time with you both.'

'Aye, of course we will,' Stan answered. 'We've closed the shop early, so there's no rush back.'

'I'm sorry to have worried you.' Charlotte suddenly gripped his arm. 'Thank you. Since the first day I met you, you've put Hannah and myself first. I cannot tell you how much I love you for that. You've been a father to us.'

Stan flushed, and shyly glanced away. 'Nay, no need to get all silly now.'

'You're family,' Bessie said. 'This is what families do.'

'Shall we go up and see Hannah? We can give Miss Newtown a break.' Charlotte paused behind Stan and Bessie as they left the room so she could speak to Winslow.

'Yes, madam?'

'Could you ask Mr Formby for a moment of his time before dinner, please?'

Startled by the request, Winslow blinked in surprise. 'Mr Formby? Er…yes, of course, madam.'

'Thank you.' She knew he'd rather eat his own tongue than to ask her why she wanted to speak to the estate's gamekeeper, and usually she'd mention her thoughts, but not this time. For this time, she would have a secret. She'd have Mr Formby show her how to use a gun, a lady's gun, which she could keep with her at all times.

CHAPTER 14

On a grey afternoon, Harry crouched low behind an overturned cart. Bullets whizzed past, slamming into the stone building thirty yards behind him. His unit was spread out in a wide arc on the edge of some unknown village. It should be on his map but his map was torn, muddied and damp, the markings barely showing. Besides, the French had removed all sign posts to thwart the Germans and all it did was add to the confusion. Their objective was to take this village. However, High Command had believed it to be deserted, the Germans long moved on. They were wrong.

'Captain, Sergeant Shelley asks—' As the young corporal crept alongside the cart towards Harry, a bullet struck him in the head, and his next words were never uttered.

Cursing, Harry took the boy's identification and slipped it into his pocket. He turned to signal the waiting men who were hidden in various places behind him. A pause in the enemy fire allowed most of them to dart closer to him and hide again before another shower of bullets filled the air. Peeping around the end of the cart, Harry quickly studied the scene before them. The village main street was little more than a dirt track, with buildings on each side and a church at the top on a slight rise. Movement caught his eye. An enemy solider had scuttled from one doorway into another. Then another broke cover and ran further up the street. Harry assumed the church was where they had been barracking, and it was now his mens' meeting point.

Ahead of him was the end wall of a building, the first in a line of small shops bordering the road. He turned and found Nicholas had edged closer to the hole in the stone wall to the right of the cart. 'We're going to clear each building on either side all the way up to the church.'

'Rightio, sir.' Nicholas called back.

'We're going to go quietly. Front and back. I'll take the left, you the right.'

'Yes, sir.' Nicholas signalled with his hands to the men on his side of the stone wall. He turned back to Harry. 'There's a sniper in the trees by the church.'

'Yes, maybe more than one. He got this lad.' Harry indicated the dead youth at his feet. He looked back at two men who hid behind a stone trough. 'You two cover us as we move up. Aim for the church.'

With a nod to Nicholas, and signalling the men closest to him, Harry left the safety of the cart and sprinted towards the wall. Bullets clattered into the ground as he ran, and with a desperate lunge, he jumped behind the wall. Six men joined him.

He flattened himself against the stonework, regaining his breath, and stared at the three men at the end of the group. 'You three go along the back of the buildings, check every door, anything that can hide a man. We'll take the front. Got grenades, Sergeant Clarke?'

His mine engineer nodded. 'Yes, sir.'

'We meet at the church wall. Go.'

Once they had crept off, Harry looked at the three men remaining with him. 'This is how we do it. Sergeant Shelley and I will go under the front windows to the next building and clear it, while the rest of you will clear this first building. We do it two by two all the way up the street. The church wall is the meeting point.'

Peeking around the corner, Harry saw no movement ahead. Nicholas was organising his men, too, and the two soldiers left behind had moved up to the cart and were waiting for Harry's signal to open fire. Taking a deep breath, Harry nodded to Shelley and they slipped around the edge of the wall and scrambled up to the next building, a butcher's shop. The enemy opened fire and bullets flew past them, clanking into stone and timber, pinging into dirt and shattering glass. The soldiers behind the cart returned fire. The noise was deafening.

With his pistol aimed ready, Harry burst into the butcher's shop. He thought of nothing but securing the building. Adrenalin high, he and Shelley checked the room. The dim interior was still. The air and ground vibrated as a grenade was let off on the other side of the road. The glass in the shop window shattered, blowing in on Harry and Shelley as they ducked down.

Carefully, they checked behind the serving counter, the cupboards and storerooms, senses alert to any movement. Finding it clear and there being no floor above, they moved onto the next building.

Again, crouching low, they scurried low up to next building they had to clear. Harry paused long enough to check the two men covering them were also moving up, then he kicked open the door of the building and entered the room. Not a shop this time but a house. The front room empty, Harry cautiously made his way into the kitchen beyond. Shelley checked the larder, which had been stripped bare of all food. They returned to the front room and, like stalking cats, they inched their way upstairs to the bedrooms above. Harry let out a breath as each of the two rooms was depleted of all furniture, the only movement was the torn curtains blowing in the breeze coming through glassless windows.

As they made their way out of the house, a shout came from across the street, another grenade was thrown, and the force of the blast ripped the front door from Harry's hands. Instinctively he and Shelley knelt, waiting for the debris to stop raining down on them and the dust and smoke to clear.

'It's a bit like the blasting we do down the pit back home, Captain.' Shelley grinned.

'How I wish it were, Sergeant.' Harry stood, his ears ringing. 'Let's go.' He didn't want to dwell on thoughts of back home. A bullet struck into the timber door frame just inches from Harry's head. He ducked. A burning sensation gripped his side, just above his hip. 'Let's go, Sergeant!'

They ran to the next building, but the doorway gave them no shelter. They barged the door open and instantly opened fire on an enemy soldier who loomed up before them. Through a haze of smoke and pain, Harry saw they'd killed the German. He felt only relief. Sergeant Shelley checked the kitchen and they both checked the bedrooms upstairs. Once more in the front room, Harry searched the dead soldier's pockets, but found nothing of importance, a photograph of an old couple, a small bar of chocolate and a half packet of cigarettes and a box of matches.

He stood and stared through the open doorway. Nicholas was clear of his row of buildings and under a blaze of fire, edged his men towards the church. Harry took a step and winced in pain. Putting fingers to his side, they came away bloodied.

'You've been hit, sir.' Concerned, Shelley pulled out his medical kit.

'It's nothing, put that away. Let's finish this first.' Taking a deep breath, Harry left the house.

* * *

CHARLOTTE HELD the pistol with both hands shoulder high and aimed at the paper target nailed to the tree some distance away.

She pulled the trigger. There was no comforting thud. She'd missed.

'Never mind, madam. Try again.' Mr Formby stood beside her full of quiet confidence. 'Look directly at that target. Block out everything else. Steady... Squeeze the trigger.'

The bullet nicked the edge of the tree, shearing off a piece of bark.

'Good work, madam.'

'I'm getting better,' she said it to herself more than Formby. She'd been practising for an hour every day for three weeks now. Mr Formby had bought her the little silver ladies gun on a discreet visit to York, and every afternoon in the shade of the woods, he taught her how to load, to aim and to shoot at different targets. He had been brought into the McBride ordeal when the rock had been thrown through the window the year before and he and the estate men had searched for the culprit. Only the senior estate workers knew of the threat of McBride, and Winslow had spoken to them again since the incident on the pit road. However, only Mr Formby knew she had a gun.

She shot again and this time got the right side of the paper target. 'That is better.'

'Much better. You're growing in confidence, madam. You hold the pistol more calmly than you did.'

'I'm not scared of it so much now.' She grimaced, remembering the first week of handling the pistol and being in awe of its power.

'That's because it's becoming familiar in your hand.' He paused, ear cocked. 'Someone is coming.' Mr Formby ran to the tree to take down the target.

Charlotte hid the gun in her dress pocket, listening for sound. She heard talking, the creaking of leather. Then, in between the trees, she saw two riders.

Mr Formby came to her side. 'Madam, if they asked us what

we're doing say I'm giving you a tour of the woods, inspecting the bird control.'

'They'd have heard the gun shots.'

'If asked, I saw a rabbit.' He patted the rifle broken over his arm, as the estate's gamekeeper a rifle was his natural possession.

She nodded, and straightened her shoulders. She had no need to cower. The repetitive handling of the gun and feeling the weight of it in her pocket gave her confidence. Though her heart sank as Petra and Bertram rode into view, arguing fiercely. They'd been at the Hall for the last week, driving her slightly crazy with their petty demands of Winslow and the staff, and their trivial squabbles, and their irrelevant opinions about everything and everyone. Charlotte tried to encourage them to go back to London, but Petra complained that London was too hot in summer.

Now as Charlotte sat on a log in the shade, she waited for them to notice her but they were too busy having their heated discussion. Mr Formby melted into the trees behind Charlotte, while she remained as still as statue. That she wore a dark green walking outfit helped to conceal her.

They hadn't seen her and were turning their horses away to take the south track back to the Hall when Petra, resplendent in a red and blue striped riding habit, suddenly jerked on the reins. She swung around to Bertram. 'I hate you,' she yelled. 'Why do you interfere? It has nothing to do with you!'

'It has everything to do with me,' he defended hotly. 'You're my cousin. I care about your welfare.'

'Well do not! I am sick and tired of you following me around like a lost puppy. Go away. Find your own life.'

'And should I do that, cousin, how will you get on conducting your sordid little affair with Alastair? I'm your cover, your token of respectability when you're meeting him. You need me.'

'I need no one.' Her face twisted in fury. 'Least of all you!'

'No?' Bertram rested in the saddle and it was the first time

Charlotte had seen him in control, not simpering to Petra's every whim. 'Tell me, Petra. How do you propose to deal with this unwanted child on your own?'

'I will go away.'

'During a war?'

'America isn't at war, stupid.' Petra jerked again on the reins, making her horse skitter to one side.

'Will you keep this child, or give it away?'

'Shut up! Just shut up!' Petra dug her heels in the horse and raced away through the trees in a mad dash that for a lesser rider would have been dangerous.

Expecting Bertram to follow her, Charlotte was surprised when he dismounted and walked the horse in the opposite direction, coming closer to her. He looked up and saw her and he gave a sad smile.

'You heard all that I suppose?'

'I did.' She turned to Mr Formby. 'I'll walk home with Mr Bertram, thank you, Mr Formby.'

'As you wish, madam.' He touched his hat in respect and walked away.

Charlotte dropped into step with Bertram who led his horse. She noticed that he'd lost weight recently, which gave him claim to some better features. He'd lost his double chin, and pot belly. He'd had a haircut and shaved off his moustache. The transformation suited him, gave him an air of sophistication that had been sorely lacking as Petra's little lapdog. 'So, she is with child for certain?'

'I'm afraid so. She had it confirmed in York last week.'

'No wonder she has been vicious and quarrelsome lately. She has much to deal with.' Charlotte ducked under a low branch.

'You don't seem surprised by this news.'

Shrugging, she stepped carefully over some roots. 'No, not really. She has been having an affair, despite promising Harry she'd stop. A child is a natural consequence of it. He'll be so disappointed in her.' She said the words easily, yet, inside, Charlotte felt different. She'd have liked to tell the selfish witch to leave the Hall and never return.

'Harry will disown her.' He shook his head and sighed.

'I will talk to him.'

'The disgrace of it.'

'She will have to go away, have the child, and give it up for adoption. No one will know. She is hardly the first woman to do such a thing.'

Bertram played with the reins in his fingers. 'I cannot believe how well you are taking this. You are so...matter-of-fact.'

As they broke out of the wood and into a meadow full of wild flowers, Charlotte thought of her year of living on the road. She'd witness so many things, unpleasant events, heard stories from others when she worked in the tavern. She fended off her share of men wanting to get their hands on her body, and through sheer luck had managed not to get into the same trouble as Petra was in now. An unwanted baby didn't shock her, what shocked her was Petra's lack of respect for herself and her family. 'I have not known Petra long, only a year, but quite quickly I knew the measure of her. She is spoilt and selfish, and gives no thought to the consequences of her actions. She has to stop seeing Alastair. If she wants the baby, I will help her, if she'll let me, but the affair must stop. Harry will kill Alastair.'

'She won't stop. I have tried, God knows how much I have tried, but she is a law unto herself. Too much freedom she's had, all her life. Her father was never about or interested in her or her brothers, and once their grandfather died she had no one to control her. Harry cannot stand the sight of her and she knows it. He blames her for the death of his brothers... She got involved with Alastair just to annoy Harry, but I do think she truly loves the man. It is all such a mess really.'

She frowned at the mention of the brothers, long dead. Harry didn't mention them much and there never seemed a time for them to discuss what happened to the two Belmont boys. She only knew Petra was involved. 'I can talk to her. Not that she likes me, or I her, but I will try to help her. Harry would want me to, even though she isn't his favourite person, she's still family.'

'Good luck. You will get your head bitten off, but I thank you for trying.'

'When she goes away, will you go with her?'

He didn't reply for a long time; the only sound was the jingle of the horse's bridle and the swishing of her skirt in the grass. 'At this particular moment I do not know. I am tired, Charlotte, so tired of being bossed about by her, of being the target for her anger, her jokes, her secrets, her moods. I want what Harry has.'

'What Harry has?' She stared at him. 'What do you mean?'

'I want a loving, beautiful wife.' He smiled shyly at her. 'I want someone to love and who loves me in return. I want a home of my own. Oh, I do not mean a house, I have plenty of those. No, I want to make a home with someone. I want to make my life seem worthwhile. I would like children. It is time.'

'They are all quality aspirations.' They walked over a rise and the Hall was before them in all its splendour. 'But you won't achieve those things while ever you follow Petra about like some lackey.'

'True.' He raised his face to the sun for a moment. 'That is why I intend to join the army. I am going to buy a commission.'

'Really?'

'I need to escape Petra. Since we were children she has been everything to me. I loved her so much, I would do anything for her. I always felt sorry for her, she was the only girl in the family and after the boys' death she had no one but me.'

'So, what has changed?'

'I have changed, and so has she. Her affair with Alastair sickens me. His wife, Susannah, is a lovely lady, and does not deserve to be treated like this. Petra won't see sense, and I am tired of the lying, of being mixed up in the seediness of it all. Our fun used to be all harmless. We had such good times, but now, with the war, and the affair… There is too much pain. I won't stand by and watch Petra destroy herself over Alastair. She won't listen to me.'

'She listens to no one.'

'No, and I won't be party to her inflicting such hurt on people any more. I feel the time has come to grow up. Men are dying in their thousands. I need to do my bit. I need to break away from her and stand on my own two feet.'

'What changed your mind about joining the war?'

'We were in a club the other week and there were soldiers, officers sitting at a table, and they just seemed to be epitome of what a gentleman is – of what I too, should be, as a gentleman. I felt ashamed. A coward. What have I done but drink and eat and merrymake my way around the country with Petra leading the way. I have written to Harry and told him. I need to be mature and face my responsibilities.'

Charlotte chuckled, startling him. 'I'm sorry, I'm not laughing at you, but I said the same things not so long ago.'

'You did?'

She nodded and grinned at him. Slipping her arm though his, she gazed up at him. 'You and I both are starting a new chapter in our lives. I wonder where it will take us?'

CHAPTER 15

*C*harlotte and Hannah, with Miss Newtown trailing behind them, walked down the aisle of the greenhouse, looking for a suitable flower to paint. Rain pelted on the glass above their heads, echoing loudly like a drumbeat. They had to raise their voices to be heard above the noise.

'What is Harry's favourite flower?' Hannah asked.

'I don't think he has one. Flowers aren't really an interesting enough topic for him.' Charlotte bent to sniff a delicate purple violet. 'His father, Mr Belmont, is the botanist in the family.'

'Will Harry's father ever come back?'

Charlotte bent to peer closely at an orchid. 'I don't know. The war may bring him back to England, but no one knows exactly where he is, so it's doubtful.'

'Imagine the stories he'd tell.'

'Yes, and the places he's seen. He's travelled extensively.'

They turned as the door at the end of the greenhouse opened and Bertram walked in. He was dressed for going out.

'Where are you off to in this weather?' Charlotte asked him. Last night, after dinner, which Petra had refused to join them, Charlotte and Bertram sat in the library and talked for hours, getting to know each other better. She found she liked this new Bertram very much.

He took off his hat, raindrops splattered the floor. 'I'm leaving for London.'

'Now?' She was surprised. 'You never said last night you'd go today.'

'Well, it seems sensible to go today. Petra is being awkward and I wanted to get my commission in progress. I have business to attend to as well, affairs to put in order while I am away.'

'Of course.'

Bertram took Hannah's hand, bowed and kissed it like a gallant knight. 'Be good, dearest Hannah and listen to Miss Newtown.' The governess blushed at his words.

'I will, Bertram. Will you write to me?'

'Indeed, I will, and I will look forward to receiving your letters.' He bowed slightly to Miss Newtown who blushed deeper and shyly glanced away.

He turned to Charlotte. 'Walk with me?'

Together they strolled down the length of the long green-house to the door. Bertram paused, his hat clenched in his hand. 'I will write to you every week. But, and going back to what we discussed last night, I will be organising for the telephone system to be installed in the Hall as well as Belmont Mews. It makes sense for your two houses to be joined by telephone. I am also putting one in my house in Mayfair. That way, this family can keep in contact easier.'

'I shall be anticipating the installation of it. Harry will be most impressed at our advancement.'

'It needs to be a priority. You could use it to call the police should McBride show his evil face.'

She sobered. 'Yes, I know.'

Bertram stared at the pouring rain for a moment. 'Petra was rather nasty to me just now when I went to say goodbye. I know she doesn't mean it.' He took Charlotte's hand. 'Try to be patient with her. She will need help, but will not ask nor thank you for it.'

'I will do all I can.'

'Of course, you will, you are too kind not to. Now, I've listed you and Harry as my next of kin since I have no living parents or kin...or wife.' He gave a wry smile and kissed both her cheeks. 'Well, this is it. I am going into the unknown. Wish me luck.'

'I wish you all the luck in the world. Take care of yourself and come back safe.' She squeezed his hand and then he walked out into the rain.

For half an hour, Charlotte tried to show interest in painting with Hannah and Miss Newtown, but her heart wasn't in it. Bertram's leaving reminded her of Harry's deployment and she was consumed with the feeling of loss.

Packing up her paints, Charlotte tidied away her easel. She was a dreadful painter and her little canvas was pitiful. Hannah was by far the better artist, and she left the two of them to continue, while she ran back to the Hall in the rain.

Instinct made her seek out Petra, and she found her in the library. A fire had been lit and, due to the darkness of the heavy downpour, two lamps had also been turned on. Petra sat curled up on the sofa before the fire, staring moodily into it. On the floor was an array of magazines and newspapers.

Charlotte stood in front of the fire and held her hands out to it. The hem of her blue day dress was damp. 'I don't think this rain will stop today.'

Petra didn't acknowledge her presence and just kept watching the dancing flames.

'I shall miss Bertram.'

Petra flinched but remained silent.

'Shall I ring for tea?'

Again silence.

Charlotte rang the bell pull beside the fireplace. Within a few moments Winslow knocked and entered. 'Winslow could we have a tea tray, please?'

'Very good, madam.' He silently left.

'Bertram is arranging for a telephone to be installed here and at the London townhouse, as well as one installed at his house. Won't that be exciting?'

'Stop talking.'

'Why?'

Petra sighed, and swung her slippered feet down to the floor. 'I do not want tea. I do not want to talk.'

'What do you want to do then?'

'Escape!'

'I have tried that. It's awfully difficult.'

Petra glared at her. 'I do not care what you did or how you did it. You are not me!'

'No, and I'm pleased for it.'

Surprised, Petra's eyebrows rose. 'What do you mean by that?'

'I mean I wouldn't like to be you at all.'

'You think yourself so smug. You would be nothing without my brother. You would be in the gutter where he found you!'

Charlotte looked her straight in the eye. 'No one found me in the gutter. No matter what happened to me I kept striving to improve my life. I kept trying to better my situation and I took care of my sister.'

'You had to rely on strangers, on stumbling into a village shop and poor people taking pity on you.'

'Perhaps that is true, but never at any time did I lose my self-respect or treat people as though they were beneath me.'

'Unlike me, you believe?'

Winslow entered with a tea tray and Lucy followed him with another tray of small delicate pastries and finger sandwiches, which they placed on a small table near the sofa used for that purpose.

'Thank you.' Charlotte poured out the tea once Winslow and

Lucy had left. She passed Petra the teacup and saucer, but she ignored her and so Charlotte put it on the table beside her. 'So, if we can finish with the insults now, perhaps we can talk about the real problem?'

'I am not talking to you about anything.' Petra stared into the fire once more.

'When is the child due to be born,' Charlotte asked quietly.

Petra jerked, but kept staring at the flames. 'Bertram has a very large mouth.'

'Bertram told me nothing.' Charlotte sipped her tea. She wasn't going to reveal that she'd heard them in the woods. She suddenly felt older and wiser than her sister-in-law, when in fact Petra was her senior by three years. She selected a sandwich. 'Why, with your looks and breeding, aren't you married by now and filling some grand house's nursery with babies?'

'Because I refuse to marry just anyone.' Petra's back was stiff and straight as a pole.

'Surely in your circle there must have been many wealthy gentlemen wanting to marry you and from them at least one should have been suitable?'

'Please stop talking.'

Charlotte sighed. 'You're right, that subject doesn't matter now. The most important issue is where you are having this child, here or away somewhere.'

'It is of no concern to you at all.'

'I'm mistress of this house, your brother's wife, and whether you like it or not, we are now family, which means we must support each other through the good and bad times. Therefore, it is my concern.'

'I shall go away.'

'Where?'

'I do not know yet.'

'Who will you take with you?' Charlotte sipped her tea.

'My maid.'

'And a friend, now Bertram has left?'

'No.'

The fire hissed and crackled as a log fell in the grate.

'Why?'

'There is no one I trust to know about my situation. It is bad enough you know, and you will tell Harry.'

'No, I won't. *We* will not burden him with this disaster. He has enough to cope with and he already worries enough about us here at home.'

Petra reached for a strawberry tartlet and nibbled on it. 'I thought America.'

'It isn't safe to cross the Atlantic. The Germans have sunk the *Lusitania*, an American liner that was of no threat to them. Yet, they still attacked it.'

'They cannot attack every ship, can they?'

'You are willing to risk it?'

'Yes.'

'Do you know anyone in America?'

'Distant friends, no one close.'

'You'll be alone.'

'I will manage.'

'No doubt you will.' Charlotte eyed Petra's waistline but she wore a loose patterned dress with a drop waist and it was hard to tell. 'When is the baby due?'

'Who cares?'

'Petra…' Charlotte couldn't hide her shock, her gaze straying to Petra's stomach again.

'I try not to eat, so I won't resemble a balloon.' She continued to nibble at the tartlet. 'This is the first thing I have eaten today. I survive on cups of tea.'

'Oh, Petra, how silly of you.'

'*Silly*? Yes, I am silly! I am down right stupid!' She burst into tears, which amazed Charlotte for she knew Petra never cried, Harry and Bertram told her that.

Charlotte let her cry for a moment then just as she was about to move over to comfort her, Petra jerked to her feet, and ran from the room.

Sighing, Charlotte finished her tea and ate an egg custard tart. Then, knowing she had to, she went upstairs to Petra.

She found her sprawled on her large four-poster bed facing away from the door. 'Petra.'

'Go away.'

Closing the door behind her, Charlotte stepped into the room. 'We need to discuss this. Burying our heads in the sand will not make it disappear.'

Sitting up, Petra's features twisted into a sneer. 'I bet you are enjoying this immensely, aren't you?'

'Why on earth should I? You bring dishonour to this family with your selfishness.'

'This family? You are talking like you were born here. How ridiculous you are, you have been here less than five minutes! Besides, Harry has already brought dishonour by marrying a shop girl.'

'We are back to insults again, are we? How terribly bothersome.' Charlotte sat on a pink silk covered chair next to the walnut dressing table. She'd never been in this room properly before, having only peeked her head around the door when she first came to live here.

'Just go away. I did not ask for your help.'

'You have only months in which to sort yourself out. I think you require all the help you can get. And I cannot see any other friends lining up to assist you in your time of need. What is Alastair doing to help?'

Petra looked away.

'Oh Lord, he doesn't know, does he?'

'I will deal with this on my own.'

'He needs to know and be held accountable.'

'What do you know about any of this anyway?' Petra snarled

175

like a dog caught in a trap.

Charlotte waited for a moment, not wanting to always argue with her, for it got them nowhere. 'If you want to go to America, Hannah and I can come with you, to help you get settled, and then we shall return.'

'You and Hannah? I think not.' Scorn dripped from Petra like venom.

'You must have someone with you, and it seems as though it has to be me, but I cannot leave Hannah alone, so she comes too.'

'I could not think of anything worse.'

'Believe me, I'd rather forgo your company too, but this situation calls for desperate measures.'

'I can manage on my own.'

'I doubt Harry would forgive me for allowing you to wander off and have a baby on your own if something were to happen to you.' Charlotte took a deep breath, trying not to let her frustration show. 'Alternatively, you can stay here. We are not entertaining while the war is on. You can stay here at the Hall and should visitors arrive then you can simply go up to your room.'

A spark of interest flashed in Petra's dull eyes. 'Stay here?'

'It'll be no different to what you're doing now. So far, you've gotten away with it. You're still riding, and there are the gardens to sit amongst as you get bigger. Wearing clever clothes and coats will hide the bump. With care and attention, it could be done.'

'My maid is sworn to secrecy. I have threatened to let her go immediately with no reference should she tell a soul, but what about the others when they see me?'

'The staff numbers are vastly reduced, as you are aware. Most of the men have gone to war, and a few of the single women have gone to the factories. Lucy is the only upstairs maid now. You don't venture to the kitchen, so you'll not encounter any of the staff working in either the kitchen or laundry. Anyway, we will deal with that should the subject come up.'

'It is an option, I suppose. Not the best option, to be certain, but an option.'

'You don't have many.' Charlotte clenched her jaw, the woman was impossible.

Petra sighed dramatically. 'If I do stay here, I am going to get thoroughly fed up and bored stuck in this house with you.'

'No, you won't. You can help me manage the Hall and estate, which will free up my time for the mine and other businesses. The village women and I create parcels of little home comforts to send to the men. The parcels are dropped off here at the Hall and Winslow and I organise to ship them out to France. There's so much to do. Socks and scarfs to knit and—'

'I will not skivvy!'

'Oh yes you will. It's about time you did something for this family instead of swanning off and doing whatever you like, because look at the state that has got you in.'

Petra scrambled off the bed and glared at her. 'Who do you think you are talking to me like this? You cannot control me, you jumped up little trollop.'

'No, I can't control you, but this is my house now, and I can make your life easy or difficult. It's your choice.'

'How dare you threaten me!'

'Oh, I dare all right. Harry has entrusted the care of everything related to the Belmont name to me, unfortunately, that includes you, too.'

'I do not know what Harry was thinking of marrying you. He could have had anyone.'

'But he chose me. Live with it or don't, I really couldn't care less either way.' Charlotte stood and headed for the door. She had reached the limit of her tolerance with Petra for one day.

'When the child is born I want it sent away instantly,' Petra said suddenly.

Charlotte paused and glanced back at her. 'I see. Well, we shall have to find a suitable family to adopt the baby.'

'Not nearby. I do not want to see it every time I enter the village.'

'I will contact our solicitor and instruct him to start enquiring at different adoption agencies.'

'I insist that no one else must know!'

'At some point we will need a midwife, if you don't want Dr Neville. I'll have to bring Winslow into our confidence.' She left the room before Petra could reply.

Out in the corridor, Charlotte noticed her hands were shaking. She didn't like confrontations, hated them in fact. However, she had to stand up to Petra, otherwise she'd never be taken seriously by her. She was the Hall's mistress. She had to act like it or risk ridicule. For the sake of the family's reputation she had to behave as though she'd been born for this role. She'd do it for Harry.

CHAPTER 16

*H*arry eagerly watched the landscape change as the train rattled its way through Yorkshire. Every mile took him one step closer to Charlotte and home. He'd quickly visited Belmont Mews when the train from Dover pulled in at Victoria Station. And as tempting as the clean bed and wholesome food that welcomed him by the housekeeper there, he had insisted on travelling on to Yorkshire, to Belmont Hall, to Charlotte.

As the train rocked, Harry fought the exhaustion that seemed to want to overwhelm him and suck him into a peaceful oblivion. But he was close to home now and didn't want to miss his stop. Not that any of his men would let that happen. Most like him had decided to spend their four-day pass by going home, though some of his men had stayed in London to eat sleep and drink and forget all they had experienced over the Channel.

'Harry.' Nicholas nudged him and Harry stood, collecting his hat and small leather bag, which held a change of uniform. He'd instructed his housekeeper at the townhouse to re-order from his tailor a new uniform for him to collect on his return to the front.

Once on the station platform, Harry looked around for some

form of transport. The best he could find was an old farmer and his cart from the next village to Belmont and who was happy to give him and his men a lift.

They saw no one on the ten-minute journey to Belthorpe, but once they were heading down the village High Street, people came out of homes and shops as word spread down the road quicker than the old horse could walk it. Children ran yelling and calling out, looking for returned fathers. Harry had to glance away from their disappointed faces when they realised a loved one was not amongst them. Some women stood weeping, the ghost of their dead husbands bringing fresh grief.

Bessie, sweeping the step outside of the shop, stopped and ran to the cart to reach and grab Harry's hand. 'You're back! Thank God!'

'Only for two days, Bessie. Are you and Stan well?' He smiled at seeing her friendly face.

Around him wives, mothers and daughters gathered to welcome home their husbands, brothers and sons.

She squeezed his hand, which before the war and his marriage to Charlotte he doubted she'd have ever imagined doing. 'We are, and you? Not wounded?'

'I'm fine.'

'Shall I take you on to the Hall, sir?' the farmer asked now the men had offloaded from his cart.

'Please.' Harry nodded tiredly. He waved goodbye to his men and then looked down at Bessie. 'Come to the Hall tomorrow, for dinner.'

Her eyes were filling with tears, she nodded mutely and let go of his hand. 'Go to her.'

'Is she well, Bessie?'

'Aye, lad.' Bessie dropped the formal address as they'd come closer since his marriage. 'Charlotte is one in a million. How she does it all I don't know. She's busy from morning to night now. She never stops for a minute.'

'I'll see you tomorrow.' He waved as the cart trundled on.

The two miles to the Hall seemed to last forever, and Harry grew nervous and terribly excited at seeing his wife for the first time.

The drive and gardens looked the same, but it was eerily quiet. After so long listening to shelling and explosions and constant gun firing, he struggled to understand the quietness assaulting his ears.

'There we are, sir.' The farmer halted the horse in front of the steps.

'Thank you.' Harry tipped him well.

'Thank you, sir, and good luck to you.'

For a moment, Harry faltered. He desperately wanted to go inside, but he also felt the urge to walk and keep on walking. As the seconds dragged on, he wondered why Winslow wasn't opening the door. Usually the butler had the hearing of a fox and knew when a carriage or car was turning into the drive. Senses alert, Harry went carefully up the wide steps and gently opened the door. Caution, borne of being hunted by Germans, made him creep over the threshold into the silent house.

The drawing room was empty, as was the parlour opposite. At the bottom of the stairs, he paused and looked up. No noise came from the landing above. He wanted to shout, but couldn't open his mouth to do so. Months of being quiet, vigilant and restrained kept him still and watchful.

He jumped violently as a door slammed somewhere in the house and voices in heated debate drifted to him. He walked down the hallway towards the study. The dining room door was open and the room empty. The voices came more clearly now and he stood outside the study for a moment before turning the door handle softly and stepping into the room that used to be his sanctuary.

His view was blocked by a woman in front of him; Petra, who had her back to him and was berating Charlotte who stood behind his mahogany desk. Neither woman noticed he was there.

'How many times must I repeat myself?' Petra stood hands on hips. 'You do not control me!'

'And how many times do I have to repeat myself that if you insist on roaming the countryside you will be seen!' Charlotte flung back. Harry had never heard her speak so harshly before. He moved slightly so he could glimpse her and was shocked by her appearance. She'd lost weight, but gained something else, he wasn't sure what, but he'd left her as a young woman and now she projected a vibe of a strong confident woman in control.

'I cannot stand this another moment,' Petra hissed. 'I am leaving.'

'Good, go. I'm sick of the sight of you!'

Petra spun around and both women gasped as they saw him standing in the doorway. Several seconds went by before Charlotte cried out and ran into his arms. She held him so tight he thought he'd never breathe again and didn't care at all. If he had a choice of where he would die, his wife's arms and not a battlefield was the top of his list.

'Why didn't you send word?' Charlotte asked between raining kisses over his face.

'I was going to telephone you from Belmont Mews, since I see Bertram's influence has been installed, but then I thought to surprise you.'

'You are here. It is unbelievable.'

He kissed her back, all the pent-up passion and longing for her for months gripped him and he squeezed her into him, loving the soft feel and clean smell of her.

Charlotte pulled back a little and smiled radiantly. 'Welcome home, my love.'

'I'm glad to be home.' He kissed her again, feasting his eyes on her beautiful face.

'It's good to see you, brother.'

Harry slowly turned to Petra, but on seeing her fully his greeting dried in his mouth as he stared at her round stomach. 'Good God.'

Petra had the grace to look ashamed. Her hands fluttered over the folds of her burgundy dress trying to hide the pregnancy. 'Harry... I...'

'Why wasn't I told?' Harry addressed the question to them both.

'We didn't want to worry you,' Charlotte murmured.

The tiredness returned to hit him even harder and it took all his remaining strength to stay upright. 'I need to rest. Then we will talk.'

With his arm around Charlotte they went upstairs to their bedroom. The clean, orderly room with its lush bed linen looked too good for him to touch. He paused by the bed. 'Though I had a quick wash in London, I should sleep in a spare bedroom, I'm filthy and no doubt have the odd louse or two.'

'Nonsense. Do you think I'm worried about lice? They can always be gotten rid of. It's more important you sleep well in your own bed,' she replied, helping him undress and take off his boots.

'I've slept in disgusting places no decent man should ever be in,' he murmured sleepily as he sank onto their soft bed.

'How many days are you home for?'

'Two.'

'Two?' Her eyes couldn't hide the disappointment.

He pulled her close to him. 'Stay with me, sweetheart...' The willpower to remain awake deserted him. He remembered nothing else.

Charlotte lay down beside him and studied him sleeping, her heart swelling with love. It had been so long since he was in their bed. So long since she could gaze at his handsome face. The lines at the corner of his eyes were a little deeper now and his cheeks hollow. Small amounts of grey peppered his hair at the temples, and yes, she saw the odd louse in his hair. He needed a shave and a good wash for he smelt of earth and damp and something else she couldn't identify but was just the smell of war.

After a while she rose and slipped from the room. Winslow was hovering at the end of the corridor and she wondered if he'd been there the whole time.

'Ah, madam. I do apologise for not being in attendance when the master arrived home.' Winslow appeared a trifle upset. His usually immaculately combed white hair was a little ruffled as though he'd run his fingers through it. Worry filled his soft grey eyes. 'I was in the kitchens, a slight drama, but nothing to worry about. I am greatly alarmed to think the master had to see to himself, to actually have to open the door himself and no one there to welcome him home.'

'He took us all by surprise.' They fell into step towards the staircase.

'I will apologise, naturally.' Winslow clasped his hands behind his back, his face stern.

'You cannot be everywhere at once, Winslow, the hall is too big and we are too understaffed. You are on your own now at the front of the house, it's completely understandable.'

'It is no excuse. Is Master Harry well?'

'Tired. So tired, Winslow, and thin.' She gave a sad smile. Poor Winslow, he was very out of sorts at what he felt was a fail of duty.

He hesitated at the top of the stairs. 'Do we have him home for long, madam?'

'Two days only, I believe.' She sighed, thinking of Petra and the conversations with Harry to come. 'We must try to not subject my husband to any more worries and burdens than he already carries. When he asks you how things are, you tell him we are managing very well.'

'Agreed, madam.'

'His uniform needs boiling. Unfortunately, the war has come

home with him. When he wakes, he'll need a bath and a hearty meal, nothing fancy tell Mrs Morrissey, but plenty of meat and… appetising…' She suddenly wanted to cry.

'I'll see to everything, madam.' Winslow nodded stiffly, obviously fighting his own emotions. 'Between the two of us we will have Master Harry fit and well.'

Charlotte blinked back her tears. 'I don't know how I'll bear for him to leave again, Winslow.'

'We will cope, madam. We have no choice.'

Charlotte kept busy for the rest of the evening as Harry continued to sleep. She, Hannah and Petra ate their dinner in a subdued manner, while Winslow paced the Hall like a caged tiger, looking up at the stairs every few minutes waiting for his master to appear. Yet Harry slept on.

By ten o'clock, Charlotte sent Hannah to bed in tears for she'd not seen Harry. Petra too retired, and Charlotte told Winslow to do the same. If Harry woke during the night she would see to anything he needed. As it happened, Harry didn't move or murmur as Charlotte changed into her nightgown and slipped into bed beside him. He slept deeply, the mental and physical exhaustion claiming him tight in its clutches.

Wrapping one arm over him, she softly kissed his cheek and watched him until she fell asleep.

* * *

SLUGGISHLY HARRY WOKE and for a moment didn't know where he was. He laid still and got his bearings. His bedroom. He then turned his head to gaze at Charlotte sleeping. Her chestnut hair was spread across the white pillow and the morning sun peeking through a crack in the curtains, highlighted the copper strands in it. Her delicate beauty stole his breath. His heart thudded in his chest with love and need of her. As much as he wanted to wake her with kisses, he knew he needed to wash first.

Not wanting to disturb her, he slipped from the bed, grabbed his dressing gown and headed out into the corridor for the bathroom. He spied Lucy coming from the other corridor leading to Hannah's rooms, her arms full of linen.

'Good morning, Lucy,' he said quietly

She dropped a quick bob. 'Good morning, sir.'

'Mrs Belmont is still sleeping.'

'Yes, sir. I'll leave your room till later.'

'Much later.' He winked.

Giggling, she hurried off and he entered the bathroom. Installing the bathroom a year ago, while they had been on their honeymoon, had been a huge expense and extravagance, yet worth it. It took a while for the hot water to arrive through the new pipe system, but it was soon filling the bath and while he waited, he shaved off his stubble. A discreet knock sounded on the door and he opened it to reveal Winslow.

'Good morning, Master Harry. Welcome home.'

'Good to see you, Winslow, come in.'

'I had hoped to have the bath drawn for you before you woke. Do you have everything you need, sir?'

'I do. Thank you.' Harry continued shaving while Winslow arranged warmed towels and opened a new cake of soap and placed it beside the bath.

'I must apologise for not being able to attend you on your arrival yesterday. Forgive me, sir.'

'Nonsense, Winslow. We no longer have the amount of staff to run the Hall as before.'

'Nevertheless, standards must be upheld.'

Finishing shaving, Harry turned to his trusted butler. 'Thank you for your letters. They give me comfort.'

'I do my best to inform you, sir, of what happens here. Mrs Belmont would not be pleased with me if she were to know I did so.'

'I understand. Yet, you did not mention to me about my sister's condition.'

Winslow blushed, his hands held tight behind his back. 'Forgive me, sir, I have only just been taken into their confidence. Miss Petra has done well to hide her condition for so long. I have a half-formed letter to you on my desk as we speak, but finding the right words to write about this delicate matter has been a challenge to me.'

'I understand, of course. That is a matter I shall deal with after breakfast.' He stripped and climbed into the bath to start vigorous scrubbing of the muck from the battlefield. 'And McBride?'

'No news, sir, nothing since the meeting on the road.'

'I have friends in high places, and I have made valuable connections within the army. People are keeping a watch out for him. I will see it is finished with as quickly as I can, but being in France makes things appalling difficult.'

'I worry every time Mrs Belmont leaves the Hall, sir, but she refuses to be contained by his threats, or my pleas.'

'My wife is stronger than any of us ever realised, Winslow.'

'Indeed, she is, sir.' Winslow started scrubbing Harry's back.

'I believe she and Miss Petra are not always seeing eye to eye?' Harry hung his head forward as Winslow poured a jug of soapy water over his head.

'There are times, sir, when I fear they will turn to physical violence towards each other.'

'And you are the only calm head in the house.'

A flicker of a smile lifted Winslow's lips. 'I try my best, sir.'

Harry shook his head and gave a wry smile. 'Women, hey Winslow?'

Winslow raised his eyebrows wryly. 'Indeed, sir, indeed.'

* * *

CHARLOTTE WOKE to fingers lightly stroking her cheek. Turning her head on the pillow, she opened her eyes to smile lovingly at Harry, who smiled back and kissed her.

'Good morning, wife.' He kissed her again.

'Good morning. You've shaved?' She yawned and stretched.

'And bathed. I've been up just over an hour. Winslow will bring us up some breakfast in half an hour.' He climbed under the covers with her and pulled her close.

'Breakfast in bed? How decadent.'

'Yes. Very.' His hands slipped under her nightdress and traced the curves of her body. 'And it's enough time to satisfy one of my hungers. For the moment anyway!' His voice was deep with need.

She laughed and hugged him to her, delighting in his amorous attentions and returning them tenfold. It had been too long since she had rejoiced in his love. Her skin tingled under his fingertips. Her body was as eager for him as he was for hers. As much as she wanted to take it slowly and savour the moment, she ached for the release he could give her.

'I have missed you so much,' he whispered against her mouth.

She ran her fingers through his hair and kissed him intensely, showing him just how much she had missed him. 'I don't think we are going to need half an hour,' she joked.

He laughed as he rolled her on top of him and slapped her bottom gently. 'I will try my best but I cannot give you false hopes.'

'Thankfully we have two days!' She chuckled as she kissed him and hoped this moment would never end.

CHAPTER 17

Charlotte stood by the window in the study while Harry sat at his desk looking over the estate ledgers while they waited for Petra to grace them with her presence. Hannah, so excited to see Harry, spent the morning with them chatting away, and only on the promise of going for a horse ride with Harry later, had she left them to go do her lessons.

'They are in good order.' Harry closed the last ledger.

'You were in doubt?' Charlotte grinned at him.

'Not at all. I know how intelligent my wife is. Come here so I can show my appreciation.' He held an arm out to her.

Laughing she went to join him, but the door opened and Petra walked in with a face like thunder. Charlotte returned to the window as Petra sat stiff backed on a chair opposite the desk.

'So, brother. Am I here to face the firing squad?' Petra snapped. She wore a dark blue dress in a style that had been specially made for her in York in a variety of colours, and which hid her stomach reasonably well, despite her getting close to her time.

'I'm not going to argue with you.' Harry sighed. 'I've learnt just how precious life is and how little time any one of us have. Shall we simply talk as adults?'

'We can try but we do not seem able to do that normally.' Petra glanced from Harry to Charlotte and back again. 'I assume she has filled you in on all the details?'

'Very little. It isn't my wife's place to tell me, it is yours. Charlotte has left it for you to tell me more.'

'That is surprising. I had imagined you and she would have had a most agreeable discussion about my fall from grace.'

'Believe it or not, you aren't the centre of our world, my dear sister. We have other things to discuss.'

Petra played with the folds of her skirt. 'What do you want to know?'

'Many things.' Harry tapped his fingers gently on the desk. 'Alastair. What does he intend to do about this situation?'

'He does not know.'

'Are you still in contact with him?'

'Yes, by letter, since he is away fighting.'

'I heard he had a commission. I will also write to him. He is to pay for the child's upbringing.'

'I am having it adopted.'

'No, you are not.'

Surprised, Charlotte stared at Harry as if he'd gone mad. 'Darling…'

Petra gripped the arms of her chair, her knuckles white. Her eyes were wide in disbelief. 'Oh, yes I am!'

He pounded the desk with a fist. 'No, you are not!'

'Harry?' Charlotte took a step forward, seeing the controlled anger on Harry's face, the tension in his body.

'The child will be *adopted*.' Petra grounded out between clenched teeth. 'Charlotte and I have already made inquiries.'

'That was before I was made aware of the situation.'

'You knowing does nothing to change our plans.' Petra sat on the edge of the chair, as though ready to either pounce or flee at a moment's notice.

'Harry, having the baby placed with a loving family is the right decision.' Charlotte put her hand on Harry's shoulder. 'It is the only decision.'

'You are both wrong. The child is a Belmont and will remain here with its family. Unless Alastair wishes to take it into his home with his wife and daughter.'

'I will not have it that way!'

'You have no choice!' he snapped.

'You are wrong. I have every choice as it is my child.'

He glared at her. 'Then you will be on the street with nothing. If you give that child away, you will be sent from this house without a penny to your name. Will Alastair help you then?'

Petra gasped. 'How could you be so cruel?'

'And how can you be so blatantly disrespectful to this family with your adulteress affair? I warned you, did I not? I warned you repeatedly to give him up. I have lost my best friend because of your selfishness. You have brought shame and disgrace to this family.' Harry leaned forward on his elbows, but talked coldly as though reading out an article from the newspaper. 'You have never cared for anyone or anything in your life, Petra, and I am telling you now that it stops today. You flaunted yourself and your dirty secrets to the whole world and you will now face the consequences of those actions.'

'I will kill myself.' Her eyes were pools of hate.

'Do it. I will bury you alongside our brothers and mother, shall I?'

'Harry! That is enough!' Charlotte aghast at his words went to Petra, who let her hold her for she was shaking so much it alarmed Charlotte.

Harry leaned back in his chair. 'So, sister, do we have an understanding?'

'All I understand is that I hate you.'

He nodded. 'The feeling is entirely mutual.'

Charlotte helped Petra to her feet. She'd never seen her sister-in-law's spirit broken before and was dreadfully upset and angry that it had been Harry who had done it. She turned to the man who only hours before had made love to her so tenderly. 'I am wondering who it is that has returned to us because you are not the man I married.' She left the room with Petra.

At the bottom of the stairs, Petra gazed at her, the fight gone from her leaving only pain and sadness in her eyes. 'Charlotte, you must make him change his mind.'

'I'll try.'

'I will stay in my room until he has gone back to France.'

'Yes, it might be best.' Charlotte kept her arm around Petra's waist and helped her up the staircase.

At the doorway to her bedroom, Petra stopped. 'I have paid every day for my brothers' deaths. Their deaths led to my mother dying of a broken heart and for my father to go travelling and never return. Harry cannot punish me more than I already do myself. I know I am not a nice person. I've tried to change, but...' She shrugged her bowed shoulders and entered her room and shut the door.

Back downstairs, Charlotte asked Winslow to take a tea tray up to Petra while she went in search of her husband. She found him in the library studying an atlas opened on the table. He turned as she walked in, his expression one of apology.

'I am sorry, Charlotte.'

'And so you should be, but it's not me you need to apologise to, it's to your sister.'

He looked back at the atlas and she walked close enough to see it was a map of France. 'I go back to hell tomorrow evening.'

She suddenly held him tight to her, not wanting him to go. For a moment they just embraced before Charlotte pulled back. 'What happened with your brothers? I need to understand.'

Harry sighed and moved away. 'They drowned in the river

that runs along the boundary of the estate.'

'I want to know it all.'

Harry sighed and ran his fingers through his short hair. 'The four of us had been out riding, and as always there were little competitions between us. Who could jump our horse over the highest wall or widest ditch. No challenge was ignored. It was summer. A very hot day, but it had been raining heavily previously, for a good week we had huge thunderstorms and hail. The river was flowing fast. It was churned up and full of debris from the storms. Mother had warned us to stay away from it.' He paused, staring at nothing as he remembered.

'I cannot recall how it started, but an argument between Terry and Raymond began and Petra joined in as she can never not be in the middle of something. I had dismounted to adjust my saddle when the next minute Raymond was in the water, encouraged by Petra to swim to the other side. It was madness. Petra was laughing, so was Terry, as Raymond made a joke of river monsters. Petra urged Terry to join him, but he wasn't a strong swimmer like Raymond. I told Raymond to get out, but he wasn't frightened by the surging water. Petra kept laughing, always laughing. She and Raymond were much alike, pranksters...'

Harry stared out of the window. 'Then she pushed Terry in. He slipped and went fully under the water and stayed under. I yelled at Raymond to get him, and he dived under, but he kept coming up empty-handed. Then on his last dive he never surfaced. I remember staring at the water in such surprise. One minute my brothers were there and the next they were gone. Nothing. Vanished. In a heartbeat. And all I heard was Petra's laughter. She thought they were staying under on purpose.'

'Oh, Harry.' Charlotte rested her head against his shoulder.

'When I have nightmares of that day sometimes, all I hear is her wretched laughter.' Harry wiped a hand over his face. 'I jumped into the water. Raymond surfaced first, floating face down. He was a hundred yards downstream. I tried to swim out to him, but the current took him into the middle and away from me so fast. A large branch hit me and I grabbed it to keep from going under, it took me down the river. I called their names until I was hoarse. I searched as best as I could for hours. I climbed out of the river and walked the banks for miles. I never saw them alive again.'

'Dear God. Oh, Harry.'

He stood very still, his face showing the torture of reliving that day. 'Later that afternoon Terry's body was found five miles downstream. He had a cut to his head. It is thought that when Petra pushed him in, he hit his head straight away and that's why he never surfaced, the current took him underwater and he was unconscious. Raymond was found around midnight. Everyone was out searching. He was tangled up in fallen tree branches and wedged under the bridge.' Harry looked painfully at her. 'You know of the stone bridge on the other side of the village?'

'Yes,' she murmured. 'It all sounds so ghastly.'

'Our mother, who, at the time had been battling a nasty chest cough took to her bed and never left it again. She died four months later. The doctor believes it was a lung complaint, or perhaps some sort of cancer of the blood, as she wasted away to a mere skeleton. But my father believes it was the boys' deaths that caused her to not fight to get well again. She stopped eating. Six months after we buried mother, my father left to pursue his dream of being a botanist in far-flung lands. He has never returned.'

'How long ago did it happen?'

'Ten years ago.'

'Ten years is a long time. Petra would have been fourteen when the tragedy happened? Isn't it time you forgave her?'

'I know I should. Maybe I could have if she had shown remorse. Yet, she never acknowledged that she was to blame for pushing Terry in. Not once did she apologise for it. Everyone says it was an accident. A prank gone wrong. I can't think of it like that. She pushed him in, knowing he wasn't a strong swimmer and she laughed. If she had not have done it, he would still be alive. I find it so very hard to forget that day. I blame myself too. I should have stopped it from happening somehow, or found them in the water…'

'My love…'

He sighed. 'After father left, Petra went wild. Especially when our grandfather died a few years later. That left just her and I living here in mutual hate of each other. I blame her completely for that stupid dare. I couldn't stand the sight of her. I was grateful that Bertram stayed so often. They became inseparable and I could ignore her. I was busy with the estate and getting the mine up and running and I didn't want to deal with her at all.'

'She was a young girl.'

'She was, and still is, a hellion. Petra knew what she was doing. Always making them fight and argue. It was as though they needed to prove to her which was the better brother. It is how she is even now with Bertram, and possibly with Alastair. Always needing attention, needing to have men think they have something to prove to her.'

'Still, she wouldn't have wanted her brothers to die.' She grabbed hold of his arm. 'Enough, Harry. You need to put this in the past.'

'Do you think I don't want to?' He sighed heavily. 'The problem is I simply don't like her. I don't believe I ever have. How can I? She's never done anything likeable.'

'That's harsh.'

'It's the truth.'

Silence stretched between them.

Charlotte touched Harry's cheek softly. 'Petra's baby… it can't stay here. She may hate it and that's not fair to her or the child.'

'Then she should have thought of that, shouldn't she?'

'You are punishing her.'

'Yes! Because she needs to learn, Charlotte. There are consequences to her actions! It is a lesson she refuses to understand.'

'And what of the child? Roaming around the estate being talked about. Will you love it? Will she? Is it to spend its whole life unloved and unwanted just so you can teach her a lesson?'

His shoulders sagged as her argument hit home. 'Do as you please. I don't care. I could be killed any day. Petra or the child are of no concern to me.'

She rushed to hold him tight. 'Please don't talk in such a way.'

'It has to be faced.'

'You will come home and life will go on as before. I know it.'

'Life will never be as before.' Harry kissed her tenderly. 'I have one night left. Bessie and Stan and Hannah, plus you and I are going to enjoy a lovely dinner and then we are going to go to bed. That is all I want to think about.'

'And Petra?'

He didn't answer her for a long time, then he took her by the hand and they went up to Petra's bedroom. She was sitting on the window seat, reading a lady's fashion magazine.

'Charlotte and I have been talking,' Harry said in a tone that brooked no argument. 'And I have an idea.'

'And what have you decided?' Petra's tone was low and uncaring.

'The house in Brighton, mother's cottage, she willed it to me, remember?'

'Yes.' Her voice was only above a whisper.

'It will be your home from now on. You can either keep the child or have it adopted, but whatever decision you make, you will not consider Belmont Hall or Belmont Mews your homes any longer.'

Petra's eyes grew wide with shock. 'Not ever?'

'You are not welcome at either house. I will still support you, for I doubt you will find a husband now, not with your behaviour and simply because men are dying by the thousands. And should I also be killed, this estate will continue to keep you. Charlotte will instruct our solicitors on my behalf, but I will also write them a letter.'

Petra glanced at Charlotte. 'Did you not talk to him?'

Harry stepped forward. 'This is the best decision that I could allow to happen. I don't want to see you again, Petra. I don't want you here in my home. If you do not want Mother's cottage, then you are free to find your own solution.'

'And what of Father's opinion? This is his estate, not yours. You are just the caretaker.' She flung at him.

Harry chuckled. 'You have always had this opinion and I have let you foster it because I did not wish to enlighten you to the truth. But it will be a surprise to you to know that Father signed everything over to me five years ago. He has no wish to live here and run the estate. Therefore, he gave it to me.' He turned and walked from the bedroom, ignoring Petra's gasp.

Charlotte lingered, not knowing what to say or do. She knew of the terms of the ownership of the estate for Harry had told her before they married, but banishing Petra from the Hall was a surprise. Yet, Harry had made up his mind and she wouldn't be able to change it and she wasn't too certain she wanted to. Living with Petra was a daily chore. Sometimes she was in a favourable mood but most times she was sullen, argumentative and downright rude. The Hall was always more pleasant without her presence.

She gave Petra a small smile of pity. 'Do you wish for me to accompany you to Brighton to settle in?'

'No,' Petra snapped. 'Get out.'

Sighing, Charlotte left the room and found Harry waiting for her.

He took her hand. 'It is done. She will go to Brighton by the end of the week. I will not discuss it any more. Can we enjoy what time I have left please?'

'Yes, of course.' She gave him a weak smile and they went in search of Hannah and the promised horse ride.

CHAPTER 18

December 1915

'Charlotte!' Hannah ran into the morning room full of excitement.

'Hannah, do not run. You are not a small child,' Charlotte admonished, looking up from her small pile of correspondence of mainly household invoices. For weeks after Harry's return to the front, she found it difficult to lift her spirits. Everyday reports came through the newspapers of battles and men lost. Letters from Harry and Bertram were full of the awful truth of what was really happening, and not the 'glory' of what the newspapers and movie reels showed the population. And as the end of the year approached, Charlotte felt depressed at the thought of a long cold winter and Christmas without Harry.

Hannah dithered by her desk. 'Bessie is here. Can I stay with you both instead of practising my writing?'

'Let us see how long Bessie is staying for first, shall we?'

Together they walked into the hallway to see Bessie chatting away with Winslow by the front door.

'Bessie this is a lovely surprise.' Charlotte kissed her cheek as did Hannah.

'Well, I thought I'd slip away for a bit while Stan holds the fort.' Bessie's eyes looked troubled and she gave a slight nod of her head towards Hannah.

Understanding the signal, Charlotte turned to Hannah. 'You need to go practise your writing for half an hour then you can come back down and have tea with us.'

'You'll still be here, Bessie?' Hannah pouted.

'Aye, my chicken, I will. Now run along to Miss Newtown, and I'll see you shortly.'

Once Hannah had left them, Bessie looked from Charlotte to Winslow and back again. 'We've two fellas in the village, strangers. They seemed a little suspicious, hanging around the pub or in the streets.'

Charlotte's chest tightened. 'Were they asking questions?'

'No, they've kept to themselves so far. Stan spoke to several people in the village and they've all said the two of them are laying low.'

'They might not be connected to McBride,' Winslow stated, indicating for them to go into the drawing room as Lucy appeared at the end of the hallway.

Sitting on the sofa, Charlotte felt the roiling in her stomach again that always happened when McBride was mentioned.

'They might not be,' Bessie agreed, 'but Stan and myself thought it would be wise to let you know, so you can be on your guard.'

'Thank you.' Charlotte tried to think positively. 'They could be totally unrelated to anything concerning McBride.'

'True.' Winslow nodded. 'Yet, it is strange that two young men should be in our village and not at the front or in work.'

'But if they are to do with McBride, why stay in the village? McBride knows I live here. He'd have told them to come here.'

'Think, lass.' Bessie tutted. 'They can't get to you here. They don't know what staff is inside, but if you're out and about in the village they could watch you and follow you along the roads. It's easier to take you or Hannah that way.'

The blood drained from Charlotte's face and she thought she'd bring up what little breakfast she managed to eat this morning.

'Water, Mr Winslow!' Bessie grabbed Charlotte and thrust her head down over her knees. 'Take deep breaths, lass. You look green as grass. That's it, deep breaths.'

It took several minutes for Charlotte to steady her stomach and the sips of water barely stayed down. 'I'm fine, Bessie.'

'You thought he'd forgotten you with the war on, didn't you?'

'No, he is always in the back of my mind.' She took a deep calming breath. 'I think I'm coming down with something.'

'You are pale.'

Winslow frowned. 'I noticed, madam, that you ate very little breakfast this morning.'

Bessie sniffed with disapproval. 'Eating a good breakfast was what everyone should do in my opinion. It stands you up for the rest of the day. Mr Winslow, could we have a tray of tea, and perhaps something to tempt the appetite, please?'

'Of course, Mrs Wheeler.'

Once Winslow had left the room, Bessie turned to Charlotte. 'Six weeks since Harry's leave, isn't it?'

'Um...yes, about that, nearly seven.'

'And when did you have your last show?' Bessie nodded meaningfully at Charlotte's stomach.

'Oh, er...' Charlotte blushed. The thought had crossed her mind only this morning. 'A week or two before Harry came home.'

'A visit from the doctor is in order, I believe.' Bessie's expression was triumphant.

'A baby...'

'It happens, lass.'

Charlotte smiled. A baby. She was instantly afraid and excited at the same time. 'I did wonder if there might have been something wrong with me as there was no sign of a baby after the wedding or honeymoon or before Harry went away.'

'Some women fall quicker than others. I do think you should see the doctor first.'

'Yes, I will.'

Winslow entered. 'Madam, I have arranged tea in the morning room. Miss Hannah is hovering on the stairs. I wasn't sure you wanted her to interrupt you at this moment.'

Charlotte rose. 'Thank you, Winslow, the morning room will be fine.'

'Lass,' Bessie held her back, 'until we know who those men are, you and Hannah need to stay here at the Hall.'

Feeling better, Charlotte nodded, but she had no intention of staying at the Hall. She had to visit the mine tomorrow and collect food parcels from neighbouring friends which would be sent to the front. McBride's bullies weren't going to stop her getting much needed parcels to their boys on the front, though she'd make sure she carried her pistol.

'On a lighter note, Stan brought home from Leeds a large order of wool,' Bessie said. 'Nearly every woman in the village is knitting socks, as well as some of the old men. By the end of the week, we will have a good few dozen pairs.'

'Oh, wonderful. I'll collect them and send them to Harry. He'll distribute them amongst his men.'

As they left the drawing room and walked into the hallway the front door opened and Petra strode towards them. In her arms she held a baby.

'Petra!' Charlotte stared at her. She'd heard nothing from her sister in law since she left the Hall six weeks ago, despite sending a letter every week to her.

Petra glanced at Bessie, then up the stairs at Hannah who stood at the top with Miss Newton, before back to Charlotte. 'I need to talk to you…please.'

Charlotte nodded and re-entered the drawing room. 'I see your child is safely born.'

'Yes.' Petra hugged the shawl-wrapped baby closer. 'She was born three days ago.'

'Three days ago? Why are you out of bed? What has happened? Why have you left Brighton? The weather is too cold to bring a new baby out.'

Raising her chin in defiance, Petra's hard stance wasn't as convincing as usual when her bottom lip quivered. 'Alastair is dead.'

Charlotte's heart sank. Harry would be upset to hear the news, even though they had fought bitterly over his behaviour with Petra and Harry had announced their friendship over, he would still be upset. 'I am sorry to hear it, truly.'

A tear ran down Petra's cheek. 'We found out that he had died the day she was born. A friend wrote to me, telling me. Susannah had received a telegram that morning. I received nothing.'

'You weren't his wife,' Charlotte said gently.

'He loved me!' she shouted loud enough to wake the baby and cause it to whimper. Petra rocked her arms. 'Shush, dearest, I am sorry.'

'The baby…'

The look Petra gave Charlotte was feral. 'I am not giving her away. Do you hear me! She is all I have.' She glanced at the baby. 'She is his image. I refuse to give her up.'

Alarmed at the change, Charlotte lifted her hands helplessly. 'But I thought you wanted nothing to do with the child?'

'I thought so too, but once I held her and saw she was just like

Alastair, and now he is gone from me forever… I could not bear to part with her. You can't make me.'

'Very well.' Charlotte took a deep breath. 'It is not going to be easy explaining her presence.'

'I know Harry will not allow me to stay here, but I…I needed to come home…when I received the news…I could not stay there by myself, friendless. I know no one in Brighton. It is dismal. The place is deserted in winter.'

'And you thought to come back here because Harry is away.'

'I could have gone to the Mews and you would not have known for weeks,' Petra said defiantly.

'Then why didn't you?' Charlotte raised an eyebrow at the question, already knowing the answer. 'You didn't stay there because you are lonely. Aren't you? You do not like your own company.'

Petra tossed her head. 'You believe yourself to be so clever.'

'I know you well enough by now.'

'Yes, if you must know. I hate being on my own with no one to talk to.'

'And you thought I would be favourable to aloneness; despite that we get on each other's nerves?'

'This is my home!'

'And mine, you forget that, Petra.'

'How can I possibly forget such a thing!'

Charlotte gritted her teeth. 'If I allow you to stay here you will be civil. I'll not be the target of your vile rude manner, do you understand?'

'God, you were such a mouse when my brother married you. In a year you have become a tyrant.'

'There you are quite wrong. I was always strong-willed or I wouldn't have survived as I did. I just do not feel the need to bully people as you do, or be loud and aggressive to get what I want.'

Silence descended in the room for several moments, then the

baby whimpered and Petra glanced down at her and Charlotte saw the love in her tender expression. 'May I see her?'

Nodding, Petra lowered the shawl and Charlotte took a step closer to see the tiny baby that had such small features and a patch of black hair. 'She is beautiful. What did you call her?'

'She is beautiful,' Petra boasted. 'And I have called her Alice Mary, my mother's middle names.'

'If you stay, Petra, people will find out about the baby. I am not going to lie for you. There will be scandalous talk.'

'I do not care!' Petra's voice rose again and she rocked the baby harder as it cried. 'As if I care for stupid people's opinions.' She lowered her voice. 'Please...Charlotte. Please...can I stay just for a short time? I cannot...I am not very good at being on my own... And with Alastair gone... I have no one...'

'Yes, very well.' Charlotte sighed. She was going against her husband's wishes, but what else could she do? Petra could hardly be turned away at the door, could she? Though how she was going to explain a baby to Hannah, she didn't know. 'Go up to your room. I cannot be rude to Bessie any more than I have been. I will come up when she has gone. I must write to Harry though and tell him.'

'Of course you will,' Petra snapped. 'God forbid you do anything unsaintly!'

At the door, Charlotte spun back to her. 'I repeat, if you want to stay here, then I suggest you curb your tongue!'

Charlotte ignored the lady's maid and the nursemaid, who lingered by the front door, looking as though they were ready to be sent away at a moment's notice. She gave Winslow a tired smile. 'Miss Petra and her baby will be staying for a short time.'

'Very good, madam.' He bowed stiffly, clearly showing his disapproval.

In the morning room, Hannah chatted like a monkey to Bessie and as Charlotte sat down, Bessie poured her a cup of tea.

'So, lass, is the wildcat here to stay?'

'Just a few weeks, if that, for we will no doubt be at each other's throats soon enough.'

Hannah selected a triangle sandwich. 'Charlotte and Petra fought so much before. Petra can say bad words too, like a man, when she thinks no one is listening.'

'Enough, Hannah,' Charlotte warned.

She tilted her head inquisitively. 'Does that baby belong to Petra? What's it called? I do like babies.'

'She is Petra's baby girl and is called Alice. You will have to give up the nursery for her.' Charlotte savoured the taste of the crumbly pastry she'd chosen. Confusingly she was dreadfully hungry now, whereas half an hour ago she thought she'd be sick.

'My bedroom is large enough to do my lessons in. Miss Newton won't mind.'

'There are plenty of rooms to study in. We can convert another bedroom or just use the library.'

Hannah finished the rest of her cordial. 'May I go up and see the baby?'

Charlotte paused and then smiled cheekily as Petra would not want company, but tough for her. If she wanted to be at the Hall, then she'd have to deal with having family about her. 'Yes. I don't see why not.'

Once Hannah had left them, Bessie refilled their cups. 'That's going to put the cat amongst the pigeons, isn't it? A baby born out of wedlock.'

'I couldn't turn her away. Harry will not be happy about it, but he is not here to deal with it. Alastair has been killed. She has no one.'

'I doubt she really had him, considering he was already married. That woman had better change her ways. You have enough to deal with without her tantrums and abuse.'

'If she causes me too much bother, I'll threaten her with Brighton again.'

Bessie huffed. 'Spoilt madam that she is. The house in

Brighton is too good for her. If she didn't come from a wealthy family, she'd be tossed onto the streets. She'll never get any respect in the village now, you know. If she'd stayed away she could have pretended to be a widow to those people she met, but here? Here everyone knows her, and she wasn't liked before, it'll be interesting to see how people will treat her now.'

'Well, I don't know what the future will bring.' Charlotte ate a triangle sandwich of thin beef and pickle. 'I just want this war to end and Harry to come home.'

'And for your own baby to be born healthy and whole.'

'Yes...' It was still amazing for her to think of having a baby.

'And for Petra to be civil.' Bessie chuckled.

'And for Hannah to marry well.' Charlotte frowned. 'And for McBride to go away. Lord, the list is long.'

Bessie patted Charlotte's hand. 'Let's tick them off one by one, shall we?'

CHAPTER 19

April 1916

In pouring rain, Charlotte hurried from the car to the mine office, dodging puddles and trying to keep dry under the umbrella. They'd had rain for weeks, the April showers were more like April downpours.

One of the pitmen acknowledged her and she asked him to alert Mr Blaneley to her presence. The office was deserted, so she stood by the small fire, holding her hands out to its limited warmth and waited for Mr Blaneley to show up. The baby moved, pressing against her ribs and she rubbed the spot on her stomach. When she'd received the note that there had been an accident, she'd been visiting Bessie and Stan and for once had been relaxed after hearing Stan tell her that the two men loitering around the village for months had not been McBride's men but were war dodgers. It seems the two men were against joining up and had been hounded out of their village. The relief that McBride didn't have men watching her was great indeed.

The office door opened and a blast of cold air followed filling the room. Mr Blaneley shook his head at her. 'Nay, Mrs Belmont. What possessed you to come out in this weather?'

'Your note sounded urgent. An accident?' Now warmer, Charlotte shrugged off her cape and hung it up to dry in the corner of the office.

'I never expected you to come out yourself.'

'Well, I'm here now. Tell me what has happened.'

'Cave in, again. D level.' Blaneley poured out black tea from a brown earthen ware pot and handed her a cup. 'Al Easton has a broken leg and a crushed hand. The Doc thinks the fingers might have to come off. Rob Wright has lost a few toes. John Thorpe has a broken wrist and young Henry Carter has broken ribs. All have the normal cuts and bruises to add to their injuries.'

'Thank heavens no one died.' Charlotte closed her eyes momentarily in wonder. 'Have they been taken to the village hospital?' She spoke of the small building that adjoined the doctor's house, which served as his office and surgery and mini hospital.

'Yes, they have.'

'I'll arrange food baskets to be sent to their homes. Their wives, or mothers, aren't to be worried about their wages while they are recuperating either.'

'Very good, madam.'

'What do we do about D level? Did it flood?'

'No, it didn't, thankfully. But whether you feel it is worth shoring up and starting again, is something we must discuss.' He showed her on a large map of the mine where the incident occurred.

'What is your opinion?'

'I haven't made up my mind yet, madam. The vein is rich, there is no doubt, but the level is unstable. Is it worth the risk?'

Charlotte paused before answering. She had to make a judgement call on something she felt she wasn't knowledgeable enough about. The money from that level would be great, and keep the mine profitable for years to come, but at what cost? 'I would hate to walk away from that seam. Are we able to shore the level up adequately?'

'To be honest, madam, I don't know. The men don't like the level. We've had trouble in it from the start.'

'All mines are dangerous, we know that, but if we can make it as safe as we possibly can, then perhaps we should continue with it. What do you think?'

Blaneley scratched his head. 'No miner wants to walk away from a good seam. I suggest we drive another level parallel to D and see if it's more secure. We can easily work both levels on that seam. If D falls in again, we will continue on with the new level.'

'Yes, I agree. That is a good plan, Mr Blaneley.'

'We will need new equipment. Ideally, more men too.'

'Equipment I can supply. Men I cannot.' She gave a wry smile. 'We need this war to be over and the men returned.'

'Agreed. Do I have your permission to order what we need?'

She took a sip of hot tea. 'Send the list to the Hall when it is compiled. I will buy what you need.'

'You, madam?' Blaneley's eyes widened. 'I can manage it perfectly well, madam.'

'I'm sure you can, Mr Blaneley, but unfortunately many businesses these days are making huge profits because of the war. Prices are getting ridiculous. Through my husband's contacts I might be able to get a better deal if I approached them rather than you.'

'As you wish, Mrs Belmont.' He didn't look too happy about it.

'You have a problem with that decision, Mr Blaneley?' She was tired and snappy. Charlotte rubbed her back and sighed.

He shook his head, but his gaze strayed to her swollen stomach. 'No, Mrs Belmont, only I wouldn't like to see you take on so much. I know how busy you are. Mrs Wheeler was telling me only yesterday how worried she is over you. You're doing so much for the war effort now. Mrs Wheeler told me as well as all the parcels you are sending over, you have also ordered for the gardens at the Hall to be ploughed up and planted with vegetables?'

'It is our duty to feed the nation and we have land to spare. It makes sense.'

'And Belmont Mews has been given over to the War Office as a recovery home for wounded soldiers?'

'Yes. Again, it made sense. We have a perfectly good town-house standing empty when it could be put to good use. Miss Petra and I returned from London last week after finalising the changes to the house. We can accommodate at least twenty soldiers and a couple of nurses.'

'Have you offered the Hall too?'

'I have, but as yet the War Office hasn't been in contact about it.'

'This war has brought so many changes.' He drank some of his tea. 'You must rest though, madam. Your husband wouldn't want you overtaxing yourself.'

'I am perfectly fine,' Charlotte lied. She was anything but fine. The pregnancy was nothing as she expected. Petra had breezed through her pregnancy, yet Charlotte felt ill most of the time. Bessie said she was carrying high, and so the baby was up under her ribs making her breath short and give her dreadful heartburn. She couldn't sleep very well and as a result her days were long, busy and exhausting. Doctor Neville believed her to be due the end of June, two months away and she was already counting down the days.

'Mrs Belmont, madam, please, let me help by sorting out this order.' Blaneley's tone was kind and Charlotte reluctantly nodded.

Her back aching, Charlotte sat at Blaneley's desk. 'Thank you, yes that would be good of you.'

'Good. I'll make a start this afternoon. Have you heard recently from Mr Belmont?'

'Yes, only yesterday. As you know he's always in the thick of things so letters are few and far between sometimes. However, two letters arrived at once yesterday. A real treat.'

'Is he well, and the pitmen?'

'He is tired, as they all are, and sick of fighting. Mr Shelley got a wound to his side, but after a week in hospital he was back with them. Nicholas was also hit, shrapnel from a bomb blast. Apparently, he was peppered with it but he was bandaged up and is fine. Did you hear the Price's son from the village got killed? Just eighteen years old.'

'Aye, I did. Sad business. And Lenny Turner last week.'

Charlotte shivered. 'That's eight men killed from the village now.'

'Let's hope they'll be no more.'

They remained silent, knowing the chances of that happening were slim.

Standing, Charlotte collected her cape. 'Well, Mr Blaneley. I shall go and visit the hurt men and ask Doctor Neville if he needs anything. I have enough petrol to drive into York and purchase what he needs should he want me to. Everything is so hard to come by now, and expensive. Good day to you.' She smiled and left the office.

After spending a couple hours in the village, first at the little hospital visiting the men who were thankfully all going to make a recovery, and with Doctor Neville not needing her services, she returned to the car as rain started to fall again.

'Charlotte.'

She turned, thinking it was someone from the village, but her hand froze on the car's door handle as she stared at McBride. She'd failed to notice the big black car parked further down the road.

'Don't be frightened.' He gave a cold smile. 'I'm just passing through on my way to London from York. I thought I'd stop by on the chance I might see you, and perhaps stay the night for this weather is getting worse.' His gaze dropped to her stomach. 'It seems your husband did his duty on his last visit home?'

Charlotte slipped her hand into her dress pocket and felt for her small pistol she carried whenever she was outside.

'Good day to you, Mrs Belmont!' An elderly woman walking past on the opposite side of the road called out to her. 'How are the men doing?' She pointed to the hospital behind her.

'Um...they are well, thank you, Mrs Jones.' Charlotte looked at the woman's concerned face, but was aware of McBride standing only a few feet away. 'They...they were very lucky.'

'Aye, you're right there, Mrs Belmont. I'm glad my George is too old to be down there anymore.' Raising her hand in farewell, the old woman kept walking, her head down against the drizzle.

'An incident at the mine?' McBride inquired, taking a step closer. 'Can I be of assistance?'

Charlotte opened the door and edged closer to the car. She glared at him, the first spasm of fear receding to be replaced with a white-hot anger. 'Help?' she rounded on him. 'Help? *You*, the man who has stalked and haunted me, now wants to *help* me?'

'Charlotte. We can be friends. I know things have been difficult, and I have lost my temper...'

'Friends?' Suddenly she laughed. She laughed in his face and laughed harder as the shock of it made his eyes widen. 'You stupid, ugly, horrible monster! You should be locked up in an asylum! You're mad, you know that, don't you?'

'Charlotte!' His cheeks grew red and he glanced about to see if anyone was watching but the street was deserted as the rain fell heavier. 'Charlotte, please.'

The laughter left her as quickly as it came and the burning rage grew inside her again. She drew out her pistol and pointed it directly at his fat barrelled chest. 'I will kill you.'

Eyes wide, he stumbled back, his hands held out in front of him. 'No!'

White hot anger gripped her as she ran at him, but gathering his senses, he warded her off, and faster than she expected, he grabbed her wrist and bent it behind her, making her drop the pistol, which he kicked into a puddle.

'Attack me, will you?' he whispered harshly in her ear.

He spun her around and brought her close to him, his eyes narrow and spittle flecked his mouth and her face as he spoke. 'You won't kill me, bitch, but I'll kill you. One day, I *will* kill you and I'll have your sister.'

A dog barked from somewhere further down the street and he let her go and straightened his coat. Without a backward look he climbed into his car and drove away.

Shaking, Charlotte walked over to her pistol and retrieved it from the puddle. A lot of good this did her. When it had come to it she hadn't been able to pull the trigger. Pathetic.

Rain fell in grey sheets, shrouding the landscape. She had to get home before driving became impossible. However, once behind the wheel, she couldn't stop shaking. Her wet clothes were ignored as she sat crying.

She jumped when someone knocked on the fogged-up window.

The smiling face of Stan appeared. 'What you are doing, lass?'

Tears rolled down her cheeks. 'Will you take me home?'

Stan opened the car door and bent down to be at face level to her. 'What's happened? The baby?'

Numb, she shook her head. She didn't want to tell Stan and worry him more than he already did. He and Bessie had worried enough over the two men hiding in the village without this now. She summoned a shaky smile. 'I just don't like driving in the rain,' she lied.

'No, of course you wouldn't. Why are you out in it anyway?

Were you visiting the men at the hospital? The village is talking of nothing else at the minute.'

'Yes, I came to see them.' She left the car and linked her arm through Stan's. Through the gloom, she gave a last look down the road, but McBride's car was long gone.

'You're shaking, lass.'

'I'm cold.'

'Right, come on, let's get you home. You have a cup of tea with Bessie while I get the cart out. I should learn to drive the motor car, shouldn't I? We'll have to be quick, mind, this weather looks like it's settling in for the afternoon.'

Half an hour later, she was at the Hall, and Stan was disappearing down the drive into the grey fog, hurrying back to the shop before darkness fell.

'You're finally home, madam.' Winslow stiff with disapproval of what he termed, 'her gallivanting about', took her damp cape and gloves. 'Mr Wheeler brought you home? The car has broken down?'

After such a long and eventful day, she had no energy left to inform him about McBride. The beast was gone again and that's all that mattered. That he threatened to kill her, was pushed to the back of her mind for now. 'I didn't want to drive in the heavy rain. I left the car in the village. I'll go up and change. Is everything here all right?'

'We have a visitor, madam. Mr Adams is here on leave.' He indicted towards the drawing room. 'He's within. Miss Petra has been keeping him company.'

Unexpected happiness burst inside her and she hurried into the room. 'Nicholas!'

His face broke into a smile as he awkwardly stood, his left leg stiff, and accepted her tight embrace. 'Charlotte. It is lovely to see you.'

'Oh, it is so good to see you!' She stepped back a little, her eyes filling with tears. He had lost weight. 'I was only telling Mr

Blaneley about you today. Harry said you got hit by shrapnel, but you are fine now.'

He laughed. 'I was but my first day back and I got this.' He tapped his leg.

'You're wounded again?'

'Left thigh stopped a bullet. Nothing to worry about.' He waited for her to sit on the sofa before sitting beside her, his face grimaced with the effort.

Petra glanced out of the window at the darkening evening. 'You have been gone all day, Charlotte,' she reprimanded.

'Yes, there was an accident at the mine.'

'Oh?' Nicholas gave her his full attention. 'How bad?'

'No one killed, thankfully, but several hurt and are at the village hospital. D level is causing problems again.'

Frowning, Nicholas tapped his fingers together. 'I'll go tomorrow and see Blaneley.'

'Is that wise, with your leg as it is?' Petra raised her eyebrows at him.

'I'll manage. I'd like to see the place. I miss it.' He grinned.

'You'll stay for dinner?' Charlotte asked, taking his hand. He was like a brother to her now, and a link to Harry. 'In fact, why don't you stay here?' She was close to crying again and smiled to lighten her voice. 'I doubt your cottage is very welcoming after being left empty for so long.'

'Thank you, I would like that. I was going to be very cheeky and ask you if I could stay as I've rented my cottage out while I'm away fighting. Harry did say I could stay, but it's only fair to ask you.'

'Of course, you can stay. For as long as the War Office allows you to. It'll be wonderful to have you here with us.'

'I've got a fortnight to heal before I'm due back at the hospital in London and then shipped over to Harry and the boys.'

'How is he?' Her voice caught again, and Nicholas squeezed her hand.

A shadow passed over his face. 'Tired. Worn out. Fed up. I've brought you a letter from him. It's just a note really as he saw me quickly as I was boarding the hospital train. He sends his love, of course. Shall I get it?'

'No, I can read it later. He's not hurt?' An ache settled on her heart. She was desperate to see him.

'He's had a few nicks, as we all have. The worst was a scrape he got taking a village a few months ago. A bullet shaved along his hip bone. But he got sewed up and carried on. As everyone does.'

'He writes a great deal to me about it all, but never mentions if he is hurt. I know it is to spare me the worry, but I would rather know.' Goosebumps rose along Charlotte's skin at the thought of her darling man being subjected to constant gunfire and the stress of leading men into battle. She missed him so terribly. It was as though a part of her was gone.

Petra played with her necklace. 'How bad is it really over there?'

Nicholas stared at her. 'Do you really want to know?'

She nodded and looked at Charlotte who nodded also. 'We want to know all of it.'

Charlotte stood. 'However, let me go and change for dinner first. I'll have Winslow ready a room for you, and set another place at the table.'

Over dinner, Nicholas told them about the war, the real war he was fighting and not the stuff that they read in the newspapers or watched in newsreels at the theatre in York. He told them of the endless boredom between battles. Days of sitting around waiting for orders, or worse still being sent from one place to another, then the orders were changed and they'd be sent to another place only to return to the first original place days later. He told them about the lack of decent food, drinking cold tea, wearing the same uniforms for days, of not bathing, of sleeping rough in trenches filled with water, of the desperate ache of missing home.

He spoke of the battles, the tough fighting in muddy fields, where men sink up to their knees in cloying mud, the fear of the burning gas bombs that drifted silently unseeingly on the breeze on pleasant sunny days. He prided in the men he fought with, and Harry who led them, as strong, dependable and loyal courageous men who he loved as brothers.

He recalled the French villages wiped out by bombing, of forests depleted of trees, of the mass of humanity fleeing the conflict carrying their only possessions, of animals dead on the roadsides.

As they night wore on, they finished eating and retired to the library where they sat before a raging fire and talked until the early hours of the morning, until their eyes grew tired and Nicholas's voice grew hoarse from talking. From him, Charlotte learned more than she could from censored letters and newsreels.

As Winslow came to assist Nicholas upstairs to bed, Petra slipped her arm through Charlotte's as they followed them upstairs. 'Pray that this ghastly business is over soon.'

Touched by the closeness that Petra rarely showed, but since the birth of her daughter she had, slowly, started to demonstrate, Charlotte smiled sadly at her. 'I have long stopped praying for I do not believe there is a God. How can there be to allow this horrific war to happen?'

Petra paused outside her bedroom. 'Why do you go to church then?'

'Because it is expected. I have to set an example, but in my mind, it's all nonsense.'

'Are you a Darwinian?'

'Definitely!'

Petra grinned. 'You really are a rebel underneath your sensible manner, aren't you?'

Before Charlotte could answer, Nicholas turned and bid them goodnight. Petra went along to the staircase leading up to the nursery to check on the baby.

Charlotte entered her bedroom. Lucy had drawn the curtains and turned back the bed. A lamp was lit and a small fire burned in the grate. It was cosy and comfortable, making her feel guilty for the dreadful situation Harry would sleep in tonight.

A small knock on the door preceded Lucy as she came in to help Charlotte undress. 'Did you have a pleasant evening, madam?'

Sitting on the stool in front of the dressing table, Charlotte took out her earrings. 'Yes, it is so lovely to have Mr Adams here.'

'Oh, yes. He is so nice,' Lucy said in a dreamlike fashion and Charlotte smiled. Nicholas was a catch for any young woman.

'Mr Adams brought home lots of letters for families in the village. I got one from my brother, Sid. So did my mam. Wasn't that wonderful of Mr Adams to do that?'

'He is a good man.' Having taken off her jewellery and the pins holding up her hair, Charlotte allowed Lucy to brush out its length before helping her to take off her dress, and while she hung it up, Charlotte changed into her nightgown. 'I'm ready now, Lucy. Go help Miss Petra, she'll be waiting.'

'Good night, madam.'

Once Lucy had left, Charlotte climbed into bed. Alone at last, her shoulders sagged. She no longer had to pretend. She gave in to the deep unhappiness that she'd fought to keep at bay. Her stomach made a large mound under the covers and she smoothed her hands over it in comfort. The baby was restless inside. Was it aware of how she was feeling? She turned her head to where Harry's pillow lay beside hers and lightly touched it. An overwhelming sadness filled her. She bit her lip to stop crying out. She missed him terribly.

A dull pain of longing circled her chest. She wanted her husband home. She needed his arms about her, his lips on hers and the whispers of love he spoke only to her. Tears slipped from her lashes as she cried silently. She had to be positive that she would have him home again, but at times it was so hard. Harry would keep her safe from McBride, but who would keep him safe from a German bullet?

CHAPTER 20

May 1916

*H*arry left the little restaurant and headed back to his lodgings. The road was wet with recent rain, but not too cold. May was becoming warmer every day, for which he was thankful. He had spent the day in meetings and attending briefs on the outskirts of Paris and now, after a welcome meal and a passable glass of wine, he wanted nothing more than a few hours' sleep before he would travel back to his men. Nicholas was due to return to the unit and he was eager to see him and talk of his stay at the Hall and of Charlotte. From Nicholas he could get the true state of affairs there, especially since Petra's return. He needed to know Charlotte was coping. His thoughts turned to the coming baby and he smiled in the darkness. A baby. He was to be a father. The sweet joy of it was suddenly swept away by a deep longing to be home. What he wouldn't give this minute to be in Charlotte's arms, feeling her fingers trailing across his body, her lips kissing him...

With no street lighting and very few signs, he paused at the corner of the road to get his bearings. A small group of noisy soldiers, Australians by the look of their slouched hat, disappeared into a public house on the opposite side of the road. Harry remembered he had turned here and that his lodgings were down to his right. Satisfied, he wasn't lost, he continued on and passed a few boarded-up shops. Music came from within the next building, another lodging house. Passing the entrance to an alley, he was roughly jostled as a man loomed out of the dark.

'Steady on there, friend.' Harry could smell the alcohol on him as he stumbled.

The man pushed Harry away. 'Leave me alone.'

'Listen, you need to get back to your lodgings.' Harry frowned, as his eyes made out in the dark that the man wore no uniform. Wary, Harry took a step back. 'I'll leave you to it then, shall I?'

'You…can't…tell me, whath- whath to do!' His slurred speech matched his swaying stagger. The man was drunk.

'I wouldn't dream of it, mate.'

'I do…as…I pleaseth!'

'Right you are.' As Harry tried to walk away the fellow grabbed his arm, peering into his face.

'I told him.' He swayed and nearly fell on Harry. 'I told him to stick his…his…his money! Jumped…up nobody!'

'All right fella.'

'Kill his own…ma…ma…mother, he would. Filth!' The drunk wheeled backwards and only the wall of the building stopped him from falling. 'If I wanted…orders… I'd join up!'

A light shone from an opened door down in the alley. There were voices and Harry saw two civilian men slip away down the alley and out of sight. He peered down at the drunken man leaning against the wall. 'You are English?'

'Aye. Who's askin…? If it's McBride, tell him…him go to…hell.'

Harry stepped back at the mention of McBride. No, surely not, he couldn't be talking about the same man. 'McBride?'

'What…of…him?' He closed his eyes, swaying.

'You work for Vernon McBride, an Englishman?'

'Maybe…did…not now.'

'Is McBride in Paris?'

The man's blurred eyes tried to focus on Harry. 'Who are you?'

'I'm a good friend of McBride's. He is a distant relative to my wife.'

'Ahhh…' The man closed his eyes again, not caring.

'Well? Where is he? I'd like to see him.'

'Down there.' He thumbed over his shoulder, indicating the dark alley.

Harry couldn't believe it. 'Does he have many men with him?'

'Enough.' The man shrugged and burped loudly. 'I feel sick…'

Ignoring him, Harry crept down the alley to the side entrance of the lodging house. His heart pounded. It was hard to comprehend that McBride was so close.

The door suddenly opened again spilling light onto the cobbles. A thin man not wearing a uniform stepped into the alley. He glanced at Harry then stopped. 'What you want? Soldier boys don't need to be down here. There's no knocking shop here.'

Harry moved back into the darkness, his hand resting on his pistol. 'Right, sorry. My mistake.'

The man was quick-witted and shut the door enclosing them in the murky light of the alley. 'You'd best get on then, hadn't you?'

'I suppose so.' Harry remained still. The shadows hiding him.

Angered, the man advanced a little. 'Go on then. What are you waiting for?'

'A friend.'

'You have no friends here, mate. Now get going.'

A bang came from an upstairs window. Harry had no idea

how many men were in the lodging with McBride. He couldn't take them all on.

'Who are you?'

Harry stepped back, keeping to the shadows. 'That's no concern of yours.'

The man came at him, but his punch missed Harry's cheek. Back against the wall, Harry defended more punches and shifted his weight in time to miss a head butt. With a quick move, he twisted free and got a clear punch to the man's stomach, knocking the wind from him. Without looking back, Harry ran from the alley before the fellow could raise the alarm and he didn't stop running until he reached his own lodgings.

Once up in his own room, he stood by the window, chest heaving, watching in case anyone had followed him. Satisfied he'd drawn no attention, he sat on the bed. McBride was in Paris. He had henchmen and was probably here on dodgy business, likely black market, for none of the men he'd seen were in uniform. How could he get to him though? In the morning he was to report to his commanding officer and receive his final orders before boarding a train back to his men. He had no time to hunt down McBride.

After a sleepless night, Harry rose early to wash and dress. Already paid up, he left his lodgings just as the sun was rising over the rooftops. The street outside was deserted, but standing on the corner was a man in a long grey coat, a hat pulled low. Instinctively, Harry turned the other way and strode quickly towards the next street. Rounding the corner, he stopped and peeked around the edge of the building. The man in the grey coat was following him.

Thrusting the strap of his satchel over his shoulder to secure it, Harry ran down the street and turned another corner. Again, he stopped and looked back, and again his follower was not far behind him. He was a threat and he wanted Harry.

Needing to lose him, Harry sprinted down a small side lane,

and into the back of a shop, where thankfully, the goods entrance was open.

The owner jumped in surprise as Harry dashed into the store and hid behind her counter. She spoke in French, but then realised he wore a British officer's uniform. 'You in trouble, oui?'

'Oui.' Steadying his breath, he watched through the open back door and saw the grey-coated man running past. He nodded his thanks to her. 'I apologise, madame.'

The woman, in her late fifties, had also seen the man running past. 'He not a German soldier?'

'No. He is bad though.'

'Bad to wear no uniform.' She sniffed in clear condemnation. 'All men to fight.'

'I agree.'

She folded her arms, her expression full of loathing. 'Villain?'

'Oui.' Harry nodded, still watching the door in case the fellow doubled back this way. 'Black market more likely.'

'You military police?' She continued her job of stocking shelves with tins from a crate as though having a British officer hiding in her shop was a common every day thing.

'No, madame.' He stood cautiously, watchful. The shop sold different goods mainly for the house. It was pitifully stocked with bits and pieces placed here and there on the bare shelves to try and make it seem fuller than it was.

She turned and looked out of her front window. The other shop owners were opening their businesses for the day. The light was getting brighter, and more people were walking in the street. 'My husband. He come soon. In cart. Take you away.'

'Thank you. Merci.'

'Coffee?' She grinned.

He gave a strained smile. 'Thank you. Merci.'

* * *

CHARLOTTE FOLDED the letter she had been reading from her solicitor and rubbed her back, grimacing at the sudden spasm that held her body rigid. Once it had passed, she continued reading. Since McBride's last visit she had dwelled a little in self-pity before straightening her shoulders and deciding to make a plan. Her gun, she realised, was not the answer. She couldn't fire it at McBride simply because she shook so much when he confronted her.

She had to think of a new plan. Something that would hurt McBride, and the one thing he cared about was money. With this in mind, she had instructed her solicitor to find out on the quiet all McBride's business dealings, the legal and illegal. She would use her inherited fortune to buy him out, only he would never know it was her. The aim was to wipe out his assets. He would receive generous offers from unfamiliar companies with invented figureheads. All would be owned by her. She would ruin him.

Another pain gripped her. She stood and shuffled across the floor holding on to furniture as she breathed through the pain. Darkness had fallen an hour ago. Rain lashed against the library windows.

'Was that another one?' Petra demanded. 'Stop hiding them from me.'

'Yes,' Charlotte managed to say through gritted teeth.

'I think you should go up to bed and I'll send Winslow for Doctor Neville.'

'Not yet.' The pain receding a little, she took a deep breath. 'I can't send Winslow out in this dreadful weather.'

'He'll get one of the gardening boys to go.' Petra threw down her embroidering in disgust. 'I cannot concentrate on that while you are pacing.'

'I'm sorry.'

'Don't be sorry. I loathe embroidering anyway, even on Alice's little clothes. But you should be upstairs. This has been going on for hours now.'

'I'll go up soon.' Charlotte rested a moment, leaning against a table in the corner of the room. She had no wish to go upstairs, for that would mean the birth was really happening and the pain would intensify. Since early morning pains had been plaguing her body. For hours she kept it from Petra and Hannah, but this afternoon when she declined to go to a war fundraiser in York, Petra had realised that her quietness was due to her fighting the contractions gripping her.

In her brusque way, Petra tried to be helpful and Charlotte appreciated it, but their relationship was not yet close enough to foster Charlotte's need to confide in her properly yet. She suffered alone, in quiet.

A small knock on the door preceded Winslow. 'Madam, would you be taking coffee?'

'Ah, Winslow!' Petra jumped up from the sofa. 'You must send word to Doctor Neville. Your mistress is in labour.'

Winslow's eyes widened before he controlled himself again. 'Indeed. It'll be done immediately.'

'Wait.' Charlotte bent over, the pain nearly driving her to her knees. 'I want Bessie.'

'Yes, of course, madam.' Winslow hovered beside her, his concern evident in his expression. 'You must not worry.'

'Come now.' Petra took Charlotte's arm. 'I insist you go up to bed. Otherwise the baby will be born in the library.'

As they made their way into the corridor, Hannah came down the stairs and the front door opened and a bearded stranger walked in.

Heart racing, Charlotte stared, thinking at first that one of McBride's men had entered the house.

Winslow rushed to the man. 'Mr Belmont, sir!'

'Papa?' Petra murmured quizzically.

The man dropped the three large travelling bags he held,

removed his sodden hat and beamed a warm smile, taking in everybody. 'Well, good evening!'

'Papa!' Petra abandoned Charlotte and ran into her father's arms.

'Daughter. I am wet through.' After a brief hug he held her at arm's length. 'Let me look at you. My, you're the image of your mother.' He touched her cheek tenderly before turning and shaking hands with Winslow. 'Sorry to be a pest, dear fellow, I've arrived unannounced.'

'No trouble at all, sir.' Winslow beamed. 'It is good to have you home, sir.'

'Indeed. I felt that with the war involving so many countries that I should perhaps head for the safety of home until it all calms down.' He gazed kindly at Charlotte. 'And you must be my son's wife. I'm Francis Belmont, Frank.'

A pain circled her stomach and she bent over with a gasp.

'Papa she is in labour.' Petra hurried back to her. 'Winslow, hurry now.'

Frank took Charlotte's other elbow and between him and Petra they helped her upstairs. 'This is a great evening to arrive home. In time to see my first grandchild born.'

Charlotte stole a look at Petra, for she'd not written to her father informing him of Alice's birth, and Petra gave a weak smile full of worry. Glancing at her father-in-law, Charlotte looked for Harry in him. Frank Belmont was tall and thin, dressed in pale linen clothes as though he'd just stepped out of the African jungle he'd called home for the last ten years. His tanned angled face only resembled Harry's a little and his eyes were grey not blue like his son's. For a moment Charlotte was disappointed, but the onset of more pain wiped out further thoughts and she stumbled to her bed with a groan.

Time lost meaning to her as Petra helped her undress and don a nightgown. Hannah was allowed to briefly give Charlotte a kiss before Miss Newtown whisked her away up to the nursery where they were to spend the night with baby Alice, away from the cries of childbirth.

Then suddenly Bessie was beside her, holding her hand. 'Now then, my pet. You're managing?'

'Yes. Thank you for coming.'

Bessie huffed. 'Where else would I be at a time like this? You're like my own daughter. Stan is downstairs talking to Mr Belmont. We were floored to see him here. But he remembered us. The man always did have an amazing memory. He was quite happy to have Stan sit with him in the drawing room as though Stan was a member of the gentry himself!' Bessie laughed and patted Charlotte's hand. 'Frank Belmont never had any airs about him.'

'Bessie?'

'Yes, pet?'

'If I don't survive then you are to take Hannah home with you.'

Bessie reared back as though she'd been slapped. 'I'll have none of that talk thank you very much. Get that nonsense right out your head!'

Petra entered, escorting Doctor Neville and with his gentle confident manner, Charlotte relaxed as best she could.

Petra stood on the opposite side of the bed to Bessie. Her face betrayed her unease. 'Now that Mrs Wheeler is here I can go or stay as you wish.'

'What would you like to do?' Charlotte asked as another contraction grew.

'Stay. If it pleases you.'

Reaching out, Charlotte gripped her hand. 'I'd like that too.'

Having washed his hands in the bowl on the table, Doctor Neville came to the end of the bed. 'Right then. Let us get on with the business of safely delivering the next Belmont generation into the world, shall we?'

CHAPTER 21

August 1916

*H*arry rested against the back of the trench. He'd spent the last hour completing paperwork and writing letters to the family of deceased soldiers. His hand ached from writing. The midday sun shone and for once it was quiet. No bombs landed, no guns fired. The trench, although inches deep in cloying mud, was drying out slowly. Around him the men sat at ease, smoking, drinking tea and cleaning their weapons.

Taking a moment, Harry pulled a letter out of his jacket pocket.

My darling,

How I miss you. Especially at this moment as I write this letter while your son sleeps in his crib by my side. He was born seven hours ago at three fifteen in the morning of June 18th. He is without doubt the most beautiful baby I have ever seen, and the image of you, in my mind anyway. In your previous letter you gave me suggestions as to what to call our child, and since he is a boy I have gone with what we previously agreed on, my father's name. He is to be called Jeremy Henry Belmont. Doesn't that sound simply marvellous?

I cannot stop staring at him. He is so small. Not as tiny as Alice was, but still small and delicate. You will love him immediately as I do. The birth was rather intense and not something I would quickly agree to do again, but the end result is pure joy. Bessie and Petra were a wonderful help to me. Doctor Neville was excellent. Hannah is besotted by Jeremy as she is with Alice. She says she feels very grown up now that she is an aunt.

It is truly unbelievable our son is here. I wish you were home. Can you see if it is possible to come home just for a short time?

What is also unbelievable is that last night your father arrived unannounced! We were all shocked. I imagine you are shocked to hear this too. The war has brought him home apparently. I haven't had the chance to talk to him properly yet, naturally. About an hour ago, he popped in to see the baby very briefly and he says he is smashing! I do not know how long he is staying, or what his thoughts were about Alice, as Petra had not told him about her. He has come home to two grand-children.

The new Nanny, Miss Blewitt, arrived two days ago and I am pleased with her. She seems very sensible and capable. She will join Nanny Smith whom Petra brought from Brighton. I've also taken on another young girl to help in the nursery. She is called Gilly and is known to Bessie quite well as she is from the village. Mrs Morrissey is enjoying having more people to cook for. She has taken the newcomers under her wing. I suppose we should advertise for a housekeeper, though Winslow insists there is no need, as between him, Edith and Mrs Morrissey they have the small staff under their control. However, it is nice to see the Hall filling up again, my love. I just wish you were here too.

I send this letter filled with such wonderful news and all my love. Keep safe and well, my darling. We hope to see you soon.

Lots of love,
Your wife & son.

HARRY FOLDED the dog-eared letter and placed it in his jacket pocket, the envelope long torn and discarded. He'd read it a dozen times now and still his heart swelled with emotion to think that he had a son, that Charlotte and his son had survived childbirth and were well and healthy. He had to try and get home. He needed to see his son, Charlotte and now his father. The letter was two months old, and he was frustrated not to be home with them. His son was already four weeks old and he'd not seen him. He didn't know for how much longer he could stand not seeing them.

It also worried him that since that letter, he'd only received one short letter from Charlotte and one from Winslow. Naturally, it wasn't easy getting mail to the troops, many things got in the way of safe delivery, boats being sunk, mail trucks bombed and the like, but it didn't lessen his anguish of not hearing from home.

Although he had written to Charlotte every couple of days when the war allowed him five minutes to himself, he omitted in telling her about the run in with McBride's man. She would only worry and what good would that do? Besides, after pulling in some favours at the War Office, Harry had learned that McBride wasn't enlisted but had travelled several times to Paris for business. His contacts in London told him that McBride was becoming a very wealthy man on the back of this war.

That news concerned Harry more than anything, for with money he could buy unscrupulous men's loyalty and silence.

'Harry,' Nicholas whispered, coming into the corner of the trench were Harry had been sitting, reading the letter by the light of a candle stub stick into the mud. Nicholas handed Harry a sheet of paper. 'New orders.'

Harry read them quickly. 'We are to stay here until relief comes at 0400.'

Nicholas yawned. 'Then where are we going?'

Rubbing the tiredness from his eyes, Harry sighed. 'There is a new offensive being organised. We have been given thirty-six hours leave first though.'

'Thirty-six hours? Not enough time to get home and back again.'

Shaking his head, Harry tucked the orders away into a pocket. 'Nope, unfortunately. I would like to go home and see Charlotte and my son. The best we can hope for is to find a decent place to eat and sleep for the night.'

'Well, at least we'll be out of this hellhole.' Nicholas gazed around at the mud and timber trench, the tired men lying against sandbags. 'I'll go tell the men the good news.'

'Nicholas.'

'Yes?'

'I want the men vigilant as we're walking out. It is the changeover with the relief that usually causes casualties. Men are thinking of other things and forget to keep their heads down.'

'Aye, I know.' As if to make a point of their words a random German shot rang out in the still night and the bullet pinged off the timber structure above their heads making them duck low.

Nicholas swore. 'God, I hate this place!'

* * *

WITH HER EYES CLOSED, Charlotte raised her face to the warm sun. Bees buzzed in search of the flowers that once used to populate the gardens but which now had been transformed into vegetable plots. High in the trees birds trilled, such a happy sound. Summer was her favourite time of the year, August days like this one especially, before the weather became too hot.

She stifled a yawn. Jeremy had had a restless night last night and although Nanny wanted to take him from her, she had resisted and walked the floor to soothe him. She smiled to herself at the thought of Nanny, who didn't think it was proper for Charlotte to feed her son herself, yet she did. Her breasts were made to feed her babies. It was as simple as that, so Bessie said loudly and proudly to anyone who would listen. Charlotte fed him herself and earned the disapproval of the nursery staff. Though, after eight weeks of breastfeeding, Charlotte could admit that she was feeling the strain of it. Her days were so busy that waking up during the night to feed was a chore. Soon she must decide whether she wanted to continue to do it.

Despite her drowsiness, she couldn't fall into a doze. Her mind was restless still processing the news of this morning. She'd received letters from her solicitor informing her that she had bought a fourth property from McBride. Also, she now had forty-eight per cent share in his cotton mill and a forty-nine percent share in his candle factory.

Word from her solicitor was that McBride was spending a lot of time in Paris, apparently it was reported that he was secretly friendly with some German officials. How her solicitor found this out, Charlotte had no idea. But that McBride might be seen as a spy, or hedging his bets on how the war might go, did him no favours. He obviously wanted to be known as a friend to both sides.

She heard a rustle and turned lethargically and sighed, her peace broken. Expecting someone from the house, her blood froze in her veins as she stared at McBride. Was she dreaming? Had she conjured him up? Wasn't he in Paris?

In an instant he was beside her, his hands about her throat. 'You bitch!'

Surprised, frightened, she grabbed at his hands, her breath

caught in her chest. She thrashed, eyes pleading. Was he going to kill her? She couldn't scream. She couldn't breathe!

'Did you think I wouldn't find out who had been buying into my businesses? You think yourself so clever? So many times I should have killed you and no one would have known. I wish I had!' He spat as he talked, eyes wild as he squeezed harder. 'I will kill you now!'

Stars floated before her eyes, his face blurred. She gasped, her arms losing their strength.

Suddenly she was free. She wheezed air into her lungs. Her eyes watered. She couldn't get enough air. She watched McBride run away, into the bushes and gone as though he'd never been.

She gently touched her sore neck, her throat on fire, pain radiating out through her body. She had no strength to stand and so remained sitting, blinking back tears.

The soft murmur of voices came on the breeze. She froze. Was he coming back? Moments later, Petra and Frank rounded the bend in the path and found her. She sagged in relief. Their voices had scared McBride off.

'You have no hat, Charlotte.' Petra tutted.

She thought quickly, straightening her clothes and sitting upright. To tell them would have them all worrying. McBride was gone, and she had no proof that it was he who attacked her. It would be her word against his. If she told them now it would ruin their day, frighten everyone. She couldn't do that to them. 'Did-did you come from the house? Did you see any one about?' she managed to croak. She gripped her skirt to hide her shaking hands.

'No, no one. Why?' Frank looked around. 'Did we have a visitor?'

'No-no. I just thought I heard something,' her voice rasped in her throat. She steadied her breathing. There was no point in alarming them. Petra would be too dramatic and think they would be all killed in their sleep, and no doubt insist on having police camping in the grounds, and everyone being armed with rifles.

'You look very flushed. Imagine not wearing a hat.' Petra shook her head at her. 'You will burn and look like a peasant who works in the fields.'

Charlotte smiled weakly at them both, thankfully her dress's lace collar was high on her neck and they'd not see McBride's finger marks. 'Five minutes won't hurt. And five minutes is all I've been out here for. I've had the ladies from the York Women's Institute here all morning talking about the next fundraiser and they've worn me out. I needed some air.' She prided herself on being normal, though she couldn't help but to keep glancing at the bushes.

'We have interrupted your solitude, my dear,' Frank said in a way of an apology, sitting on the grass at her feet.

'You should tell them next time to have their meeting without you and send you a letter detailing the outcome!' Petra sat beside Charlotte, her parasol tilted to shade them from the sun. 'They take you for granted. Always calling in on you and pressing you to help them. You have enough to do.'

'I might do that, and perhaps volunteer *your* services to help them?' Charlotte wondered if she was in a dream. Had McBride really been here? Then she touched her neck and felt the pain. She took a deep breath, wondering he McBride was watching her from somewhere close by.

Petra reared back. 'Good Lord, why would you want to do that? Those ladies bore me, and although their cause is a good one, I do more than my share of war work. No thanks to you.'

Charlotte swallowed, the ache in her throat making her want to cry, but she fought it. 'I hardly think the odd day here and there helping me in the village packing up parcels for the men is very taxing on you, is it?' How was she acting so ordinary after everything that just happened only moments ago?

'Are you saying I don't do enough?' Petra frowned at her.

'Would you have me run off to France and drive an ambulance, which is obviously the *latest* thing to do amongst the ladies of our class, or should I become a nurse?'

'If I wasn't married it is something I would have done.' Charlotte murmured, wishing right now she was in France, or anywhere, but here.

'Of course, *you* would,' Petra scoffed. 'Any opportunity to get your hands dirty and you are in the thick of it. Just look at all that mine business.'

Frank laughed. 'That *mine business* keeps this estate going successfully. We cannot simply rely on sheep now like we did when my grandfather was a boy.'

Petra flapped a fly away from her face. 'Anyway, enough talk of such things. They bore me. The babies are asleep, so we thought we would come find you and have tea out here. Lucy will be along shortly with it. Hannah and Miss Newton have gone into the village to see Bessie and Stan.'

'Alone?' Charlotte, mindful of McBride, felt a frisson of alarm. Would he find Hannah? 'I think I'll go and find them.' She rose, her legs still a bit like jelly.

'Winslow has gone with them, as it is his day off. He won't let Hannah out of his sight, you know what he's like.'

Grateful to Winslow, Charlotte relaxed slightly. She looked at Frank who had stood and wandered over to inspect the row of lettuce bordering what once was a rose garden, not far from the bushes McBride had fled into. She relaxed a little. If McBride was still in the bushes, Frank would probably see him. No, he'd have gone by now.

She sighed and eased her shoulders. Frank was speaking of the snails eating the plants. She let his words wash over her. Her father-in-law was a strange man. Content to spend hours in the library reading botany books, or hours in one of the rooms writing about botany, and hours in the garden drawing botany. He got along well with Miss Newton and Hannah, often accompanying them when they painted in the garden. Perhaps she should tell him about McBride, so he could keep an eye on Hannah when he was with her.

Frank, although friendly and agreeable to everyone, enjoyed his own company much more than being with others. Thankfully he had taken Petra's news about Alice quite well. After years living in the jungle amongst tribes and indigenous people around the world, where social rules were very different to what he knew, his attitude wasn't as strict about illegitimate babies as most gentlemen of his class.

Petra had lost a great many friends since Alice's birth, but she hadn't lost her father's love. Her shame would never be forgotten, and her life was completely changed from the one she used to lead, but she knew she had the love of her family and for now it was enough, or so it seemed to Charlotte. Perhaps one day, Petra might think that her sacrifice had been too much, but at the moment, she was content being a good mother to Alice, which astonished everyone.

Charlotte liked Petra much more now than she ever did, and despite her fall from grace, Alice's birth and Alastair's death had softened Petra somewhat. Though, of course, she still had a sharp tongue when she was in the mood.

'Are you quite well, Charlotte? You seem somewhat subdued.'

'I'm fine,' she lied.

'I want to talk to you about something rather serious. I have been thinking,' Petra said now, drawing Charlotte's attention away from watching Frank tending to the row of carrots behind the lettuce.

'Oh?'

'Papa and I have been talking, and I believe, after the war is over, I may go with him when he leaves.'

Having got her full attention, Charlotte stared at Petra. 'Go with him where?'

'Africa.'

'Africa!' Charlotte gaped in surprise. Her thoughts only moments ago fresh in her mind. 'Why?'

'To start again.' Petra shrugged one shoulder, as though that was the only answer she needed to give.

'You have a home here. Even Harry agrees with me on this now.'

Petra chuckled. 'Harry would agree to whatever you said since you have given him a son. But we both know that he and I will never be close. Too much has happened.'

'But Africa? Why so far away? You won't know anyone.'

'She will have me,' Frank said, coming to stand beside them.

Turning to him, Charlotte raised an eyebrow in question. 'You? I don't wish to be offensive, but you go and live in jungles. How can Petra possibly do that?'

Petra laughed and Charlotte finally realised that since her father's return, Petra had been the happiest she'd ever been.

Frank smiled. 'I shan't be doing that anymore. I am getting too old to be traipsing the jungles now. Yes, I will go on some small expeditions, but only for short amounts of time. I need to start cataloguing my findings. I have years of notes that I must write up properly. Petra will run my house in Antananavivo, which is not in Africa.' He gave Petra a gentle reproving look. 'She needs to learn her geography.'

'Antananavivo? Where is that?' Charlotte asked, amazed how much she didn't like the news of Petra leaving.

'Madagascar.'

'Madagascar?' Charlotte wasn't even sure she had heard of it.

'It is a large island off the coast of Africa. I have a house there. The town of Antananavivo is quite large, it is the capital. I have made a few friends. However, I am sure we will make more. The island is stunning. Very exotic. I think Petra will enjoy it.'

'I need to do this, Charlotte.' Petra briefly touched her hand. 'I cannot stay in England. Everything has changed. I will take Alice and we shall go with Papa. I will conveniently become a widow, and no one will treat Alice differently, unlike here.' Suddenly hearing voices, Petra straightened. 'Besides, it is not until the war has finished. We still have some time together.'

They all turned as Lucy came into view carry a tea and coffee tray and walking next to her, carrying another tray of cakes and sandwiches, was Bertram.

With little shouts of joy, Charlotte and Petra rushed to hug him and welcome him home. Charlotte held him tight, the suppressed tears from McBride's attack ran down her cheeks.

Bertram gazed at her. 'Charlotte?'

'I'm fine,' she whispered. 'Just glad you're home.'

Frank shook his hand as everyone talked at once and another chair was carried down from the terrace.

'How long will you be home for, Bertram?' Frank asked, as they settled themselves.

'Three days only,' Bertram replied. 'I wish it was longer.'

'I read that your regiment got hit hard in your last battle,' Charlotte said quietly. Bertram had written to her over the months, but his appearance today shocked her. He was so much thinner, the flesh taken off him and his skin drawn tight over his bones. His eyes were hooded now, wary. Gone was the childish innocence in him that used to drive Harry crazy. Maturity and grief had replaced that, and the effects of the war had aged him. There was no denying that he had evolved into a man that would now draw ladies' attention, whereas before he appeared a tubby buffoon.

Bertram stared into his teacup. 'It was bad, yes. There are not many of us left. We will merge with another regiment probably, on our return.' He gazed at Charlotte. 'Harry is well? And the new baby?'

She smiled, waving away the cake that Petra passed to her. 'Jeremy is such a joy and resembles his father very much. I received a letter from Harry just yesterday. He says my letters aren't getting through to him, which saddens us both as I had put in a photograph of Jeremy and I.'

'Blame the Germans. They are menacing our ships in the Channel.'

'I blame the Germans for everything!' Petra sneered.

Charlotte drank the last of her coffee. 'After you are finished your tea, would you like to visit the nursery and meet your new cousin?'

'Absolutely.'

'Alice is growing, perhaps you'd like to give her a minute of your time too?' Petra put in tartly.

'Of course. I want to see them both,' Bertram replied patiently, biting into a sandwich. 'I am here for three days, if that suits you all. I have plenty of time to play with the babies.'

'This is your home, you know that. You can stay as long as you want.' Charlotte patted his arm, then looked at Frank, for rightly he was head of the house while Harry was absent. Or was he? She didn't know the correct etiquette in this circumstance.

Frank doffed his straw hat at her, reading her thoughts. 'This is not my house, remember. It belongs to you and Harry. I am but a guest.'

'Hardly.' Charlotte smiled at him then turned to Bertram. 'Hannah will be pleased to see you.'

He took a sip of tea and leaned back into his chair with a pleased expression on his face. 'I am happy about that. She writes the most delightful letters to me, as does Miss Newtown.'

'Miss Newtown?' Petra jerked forward, nearly spilling her plate of crumbs off her lap. 'Heavens, why are you writing to the governess?'

Bertram crossed one leg over the other. 'Because, dear cousin, I want to.'

'But why?' Puzzled, Petra stared at him.

'We got to know each other a little before I left to enlist. I asked her if she would be willing to write to me and she was. We have been corresponding for a year now.'

'What on earth have you to say to each other?'

'Actually, quite a lot. Miss Newtown is knowledgeable on many subjects.'

'She is a governess,' Petra frowned, 'she is *expected* to know things.'

Charlotte stood, as did the men, and she waved them back into their seats. 'I must see Mrs Morrissey and let her know you are home. And, Petra, remember, you now dine with me, a solicitor's daughter, and the Wheelers', simple shopkeepers. A governess should be no hardship.'

'That is different!'

'How so?' Bertram asked with a tilt of his head. 'The whole world is changing, Petra. Besides, you are in no position to cast aspersions.'

Ignoring the slight, but not finished on the subject, Petra continued, 'You will give her ideas, Bertram. She would no more think herself capable of marrying into this family than she would of marrying a prince. That is not the correct thing to do to her, surely?'

'I will give her ideas?' he teased, winking at Charlotte.

'Do not be obtuse. You know what I mean.' Petra took another slice of lemon cake. 'You must be kind to Miss Newtown, Cousin, and desist with all this correspondence, for her benefit.'

'I do not think so.' Bertram stood and took Charlotte's arm to link through his. 'I will come in with you.'

Petra scowled up at him. 'Bertram, you must listen to me, Miss Newtown will have designs above herself.'

Taking a deep breath, he took a moment to consider her words. 'I certainly hope she does. For I intend to ask her to marry me.'

CHAPTER 22

November 1916

*H*arry threw himself into a bomb crater. Rolling onto his back, he waited for his men to join him, and one by one amongst the hail of bullets they fell into the crater beside him. In the half-light of dawn, he mentally calculated the time since he had blown the whistle to start the attack for his section. Walking across a field riddled with shell holes and hearing the machine guns up ahead had been the stuff of nightmares. The horror of the slaughter would never be forgotten. How had they got it so wrong? The Germans were meant to be wiped out and fleeing. Instead they had survived the hours of Allied barrage and still been there in the trenches, waiting for their approach, ready to mow them down like ducks on a pond. Why hadn't our big guns done the job?

Glancing up as another solider slid into the crater, his arm all bloodied and torn, Harry cursed the fates that had sent them to this hell. His orders were to advance his men across no man's land and into the enemy trenches, where he would find little resistance, if any, and move on. Advance. Advance. Advance.

Chuckling at the insanity of the war, then suddenly swearing violently, Harry knelt up. His men were in a state of shock as well as resigned to the fact they were in a mess. He looked around at each of them, men he could rely on with his life. Nicholas, Shelley, Clarke, Kemp, Patterson, and so many others from the village and the mine.

He was leading them to their deaths.

For a moment he froze. His heart raced and his stomach clenched.

'Harry!' Nicholas pulled at his arm. 'Harry!'

Turning, Harry stared at him, then blinked. The deafening noise of the machine guns, bombs exploding and cries of men burst into his brain.

A shower of dirt rained over them as another shell erupted just yards away from their hole. A small pebble struck Harry in the face. The sting brought him to life and a rage engulfed him. So many times in the past, he had got his men out of difficult scrapes, and today would be no different. No matter what the odds.

'How many wounded?' he asked Nicholas.

'Just two in this hole. We are spread far, Harry.'

'Get the wounded to the back. Take their ammunition. They will have to wait for stretcher-bearers. We cannot stay here any longer, the Germans know where we are hiding.' Another shower of earth fell on them. Their ears hurting with the sound of bombs.

Harry scrambled to the lip of the crater and peeped over the edge. Ahead was nothing but smoke and dust. Distant figures were running, dodging bullets and jumping in and out of shell holes. He thought quickly, watching men die by the second.

Sliding back down, Harry had the attention of the men trapped with him. 'Right, we aren't going straight ahead. We play this smart. We are going to go sideways.' He pulled out a crumbled map of the area, which no doubt was now completely different to when it was first drawn up. He pointed to the enemy trenches that were marked on the map. 'Our objective was to take these. They were meant to be empty, the Germans fleeing. Not so. Therefore, we are going to the right. We will flank them and head for that small copse.' He pointed again to a tiny wood on the map.

They all jumped as two more soldiers scrambled into the hole. One was bleeding from a cut in the face, but nodded to Harry that he was fine to continue.

'We go out in twos. We are running this time, men, not walking like we were just an hour ago as though it was a bloody stroll at a picnic. Weave and dodge, make yourself a hard target to aim at. Do not stop! Do not drop into a shell hole. Just run. The smoke will give us cover. They are expecting a full-frontal attack. And other divisions will do that, but not me and not you.'

Crawling up the right side of the hole, Harry peered over again. A barrage of machine guns were firing on a group of men trying to cut through rolls of wire a hundred yards ahead of them. 'Let's go.'

He ran as fast as he could, weaving between fallen men, blown up ground and rolls of barbed wire. Bullets whistled past him, pinging the ground around his feet. He dodged around a shell hole and yelled at the two men crouching inside it. 'Get up! Follow me!'

He kept running as they scrambled to their feet.

At each bomb crater and to every man he saw lying on the ground waiting, he'd yell at them to get up and follow.

Ahead he saw the line of shattered trees, the copse or what remained of it. Ducking and weaving he kept going, not daring to look behind to see how the others were managing. Not all were fast runners like him, he knew, but this was the only chance they had.

Abruptly a small water filled ditch appeared in front of him, he leaped across it as easily as a gazelle might. The trees were closer now. The bullets less. He crossed a dirt farm track and then the smoke cleared. In surprise he saw too late the shallow trench dug in a line before the start of the trees.

Two Germans manned a machine gun, but both were looking at it, talking rapidly and banging at it with a hammer. Instinctively Harry yelled as he jumped into the trench. He shot the first German in the head, the next one through the chest as the soldier turned to look for his own weapon. Noise behind him made him swing around and raise his pistol but it was his own men jumping, falling into the trench.

Watching the last few men run across to them, Harry counted there was one missing. 'Who is down?'

'Kemp.' Nicholas panted.

'Bad?'

'Dead. Shot through the head right beside me. A good man.'

Harry bowed his head. Kemp, his footman at the Hall in a former life – in a world he was fast forgetting had even existed. Charlotte will be upset. She liked Kemp. But he would think about that later.

Nicholas passed him a water canteen and he took a long swig at it. 'Patterson, see if this is of any use.' He pointed to the mounted machine gun that had saved his life. It being jammed and the two Germans trying to fix it had stopped Harry and his men from being mown down.

Walking further up the trench, he studied his map and the terrain around him. Bombs had destroyed most of the trees, leaving only shattered trunks and stumps, and that gave him a view of the countryside on the other side.

Nicholas joined him. 'My God, Harry, I've never seen a man run as fast as you did just then.' He grinned.

Harry gave a wry smile. 'Being chased by my brothers made me fast. Sometimes they were faster than me though and a beating usually was the prize for being caught. I am not letting any German beat me.'

A plane flew overhead, one of theirs, and they gazed at it for a moment. It appeared so peaceful and serene up there.

Harry sighed. 'Let us get moving. We'll aim for that ridge over there. It looks like our fellows could do with our help.' He pointed into the distance where the terrain rose to a long ridge. 'Spread the men out.'

They set off at a steady pace, guns ready, and eyes watchful. Allied soldiers were ahead, battling fiercely. Gunfire vibrated the ground beneath their boots, the sound so loud, Harry had to shout his orders, and was fast losing his voice. As they walked closer to the fighting, bullets began pinging around them.

'Step up the pace!' Harry shouted, jogging now. His focus was on a group of men laying in a slight depression in the hill and bogged down by heavy fire. The enemy was further up the incline, hidden behind a sandbagged trench and in full use of their machine gun.

One of his men was hit suddenly, now they were in the German's range, and Harry screamed at them to get down.

On their stomachs they crawled on. The smell of earth, and crushed grass filled his nose, but he preferred that to the acrid smell of gunpowder. Another plane flew overhead, the enemy this time, and the pilot was dropping bombs with devastating effect. The men ahead of him was targeted. Harry yelled at them to take cover as bombs rained down. Only one bomb landed near them and as Harry watched, he saw other missiles land around them. However, these bombs didn't explode, instead smoke erupted like a cloud.

Suddenly, the soldiers ahead started scrambling about, yelling. The noise of enemy fire drowned out the words, but as the smoke disappeared, Harry watched as one man pulled at something on his kit.

The truth dawned abruptly, and Harry's blood turned to ice.

'Gas! Gas! Nicholas, tell them masks on! Gas!' he shouted as loudly as his damaged voice would allow, as he too, pulled his mask free from his belt and rammed it over his head. Of all the things he feared in this ghastly war it was the silent deadly gas that destroyed lungs and chests, blinded and burned eyes and skin.

Unable to yell now the mask was on, he hand-signalled to the men his orders. They continued on. When they were within a few yards of the holed-up soldiers, Harry urged the men to quickly lie in the depression and open fire on the German line up on the ridge.

While his men fired, Harry, keeping low, found the commanding officer of the small outfit and introduced himself as best he could with his croaking voice and wearing the mask.

'A rum deal this, isn't it?' The other officer, a Captain Hibbleston, remarked, kneeling beside Harry and taking out his map to show him their position.

Harry nodded, went to speak and then felt something slam into his shoulder and again in his left arm, knocking him onto his back in surprise.

A pain so excruciating radiated throughout his body. His mind went black. When he opened his eyes, all he saw was several gas masks leaning over him, he couldn't tell who was who. Muffled shouting and intense firing filled his ears. Fingers and hands pulled at his body, he was being dragged. He wanted to stop them for the pain was extreme, but he didn't know how to speak. Inside his head the words, stop! stop! stop! screamed repeatedly, but nothing came out.

He blinked rapidly, his eyesight blurring. The gas mask. He had to get it off, he couldn't breathe. Hands grabbed him, pinning him down. Pain shot through his entire body and he yelled. He felt as though someone was stabbing him with a red-hot poker. He grabbed the nearest solider to him and saw his fingers were bright red, covered with blood. Lifting his head, he stared down.

Everything was red, his chest, his arms, and the hands of the soldiers tending to him. His blood. He'd been shot. A tremor rippled through him, and then another. Agony. All he felt was agony. The edges of his vision blurred, softened, darkened.

Someone shook him. He fought to focus on their words as they shouted at him, but the need to close his eyes was too powerful. He gave into it gladly.

CHAPTER 23

*C*harlotte forked the last of her bacon into her mouth and folded the newspaper. A weak sun streamed through the windows. She glanced up as Winslow brought the coffee pot over and refilled her cup. 'Thank you.'

'Do you require anything else, madam?'

'No, thank you.' She smiled at him.

She had finally told Frank, Winslow and the Wheelers about McBride's attack. Winslow had alerted what men that still worked on the estate to keep a special eye out for strangers wondering about. Charlotte had informed her solicitor about the attack as well, in case anything else happened to her. Thankfully, since that day in the garden she'd not seen McBride again. However, she'd received a hate letter from him, which she'd stupidly thrown straight into the fire. Later, Frank had told her to keep any letters that arrived as evidence, and she could have slapped herself for being so thoughtless.

She kept Hannah close, using the cold winter weather as an excuse to keep her indoors. Frank insisted he accompanied Charlotte whenever she left the Hall and she was so grateful he did.

And he agreed with her that Harry mustn't know until after the war.

A sigh from Petra opposite was loud in the room. 'Papa, do you remember Jonathan Pope-Brown? He was good friends with Terrance, were in the same House at school. His sister Abigail has written to me that Jonathan was killed recently. His ship was sunk by a German U-boat. How ghastly.'

'Another good family loses a son.' Frank shook his head sadly.

'Have I met them, Petra?' Charlotte asked. She had been introduced to so many people since marrying Harry that she soon forgot their names unless they lived locally, and she visited them often.

'No, I do not think so. They live in London mostly, though they do have a pile in Norwich. I have only been there once with Terrance for a summer party.'

Frank buttered a slice of toast. 'Such a nice family, the Pope-Browns. I attended Cambridge with one of the cousins, and Terrance and Jonathan were good friends indeed. Jonathan was most upset at the boys' funeral.'

Sadness filled Petra's eyes. 'What a day that was. So many people, hundreds, came to the boys' funeral. Now death is touching so many more families. How many of those that attended are alive now?'

'Young men cut down in their prime. Unheard of.' Frank sipped his tea. 'I shall write to the Pope-Browns and offer our condolences.'

Hannah walked into the room, with Miss Newtown a step behind her. 'Good morning. Sorry we are late. We went up the nursery to watch Alice and Jeremy have their baths. I got wet by Jeremy and had to change.'

Charlotte smiled. 'He's a little tinker when having his bath. I'm sure he is splashing us on purpose.'

'He giggled so much.' Hannah laughed, helping herself to

scrambled eggs and toast from the sideboard. She sat next to Petra. 'Do you think Alice has another tooth coming through?'

'Yes!' Petra folded her letter away. 'Isn't she so clever?'

'It's stopped raining, shall we take them out for a walk after breakfast?' Hannah asked the table in general as Winslow poured her a cup of tea.

'An excellent idea,' Petra agreed.

'I have a meeting in York this afternoon, so I've time this morning.' Charlotte pushed the newspaper over to Miss Newtown. 'There are some interesting articles in there for you and Hannah to discuss.'

Hannah pouted. 'I don't like reading about the war. It makes me sad.'

'It makes us all sad, but you must learn what is happening in the world. I won't have you growing up ignorant of what is important.'

'She is a child, Charlotte,' Petra reprimanded.

Raising her chin in defiance, Charlotte stared at her sister-in-law. 'You sound like Stan, who thinks she is a baby to be spoilt and petted. Hannah is not a child, she is fourteen, a young lady, and she needs to know about the world. She will be educated as thoroughly as possible and become an adult with more thoughts in her head than running a house and what the latest fashion is.'

'Like me, you mean?' Petra scoffed.

Forking up some egg, Hannah gave a wry look. 'No point arguing with her, Petra, you won't win.'

Charlotte was about to retaliate, but stopped on seeing Winslow hesitate at the doorway before walking towards her, his eyes not leaving her face. Her heartbeat slowed as he walked, his hand visibly shaking.

'Madam, there is a telephone call from the War Office.'

Everyone stopped what they were doing and stared at Winslow.

Charlotte couldn't move. Her brain refused to think.

A sob escaped Petra, making Charlotte jump.

'I'll take the call,' Frank murmured, his voice seemingly coming from far away.

Charlotte watched him leave the room, her body stiff with tension.

What seemed like an eternity passed before Frank returned to the dining room.

'Well?' Petra fairly shrieked in her anguish. 'Who is it, Harry or Bertram?'

She heard nothing of what Frank said except for two words.

Harry wounded

Frank knelt beside Charlotte's chair. 'One of my friends, George Butte in the War Office just got news of the latest casualties and thought to ring us immediately. Harry was wounded in a battle. We are allowed to visit him once he's been assigned to a base hospital. I'll receive further news then.'

'How badly is he wounded?' Petra demanded.

'George didn't say. We must wait.'

Petra jerked to her feet. 'Wait? Wait? Why? Why must we wait with no news? How maddening is that? And how cruel to leave us in suspense?'

'Daughter, calm down.' Frank touched Charlotte's hand, his face pale. 'Did you want to go to France, my dear?'

Frozen, Charlotte gazed around the breakfast table. Hannah was crying softly, Miss Newtown comforting her, while Petra looked fit to burst with anger.

'Petra…' Charlotte put up her hand, for she could not deal with Petra's volcanic temper at this moment.

'Dearest!' In seconds, Petra came around the table and was crushing her into a tight embrace. 'He'll be fine. He's strong.'

'He must survive…' Charlotte shook, her whole body trembling so much she caused Petra's body to shake too with the force of it.

'Winslow!' Petra shouted for him even though he was still standing by the table. 'Brandy, man, get it! Quickly!' Petra turned to Miss Newtown, whom she had barely spoken to or acknowledged her presence since Bertram had revealed his marriage plans. 'Miss Newtown take Hannah upstairs. Go to the nursery, the babies will comfort her.'

Hannah left the table, however, instead of making for the door, she wrapped her arms around Charlotte. 'Harry will be fine. I know it. He wouldn't die and leave us.'

Charlotte nodded, her world shattered, her body trembling.

As Hannah and Miss Newtown left the room, Frank paced the floor. 'I couldn't find out much. There has been another large battle on the Somme. It began yesterday. Reports are suggesting immense casualties. The War Office is struggling with the details. Why do they repeat the same senseless battles over and over?'

Winslow came to stand next to Charlotte and offered her the brandy, which she sipped with shaky hands, spilling some down her front. The fiery taste burned down her throat, awakening her senses. She leaned out of Petra's embrace a little. 'I need to be in France.'

'Yes, indeed.' Petra looked to Winslow. 'When is the next train to London?'

'I believe there is a ten-thirty train running every day now from York to London. The other times have been abolished until after the war to save on coal unless it is to move troops or war supplies.'

'We need to be on it. Have Lucy pack quickly.'

'Jeremy?' Charlotte thought of her baby. 'I'm still feeding him his evening feed. He'll have to come.'

'Really? All that way in the cold?' Petra frowned. 'Will you have the time to focus on him once you're with Harry at the hospital? You will be there every day. Shall we not give Jeremy the bottle all the time now? He has it for his other feeds. Nanny can see to him and he'll be far more comfortable here.'

'Yes, of course. I didn't think…'

'I will drive the car to York, we can leave it there.' Frank headed for the door.

'Let us go upstairs and pack.' Petra took Charlotte's arm.

Charlotte shook her head. 'You must stay here, Petra. I can't be worrying about everything here, not when I need to concentrate on Harry. You need to stay as I don't know how long he'll be in hospital for.'

'You do not want me with you?'

'I do, but I need you here more.' They walked out of the room. 'Petra, you need to run the house, stay with the babies, and Hannah. Never leave Hannah alone, promise me. She's not to go out anywhere on her own. I need you to fill my role while I'm away. Can you do that for me please?'

Petra straightened her back. 'Naturally I can. I will see to everything.' They climbed the stairs. 'You go with Papa and be with Harry. You must not worry about anything here.' She paused on the landing. 'I will not have to go to the mine, will I?' She shuddered with distaste.

In other circumstances, Charlotte would have laughed and made her go just to be cheeky, but this was too serious a matter for jokes. 'No, just write a note to Mr Blaneley and inform him of the details. He'll cope. Oh, and my diary is the top drawer of my desk, you'll have to take my place in the committees, and cancel any appointments and invitations you don't want to be involved in.'

'I will see to it all. Do not worry.'

She entered her bedroom and saw Lucy flitting from drawers to wardrobe. 'Thank you, Lucy. I won't need much, there are some clothes I left at The Mews after the honeymoon, I can collect them before we get on the boat.'

'Come say goodbye in the nursery.' Petra pulled her from the packing case. 'We haven't much time.'

Upstairs, Charlotte held Jeremy close to her, smelling his sweet baby smell. His fingers grasped the lace of her blouse and he stared intently at her. He had his father's blue eyes.

'I love you little one. I'll be home soon with your Papa.' She kissed his soft hair and hurriedly gave him back to his Nanny before she burst into tears.

In quick succession she kissed Alice and Petra, smiled warmly to Miss Newtown, squeezing her hands and then hugged Hannah. 'Help Petra, won't you dearest? She'll need you.'

'Yes, I will.' Hannah nodded and Charlotte kissed her cheek before another last kiss for Jeremy and then she was hurrying from the nursery down to the bedroom, there Lucy was lifting her suitcase and a smaller bag from the bed.

'All ready, madam.'

'Thank you, Lucy.' Taking the smaller bag, she turned as Winslow came in to take the suitcase.

'Is Mr Belmont ready, Winslow?' she asked as they went down the staircase.

'In the car waiting, madam. Mrs Morrissey has packed you a small hamper for the journey as you'll not get anything decent until you're at The Mews. I'll ring ahead and let them know you're coming and to be ready for you.' Winslow opened the front door.

'Ask Mrs Jones to put some of my clothes in a case for me, I've not had time to pack too much.'

'I will. You mustn't worry about anything here. I will make sure it all runs smoothly while you're away.' He gave her a nod which spoke volumes. 'I won't let anything happen.'

'Thank you, Winslow. I rely on you too much.' Charlotte smiled at him in gratitude as she went out into the weak sunshine and climbed into the car. Winslow secured the baggage and then Frank was driving them off at speed down the drive. They had to make a dash to York to not miss the train.

'He will be all right, my dear.' Frank gave her an encouraging smile. 'He is not ready to leave his beautiful wife and son just yet, I can assure you of that.'

She nodded and hoped her father-in-law was correct because she wasn't ready for him to leave her either.

Morning traffic in York interrupted their progress to the station, but they finally made the train with barely a minute to spare. During the journey down to London she kept her thoughts from drifting into the uncertainties of how badly wounded he was, and instead focused on how wonderful it will be to see him, to tell him about Jeremy. Perhaps she should have brought the baby, it might have given Harry something to concentrate on, to take his mind of his injuries.

They caught a taxi from Kings Cross Station to the Belmont's London residence, The Mews, a four-storey townhouse on the edge of Knightsbridge. It was early evening when they walked through the front door, but after greeting Mrs Jones, the house-keeper, Frank got straight onto the telephone to ring his contacts at the War Office.

Thankfully, the house was in between a flux of soldiers. Mrs Jones, welcomed them warmly, stating the last load of soldiers had left the week before and she wasn't expecting another intake until the weekend.

Charlotte walked upstairs to the drawing room and looked around, most of the expensive ornate furniture and valuable paintings and ornaments had been stored up in the attics, stripping the house of its warmth and character. Now it was just a boarding house for soldiers recuperating from minor wounds, or those on leave who lived too far away to return home. The place depressed her, and she had no wish to bring Harry home to this, especially once another batch of soldiers filled the rooms. However, she had little choice, and once he was well enough to travel they'd go home to Belmont Hall.

She returned downstairs to Frank, who was hanging up the

telephone. He glanced at her. 'George has news that Harry is at a hospital in Abbeville.'

Nodding, Charlotte fought back tears. She was so eager to see him. 'And his condition?'

'George didn't know.' Frank looked apologetic. 'He has pulled many strings and been on the phone all day to find out where Harry is. George has managed to get us two tickets on a steamer to Le Touquet. It leaves Dover tonight. We need to get on the next train to Dover.'

'How wonderful your friend is to do that for us.' Charlotte was eager to continue their journey. The sooner they did, the sooner they'd be with Harry.

Frank nodded. 'George has been a friend since school.'

'Shall I have a tea tray made up?' Mrs Jones asked.

'There's no time, Mrs Jones. We need a cab.'

'I have your extra case here, madam.' Mrs Jones hesitated before turning away. 'How is Master Jeremy, madam?'

'As handsome as his father.' Charlotte smiled tearfully, thinking of her darling son. 'I will bring him down to see you on my next visit.'

* * *

CHARLOTTE AND FRANK made it to Abbeville the following evening. They'd crossed the Channel during the night, alert to every noise as the steamer traversed waters filled with unseen enemy boats. By morning, the boat safely docked in Le Touquet and Frank used vast amounts of money and convincing talk to secure them seats on a medical train travelling back to Abbeville.

Again, Frank used his money and influence to rent two rooms in a small lodging house on the outskirts of town, but close to where the new city of tents had been created which made up the hospitals of the British, Australian and South African wounded.

After a quick wash and change of clothes, Charlotte and

Frank left their rooms and headed for the wooden administration building.

Nervous and excited at the same time, Charlotte walked on shaky legs to the hospital with Frank. She clutched a small basket of treats for Harry, her mouth dry as they entered the building.

For two days she had thought about his injuries. What if he was missing limbs, or his face was shattered, or he was paralysed? She would deal with it all, but would he? How would Harry cope not being the man he once was?

'Ready, my dear?' Frank smiled reassuringly. 'Remember, no matter what state he is in, he is still our Harry. We will make him better.'

She nodded as an orderly greeted them, told them to wait and he'd get the matron.

A solider in pyjamas sitting in a wheelchair came out of another room next to the foyer. He nodded to Charlotte and Frank before wheeling himself down a ramp and outside. Two nurses exited one room and disappeared into another room opposite. There was a yell and a cry of pain coming from that room until the door closed shutting off the noise. Behind them a young woman came through the front door carrying a box.

'It's very busy.' Charlotte watched as a young nurse and an older woman came towards them, discussing the papers they held.

'Good morning to you both.' The older woman having dismissed the young nurse came to stand before them. 'I am Matron Donaldson. Can I be of assistance?'

Frank bowed slightly. 'Matron, I am Mr Francis Belmont and this is my daughter-in-law, Mrs Charlotte Belmont. We have come to visit my son, Captain Henry Belmont.'

'Ah, Captain Belmont. He arrived straight from a CCS.'

'CCS?' Charlotte enquired.

'Casualty clearing station, a hospital a few miles from the

frontline of battle.' The matron glanced at Frank. 'You received word quickly, Mr Belmont.'

'Friends in certain places, Matron.'

She inclined her head. 'Of course.' She read through her list of papers. 'Belmont. Yes, come this way. You will have to forgive us today as we have been run off our feet with this new intake of wounded. They sent us more than we were expecting.' She led them outside and across a small grassed area and into the edge of a vast network of marquees.

Inside one of the marquees, she stopped by a small desk near the entrance. 'Captain Belmont is very weak. Infection has entered his wounds.' Matron read from a piece of paper on the desk. 'His bullet wounds are severe, and now this infection... but I'll have the doctor tell you more when he sees you later.'

'He will survive though?' Charlotte whispered, her breath suspended in her throat.

'He has the best chance now he is here with us. Come this way.'

Charlotte felt Frank's hand on the small of her back as they walked past wounded men in the white sheeted beds. Those that were awake watched them pass with no expression on their faces.

At the last bed on the right, Matron stopped.

Charlotte put her hand over mouth to stifle a gasp. Harry lay there eyes closed, or someone who vaguely resembled Harry.

Matron adjusted the already straight sheet. 'Usually our men are not so dirty but apparently the battle was a large one, a big push before winter sets in, and the medical staff were overwhelmed. We will wash him properly once he's fully awake. His wounds are sterile now, but the infection would have got in on the battlefield or the casualty clearing station long before he reached us. They do the best they can out there but there are more wounded than staff.' Matron brought over another chair so they each had one. 'Sit beside him and talk to him. Let him know you're here. I'll be back shortly.'

Charlotte sat on the edge of the chair, placing the basket at her feet. She took Harry's hand and stared at her husband. Even under the grime of the battlefield, his skin was the colour of ash, except for his thin face, which was patchy red and flushed. His dark hair held more grey now than last time she saw him, and was matted in places. Tiny spots of blood were splattered across his neck and through his beard stubble. He stank. There was no other word for it. He smelled of dirt and blood and gunpowder and acrid body odour and other smells Charlotte couldn't identify.

Tears fell over her lashes and ran unchecked down her cheeks.

Frank, too, was crying, holding Harry's other hand. 'I do not recognise him. He is my son, and I know I have not seen him for ten years, but I thought I would know him.'

'He doesn't usually look like this.' Charlotte whispered. 'He was strong and handsome, so handsome... and healthy. He...he...' Her voice broke. Instinctively she bent over him and kissed his dry lips. 'Harry, darling, it's me, Charlotte. I'm here, and I won't leave you.'

They sat beside him for an hour before the Matron brought the doctor to them. Major Moore appeared tired and stressed, but he shook their hands, gave a small smile and read from a thin file he carried. 'Captain Belmont was shot by a machine gun. The bullets hit fast and explosive as you can imagine. The spray of bullets hit him here,' the doctor pointed to Harry's bandaged upper arm, 'then went across his chest, narrowly missing his heart and throat and across to his other shoulder. Thankfully no important arteries were hit, otherwise he wouldn't be with us now. From his notes, he was on the battlefield for some time before the stretcher-bearers could get to him and so his men carried him to the casualty clearing station.'

'Are all the bullets out?' Frank asked quietly.

'No. The battle was a large offensive and the medical staff

could not cope with the sheer numbers of casualties, I've been told. A doctor there was able to take out three bullets before the Captain was loaded onto transport, but two are lodged deeper in his chest. If they had tried to do it in the clearing station, he would likely have died on the table. He was transported here last night. However, I'm afraid infection has set in. He will go into theatre very shortly to have the other bullets removed.' Major Moore sighed. 'I will not give you any falsehoods. Captain Belmont is very ill. He is lucky to still be alive. I cannot give you my word that he is out of danger. It will be a waiting game. His body and mind has been through a great deal...' He fiddled with the file he held. 'You must, of course, think positively. Only, I—'

'We understand, Doctor,' Charlotte interrupted, knowing what he was going to say, yet she didn't want the words spoken out loud. 'We are here now and although I am not a nurse, I can assist the nursing staff here and I can give my husband all the attention he needs.'

'Indeed, Mrs Belmont, but...'

Charlotte stopped him with a smile. 'My husband will not leave me, Major Moore. I simply will not allow it. I need him and he needs me.'

The major nodded. 'Then I will say no more and leave you to it, Mrs Belmont. Your husband will be taken soon and you may wait until he returns.'

Once he and the Matron had left, Charlotte turned back to Frank. 'I will stay here. Did you want to go back to the lodging to rest?'

'Dearest, we can take it in turns. You'll exhaust yourself if you don't get enough rest. Let us take it one day at a time.'

'The nursing staff have so many men to take care of, I can do this. I can stay with him so he's not alone.'

'We will do it together. You are not alone in this.'

'Thank you.'

'Now, I will go and see if I can cajole a cup of tea out of one of the nurses.' He gave her a grin and left her alone to sit with Harry.

After a few minutes, Charlotte stopped a passing nurse. 'Excuse me, could I have a bowl, soap, hot water and a cloth please? I want to wash my husband.'

'I don't think that is allowed, I'm sorry.' The nurse looked no more than eighteen years old and as timid as a mouse.

'My husband needs washing. I'm not asking anyone to do it, just show me where to get what I need, and I'll see to him.'

'Matron won't like it, I'm sorry, I can't help you.' The nurse scuttled off.

'Hey, missus.' The man in the bed next to Harry, spoke in a loud whisper. His legs were under a cage, keeping the blankets off him.

Distracted, Charlotte turned to him. 'Yes?'

'In that little curtained room over there, you'll find what you need, though not hot water.'

'Thank you.' She smiled at him and hurried to the curtain opposite, which was simply a large pantry filled with medical supplies. Taking a small bowl, soap and a cloth, plus a clean white towel. Charlotte slipped out of the pantry and back to Harry's bed without being seen.

'There's water in that jug, missus.' The man pointed again at the bedside table a few beds down from his. 'It won't be hot though, just room temperature.'

Charlotte retrieved the jug and set about washing Harry. The cool water must have felt refreshing on his hot flushed face, though he didn't move as she wiped the soapy cloth over his bristled chin and jaw, his cheeks and forehead and lastly, she tenderly wiped his eyes. The water in the bowl turned a dingy grey brown.

The man in the next bed laughed. 'Matron will have you thrown out!'

'She can try!' Charlotte grinned back, hoping she wasn't hurting him in any way. She couldn't wash his hair or shave him yet, but at least his face was clean and the flush redness had receded a little. His forehead felt a little cooler to the touch.

When she had finished, she sat down, and pulled the newspaper from the basket and began to read softly to Harry, hoping that the sound of her voice would wake him.

Frank returned with a cup of tea for her. 'Are you hungry?'

'Thank you.' She took the tea from him. 'No, I'm not, besides, there are some oat biscuits in the basket I brought. Do you want one?'

'I will, yes, for Harry won't be having them today and we can always bring him more.' Frank took two and Charlotte offered some to the man in the next bed, which he gratefully took with a smile of thanks.

Frank sipped his tea. 'Harry looks a little better. Not so red in the face… Has he had a wash while I have been gone?'

'Yes. I did it.'

'You?' His eyes widened, but as another nurse came to check on the man in the next bed, Frank quickly changed the subject. 'What else is in the basket?'

Charlotte blushed. 'I was silly really, bringing all this when I didn't know the extent of his injuries. I just thought he might want some comforts. I feel foolish now. He is in no state…'

'You were thinking of him, my dear, there is nothing wrong in that. Tell me what you brought.'

'An Anthony Trollope book, a photograph of Jeremy, a small flask of whiskey, in case he fancied a tot at night, those biscuits, and some of Mrs Morrissey's chutney from home. This newspaper, clean pyjamas and a new shaving kit.'

'Well, I am sure he will enjoy it all when he wakes up.' Frank smiled.

If he wakes up.

No, she mustn't think like that.

Charlotte sipped her tea, shying away from the thoughts of Harry not ever waking up. He *would* open his eyes for her, she knew it.

CHAPTER 24

Abbeville, France

*H*arry opened his eyes to a bright room, sunshine streaming in through the window, hurting his eyes for a moment until they adjusted. He was in a wooden hut, bare of comforts. Without moving his head, and scared at what he might find, he gazed slowly down at his body covered in a white sheet and blanket. He gently flexed his feet a little and closed his eyes in grateful relief that he still had his legs.

He lay completely still for he could feel the restricting bandages about his upper body and arms and he didn't want to move in case he caused pain. Yet his mind worked overtime, his eyes scanning about the room. He remembered bits of the battle, of talking to Nicholas, the bombardment, running, smoke and gunfire, a plane, of being under attack, more running…

Was he still in France, or had he been taken prisoner by the Germans? A shiver of fear ran down his body. A dragging ache

265

started to radiate from his chest. Sweat broke out on his forehead.

Noises came from outside, he turned his head, bracing himself to see an enemy uniform. As the door opened and a figure came closer, he blinked rapidly, not believing his eyes, Charlotte? No, it couldn't be. She wasn't in France. Was he dreaming then, or even dead?

His beautiful beloved wife came closer, tears filling her eyes, her smile wide and full of love. Then she was kissing him, raining kisses all over his face, telling him how much she loved him and he relaxed, for if he was dead or dreaming then he was happy to stay that way.

He raised his arms up to hold her and a sharp intense pain hit his body. He yelled, frightening Charlotte. Pain washed over him in waves. As though someone was opening his chest up with a knife, the agony rendered him speechless and out of breath. He vomited over the side of the bed. The action sending the pain up another level. He cried out and then all was black.

* * *

CHARLOTTE RAN OUTSIDE for the doctor or a nurse, her heart pounding in her chest. The wooden huts available for wounded officers lined the edge of the bigger marquees where recovering soldiers rested. She ran into the first marquee. In the far corner she spotted Major Moore and hurried to him. He rushed with her back to Harry, who lay unconscious.

Major Moore frantically examined him for a pulse. 'It's there and strong. He's just passed out from the pain I would think.' He rattled off instructions to Matron who just entered the hut and then turned to Charlotte with a small smile. 'He woke, Mrs Belmont. That is a good sign.'

'But he...' She waved her hand shakily towards Harry, not

finding the words. The shock in seeing him awake and then collapse shook her badly.

'He will be better now, Mrs Belmont, I believe it and so must you. He survived the operation and has woken after two days and his temperature has gone. We must let him sleep again, a natural healthy sleep and you will see a difference in him, I am sure.'

She looked over at her darling man, whose face had been ash grey but now the colour was seeping back to his cheeks. Her joy at finding him awake had been momentous, only for it all to be shattered so quickly.

'Mrs Belmont. Please, return to your lodgings and rest. The hard work will begin when your husband wakes again, for he is going to need help and understanding as he recovers from his injuries. I insist you do not come back here until tomorrow morning, when you've had a good night's sleep and food. Will you do that for me please?'

'But I can—'

'No, Mrs Belmont, I insist this time. You've been wonderful sitting by your husband's side night and day, but as I just mentioned, you're going to need your strength now. Please, go and rest. I will see you tomorrow.'

'Very well. His father will come and sit with him. However, if there is any change in him you will send for me straight away?' At his nod, she went to the bed and placed a kiss on Harry's forehead, touching his cheek softly. 'I'll be back in the morning, darling.'

Reluctantly, she left the hospital and strolled along the dirt roads, heading for the town. Instead of going to the lodging house, she made her way into the old town. The sun shone from a cloudless blue sky and although it wasn't very warm, many town's people and soldiers were out enjoying the weak sunshine and the moment of peace. If you ignored the fact there were soldiers walking the streets, you wouldn't know there was a war on.

Taking a deep breath, Charlotte smiled at nothing, just happy that Harry had woken. She couldn't wait to tell Frank and to telephone the Hall and let them all know he had opened his eyes and looked at her. The doctor had faith that Harry was over the worst, so she had to believe that too.

She turned the corner and waited for a black car to drive past, only for it to slow and stop in front of her. Her mind full of Harry, she failed to recognise McBride at first, and then awareness of him had her stepping back, the old fear churning her stomach.

He smiled evilly, looking her up and down. 'I knew if I waited around these streets long enough I would see you, but this was quicker than I expected. I only found out yesterday that Belmont was wounded and that you had actually travelled here to be with him.'

'Leave me alone.' Her throat dried, remembering his attack. Was he to finish the job now?

'I will never leave you alone. I only wish I had succeed to choking the life out of you months ago. You've cost me a lot of money, my dear.'

'Go away.' Charlotte started walking, forcing her frozen legs to work.

McBride caught up with her, walking beside her as though they were best of friends. 'So, tell me, how is it being a mother?'

'I will not tell you anything.' She crossed the street. Ahead was a small grassland that people used as a park, and as a short cut to the next road. Charlotte hurried her steps, eager to cross the park, bringing her another street closer to the lodgings.

He laughed at her efforts. 'You can't outrun me, sweet Charlotte. I will always dog your every step until the day you die, which if I have my way will be sooner rather than later.'

His words chilled her, she stumbled, but kept going.

'So, my girl, what about your husband? Is he in a bad way? I heard his injuries were severe.'

Incensed suddenly, she rounded on him. 'Who told you? How do you always know everything about me?'

He laughed as though it was a huge joke. 'I have eyes and ears everywhere, my dear. My money passes through a lot of hands and I have friends in high places. You must surely understand that by now? I was heading back to London from Paris when I got word of Belmont. I changed my plans so I could see you.'

'Why though?' she muttered through clenched teeth. 'Why do you still care? Why can't you forget about me? Are you still after my inheritance? Because you're wasting your time. I've willed it all to my son.'

'Then I'll have to take your son then, won't I?' He laughed maliciously, then grew serious. 'It's not about money any more. You wronged me, Charlotte. I changed *everything* for you. We would have been happy if you'd just given me a *chance*. Now, I want what is mine. And that is *you*. I'll even take on your brat.'

She stiffened at the mention of her baby. She'd never let McBride near Jeremy. 'You want to kill me, then do it! Do it!' She raised her chin in anger. If getting killed would rid Harry, Hannah and Jeremy of this man, then she'd do it.

He spread his arms wide. 'I was in a rage when I said that. I didn't mean it. Where would the fun be in killing you when tormenting is more exciting?'

'You nearly choked me to death. You meant it.' She spied a silver handled dagger inside his jacket when he opened his arms. 'I'm tired of all this. Just do it and be done with it.'

'Don't be silly, Charlotte. I don't want to harm you. I love you. And I'll love your child, and Hannah too.'

'You don't know the meaning of love.'

'Don't make me angry,' he snapped. 'Why must you always be difficult?' He grabbed her arm. 'Come let us go somewhere quiet to talk.'

'No!' With speed she didn't credit herself of having, she

whipped out the knife from his jacket pocket and plunged it into his stomach.

McBride stared at her, his mouth falling open. He looked down at the wound. 'You stabbed me...'

Dropping the knife, Charlotte backed away, horrified at what she had done. She shook her head wordless, then started running. She gathered her skirt higher so she could run faster, expecting any moment for him to grab her.

She ran the next few streets without being aware of where she was going, just needing to get to the safety of the lodging house. A stitch gripped her side as she ran. She made a wrong turn and cried out in panic of getting lost. Fearful of being caught by McBride, she ran on, turning at the next street and making her way down a dirt lane behind one of the shopping streets.

At last she found the right street and dashed through the gate of the lodging house. Crashing open the front door, Charlotte skidded to a halt on the wooden floor and stared up at Frank who was descending the stairs.

'Charlotte? What is it? Has Harry...' Frank hurried to her, taking her by the arm he led her into the front room. 'What has happened?' His face lost its colour.

'I-I-I...' she gasped, out of breath from running. Her body shook so bad so could hardly stand upright and if Frank let go of her arm, she would fall.

'Charlotte, dearest, you're scaring me.' Frank eased her onto the small sofa. Her hat was hanging on only by one pin and he took it out and placed it on the small table. 'What has happened, dear girl? Has Harry...gone?'

'No.' She swayed. 'I stabbed him.'

Frank reared away from her. 'Who? Harry?'

'No. Mc-McBride.'

'McBride?'

A sob escaped her, and like the bursting of a dam, she sobbed brokenheartedly at what she had done, the worry and the stress of not only McBride, but Harry, too.

Frank cradled her to him and let her cry. Eventually when she could talk, she told him everything.

'I want you to go upstairs and lie down for a time.' Frank kissed the top of her head. 'I shall go out and see if the fellow is still about.'

'What if I have killed him?' Charlotte shuddered, calmer now. 'I'll be hanged.'

'I doubt that you have done so. You may have only pierced his belly. Rats like him have a habit of surviving.'

'Good God. What have I done?' She groaned, her eyes wide with fear.

'McBride is a monster and obviously a criminal, he'll not go to the police. He'd not want them meddling in his business. Try not to think of it. You need to rest.' Standing, Frank helped her to her feet. 'Go upstairs. I will be as quick as I can.'

When he had left, Charlotte stood staring out of the window, finding it difficult to function properly. How had she done such a thing? In that blood heated moment, she had wanted to kill him and tried to!

'Madame Belmont?'

Charlotte glanced at the French housekeeper, but remained standing near the window.

'Monsieur Belmont…good?' she asked in her broken English.

'He woke up.' Fresh tears trickled down Charlotte's cheeks. Such a momentous thing happened and McBride had overshadowed it.

'Fantastic!'

Charlotte nodded, staring out at the deserted street. 'I want him back in England. We need to be with our son.' Her voice wobbled again but she fought more tears. Crying wouldn't help the situation. She had to forget McBride and concentrate on Harry.

A sudden thought hit her. What if McBride went to the hospital to see a doctor. He'd be close to Harry. He could harm Harry when no one was looking. Frantic at the thought that Harry could be in danger, she dashed from the room.

'Madame?'

'I'm going to the hospital.' She hurried from the house without pause for her bag or her hat. The black shoes she wore weren't meant for running in and she felt every uneven surface through the soles as she ran. Uncaring of what the neighbours or people in the streets thought of her, she ran as fast as she could in her tight skirt, lifting the hem to free her movements.

'Charlotte!'

She was hauled by the arm to an abrupt stop, Frank's astonished expression plain to see. 'What are you doing woman?'

'Harry...McBride...he might hurt Harry.' Her lungs were bursting.

Frank drew her to one side to let a young woman pass them. 'I've been to the hospital. Harry is fine, sleeping. McBride can't get to Harry. I've told the staff he is to have no visitors except you and I.' He turned her about and headed for their lodgings. 'You need to rest and change. I will go back to the hospital and stay with Harry all night. You can relieve me in the morning.'

'But—'

'No buts,' he said sternly. 'Do you want Harry to see you like this when he wakes up?'

She shook her head, aware of her hair falling about her face. Her feet throbbed. She must look a sight.

'Charlotte, I know you must be worried, I do understand. However, Harry is our priority. This McBride fellow will be tending to his wound. He won't be bothering you for a while I shouldn't think, and in my mind, he deserved to be stabbed. He's a bully and a beast who'll stop at nothing until he gets what he wants. We can no longer tolerate this man's evilness. I will not allow you to feel guilty for what you have done. He has done nothing but threaten you and those you love. He deserved what he got and more.'

Frank paused at the foot of their front steps. 'I want you to promise me something.'

'Yes, what is it?'

'Think no more of McBride. Concentrate on Harry. Yes?'

'Yes.' She nodded. 'I'll try. It's not easy, Frank.'

'I know, but leave it to me, will you? Will you trust me to sort this out?'

She nodded.

'Good. Now go on inside and I will see you in the morning.' Frank kissed her cheek and left her.

* * *

WHEN CHARLOTTE CAME DOWNSTAIRS the next morning, the house was a hive of activity. Soldiers were lodging in the other rooms and the place was overrun with them. She stood at the bottom of the stairs pulling on her gloves, and pinning on her hat. Breakfast no longer seemed appetising surrounded by so many men and she left before anyone spoke to her.

Walking fast, she scanned the streets for a large black car and McBride. At this time of the morning, the streets rang with the clip clop of horse's hooves as the bin men, the milkman and other trades started to make their rounds of the neighbourhood. The smell of freshly baked bread lingered in the air.

There was no McBride.

Charlotte entered the hospital grounds and made her way past the marquees to the row of wooden huts. At Harry's hut, she paused and smiled at a nurse and an orderly who were coming down the steps as she went up them. The orderly held the door open for her.

Inside, she relaxed her shoulders, realising how tense she'd been since leaving the house.

Major Moore stood at the end of Harry's bed reading notes in a file. He looked up. 'Mrs Belmont. You did as you were told. I am most impressed.'

She glanced at Harry, who slept, and smiled back at the doctor. 'You should be impressed. I don't often do as I'm told.'

'I don't doubt that for a moment.' He chuckled. 'But I must say you look better for it.'

'Thank you.' She had dressed carefully, wearing a navy-blue suit with the skirt and jacket having black embroidery at the hem and cuffs, a matching little navy hat with a peacock feather on the side of it. Her hair she had washed and bundled up in a net under the brim of her hat. She'd applied light makeup to her pale face, hoping it hid the shadows under her eyes, for despite the Doctor's instructions, she hadn't slept well at all.

'You'll be happy to know your husband is doing well. He woke during the night, and had a drink before sleeping again. I am most encouraged.'

Relief flowed through Charlotte like a tide on a beach. She sagged and the doctor held her elbow to steady her. Tears rose but she smiled. They were happy tears. She gazed at Harry, who had healthy colour back in his face.

'Now, Mrs Belmont, everything will be fine.' His kind voice soothed her. 'Your husband is seriously injured, that is true, but he should make a full recovery. In under a year he will be back to normal.'

'I'm so pleased to hear that. Yes, indeed I am. I'll be even more happier when he comes home to Yorkshire with me and never has to return to war again.'

'I'm afraid if the war drags on for more years, there is every chance the War Office will want your husband back out in the field. Men of his experience are hard to come by now.'

She stared at him as though he had grown two heads. 'No!' She didn't mean to shout, but the word exploded from her like a firecracker.

'Mrs Belmont—'

'No!' Her hands clenched into fists. 'He will not be going back. He's done enough, done his share.'

'I understand, really I do—'

'Then you will write a report to say he is unfit for duty!'

'We will assess that in due course. There is time yet.'

'I will not have him leave us again.' She glared at him, hating him for mentioning the possibility of Harry going back to war. 'I apologise, Major. It is just that I…' She shook her head wordlessly, overcome.

'I understand. You've been brave, hoping for the best and secretly fearing the worst. It is only natural. This process is hard for everyone.' Major Moore gathered his paperwork. 'I have sent your father-in-law for some breakfast while I did some tests on Captain Belmont. He should be back soon.'

'Thank you.'

'I'll be return this afternoon.' He closed the door softly behind him.

Charlotte took the chair next the bed and moved it a little closer so she could sit and hold Harry's hand.

Charlotte's heart leapt in her chest as Harry suddenly opened his eyes. 'My love, I've been so worried,' she whispered against his cheek.

He looked pale, unshaven and thin, but his smile for her was full of love and she kissed his hand.

'I am sorry to have put you through it, darling.' Harry cupped her cheek, his gaze roaming her face. 'You are so beautiful.'

'Well, you aren't at the minute.' She touched his bearded jaw.

He laughed then grimaced. 'Don't make me laugh, my love. I'll burst my stitches.'

'Are you in a lot of pain, my love?'

'It's not too bad. They gave me something for it during the night.' He held her hand. 'I thought I had dreamed you were here. I thought I might be dead.'

'You are far from dead,' she said with a slight shiver. 'We will get you home, back to the Hall, where you can recover. Jeremy needs to meet his papa.'

'I long to see him. Sometimes I feel as though he isn't real. That my old life is no longer.'

'Your life is there, waiting for you to return home. We are all just waiting. Waiting for this war to finish so we can get back to living our lives.'

'It was wonderful to see Father when I woke up.' Harry rubbed his thumb absentmindedly over the back of her hand he held. 'He was gone too long, and I told him so. I have missed him.'

'I like him. We have become close.'

'After the war he is going away again, and taking Petra and Alice.'

'Yes.' She had nothing else to say on the matter as she thought it a good idea for Petra to start a new life.

'We talked during the night. The pain was making it difficult for me to sleep, and poor Father was most uncomfortable on that hard chair. We talked.' Harry squeezed her hand. 'He told me of the incident with McBride yesterday, and of those that have happened while I've been away. You should have told me about them, but I do understand why you didn't tell me.'

'I didn't want you to worry.'

He lifted her hand up and kissed it. 'You must have been so scared.'

She hung her head, ashamed. 'I should never have stabbed him yesterday. If I have killed him I will go to jail, leaving you and Jeremy.'

'You should never have been put in that position, my darling. He deserves what he got, and maybe it will be enough for him to leave you alone now. He knows you'll fight back. Bullies don't like that.'

'You don't think he'll go to the police?' Fear filled her throat.

'No. Men like him don't work that way.'

Charlotte bowed her head, exhausted by the torment. 'I'm so tired of it, Harry.'

'I know, my love. It has to stop and it will.'

She stared at him. 'How? There is nothing we can do. There is no evidence he is doing anything to me. If I went to the police, it would simply be his word against mine.'

'Father has contacts.' A spasm crossed Harry's face as pain shot through him.

'I think you need to sleep. You're in pain and tired.'

'I want to talk to you though.'

She kissed him lightly. 'I'm not going anywhere. Have a little sleep.' Charlotte looked up as a nurse came into the hut.

'Captain Belmont, do you need medication for the pain?'

He nodded, his face pale.

Charlotte squeezed his hand. 'I'll go see if I can find a cup of tea while you have your medicine. I want you asleep by the time I return.'

At the door, she stopped to watch the nurse administer medicine to him and sent a silent thank you to the fates that had spared her husband.

CHAPTER 25

Belmont Hall, April 1917

*G*ingerly, Harry side-stepped Mighty, who was thrashing his head about in the courtyard of the stables. The big horse was eager to go galloping over the fields, but unable to do so. Harry wished he could jump up on his back and ride him as he used to do, but despite his injuries healing well, his body wasn't ready to be put to the test on Mighty, and nor did he want to bring attention to him.

Hoskins gathered Mighty's reins. 'I'll put him in the top field, sir, for an hour if you are happy for me to?'

'Yes, very well. If he is seen, then there is nothing much we can do about it. The poor fellow is going crazy being cooped up every day.'

'He's not doing too bad, sir, I take him on night rides at two in the morning. No one is about then.'

'Did we do the right thing, Hoskins? Hiding him from the

army? It was extremely selfish of me. But I was giving up my life, I thought that was a fair trade.'

'Aye, you did right, sir. The army got ten very good horses from our Home Farm, they even took some of the pit ponies and Miss Hannah's pony, which broke her heart. I wasn't going to let them take this stallion that is worth more than most men's yearly wage, to be cannon fodder!'

Harry smiled at Hoskins's vehemence. The older man was such a good loyal member of staff.

'Sir, I think this estate has done more than its fair share of giving to this war, don't you? Mrs Belmont works herself to skin and bone with all the work she does for her committees and running this place. We've given men, horses, coal and food. I think we can keep Mighty.'

Harry understood his meaning. 'You could be right, Hoskins, but we must all do our duty. All the land estates are being just as generous as us.'

'Aye, sir, some more than others though.' Hoskins opened the half door on Mighty's stable. 'I'd best get this irritable fellow out onto the grass. He needs to blow off some steam.'

Harry nodded. 'Don't we all, Hoskins, don't we all?' With a loving pat on Mighty's neck, Harry turned away and headed back to the house.

Winds bit deep into the countryside. Spring failed to warm the country, as though winter still wanted to linger and hinder the people.

He'd been home for nearly four months; they had seemed the longest four months of his life.

Strolling through the dismal gardens, depleted of flowers long ago, and now used as vegetable plots, he tried to summon some enthusiasm for something, anything. He wished he could be interested in the estate, the mine, the village, his other businesses, even his own family. However, it was as though his mind was now only programmed for one thing, getting back to his unit and finishing this war. He knew without a doubt that within a few more months he would return to France. He missed his men. He had a job to do. Letters from Nicholas came regularly and only heightened his sense of longing to be there with them. They were his men, men who he had fought alongside with, men he had watched die, men who had done amazing feats of bravery and survival. He missed them and he needed to go back to protect them.

He paused by the fish pond, not really seeing the red carp bob to the surface hoping for food. He glanced up at the Hall's windows, not wanting to go inside, then he saw her, Charlotte, standing on the path, watching him, waiting.

His heart thumped in his chest. How he loved her, yet they had argued so much in the last month as he became healthier and more mobile. When he first arrived home, he spent the first month mostly in their room, sleeping, eating and talking to Charlotte. For a while they could just forget everything going on outside of that room and be together with Jeremy.

But as he became better, and started leaving the bedroom, he soon grew restless. He read the newspapers every day, devouring all the details in the war articles. Worry about his men gnawed at him constantly. They needed him. He was their captain, their leader. When he voiced this to Charlotte, however, she grew angry. She refused to speak to him about returning to France and a wedge was growing between them.

Now, as Harry raised a hand to her, taking a step towards where she stood, he had a sudden urge to make everything all right between them. Only, she walked away, wiping her eyes.

Pushing his hands into his coat pockets, he sat on the pond's stone wall, surprised at how fast they had grown apart. She wanted him home, safe and well. While he wanted to be back over there fighting, doing his bit. When the war was over he'd be the man she wanted, the man he was before, but not now.

'Ah, there you are, my son.' His father rounded the path and came to sit beside him. He was wrapped warmly with a thick scarf and long coat. His father wasn't handling the spring chill very well after ten years in the tropics. 'I have been looking for you.'

'Why?'

'I need you to come with me, if you feel up to it?'

'Of course.' Anything was better than wrestling with the demons in his head.

Intrigued, Harry stood and followed his father around the side of the hall to his car parked on the drive. He hadn't even wanted to drive it since returning home.

His father pulled on his gloves. 'It will require an overnight stay, maybe two. We are using the last of our petrol horde. I have already taken the liberty of asking Winslow to pack you a bag, and I have told Charlotte we are spending the night with a friend of mine near Hull.'

Harry paused on opening the car door. 'I shall go say goodbye to her.'

'Do not bother, she has gone. She left just now with Petra, riding their bicycles to go to a meeting in the village with the war widows about the Christmas fundraiser.'

'Without saying goodbye to me when she knew I was going away for the night?' He joined his father in the car and they drove away from the Hall. Hurt knifed him, Charlotte would never normally have done that.

'Son, I cannot tell you how a woman's mind works, no one knows that. But what I will tell you is this. She loves you, and is heartbroken right now. You have pushed her away.'

'I have not.'

'Yes, you have. Do not argue with me, for I have been witnessing it since you left your bed. You have taken no interest in anything since you've been back here. Have you any idea what Charlotte has taken on in your absence? She has the Hall, the estate, the mine, the people of the village, her various war committees, not to mention the business of McBride, and the happiness of Hannah and Jeremy, Petra, myself, and now you.' His father gave him a stern look. 'Having you home should have lightened the load. But you have not cared about any of those things. You have selfishly allowed her to carry on.'

'She does not need my help. The doctor told me I was to rest and heal, nothing else!' he defended hotly, stung by his father's words.

'And it has worked, physically. But mentally? No.' His father turned the car onto a road leading north, away from the village and towards York.

Silence stretched between them until Harry took a deep breath and glanced at his father. 'I feel that I am suspended between two lives. One is here, the other is in France. My mind doesn't know what to do as I belong to neither right now.'

His father sighed. 'That makes sense.'

'I will make it up to her, when this is all over.' He winced as they bumped over a large hole.

'Yes, you will, for you will not find a better woman, I can assure you of that. You do not want to destroy your marriage and the love you have for each other. Don't do as I did with your mother. I was selfish, always going off and focusing on my own interests without thought to anyone. Her love for me died long before your brothers died. Their deaths were the final straw for her.'

'I know. I will not fail Charlotte.'

'We both won't.'

Harry looked quizzically at his father. 'What do you mean and where are we going?'

'To catch a train to London.'

'London? Why?'

'To give Charlotte one less thing to worry about. We are going to finish this McBride business.'

* * *

CHARLOTTE SIPPED HER TEA, warming her stockinged feet by the fire in the shop's back room with Bessie. Petra had gone home with a headache and Stan was outside brushing the mud off her boots, after giving her a telling off about riding to the village from the Hall with only Petra for company as her sister-in-law would be no match if McBride stopped them.

'He'll walk you home,' Bessie said, passing her another slice of currant cake.

'I have my bicycle. I can ride back by myself, it'll not be dark for hours yet.' Since the stabbing, she'd grown hard concerning McBride. She'd received no letters from him, and her solicitor hadn't found anything about his possible death. If he had survived, he'd gone underground again. And, as much as he frightened her, she'd become tired of jumping at every shadow. The state of her marriage was uppermost in her mind and it's all she could think about. McBride no longer held her in his grip.

'And what if McBride is about?' Bessie gave her a look of rebuke. 'Why did you put yourself in danger like that?'

'Because the one old horse we have left is being used in the fields, so I couldn't use the cart and Frank took the last of the petrol to go see his friend in Hull. He's taken Harry with him, get him away from the Hall for a bit. I'm rather glad they have gone in a way. The atmosphere is too tense.' Charlotte eyed the cake. 'I do not need a second slice, Bessie.'

'You do and you will eat it. I'll not have my cake go wasting and you are nothing but skin and bones. Doesn't that cook up at the Hall feed you?'

'Yes, of course. I just don't have the time to eat much lately. I'm not feeding Jeremy any more, so I don't have to worry about my milk. It's gone.'

'Then make the time for yourself.' Bessie shovelled some more coal on the fire. 'How is *he*?'

Charlotte sighed, knowing Bessie meant Harry. 'He is regaining his strength and physical movement more each day. On his last visit to London to see the doctor they encouraged him to do as much activity as he can manage. Well, you know, Harry. He has taken that as a challenge. He has increased his eating, asking Mrs Morrissey to cook him hearty beef stews and the like. He walks for miles every day, spending hours down at the stables, though he hasn't ridden Mighty yet. I think he is worried the pull of the reins might tear at his wounds. But generally, he is doing very well. I'm surprised at how fast he has recovered.'

'He ought to be grateful he still has that horse, when the army took everyone else's.'

'Yes, well, we hide him very thoroughly. It is Hoskins main task in life to not let Harry lose Mighty.'

Bessie sat down at the table and drank some of her tea. 'And what of his mind?'

'That I don't know, Bessie.' Charlotte fiddled with the teaspoon on her saucer. 'Harry doesn't talk to me now, not like he used to. And when we do talk, we argue. He thinks only of going back to France. I need him here.'

'This war!' Bessie thumped the table making Charlotte and cutlery jump. 'Do you know Mrs Tidbury lost her son? The news came through yesterday. And Elsie O'Conner's husband is gravely wounded. He's in Harry's unit.'

Charlotte closed her eyes. 'I will have to let Harry know when he comes back. It'll be another reason why he needs to get back over there as quickly as possible.'

Reaching across the table, Bessie took Charlotte's hand in her own. 'Listen to me, lass. I know it's hard. I can't imagine how I'd feel if Stan was sent over, and he probably will soon, if they keep raising the age limit. He's sixty next month and if this war keeps going, he'll be khaki before we know it.'

'God, I hope not, Bessie. They wouldn't take them that old.

Besides, I couldn't stand having another loved one in battle. I can't cope as it is with just Harry and Bertram and Nicholas.'

'Lass, this village has lost ten men, and what two from the Hall, and another four from the pit? Everyone is suffering. No one is alone in the misery that is this war. This doesn't just affect you, lass, it affects us all.'

Charlotte sat straighter. 'What are you saying?'

Taking a deep breath, Bessie let it out in a sigh. 'I'm saying, stop being so hard on him. He needs to go back for his own peace of mind. I've seen it in the other men when they come into the shop. They are happy to be home for three days or whatever, but longer than that they're eager to return and be with their pals. They carry a guilt of not being there to watch each other's back. You've got to let Harry go.'

'I have no choice!'

Bessie raised her eyebrows in reproach. 'You have a choice to let him go with your blessing or with a scowl on your face.'

Feeling like she was a child being told off, Charlotte stared into the fire. Bessie's expression reminded her of when she and Hannah first walked into the shop that rainy night nearly four years ago. 'I sometimes wonder what mine and Hannah's life would have been like if we hadn't come into your shop.'

Bessie snorted. 'Mine would have been a whole lot easier, that's for sure.'

'Oh?' Charlotte frowned.

'Yes, I was living my life without any drama at all. Just me and Stan working the shop, content as can be. Then in stumble you two and bang! Our lives changed for ever.'

'Was that such a bad thing?'

Smiling, Bessie stood and in a rare show of affection, she kissed the top of Charlotte's head. 'You and Hannah brought life and laughter and love into this house. As Stan says quite often, you both walking into our shop that night was the best thing that ever happened to us.'

'Despite the dramas?'

Bessie laughed. 'Yes, indeed. You and Hannah have become our daughters. So, of course, we will worry and love the pair of you until our dying day. We want only your happiness.'

The door opened and Stan came in carrying her clean shining boots. 'This is the best I could do with them.'

'Heavens, Stan, they look brand new!' Charlotte grinned, putting them on. 'Thank you.'

'I'll walk home with you.'

'Stan, I'll be fine. I have my bicycle.'

'I said, I'll walk home with you. No arguments.'

'Very well.' She kissed Bessie's cheek. 'You'll come for dinner on Friday?'

'Aye, of course, as normal.' Bessie wound Charlotte's scarf around her neck to her satisfaction. 'Remember what I've said, and think on. Don't spoil what time you have left with Harry by having a sour face.'

* * *

HARRY PULLED his coat collar further up and tucked his chin lower so the hat he wore hid his face better. The night shadows spilled out over the cobbled back alleys of London's south bank. A scabby cat meowed as they passed, before scaling up a high wall and disappearing into the darkness.

Like him, his father wore all black as they walked the narrow lanes towards the warehouse where McBride was meant to be. For the first time in over two years, Harry wore civilian clothes. His father forbade him to wear his uniform as it could be identified. Other than that, his father had said very little to him about what was to happen. Apparently, they were there to watch and observe as a special favour given by one of his father's friends.

Rounding a corner of a large brick warehouse, they stopped. Ahead was a group of plainly dressed men.

'Who are they?' Harry whispered to his father.

'Police, along with officials from the War Office. They are waiting for a signal from inside the warehouse.'

On the still night air, they distinctly heard a whistle blown. Harry jumped for it was the same whistle sound that sent him and his men over the top on the battlefield.

'Come on. Quickly.' His father urged Harry to run up the alley and into the warehouse where the men had gone.

Inside, the warehouse was dimly lit. Harry stayed close by his father, wishing he wore his uniform and the pistol that usually sat on his hip. Circling large crates, they slipped quietly into an area where Harry could see the men standing in a circle. In the middle of the circle stood McBride, and crowding around him, pistols drawn were his henchmen.

Edging closer, Harry ignored his father's restraining hand. He wanted to hear what was being said.

'They are arresting him,' his father whispered.

'For what?'

'War profiteering. He's been under the government's surveillance for some time. I told a few of my friends in Parliament of what he was doing to Charlotte and they stepped up their interest in him. Thankfully for us, McBride has been making too many crossings into France.'

'He was in Paris one time when I was there. I found out by accident, but he had too many men with him for me to do anything about it. If I had tried, I would have ended up dead in the Seine. McBride didn't know it was me, but he had men on the streets and one recognised me and chased me.'

'You were lucky to escape then.'

'He will be sent down for this?' Harry prayed it would be so.

'For a long time.' His father nodded towards where the men were still talking. 'McBride was brought here under false pretentions. He thought tonight he was going to be buying guns from the Irish to smuggle across to Germany, but it was all a charade organised by the War Office.'

'So, he's a traitor as well. He should be shot,' Harry murmured, angered.

'He probably will be.'

Suddenly a scuffle broke out, McBride's henchmen tried to break free of the surrounding officers. All hell broke loose as yells and shouts filled the cavernous warehouse before shots rang out, deafening them.

Harry ducked, his hand went to his hip, but he had no pistol. He swore and charged in anyway.

'Harry, no!'

But he wasn't listening. He saw McBride struggling to break free of the officers who held him and had to have his part in the matter. McBride was not going to escape if he had anything to do with it.

Another shot rang out and Harry skidded to a halt. McBride looked in surprise at him before staring down at his chest. A small liquid stain seeped through his waistcoat, growing larger with every second. McBride's legs buckled and he gripped the arms of the men who held him and he brought them down to the floor as he fell.

Harry knelt beside McBride, the hated man blinking up at him. 'May you rot where you are heading, and by my reckoning, it is only going to be downwards. Take with you that Charlotte and I will be happy for the rest of our lives.'

'You-you ...' McBride spluttered, his hand trying to reach for Harry.

His father pulled him away. 'Enough, son. Let it be now.'

Staring down at McBride, Harry felt a wave of relief wash over him as the despicable fiend breathed his last.

CHAPTER 26

*C*harlotte sipped her afternoon coffee in the drawing room. The newspaper lay unread on her knee. She had so much still to do, but the thought of moving seemed too difficult. It was nice to just sit and rest for once. She'd spent an hour this morning with Winslow and Mrs Morrissey, trying to make the food they had stretch even further, then another two hours with Mr Tyler from Home Farm and Mr Formby the gamekeeper. Between them they brought dismal news of poachers and animal husbandry bills. She had correspondence to attend to, and if she had the energy, a trip to the mine.

Through the drawing room windows, she could see it was raining, fat drops fell from pewter grey skies. In the corner of the room, Petra softly played the piano, while Miss Newtown and Hannah sat at the small occasional table playing cards, and by Miss Newtown's murmurs of discontent she was losing the game.

They all looked to the doorway as Harry and Frank walked in, smiling broadly.

Petra stopped playing. 'You both seem pleased with yourselves. Did you have a good visit in Hull, since you were gone for three days instead of one night?'

'We did not go to Hull,' Harry said, sitting beside Charlotte, taking her hand.

'Oh? Where did you go?' She was surprised he held her hand for they hadn't touched hardly at all since his injuries had healed and the arguing began.

'To London.' Harry stood. 'I want to tell you something. Shall we go upstairs?'

Charlotte followed him, a sense of foreboding filling her heart. 'Am I to be worried, Harry?' she asked as she ascended the staircase and walked towards their bedroom.

'No, quite the opposite.' He opened the bedroom door and waited for her to enter, then closed the door behind him. In two strides he was standing before her. Delicately he cupped her face and placed small kisses on her nose and eyelids, her cheeks and finally her lips.

All the pent-up love and yearning for him broke the cold barrier between them and she wrapped her arms around him, holding him tight as the kiss deepened.

'I love you,' he whispered against her mouth. 'From the moment I met you I have loved you.'

'And I love you.' She pulled at his buttons, hating the khaki uniform that defined him as a soldier and not her husband.

'Let me love you properly, please, my darling.'

She nodded, knowing that his injuries where healed enough for what they both wanted and needed to do.

Clothes were disregarded hastily, no words were said as they explored each other, reacquainting themselves with the other's body. In bed, Harry touched and kissed Charlotte with a passion she remembered of their honeymoon. Her body arched into his hands as they roamed her curves. He kissed every inch of her, his tongue sending her mad with desire for what only he could give her.

She responded in kind, luxuriating in the freedom of knowing what he liked, of feeling him respond to her fingers, her lips. There weren't any boundaries just the simple and complete trust they used to share.

Despite their urgent need of each other they took their time, not wanting the moment to end. For once everything outside of the bedroom was forgotten. Instead, the focus was on each other and recapturing the deep love they had allowed to falter.

Much later, spent and happily content, Charlotte lay in Harry's arms, her head on his good shoulder. With one finger she drew circles around his belly button. 'You haven't told me what you brought me up here to say.' She smiled up at him.

He took her hand and kissed her palm. 'McBride is dead.'

She jerked upright, pulling the sheets around her nakedness. 'Dead?'

'Yes.'

'How? Are you sure? How do you know this?'

'I saw it happen directly in front of me.'

She felt the blood drain from her face. 'You killed him?'

'No, not me.' He sat up.

'I don't understand. Why were you there?' She crawled out of bed and wrapped her champagne coloured silk dressing gown around her with shaking hands.

'Father—'

'Frank was there? He killed him?'

'Let me explain, please. Come sit back down.'

She sat on the edge of the bed, wary, her mind not accepting McBride was dead.

Harry took her hand again. 'Father has many friends in high positions, more than me, certainly, and he has been worried about this McBride business, naturally, as he admires you so much. He decided to get in contact with some of his acquaintances and see if there was something that could be done about McBride. As it happens the War Office and Government already had their eye on McBride for his underhand dealings, but then he started to dabble in war profiteering and they were rather confident that he was perhaps making friends on the wrong side.'

'The wrong side?' she asked confused.

'The Germans.'

'Doing what?'

'Buying guns from rebel Irish groups to sell to the Germans, and vice versa. They, the police and the War Office, contacted him about a 'so-called' deal and arranged to meet him. He bought the ruse. Two nights ago, in a warehouse on the south side of the Thames we, Father and I, were there when they sprung that trap and caught him.'

'Why? Why were you there? It had nothing to do with you.' Anger began to build.

'Father thought I would like to see him be taken down, so that I would have proof you were now safe from him.'

'Couldn't we have just been told by one of your father's friends that he was arrested? Wouldn't that have been proof enough? Why did you have to put yourself in danger?'

'I was not in any danger.'

She slipped her hand away from his. 'If he was to be arrested then how did he die?'

'A fight broke out. McBride tried to make a run for it. He got shot in the confusion.' Harry shrugged, unconcerned. 'My face was the last he saw and I quite like it happened that way.'

Charlotte stood and moved away from the bed, hugging herself. 'There was fighting with McBride's henchmen and guns. You could have been shot, too!'

'No, not at all.'

'You were there, close enough for McBride to see your face, so yes, you could have been shot in the mayhem.'

'I was perfectly safe, Charlotte.'

'Really? Are you saying that not a part of you was excited to be in amongst it all, to be facing danger? God knows you've been bored out of your mind here, eager to get back to the fighting.'

'Stop it.' Harry flung himself out of bed and began to dress. 'Do not pretend to know what I am thinking or feeling.'

'I have to pretend to know since you won't tell me yourself!'

'Be quiet! I bring you good news and all you do is moan about the fact that I was there. Yes, I wanted to witness it, once I knew. I wanted to see McBride arrested and rot in jail. That he was killed makes it an even better result.' He tugged on his shirt and buttoned it. 'Why can you not be happy about it? You are free of him at last!'

She glared at him. 'I am pleased to be free of him, but what I don't like is you willingly putting yourself in danger again for no need.'

'Stop going on about being in danger. I am a solider. It is what I do.'

'And you are my husband and a father, too. Do we not count? Have you any idea how it is for me? I spend my time keeping as busy as possible just so I don't have to think about you being shot at, or worse, killed. Every time the postman comes to the door, or the telephone rings, I stop breathing, hoping it isn't a buff envelope with your name inside, or a call from the War Office. You have no idea how that feels living with that threat every single day. It's exhausting. For these last four months I have been free of that weight sitting above my heart. Only, you might as well have been over there anyway because your body was here, but your mind wasn't. I felt just as alone as I did when you were in France!' She ran out of breath and patience.

'I have no control over whether I die in this war or not.' He buttoned up his uniform jacket, his demeanour stiff and distant.

'No, you don't, but you did have a choice about being in that warehouse. You have a choice about returning to France!' She snapped. Angry tears hovered on her lashes, she blinked them away.

'I do not have a choice about returning. I am fit enough to report for duty. I cannot hide away here, shirking my responsibilities.'

'You have a duty here too, to us, your family, to this estate!'

Furious, he grabbed his boots. 'I will not sit out the rest of this war on my backside while I can still hold a pistol and be of use. I am not a coward! You cannot ask that of me!' He pulled his leather boots on, and snatched his officer's cap from the dressing table.

'You are not well enough! The doctors said—'

'The doctors have given me a medical pass to return. I am well enough.'

'No, on your last appointment they said you'd have to be put through some physical tests …'

'I saw the doctors this morning. I went to the hospital before we boarded the train. I passed the tests. They are desperate for men to return to France. I am returning to active duty tomorrow. I leave tonight.'

She gasped as though she'd been punched. 'There aren't any night trains.' She was grasping at straws, she knew it.

'There is an army personnel train leaving York at ten o'clock.'

Glancing at the clock, she calculated the time left. 'It's twenty past four. And you'll leave about nine o'clock. So, four hours and forty minutes left,' she said dully. The fight left her. She had lost.

'Charlotte…' His voice was soft, his expression tender. 'Darling, please…'

Deflated she slumped onto the bed, tears flowing.

Harry knelt before her, resting his hands on her thighs. 'I'm sorry. My love, listen to me. I will come home to you. I promise. Let me finish this godawful war. Let me bring home all the men in the village, all the husbands, and sons, and fathers left. I know you don't understand how strongly this grips me, but I cannot turn my back on them, not even for you. I am a Belmont and they are Belmont men.'

She nodded, head bowed. 'I know. And I am proud of you, so very proud, but you are my world, and without you, I feel hollow and empty. Is it so wrong of me that I want you here safe with me?'

'No, darling, it isn't.' He gently wiped her wet cheeks. 'I will make this up to you, Charlotte, as soon as this madness is over. I will come home and take over everything again, giving you the rest you deserve. I will be the man you married. Please give me your blessing. I cannot go back over there with this between us. I need your love to help me face whatever is waiting for me in France.'

Placing her fingertips on his cheek, she kissed him. 'You have my blessing. You have my love, always. Just *please* come back to me.'

'I will. I promise you.' Standing, Harry began undoing the buttons on his jacket. He flung it off and then carefully pushed Charlotte back to lie on the mattress. He drew open her flimsy dressing gown and ran a finger over her nipples. 'We have four hours.'

She smiled as desire replaced her misery. 'And forty minutes.'

EPILOGUE

Easter 1919

$\mathcal{C}$harlotte smiled and kissed the top of Alice's head. 'Sleep tight, sweetheart.'

She and Petra swapped places and Charlotte bent over Jeremy's bed and hugged her little son to her. 'Good night, my darling.'

Sleepily he yawned, and settled more snugly in his blankets. 'Mama.'

She kissed him and placed his favourite toy, a wooden solider beside him, knowing that Nanny would take it away once he was asleep so the hardness of it wouldn't hurt him in the night. Charlotte wished he'd chosen a soft teddy to cuddle with, yet he preferred the soldier because papa was a solider.

Turning, she crossed over to the next smaller room on the nursery floor, there the cot was placed closer to Nanny. She peeped over and seeing Annabelle fast asleep, she tucked her blankets in more securely, trying not to wake her. Her daughter had been born over a year ago. Conceived on the last day of Harry's convalescence.

Charlotte hadn't expected to fall pregnant and the surprise took some getting used to, but on a cold snowy day last January, after a quick five-hour labour, she welcomed Annabelle into the world. Thankfully, Harry returned home for a week to see them. Since that time, she had been fortunate enough to have Harry home three more times. Each time he seemed a little more older, a little more weary, but more confident that the war was waning, and the end was near.

His last visit was six months ago, and once again he left her pregnant. In a few months she would have their third child.

'Charlotte,' Petra, wearing a beautiful blue silk gown, whispered from the doorway. 'Are you ready?'

Nodding, Charlotte gave a lingering look at Annabelle, and then followed Petra from the nursery and downstairs to the gallery landing.

'Everyone will be arriving soon.'

'Hardly everyone.' Charlotte sighed, linking her arm through Petra's. She felt a little tired tonight. The baby kicked hard against her ribs. She wore a sateen and lace gown of deep burgundy, a colour that suited her copper coloured hair, which had been newly washed and styled by Lucy.

Tonight, for Easter, she and Petra had put on a little party for friends. However, influenza, or the Spanish Flu, as it was now named, had swept through the country with devastating results. Many people had decided to stay home, away from possible infection.

'It is quite horrific that so many of our friends and neighbours will be missing tonight and for ever more.' Petra fiddled with her evening gloves. 'Now the war is over we should all be returning to our old lives, but that will never be again. This is the first proper party we have had in years.'

'That old life is lost, but a new one will replace it. It'll simply be different, that's all. However, we will still laugh and dance and the old ways will merge into new ways.' Charlotte paused at the bottom of the stairs. Winslow was reprimanding one of the new footmen. He was struggling to train the young men who were tired of taking orders after years of warfare.

Petra gave Charlotte a worried look. 'Father is talking of leaving as soon as Harry comes home.'

'Oh? I am not surprised. He is eager to travel again. He's been cooped up here for too long.'

They wandered into the dining room, which for the first time in five years was resplendent in decoration, and fully set for guests.

'I…I…' Petra stalled, moving a wine glass a half inch further to the left.

'What is it?' Charlotte asked, amazed they had found so many candles to light. She always preferred eating dinner in candlelight to the bright electric wall lights.

'If I do not like it there, in Madagascar, may I come home, back here?'

'Absolutely.'

'But Harry?'

Charlotte hugged her. 'Harry's anger at you has gone. You both have changed. You are not the spoilt madam you once were, and he is not so uptight about the past. Too much has happened.'

Petra sagged with relief. 'Thank you. I will miss you so much.'

'And I you, very much.' Charlotte grinned. 'Especially as it took me a full year to even like you!'

'Oh!' Petra laughed. 'And I hated you.'

'I'm glad we got past that.'

Petra kissed Charlotte's cheek in a rare display of affection. 'I don't know how I would have coped without you. The best thing my brother ever did was marrying you.'

Amazed at such a statement, Charlotte squeezed Petra's hand

in acknowledgement. 'Coming from you, I could ask for no better compliment.'

Laughing, they left the dining room and headed for the drawing room, just as Frank descended the stairs and the door-bell chimed.

Winslow instructed the new footman to open the door for their first guests. Bessie and Stan came in full of smiles and laughter, ribbing the young footman as they had known him since he was a boy.

'Happy Easter one and all,' Stan said, as Hannah raced down the stairs.

'Bessie! Stan! Look at my dress.' She skidded to a stop in front of them and pirouetted. The shimmering green silk of her first adult dress glistened in the golden light. With her long dark hair, she was turning into a stunning young woman.

'Hannah!' Charlotte shook her head. 'How many times must I tell you not to run? You're a young lady. Act like one.'

Stan waltzed Hannah into the drawing room and Bessie shook her head in bemusement. 'Those two!'

Miss Newtown sedately joined them. She wore a sober grey dress as befitting her station, but had added white lace and deli-cate pink flowers were pinned to her breast. 'I do apologise, Mrs Belmont. Hannah refuses to listen to me at times.'

'I know, Miss Newtown. It is not your fault. She will grow up one day. The Ladies College she'll be attending in September will help shape her.'

'And then you'll have Master Jeremy and Miss Annabelle and the new babe to sort out.' Bessie grinned.

In the drawing room, they took the flutes of champagne offered from Winslow, as Doctor and Mrs Neville were announced.

'When is Harry expected home, lass?' Bessie asked Charlotte, as Petra greeted the doctor and his wife. 'I noticed some of the men from the village are home.'

'I am not sure when to expect Harry. He telephoned me from Paris three days ago. But there is so much to do, mopping up after the armistice. Now he's loaded down with paperwork and logistics to get the areas secure and the men home. He sounded tired.'

Bessie patted her arm. 'At least he's not being shot at.'

More guests arrived, Mr Groates, the village schoolmaster, and Mr Stevens, the vicar, some families from neighbouring estates.

Charlotte circulated, making sure everyone had someone to talk to and something to drink. Discussions flowed about the flu epidemic, the effects of the war, the state of the country and what the current Government planned to do now for all these men with no jobs to go to.

'Madam,' Winslow appeared at Charlotte's side. 'Dinner is served.'

At her nod, Petra and Frank helped escort people into the dining room. In the relaxed confusion of people getting seated, it took a moment for Charlotte to notice the three officers standing in the doorway.

'Harry!' In the space of a heartbeat, Charlotte ran across the room and into Harry's arms. 'You're home!'

'I am. We are. It is done, my love.' He kissed her, then turned to Bertram and Nicholas. 'We can fit Nicholas in, can't we?'

'Of course.' Charlotte kissed Bertram and then Nicholas. 'Welcome home.'

For several minutes, chaos reigned as everyone welcomed home the heroes.

Charlotte saw Winslow wipe away a tear when he thought no one was looking and she stepped up beside him to squeeze his arm. 'He's home. Everything will be just fine now.'

'I know, madam. Happiest day of my life it is, and, madam, it has been the greatest honour to be a member of Belmont Hall staff during this time.'

'You're not a member, Winslow, you *are* Belmont Hall. I could not have done it without you.'

'It was a pleasure, madam.' He coughed with embarrassment.

Harry came to stand with them. He shook Winslow's hand. 'I owe you a great deal. You have taken care of my family and my home. I will never forget that.'

'The privilege was all mine, sir.' Clearly emotional, Winslow walked away to instruct the footmen to begin the meal.

Harry kissed her soundly, before escorting her down the table.

She embraced him tightly. 'We have everything to look forward to.'

'We do. Including a wedding.' He nodded to where Bertram was holding Miss Newtown's chair for her. Then Harry put his hand on Charlotte's stomach. 'And another little one for the nursery. We are very fortunate, darling.'

'Yes, indeed. I feel like I can breathe again for the first time in years. Maybe I can put my feet up for a bit.' She grinned.

'That you can, darling. No more visits down the mine either. Winslow kept me informed.'

She gave him a stern look as she took her seat. 'I found them rather interesting. I'll not have you curb all of my activities, Harry.'

He laughed and kissed her again. 'I would not dare, my love.'

Frank waited until Harry took his place at the head of the table, then he stood and raised his glass. 'A toast. To the gallant men and women who fought a great fight and won.'

Everyone stood, raised their glasses and sent up a loud cheer.

'To my wife,' Harry toasted, 'who never faltered despite the heavy burdens she carried.'

Along the length of the table, and with the love of friends and family between them, Charlotte smiled lovingly at Harry as they cheered.

ABOUT THE AUTHOR

AnneMarie Brear

Ms Brear has done it again. She quickly became one on my 'must read' list. –The Romance Studio

Australian born, AnneMarie Brear's ancestry is true Yorkshire going back centuries.

Her love of reading fiction started at an early age with Enid Blyton's novels, before moving on into more adult stories such as Catherine Cookson's novels as a teenager.

Living in England, she discovered her love of history by visiting the many and varied places of historical interest.

The road to publication was long and winding with a few false starts, but she finally became published in 2006.

Her books are available in ebook and paperback from bookstores, especially online bookstores, and libraries. Please feel free to leave a review online if you enjoyed this book and let her know via her social media.

To receive AnneMarie's newsletter about her books, please go to her website.

http://www.annemariebrear.com

Printed in Great Britain
by Amazon

83479442R00181